# MARROW

# MARROW

A
NOVEL

## Samantha Browning Shea

G. P. PUTNAM'S SONS
New York

**PUTNAM**
—— EST. 1838 ——

G. P. Putnam's Sons
An imprint of Penguin Random House LLC
1745 Broadway, New York, NY 10019
penguinrandomhouse.com

Book design by Laura K. Corless
Title page art: Bare trees silhouette © Eroshka/Shutterstock.com

Library of Congress Cataloging-in-Publication Data

Names: Shea, Samantha Browning, author.
Title: Marrow: a novel / Samantha Browning Shea.
Description: New York: G. P. Putnam's Sons, 2025.
Identifiers: LCCN 2024052710 | ISBN 9780593851951 (hardcover) |
ISBN 9780593851968 (epub)
Subjects: LCGFT: Witch fiction. | Novels.
Classification: LCC PS3619.H399828 M37 2025 | DDC 813/.6—dc23/eng/20250103
LC record available at https://lccn.loc.gov/2024052710

Printed in the United States of America
1st Printing

The authorized representative in the EU for product safety and compliance is
Penguin Random House Ireland, Morrison Chambers, 32 Nassau Street,
Dublin D02 YH68, Ireland, https://eu-contact.penguin.ie.

For my family

*Wanting is a powerful magic.*

—SOPHIE MACKINTOSH,
*Blue Ticket*

# MARROW

# ONE

For years, Oona had dreamt of her return to Marrow. At night, lying in bed beside Jacob, she used to fantasize about the sour brine of the marsh air, pretend she could still feel the grit of salt on her skin. It would bring her a kind of peace, she'd thought, to see the island materialize on the horizon, to catch sight of its foggy shores and rocky coast. But of course in her dreams, Oona had always imagined herself up on deck, stationed at the bow like a figurehead. In reality, though, she spent most of her first ferry ride in over a decade down in the bowels of the boat, squatting on the slick floor of the head, vomiting up her breakfast.

As yet another wave crashed into the side of the hull and the ferry lurched sideways, Oona tried blaming her nausea on the years she'd spent onshore. She blamed the storm that had rolled in earlier that afternoon, the reason they were all running late. But deep down, she knew it wasn't as simple as any of that. She'd thought it would've passed by now, but the truth was she'd been sick back in Portland too.

It had been a struggle, trying to conceal it from Jacob. She couldn't tell him yet, though. It was too soon. Something could still go wrong.

Something always went wrong.

Belowdecks, Oona braced herself once again as the captain threw the engines into reverse, but thankfully no great pitch forward followed. Instead, she heard the grinding whir of the propellers as they began churning in the water, and she realized they were docking. They'd made it. She was home.

Marrow Island was large compared to some of its neighbors— rocky outcroppings reachable only by dinghy or rowboat—but compared to towns on the mainland, compared to Portland, it was nothing. Just twenty square miles of marshland, caves, and tide pools. A tiny town that had grown up around the port where the ferries docked. As a girl, Oona had lived in awe of that small town. She'd loved its hustle and bustle: the shops that lined the cobbled main street, the dive that sold lobster rolls and french fries in the summer. She'd even loved the hawking cries of the fishermen at dusk, the way the gulls would circle overhead as customers stooped to examine the daily catches displayed in rows of coolers on the docks. Still, she was surprised to find the town largely unchanged.

It was April, offseason, so the town's only restaurant hadn't opened yet, but everything else was just as she remembered it. As she made her way down the ferry's gangplank, she could see the grocery store off to her left. Its faded green canopy still said *Albert's*, though she'd read in the papers that Al himself had died a few years back. Next to the grocery was the Robertses' pharmacy, and then after the pharmacy was the hardware store owned by the Clarks. Looking at those shops, all in a row, Oona couldn't help but remember the last time she'd seen their owners, the way those three men had stood to block her entrance to the funeral. They were only doing what the Tanakas had asked them to do, only trying to support their grieving friends and neighbors, but that didn't mean Oona couldn't hold a grudge. *Good riddance*, she thought as she turned away from Al's.

At the end of the dock, she put down her bag to rest. Her luggage wasn't heavy, but she was out of breath. That last hour in the ship's bathroom had taken a lot out of her. She leaned against the dock's railing and stared down at her duffel. She didn't even know what she'd packed. An old pair of sneakers? Her navy raincoat? Her trip— it hadn't exactly been well planned. She'd panicked, that's what Jacob would say if she was to call him, tell him what she'd done. She'd started feeling desperate, so she'd allowed herself to be lured in, once again, by the fairy-tale promise of a simple solution. If she let him, she knew he would convince her to return to the mainland.

"Mrs. Jones?"

A young woman approached Oona tentatively. And though she wasn't wearing anything all that telling—wasn't, for instance, dressed in a purple robe—still, Oona's first thought was that the girl looked like an Initiate. Only, to be an Initiate, she would have to be pregnant, and as far as Oona could tell, she was not.

"Are you Mrs. Jones?"

It took a minute before Oona remembered the name she'd assumed when she'd called the Center from Portland and found there was actually one guest not yet accounted for, her arrival time for that very weekend still unconfirmed. It was a minor miracle—though the Center technically remained open all year long, the midwives spent the offseason caring for local women. The only time they accepted outsiders was during the Summer Session, which ran roughly from just before Beltane to Lughnasadh, or from late April to August 1. Oona hadn't actually expected to be able to attend. She'd called out of sheer desperation. But when she'd discovered there was an opening, she'd made the split-second decision to claim it as her own.

"That's me," Oona said on the dock. "I'm Maggie Jones."

The girl breathed a sigh of relief. "Thank goodness! For a second, I thought I was going to have to tell them that I'd lost you." She laughed, but Oona offered only a small smile in return. "I'm Holly," the girl said. She reminded Oona of a Girl Scout—all bright helpfulness and good cheer. "I'm an Initiate here this season."

She stuck out one hand, and this time Oona smiled more genuinely. So she'd been right, she thought. The girl *was* an Initiate. That was good news. It meant that she was new to the island.

"Here," said Holly. "Let me get that bag for you. We've got a Jeep waiting just over there. You see it?"

She pointed and Oona nodded. The Jeep, though, that was also new. It even had the Center's name stenciled on the side: *Bare Root Fertility Center.* Fancy. When Oona was little, the only car the Center had owned was a truck. Red, with rusted wheel wells, it broke down at least once a month. That's how Oona got to spend so much time running wild on the docks in town, watching the fishermen. Otherwise, for many years, she'd rarely left the Center's grounds.

"You were late getting in," Holly said, as Oona followed her to the Jeep. "We were expecting you all closer to two. I was just telling the other ladies here that I'm afraid you've likely missed supper."

When Holly opened the car's back door, Oona realized there were already two other women waiting: a wealthy-looking Asian woman, who was perched on the bench seat farthest from Oona, her wrists adorned with gold; and a tall Black woman, who was holding a small spiral notebook. Once Oona finally got herself up and into the car, the woman with the notebook chuckled. "This thing needs a set of stairs or something," she offered. Oona smiled politely but didn't respond. She'd never been very good at small talk, and anyway, she figured she wasn't there to make friends. Friends were just a liability for someone like her, someone who needed to go unnoticed.

It was bad enough that she'd shown up looking like such a mess.

The two women to her left were dressed quite differently from each other—the woman seated by the window was wearing a pair of fur-lined duck boots and what looked like an expensive winter coat, while the woman with the notebook was dressed more simply—but they both looked put together, tidy, and well-groomed. Oona, on the other hand, was greasy and bloated. When she glanced down, she saw there were flecks of vomit on her coat. She hadn't bothered to look up how much a visit to the Center would cost because any amount would have been too much for her, but now she worried that her ratty duffel, her thrift-store jacket would give her away.

"Ready, gals?" Holly called from the front seat, as the Jeep's engine turned over.

The other two women chirped back, "Ready!" but Oona just slouched against her door, pressed her forehead to the window's glass.

It was after six and already the sun was dropping low in the sky, dusk drifting in like a rolling fog. As the car pulled onto the main road the other two women closed their eyes, probably grateful for the respite after the long ferry ride, but Oona found she couldn't look away. She needed to see the salt-stung, shingled buildings of Port Marrow give way to the sharp rise of the forest's towering pines, to stare out at the breathtaking expanse of rocky tide pools that stretched along the shore for miles. She told herself that she wasn't scared, she just needed the reminder that it was all real, that she was finally home, but when she glanced down she saw she was gripping her seat belt so tightly, every one of her knuckles had flushed white.

Still, despite her anxiety, Oona soon found herself lulled by the journey, drowsy by the time they pulled into the Center's long clam-shell drive. As soon as the car came to a stop, though, the fear was back in her chest, thrashing like a caged bird. She jiggled the handle on the door twice before Holly told her to wait a minute. She would come around to let them out. *Trapped*, Oona thought, briefly pan-icked, but then the door swung open and she tumbled out onto the drive.

The woman with the notebook followed, but when the other woman moved to join them Holly told her it wasn't yet her turn. She was going to be staying in a cabin on the other side of the compound, in House Imbolc. Oona and Shelly (for that was the name of the woman with the notebook, Shelly) were marked down for House Sa-mhain. Oona had nearly forgotten that the cabins were each named after one of the eight sabbats.

"Here are your keys," Holly said, as she handed first Oona and then Shelly a heavy iron key, strung on a band of soft white ribbon. "Go on in and make yourselves at home. Like I said, you've missed supper, but there should be plenty of healthy snacks in the pantry in the common room, if you're hungry. Fresh fruit and organic granola. Stuff like that. Oh, and skyr in the mini-fridge, if you eat dairy. But if none of that is to your liking, just call the kitchen. They'll send over anything you want. Okay?"

Dumbstruck, Oona nodded. The cabins had never had mini-fridges before. They'd barely had electricity, running water.

Holly turned eastward and pointed to a sandy path that wove through the trees, then she explained what Oona already knew: that the part of the compound where they were standing was still surrounded by forest, but if they were to follow that path the woods would open up onto a bluff, below which they'd find the beach. After checking her watch, Holly told them that the Welcoming Ceremony would be taking place on the beach in thirty minutes, just after sunset. "Meet us down there?" she asked.

"Of course," Shelly said, answering for them both.

And with that, Holly climbed back into the Jeep and drove off.

Oona watched her taillights disappear around a bend while Shelly picked up the handle of her rolling suitcase and turned to the cabin. "Shall we?" She didn't wait for Oona to respond, she just started walking, taking quick, purposeful steps as if she'd been there before.

Oona felt jealous of her confidence and her getup. Despite the fact that Oona had never traveled out of state, Shelly, in her heavy knee-length rain slicker and her grip-soled boots, seemed somehow better dressed for the climate. But Oona was relieved to discover that, unlike the wealthy woman from the car, none of Shelly's belongings looked particularly expensive. Rather, it appeared that she'd bought most of her gear at the army-navy store. Oona was pretty sure she even recognized the boots. Jacob had a pair just like them.

As they neared the cabin, Oona stalled so she wouldn't have to be the one to use her key. It was stupid, maybe, but she was afraid of betraying herself, afraid her breathing would turn ragged, afraid her hands would shake. As a child, tasked with changing the linens, she'd worn a whole necklace of those keys, and as she stood there at the cabin's door she once again felt the weight of them pressing against her chest.

"Coming?" Shelly prompted from inside.

Oona hurried to catch up with her in the common room.

"It looks like there's four of us staying here." Shelly pointed to a chalkboard that hung between the two bedroom doors, where the women's names were written: June, Shelly, Maggie, Gemma. "Or maybe more. . . ." She walked across the common room toward the final door, and Oona spoke without thinking.

"No," she said. "That's just the bathroom."

Shelly pulled open the door and peeked in. "So it is." She turned to smile, curious, back at Oona. "Good guess."

Oona's heart pounded, but she tried to look casual as she shrugged. "Well, it was that or start looking for an outhouse."

Shelly laughed, and Oona thought: *If you only knew.* The Center had been built on a former campground. She was thirteen by the time they'd saved enough to put in proper plumbing. Now . . . Oona turned and saw that the whole back wall had been transformed into a kitchen, like the efficiency motel where she used to work as a housekeeper. Only nicer. Much nicer. The countertops looked like they were made of real marble. Oona could hardly believe her eyes.

"The others must already be down at the beach," Shelly said, brushing her locs off her shoulder. "I'll just throw my stuff in my room and then we can walk down together."

"Together?" Oona echoed.

"Unless you don't want to." Shelly's left eyebrow ticked up, and Oona saw her gaze turn inquisitive.

No, more than inquisitive—she looked suspicious, which in turn made Oona tense. "I'd love to walk together," she hurried to say. "Let me just find my phone. One second."

She ducked into her room and closed the door behind her, hefted her duffel onto the foot of the only unclaimed bed. She'd packed underwear at least, she was relieved to discover, and two pairs of cotton shorts. Her red bathing suit and her white canvas sneakers. Her favorite fisherman sweater and her baggy jeans. It wasn't much, but it would do for the long weekend.

At the bottom of the duffel, she dug around for her cell phone, which she'd purposefully buried beneath her clothes. Zero missed calls. Oona released the breath she'd been holding. Technically, Jacob's boat was supposed to remain at sea for the next three days, but his trips were always somewhat unpredictable. It wasn't unusual for him to stay out longer if his team had trouble locating the herring population they were attempting to research. Oona's plan, if you could call it a plan, was to make it back to Portland before her husband, but she'd known when she boarded the ferry that she was taking a risk. Jacob could easily end up getting back to the house before her, and then what would she say? What would she do?

For a moment Oona felt overcome, sure she'd made the wrong decision—or at least gone about things the wrong way. After all, she wasn't trying to start a fight with Jacob. In fact, she was attempting to do the opposite. The reason she'd left the way she had was because she hadn't wanted to argue with him again. Still, she couldn't ignore the niggling feeling that she'd put in jeopardy the one thing she couldn't bear to lose: the only family she had left, her husband. Only when she stood up, ready to—what? Pack her things and leave?—she felt it, the quickening, and she dropped back down onto the bed, stunned.

Of course she'd thought about this moment before. On the message boards, one woman had claimed that when she'd first felt her baby move she'd thought she was just nervous, experiencing "butterflies," while another had said that for her it felt like gas. And so, based on their descriptions, Oona had always imagined that the feeling would be subtle, easy to miss or to mistake, and in each of her five previous pregnancies there had been moments when she'd wondered—or at least hoped. But this time was different, this *feeling* was different, something impossible to ignore. For Oona, the quickening didn't feel like butterflies or gas, it felt like what it was: a baby, *her* baby, moving inside her. Unmistakable, and yet hard to believe.

She still had her hands pressed to her belly when Shelly called her name, or her fake name. "Maggie?" It sounded like her mouth was full. "Are you almost ready?"

"Oh, yes, sorry." Oona got to her feet and grabbed her jacket. "I'm coming right now."

In the common room, she found Shelly knelt down in front of the pantry, holding her notebook and a half-eaten protein bar. "Nothing too good," she said. "But they have almonds and rice cakes. And some kind of fruit leather. Do you want anything?"

"No," Oona said. "I'm not hungry."

"You sure?"

With a heavy swallow, she nodded. Already, the smell of Shelly's protein bar had wafted her way, and for whatever reason, peanut butter was a no-go for her this time around. Even standing close to Shelly was making her nauseated.

"I missed lunch, so I'm starving," Shelly explained. She took two more bars and a handful of almonds and stuffed them into her coat pockets along with her notebook. "But this should hold me for a while. Ready?"

Oona nodded. When they left, she locked the door with her key.

The beach was only a little more than half a mile from their cluster of cabins, and as Oona trailed Shelly through the woods she caught the scent of the pine trees' sap in the air and found herself transported back to her girlhood. How many hours, she wondered, had she spent roaming that forest searching for skullcap and stinging nettle? How many nights had she used the light of the moon to follow the path to its end? She used to like to sneak out to the overlook and hide among the scrub brush, spy on the women down below in the sand. Now it was hard to believe she was going to be one of them. The thought made her feel first giddy and then terrified. She stopped short at the end of the trail, but Shelly didn't notice until she was halfway down the rocky slope.

"What's wrong?" she asked, when she realized Oona was no longer beside her.

There was a bonfire going down on the beach, but its light didn't quite reach them up on the hill, and in the dark Shelly seemed tentative. She stood with her knees bent, both hands extended in front of her as if she was bracing for a fall. When she was younger, Oona would've smirked at her cautiousness, would've clapped a hand over her eyes like a show-off and marched deadman-style straight down to the sand. But not anymore.

Shelly held out her hand. "I know it doesn't look like it, but there's a path here. I promise."

"I'm fine," Oona said. "You go on ahead. I'll catch up."

"No," Shelly said earnestly. "I'm not leaving without you."

*Christ*, thought Oona. This was why she'd wanted to walk over alone.

From where she stood she could see all the other Mothers (for they were, according to Center credo, all of them Mothers, even if their babies hadn't been born earth-side yet) mingling down below, swaying to the beat of whatever song was playing over the speakers, but she couldn't see their faces, couldn't tell much at all about them from so far away. Was she down there? Oona wondered. Was she that woman standing by the fire? Or was she the one walking barefoot by the tide?

She didn't mean to, but when Shelly said her name again she startled and accidently spoke her question out loud. "Do you see her?"

"Who?" Shelly asked.

*"Her."*

For a minute Shelly looked blank, then suddenly she seemed to recognize the awe in Oona's voice, the urgency. "Ursula?"

Oona hadn't heard anyone say her mother's name in years.

Still unsure of her footing, Shelly turned warily back to the beach. After a moment's worth of scanning, she shook her head. "I don't see her, but Vivian told me that she often doesn't join until the end of the ceremony."

"Really?" Oona asked. Her mother had never been late to a ceremony or ritual when Oona was still living on the island.

"That's just what Vivian said. You remember Vivian. From the car?" When Oona said nothing, Shelly pointed down at the beach. "There she is. The one with the black hair. I know she was quiet earlier, but before the waves picked up she was telling me all about the Center. I think maybe she's been here before? Or a friend of hers has? I can't remember. I don't think she was expecting that boat ride, though. It was rough out there, wasn't it?"

Oona hadn't noticed either Shelly or Vivian on the ferry, so she'd assumed they also hadn't noticed her, but something about Shelly's comment made her wonder if perhaps she'd been more conspicuous than she'd imagined. "It was a bad storm."

"You're telling me. My flight had to land right in the middle of it. Nearly blew us off the tarmac."

When she reached Shelly, Oona took her outstretched hand. "Where'd you fly in from?" she asked.

"SFO," Shelly said. "The Bay Area. But I'm from Portland, originally."

*Portland*, Oona thought. That wasn't good. Then again Shelly had said *originally*, so hopefully that meant she'd been out west awhile, that there was little chance she and Oona had ever crossed paths.

When they reached the sand, they took off their socks and shoes and left them at the base of the hill like everybody else. The sand was cold on Oona's feet, and damp from the storm earlier, but she knew it would be warmer once they got closer to the bonfire, which was burning hot and bright only twenty yards away.

"Do you want anything to drink first?" Shelly asked.

Not far from the fire was an old wooden picnic table with a tin tub on one side holding bottles of water and green juice, and on the other end an assortment of what Oona knew had to be nonalcoholic wines. Bare Root was a dry facility. Always had been. But from the number of women "drinking," it looked like maybe Ursula had stopped mentioning that bit in the brochures.

"White or red?" Shelly asked, once they made it across the sand.

Oona thought about explaining Ursula's policy, but then she noticed that a few of the other witches in her mother's coven were standing by the far side of the table, pouring their own drinks. She recognized them right away—Joyce with her twin gray braids, Donna in her dungarees. It had been fifteen years and still Oona could remember how it'd felt whenever Joyce had tugged on her ponytail. Standing there in the sand, she could feel the nape of her neck begin to ache and she knew that if she was able to recognize them so easily, then it stood to reason that they might recognize her in return, even despite her rushed dye job. It was safer just to stick to the shadows. Safer, too, to avoid launching into a history of Bare Root. After all, Oona was supposed to be a first-time visitor, a newbie. She wasn't supposed to know what the rules had been fifteen years ago.

"Shelly!" Oona heard someone call, and she turned around. It was the woman from the Jeep, Vivian. Somehow, though they'd been given only a few minutes in their cabins, she'd not only changed clothes but had found the time to reapply her lipstick and pull her long black hair into a perfectly messy bun.

She was standing with a group of similarly well-styled women, waving, and before Oona could think of a good excuse, Shelly took her by the arm.

"Come on," she said. "I'll introduce you. I have a few things I want to ask Vivian anyway, since she seemed to know so much about the Center." Shelly dropped Oona's arm to pull her notebook from her coat pocket, but when Oona didn't follow she reached for her again.

"Come on. They won't bite," she teased, as she dragged Oona closer.

Oona said nothing, but she knew that even sharks could look harmless from far away.

"Hey, Vivian," Shelly said, once they were within earshot of the group. "You remember Maggie. From earlier?"

Oona thought she saw Shelly and Vivian exchange a look, but it happened so fast she couldn't decipher what it might mean. Were they onto her? Already?

"Of course," Vivian said. "You were on the ferry too. Rough waters. Do you get seasick?"

"Not usually," Oona said, which was the truth.

"Lucky." Vivian took a sip from her bottle of green juice. "I can still feel the rocking." She placed her palm on her stomach and spoke to the rest of the circle. "And I think I'm still a little nauseous, but maybe that's just nerves. I can hardly believe I'm here. Like, am I really doing this?"

Every woman in the circle bobbed her head.

"But nothing else has worked," she continued. "I was telling Shelly on the ferry. We've done four rounds of IVF. Four! We've been trying for more than five years now."

"Gosh, we've been trying for eight," the woman to Oona's right admitted. Vivian held up her bottle and with a shy smile the woman clinked her own against it.

"Here's to not giving up hope," Shelly said, lifting her own glass in turn. "I know it can be difficult, but it's true that you never know what will happen. I've seen my own patients succeed when every expert told them there was no chance."

"Shelly's a doctor," Vivian explained. "A gynecologist."

Oona turned, surprised. "You are?"

"She's practically a saint," said Vivian. "She works at Planned Parenthood. Isn't that right, Shelly?"

"Yes, that's right. I do. When my older sister got pregnant at sixteen, she struggled. I went into this line of work with the goal of being able to help girls like her."

"That's so commendable," said Vivian. "Isn't that commendable?" She looked out at the rest of the circle, as if she were somehow responsible for Shelly's decency.

"So you're a doctor," said one of the other women. "And you still came . . . here? You still believe in—"

"I believe in following every lead," said Shelly, and there was something in her voice that made Oona think this was a speech she'd given many times before—to her friends, to her family, maybe even to her fellow doctors at the clinic. "Just because one person calls a thing magic, doesn't mean it isn't real. Take the ancient Egyptians, for example. They used to apply an eyeliner that they thought was a gift bestowed by the god Horus to protect them from eye disease. Today, we don't necessarily believe that the eyeliner came from Horus, but when analytical chemists at the Louvre studied the composition of that eyeliner, they were able to identify two types of lead salt that, when applied to human skin, have the potential to help activate the immune system and kill the kind of bacteria that cause eye disease."

"Wow," said one of the other women.

Across the circle, Vivian nodded sagely. "I think that's such a wise way to look at all this."

Oona prickled at Vivian's overly earnest admiration, but Shelly seemed unfazed. As a doctor, she was probably used to her words being met with a certain kind of wonder. But Oona couldn't help it, it all just rubbed her the wrong way—reminded her of the Initiates who used to follow her mother around, gathering at her feet like disciples.

When Oona looked out across the crowd, her gaze landed on Holly. Just like Oona expected, she was wearing an Initiate's robe. As was the girl beside her, who looked even younger, with a teenager's sulky pout and a thorny tangle of black hair.

It was hard to tell in the dark, with the robe, but Oona didn't notice any obvious signs of a belly on the second Initiate, either. It was all so strange, she thought. For years, Ursula had insisted that the Center could only accept Initiates who were not only pregnant but had passed the point of viability, because any potential new coven member needed to be able to be tested for power. But now it seemed that she'd relaxed her rules. Unless, of course, the two Initiates were mothers who had left their children at home for the summer?

Oona squinted at the two girls standing by the fire. She supposed it was possible they were both already mothers, but it seemed unlikely given how young they were. Plus, it wasn't just that they weren't pregnant. There was something else different about them too. When Oona was young, the Initiates had always seemed, well, desperate. They'd shown up at Bare Root looking hungry and afraid. They'd come with black eyes or busted lips or bruises. They'd come with track marks or burst veins. Holly and the other girl, though . . . they looked healthy. Well-loved, well-fed.

As she watched them, the Initiates both began stoking the fire's flames, and Oona couldn't help but think that if she'd been the one in the robe, she would have worried about the ashes, about the soot that was rising in the air to cling to their sleeves. She would have wanted to keep the robe pristine because, as a girl, there was nothing she'd wanted more than a robe of her own.

On days when her mother was out, teaching a workshop in the lodge or attending a birth in town, Oona used to sneak into her bedroom closet. She never dared to take down her mother's ceremonial whites or lay her hands on any of her ritual jewelry, but the Initiate robes were something else. Simple cotton and the same soft purple as the asters that grew in the shade of the lodge, they were lent out nearly every Summer Session when a new batch of young women—and they were usually *young* women—showed up at the Center's grounds. Most years, Ursula managed to recruit only one or two Initiates, but because the robes were rarely, if ever, replaced, it wasn't long before they started to look pretty ragged. By the time Oona was twelve, nearly every hem on every robe had begun to fray, and each robe carried its own set of mystery stains: grass or blood or berry juice. Still, when Oona pulled one out of her mother's closet and slipped it on over her head, when she tied its sash around her waist, she used to swear that she could feel the robe transform her, that as soon as she put it on she could feel her power begin to gather right there at the base of her spine.

Of course, it was only a few years later that Oona lost the chance at her own robe forever. She was eighteen when her mother expelled her from the coven and banished her to the mainland. The last thing she told her? *There's nothing left for you here.*

Now, standing on the beach, Oona could taste her own bitterness on her tongue, like copper. Or was that fear?

God, how she hoped her mother had been wrong.

In the circle by the water, the woman directly across from Oona dropped her voice and leaned in closer. "I've heard that she speaks in tongues."

A second woman added, "I had a friend who came two years ago. They tried for over a decade and never got anywhere. Not so much as a chemical pregnancy. But one summer with Ursula and that was that. She went home and got knocked up the very next day."

Distracted by Holly, by the fire, Oona had drifted out of the conversation, but at the sound of her mother's name she tuned back in.

"They say Ursula conceived a child on her own," added the woman with eight years of fertility treatments under her belt. She was so soft-spoken, it almost sounded like she was whispering.

Shelly opened her notebook. "I heard that too," she said. "Someone told me she gave birth to . . . a daughter? Is that right?"

The woman nodded. "Immaculate conception, they say."

"No," Vivian countered. It was clear to Oona, even just a few minutes into knowing her, that Vivian was the sort who liked to be an authority on things. "It wasn't immaculate conception. It wasn't religious. It was parthenogenesis. It happens all the time in the animal world. Bees, snails, even snakes and lizards—the females of those species can all reproduce on their own."

"Gosh, is that really true?" Eight Years asked, first of Vivian and then of the rest of the circle. She turned her big blue eyes on Oona. "Is that true?"

But what could Oona say? Parthenogenesis. It sounded good. And while it was the first time she had ever heard of it, that didn't mean it wasn't true. As Oona was growing up, though, her mother had always explained it differently. *I spoke you into being.* That's what she used to say. It had left Oona in awe of the sheer power of her mother's will, the dominance of her desires. But it had also left Oona feeling, in some way, proud. As she grew, she came to question a lot about her mother and their relationship, came to wonder if perhaps she wasn't a disappointment, not the daughter Ursula had imagined when she'd willed her into existence all those years before. But for all the worries and suspicions, there was one thing Oona never doubted: that once, at least, she was wanted; once, she was loved.

"I think—" Oona began, but she never got to finish her sentence because she was drowned out by the sound of a splash. Though the storm had passed some hours before, the waves were still white-capped and frothy. All the while she'd been standing there, they'd been rushing up to the shore, crashing against the rocks. The sound had been loud at first, but Oona had gotten used to it. The dull roar had faded to the background, become as gently lulling as white noise. Now that steady rumble had been punctured.

There was somebody in the water, and Oona's first instinct was to scream, to call for help like she'd been trained to do since she was little. For while the water in Casco Bay was never warm, in the summer at least it was possible to swim in. As a child Oona herself had often braved the cold. But there was nothing brave about wading out to sea in the spring. That was just stupid—suicidal. It had been a frigid winter. Oona doubted the water was any warmer than thirty-five degrees, and at that temperature a person could get hypothermia in a matter of minutes. In cold like that, the easiest thing to do was drown.

But just as she turned to cry for help, Oona felt a hand on her shoulder. Shelly was pointing back up the beach, to the base of the hill where the looming pine trees cast a long shadow against the moon's silver glow. "She's here," Shelly whispered.

Oona didn't have to ask who she meant. The reverence in Shelly's voice, the hush that had descended upon the circle, told her everything she needed to know.

On the ferry ride over from Portland, on the long drive away from the docks, Oona had tried to resist imagining this moment—her first glimpse of her mother in almost fifteen years. But when she *had* thought of it, when she'd allowed herself that small indulgence, the very idea left her clammy and cotton-mouthed. Just picturing it back in the ferry's bathroom, she'd been able to feel the blood thrumming in her throat. So to reassure herself she'd gazed into the little mirror over the sink, no bigger than a porthole. Her image there had been a comfort, proof that she was very likely unrecognizable with her hair dyed a mousy brown and cut to just above her shoulders. On Marrow Island, Oona had been known for her mane of copper curls, but as soon as she'd held that ferry ticket in her hand, she'd known that what she would need most once she reached Bare Root was the ability to blend in, to go unnoticed. If she wanted even the chance of making it through the long weekend, of receiving the protection spell at the Beltane celebration on Monday night, then she couldn't risk getting caught.

Still, when Ursula emerged from the shadows and the firelight hit her face, Oona had to fight the urge to run. Tall and square-jawed, her mother had always cut an imposing figure, and the past fifteen years seemed to have done little to dampen the effect. If anything,

Ursula appeared even more intimidating, with her eyes the color of deep sea and her long white hair styled in a fishtail braid.

Standing in the sand, Oona had never felt so exposed. A small voice in her head told her to step back, to take shelter among the circle of women surrounding her, but when she went to pick up her feet she found she couldn't move. She couldn't do anything but stare—at the new lines that creased her mother's forehead, at the long coil of white hair that whipped behind her as she strode down toward the water's edge. For one frightening moment, Oona felt as if she'd traded places with whoever had made that splash. The warmth of the fire seemed to ebb away, and without it she was left paralyzed, too stiff with cold to swim.

But just as quick as it came on, the feeling passed when Oona saw Holly stand up in the surf. She hadn't noticed either Holly or the other Initiate rush down to the water; she'd been too busy looking at her mother. But while Ursula stood on the shore, Holly waded through the waves with her arm wrapped around the waist of another woman.

*No,* Oona thought as she watched them. *Not a woman, a girl.* A tiny thing with limbs like sapling branches. She was still a ways back, but Oona could see that she was wearing some kind of long white dress. As the water swirled about her knees, her ankles, it clung to her bony chest, to the tight drum of her belly. It was enough to make Oona sick.

*Not again,* she thought. Prayed.

And then the girl was kneeling in the sand, coughing, sputtering. Shivering, but alive.

Oona closed her eyes in relief, and Shelly squeezed her shoulder. "Thank god," Shelly whispered.

Across the circle, Vivian rolled her eyes. "Of course it's her," she said.

Eight Years bobbed her head, seemingly in agreement. Oona had met them only minutes earlier, but already it seemed clear that Eight Years was the nodding type, ready to second anything someone as imperious as Vivian had to say.

"Do you know her?" Oona asked.

Vivian's eyes lit. It was unnerving. "Don't you?" Her lips curled into something like a smile. "Take another look."

Oona glanced back at the water. Both Holly and the girl had gotten to their feet and made their way back up the beach. Now they were standing, huddled together, in front of the fire. As Oona watched, Ursula draped a heavy wool blanket over each of their shoulders. Oona turned to Vivian again. "I don't know what you mean."

"She doesn't look familiar?"

"Ohh," said a woman from the other end of the circle. "She's that girl, isn't she? The one whose mother runs that magazine. What's it called? *Glow*?"

"It's a blog," Vivian said. "Well, it's practically an empire, with the website and the newsletter, her social media following, the cookbooks, and the line of candles and bath salts. But yes, that's Astrid Nystrom's daughter. Remember her? Astrid used to post pictures of her all the time in her mini-couture, with all those blond curls. Now look at her. Knocked up at sixteen, and by some junkie at rehab, or at least that's what I've heard."

"No!" the other woman gasped. "At rehab? Really?"

Vivian shrugged and smiled her Cheshire Cat smile. "That's just what I've heard."

"From whom?" Shelly asked.

"What?"

"How do you know all of this about . . ." Shelly's eyes flicked back toward the fire. "What's her name?"

"Gemma," the other woman said. "I remember seeing pictures of her when she was, like, five years old. She was the cutest thing. Big brown eyes. Rosy cheeks. She looked like an angel."

Vivian snorted. "Well, she's clearly no angel. From what I've read, she's had some serious issues with drugs. So Astrid sent her here to stay clean and wait out the pregnancy. Too late for an abortion, I guess."

"Poor girl," Shelly said, softly.

Oona touched her stomach. "How far along is she, do you think?"

"I've heard five months," Vivian said.

Shelly frowned. "Tragic."

And Vivian nodded, newly solemn. "It really is."

But Oona could tell from the pinch in her mouth, from the cant of her eyebrows, that she wasn't feeling what Shelly was feeling—some kind of pity. Instead, Vivian looked bitter. No, she looked jealous. Oona looked around the circle: They all did.

With a spike of fear, she snatched her hands back from her belly. Better not to draw attention, she thought. If her goal was to blend in, then she couldn't risk becoming the focus of these women's ire the way Gemma Nystrom had.

Oona peered over at the fire. Gemma. Where had she heard that name before? And, of course, that's when it came to her: the chalkboard between their bedroom doors. Gemma was her roommate.

Oona glanced at Shelly and found Shelly was already looking at her. Apparently, she'd arrived at the same realization. This girl—this half-drowned harpy—was theirs.

By the refreshment table the speakers cut out, and when Oona looked over her shoulder she saw that Holly was leading Gemma up the hill and into the woods. If Oona had pulled a stunt like Gemma had, back when she still lived at the Center, her mother would've dragged her away. She would've grabbed a fistful of the keys Oona wore like a necklace and pulled till the string bit into the back of her neck. But Gemma . . . Oona watched as Holly draped her arm gently around Gemma's shoulders, hugged her to her side to keep her warm. Gemma was being treated like what she was: a child in need of coddling. Fragile, delicate. Maybe even ill.

Oona turned away, surprised and more than a little embarrassed by the resentment she felt bubble up inside her. When she looked back at the beach, she saw that Joyce was standing on an overturned apple crate, waving her short, muscular arms to gather the women close. Behind her, Ursula was already sitting cross-legged in the sand, her white silk robes pooled around her so from where Oona stood it looked like her mother was floating in a circle of light.

"I think it's time," Shelly said.

Vivian's head jerked up. It appeared she hadn't noticed, but as soon as her gaze landed on Ursula she took off. Without so much as a goodbye, she started power-walking toward the fire, determined—it seemed to Oona—to beat the others and get a front-row seat.

"Hello, everyone!" Joyce called out once the thirty or so women on the beach had collected around her. They stood in a layered semicircle, row after row like shark teeth. "And welcome to those of you who came in on the later ferry today. I know you missed our traditional Welcome Talk and likely have a few questions about the layout of the Center, your schedule, and the times you'll be expected for daily meditation and meals. In your cabins, you should find a map as well as both a daily and a weekly calendar. And of course, our staff is always available to help. I'm Joyce," she said, moving aside one of her thick gray braids to gesture to her name tag. "And over there are: Lally, Donna, Carol, and Alice. We're missing Holly right now, but over by the fire you'll see our other Initiate for the summer: Inez. Inez, can you wave so everyone can see you?"

Begrudgingly, as if the act pained her, the younger, darker-haired Initiate raised one hand in a kind of salute.

"Holly and Inez will both be at morning meditation, which will be held here on the beach at seven o'clock. If you need anything, just come find them in the morning. Okay?" Joyce asked the Mothers, and around the circle Oona saw their heads jog. "Okay." She clapped once. "Then let's begin. Inez?"

At the sound of her name, Inez stepped up to the fire with a tin pail of seawater. When Joyce nodded, she cast the water out over the flames. It took a few pails, a few resolute trips back and forth from the water's edge, but eventually Inez succeeded in dousing the bonfire. As the women watched in silence, the remaining embers hissed and glowed.

Oona knew the next step so well—had spent so many summers spying from the scrub grass—that she nearly sat down before she was told. At the last moment, though, she caught herself and she waited: for Joyce to pick up the apple crate and exit her make-do stage, and for the women around her to grow quiet and shift their attention over to Ursula, who was still sitting with her eyes closed in the sand.

Only once the circle was silent did Ursula speak, and even then she didn't open her eyes. "This is a moon fertility ritual," she announced, her voice rising above the sound of the waves. "It's how I always like to begin our Summer Sessions here at Bare Root. Please." She gestured toward the beach around her. "Join me."

Immediately, Vivian rushed to sit by Ursula's side, and the rest of the women scurried after her, inching this way and that until they all sat shoulder-to-shoulder in one large circle. Without the fire, the wind coming off the water was chilling, but at least the sand, so close to where the fire had burned, was still warm.

"Now, as many of you have, I hope, noticed, tonight is a full moon. A Pink Supermoon, to be exact. So it's the perfect time to take advantage of the moon's power and the pull of the tides to cleanse ourselves of whatever negative energies we may have brought with us to Marrow. Maybe, last month, you received a disappointing diagnosis—PCOS, DOR. Maybe your IUI didn't take or your egg retrieval yielded no viable embryos. Maybe you suffered yet another miscarriage. Whatever it is that broke your heart, that brought you here, it's time to say thank you to it because we are grateful that it got you to this place of healing, and then it's time to let it go. So"—Ursula looked out over the circle, and Oona followed her gaze as her mother's eyes lifted up to the moon shimmering over the water, to the stars, now bright without the fire's flames—"I want you all to close your eyes," she said. "And listen to the waves. Do you hear them? Listen as they crash against the rocks. And then the undertow. Try to feel it, the pull of the moon, the tide. That tug, can you feel it? Feel it deep down in your belly. Now picture your negative energy. Name in your mind the thing that hurts, and force that energy down to your core. Imagine it there, like a ball of light. Feel its heat, pulsing. Then take a deep breath in through your nose, out through your mouth, and imagine pushing that ball of light out into the world, imagine you're giving birth and push, push, push!"

Oona cracked an eye and snuck a glance at the women on either side of her. To her right, Shelly was panting, breathing in short little gasps. While to Oona's left, Eight Years had furrowed her brow and screwed up her eyes, like she was attempting to make out something far in the distance. They were trying too hard, Oona knew. Vivian too. Sitting in the sand next to Ursula, she was grunting so much it sounded like she was constipated. It took everything Oona had inside her not to laugh like she had when she was little, spying from up above.

"Now," Ursula said, and afraid of getting caught, Oona clamped her eyes shut again. "Now that the bad energy is out of your body, imagine the waves carrying it away. Picture the water rushing in, and then the pull of the tide. That power. Dragging, dragging. Take a breath in through your nose, breathe in the moon's white light. And then out through your mouth, releasing those final dregs of hurt, of heartbreak. Breathe out that dingy gray light. Now open your eyes. Do you see it leaving your body?"

Around the circle, Oona heard the women begin to giggle and gasp. They could see it, they said. Look! Look! And indeed when Oona peeked open one eye, she could see it too: Each time she exhaled, a tiny cloud formed before her, gray as dirty bathwater. It was a relief, she found, to see it all made so real. All the bad energy she'd felt stewing inside her now for months, years—all the loneliness and bitterness and frustration, all the anxiety and angst, all the fear. There on the beach, she could see it all. She could reach out and touch it. And while she knew that if given the chance Jacob would find some way to sap the magic from that moment—explain that it was just condensation, their warm breath in the cold night air—seeing that cloud of fog made Oona feel better. After only a few minutes, she found that she was able to picture her last miscarriage without becoming dizzy and weak.

"When you were accepted to this year's Summer Session," Ursula said, "you were sent a packet of materials in the mail. Do you remember?"

Beside Oona, Vivian nodded. Eight Years reached for Oona's hand in the dark.

"You were asked to spend some time thinking about which fertility goddess spoke to you, which one you were going to spend your time here, and hopefully ever after, calling upon and praying to. Some of you probably chose Demeter, goddess of fertility and the harvest. Or maybe Diana, protector of childbirth. I won't ask you to name your goddess now. We'll get to that in the days to come. For now, I just want you to close your eyes again and picture her. Imagine your goddess sitting there, right in front of you. What does she look like?"

All around the circle, Oona watched the women dutifully close their eyes. Eight Years pulled her hands back into her own lap and knit her fingers together. They were all concentrating so hard to conjure their goddesses—women they likely imagined looking something like Ursula. Clad in long, billowing white robes. Hair in a loosened braid. Silver jewelry glinting in the moonlight. But Oona knew that was child's play. If a goddess were to really sit down in the sand before you, she wouldn't look like a fairy stepped out of a dream. She would be a nightmare. The sea incarnate. A woman birthed from a storm. All whipping winds and swelling waves. She would be a fury. Or at least, that was how Hekate had appeared to her.

As a girl, Oona had spent years waiting to see her first goddess. She'd expected that it would be Persephone because her mother had told her that Persephone was always the first goddess to visit a young witch. In fact, that was one way her mother tested for power: Any girl nearing puberty was instructed to report her first day of menstruation, and then the coven waited to see if Persephone would appear. But as desperate as Oona had been to gain access to Lally's herb stores and the coven's spell books, she'd never trusted herself to lie convincingly about seeing Persephone. For as long as Oona could remember, her mother had insisted that she was not, and never would be, a witch. Magic, she told Oona often and definitively, did not run through her blood. So Oona had known that if she claimed to see

Persephone, Ursula wouldn't simply take her at her word. She would demand proof; and when Oona could not provide that proof, she would be found out, humiliated, punished. So no, Oona had never even considered trying to lie. But she'd also never considered admitting the truth, because if she had, her mother would have written her off for good. So instead, for years, she'd taken each pair of her stained panties and buried them deep in the woods.

It hadn't been much of a plan, but then again Oona had never been much of a planner. That was another of Ursula's regular complaints: Too often, Oona flew by the seat of her pants. She lacked self-control and discipline. She was impulsive. Still, for a time, her plan had worked. Lally convinced her mother that Oona was just a late bloomer, and Oona, for her part, spent all her free time trying to will Persephone to appear. She wasn't allowed to attempt any real magic—she wouldn't be considered a Maiden until she saw Persephone and therefore wasn't allowed to even *study* Craft—but she tried yoga, meditation, and lucid dreaming. She tried acupuncture and Reiki. She even snuck some of Lally's herbal pills. But nothing worked. At least not until that last summer on the island, when she went on a hike with Jacob up the east-side cliffs.

They'd just reached the peak, the tallest point on the island, when Oona looked down and saw something floating in the ocean. No, not something. Some*one*. She and Jacob took off running, but Oona was the one who reached the shore first. And that's when she saw her— Hekate—rising out of the water. Her hair dark and lank as kelp. Her skin the kind of white that signals death on the water—sun-bleached, like the belly of a washed-up seal. She was carrying the body in her arms, like a sleeping child, bearing it through the waves' froth and tumult. And then, suddenly, Jacob was next to Oona in the sand, sprinting past her, kneeling over the body in the surf, and Hekate was gone.

In the circle, Ursula asked the women to call upon their goddesses to help them on their journeys, then she told them all to place their hands upon their wombs. "Picture yourself pregnant," she said. "Feel your round, full belly and the little baby kicking and rolling inside."

As Shelly began to rub her stomach, Oona placed her hands back on her belly and closed her eyes.

"Talk to your baby," Ursula commanded. "Tell them how much you love them, how much you long to be their mama. Let them know that you are ready for them now and ask them if they need anything from you before they come. Ask, and then listen."

In the sand, Oona tried to fight back her unease. All around her, she saw women mouthing messages to their children, not just unborn but unconceived. And while Oona understood their desperation—she was nothing if not desperate, sneaking back into her hometown like a thief—their sincerity, their *sweetness*, left her feeling like a fraud. She wanted the pregnancy, yes. She wanted the title of Mother. But the baby? She hadn't allowed herself to think much about what would happen after the birth. All she'd known when she'd left Portland was that she was unhappy. More than unhappy. That every morning, she'd woken up longing to go home. But was she meant to say all of that to her unborn child? Surely not.

Defeated, Oona opened her eyes and looked out at the water. When she'd first told Jacob what she'd seen that day by the cliffs, he'd assured her that she must have been mistaken. It had just been a trick of the light, he'd said, or a seal's head bobbing in the surf. He'd meant it as a comfort, of course, but looking back, Oona couldn't help but feel gaslit. Once, she'd thought that Jacob was the only person who loved her without expectation, who thought she was magic even without her mother's gifts. But now . . . now she wasn't so sure. Because it had turned out that Jacob was just like everybody else. He, too, wanted her to be different. Not the same kind of different, but different all the same. And while she'd thought it might be a relief to finally stop trying so hard to prove that her mother was wrong about her inheritance, to give up her nightly attempts at lucid dreaming, quit the acupuncture and the Reiki, the truth was that living on the mainland had been just as hard as living on the island. Harder, even.

Jacob was often gone, crewing for a research vessel out at sea, and Oona's job cleaning motel rooms had been far from fulfilling. No, as she'd tried to explain countless times to Jacob, she needed more. There had to be more to the world, she thought, than unmade beds and dirty toilets. There had to be more to *her*. That's why she'd returned.

It was clear by now, twenty years after she first got her period, that she was never going to see Persephone, but she still thought there was a chance that she had power. In another life, she might've begged her mother or Lally to test her the way they tested the Initiates at the end of every Summer Session, or the way they tested the witches who were not brought up in the coven but who joined later on in their lives. She might've been able to prove herself, she thought, if she'd been allowed to remain on Marrow. But of course she hadn't been allowed to stay. She'd been banished, exiled. And now her only hope was that she could start over. If she could just become a Mother, then even without Bare Root, she'd come into her power and gain enough strength to practice Craft on her own. Then she could start her own coven, like her mother had done. And once she had her own coven, her own community, then maybe she would be happy. Happy enough, anyway.

Sitting there in the sand, Oona heard Shelly mutter something under her breath. It sounded like "please." And without thinking, Oona reached for her belly again. *Please*, she thought. *Please be real.*

She wasn't sure whom she was talking to—the baby or Hekate—but begging felt familiar. She'd pleaded that same way a dozen times before as she lay alone on the floor of their rental's tiny bathroom, unable to stanch the flow of blood. It had never worked before, so Oona wasn't sure why she thought this time would be any different, why this *place* would be any different, but still she kept asking—praying—for help, until she felt Shelly shift beside her, heard Eight Years begin to stand up.

The ritual was over, and she felt no different. Nothing had changed for her. She was not transformed. She was just a stupid woman sitting in the dark, playing at witchcraft. She might as well have been at a sleepover, whispering "light as a feather, stiff as a board."

When Ursula stood and began her speech to end the ritual, Oona opened her eyes. The cliffs she'd hiked with Jacob were still about three miles away, but the ocean in front of her was the same ocean. If Hekate were anywhere, Oona had thought she'd be there. But that, she supposed, was just wishful thinking. No, Jacob was probably right. She hadn't seen anything that day at the cliffs. No goddess had ever appeared to her, which meant that she had no powers. The ritual she'd performed had failed and there was no curse.

She was not her mother's daughter and she didn't belong—not to the Bare Root coven or to any other. So there was no use waiting for Beltane. In the morning, she told herself, she could go.

But no sooner had she gotten to her feet then she saw something dark move out of the corner of her eye. "Did you see that?" she asked Shelly, who was standing beside her. Oona pointed at the water.

"See what?" Shelly asked.

"It looked like—" Oona started, but before she got a chance to finish her sentence she felt them: the flutters. So much stronger than before. "I thought I saw something in the water."

Vivian stepped closer. "Probably just a cormorant."

"Maybe," Oona said, but in the dark she gripped her belly tighter. The baby—she could feel it moving, *swimming* in there. It didn't make sense—it was, as Jacob would say, utterly illogical—but somehow she had the feeling that the baby had felt it, the presence of whatever Oona had thought she'd spotted offshore. Some kind of waterfowl, as Vivian had suggested, or a seal, like Jacob had guessed all those years before. But then again . . .

"Don't forget!" Ursula called as the women began filtering up the beach toward the woods. "Morning meditation is at seven tomorrow!"

Shelly turned to Oona. "Do you want to walk back with me? I'm headed home."

"Home," Oona repeated under her breath. It was hard to believe that she was finally back, finally allowed to call some tiny part of Marrow home again. It felt so good, so *right*.

She might even sleep, she thought, as she followed Shelly back up the beach. For the first time in more than a decade, she might not startle awake missing the sounds of the sea.

# TWO

When Oona was a girl, her mother's coven was small. Selective, Ursula liked to say, because it wasn't just any witch who could live according to the rules of their order: isolated, removed from the world and from its men. Each spring, she tried to find new recruits among the young women in Portland. She visited the local shelters, the food pantries, the soup kitchens, and while it was easy enough to convince those women to spend the summer out there on the island in exchange for room and board, easy enough even to convert them—Ursula had her own kind of gravitational pull—getting them to stay proved nearly impossible. When the time came, each fall, for the women to be tested for power, to see if they qualified to go through Initiation, most of them fled. Some, because they'd found out that the child they were carrying when they'd arrived was not a daughter they could raise up in the coven, a potential future Maiden, but rather a son they'd have to raise back on the mainland. Others, because they were now swimming in grief. It wasn't all that common—thankfully, it seemed to happen only every few years—but sometimes an Initiate's abuse of drugs or alcohol would result in the loss of her child, in a stillbirth. And while those women would still be considered Mothers if they joined the coven, none of them ever chose to stay. So, for the most part, the witches Oona had grown up around were older—women who had not been recruited by Ursula, but who had instead shown up one day on the Center's doorstep claiming they'd been called; women whose children were already grown or whose motherhood was complicated for various reasons. Of course, like the Initiates, those women all had to first be tested before they could go through Initiation, but if they passed, they joined the coven as Mothers rather than Maidens, which meant they were able to not only study but practice their Craft.

On the ferry ride, Oona had wondered which of the witches she'd known as a child would still be living at the Center. She'd imagined that some had likely moved on. After all, it'd been fifteen years. But as she looked around the cafeteria at lunch on her second day on the island, she realized that not only were Joyce and Donna and all the other witches she used to know still present, there were new witches too. And they were younger. One looked barely out of high school.

Oona hadn't paid much attention to these other witches at first—not at the bonfire the night before and not at breakfast earlier that morning—but as soon as she stepped out of the lunch line she spotted them. They were all sitting together at one of the long driftwood tables not too far from the doors. And while the new witches weren't dressed in any identifying clothing—as a rule, the coven reserved robes for rites and rituals—Oona recognized them as belonging to the coven just the same. It was in the way they sat: so comfortable, so easy, like they were sitting at a table in their own home. And, she supposed, they were.

It was hard not to feel jealous. As she watched them, envy curdled in her stomach, rose up her throat like bile. She wanted to take her tray and find a seat at whatever table was closest to them, sit where she could overhear their conversation, maybe pretend she was one of them for the time it took to eat her lunch. But she didn't dare get so close. If she drew attention to herself, she knew it would be only a matter of time before the women who knew her would be able to see past her short, dyed hair. And she needed her disguise to hold up for at least two more days, until she received the protection spell at the Beltane celebration.

"What's wrong?" Shelly asked, when Oona finally made it over to the table where she was sitting. If it were up to her, Oona would have chosen to eat alone, but again, she knew she couldn't risk standing out. And as nice as Shelly was—and she *was* nice, maybe the kindest person Oona had met at Bare Root—she was also nosy. They hadn't even been on the island twenty-four hours, and already Oona had lost count of the number of times Shelly had asked her who someone was, where they were going, what they were doing, and why. She carried her little spiral notebook everywhere she went, and the way she was always scribbling in it, it was like she expected to write a report on the Center when she went home.

"Nothing," said Oona, then she held her breath as she waited for Shelly to ask again.

Despite her telltale raised eyebrow, though, Shelly remained quiet. Instead, she turned her attention to Vivian, who had started telling the others at the table about Shelly's roommate, June. Apparently, June had suffered some kind of breakdown during their first lesson in grounding and was now headed home.

After breakfast that morning the women had been divided into two groups—half were sent to attend an introductory lecture on Craft given by the coven's Initiates, Inez and Holly; the other half had met with Ursula in the lodge. While the Summer Session Mothers were never taught the kind of advanced (and dangerous) witchcraft practiced by the coven, Bare Root made a promise to its attendees: By the end of the Summer Session, they would come to learn enough of the basics of fertility magic that they would be able to use Craft to help themselves. Of course, their success would depend entirely on whether they actually had power (a fact the Center, conveniently, failed to mention on its website). But for those who did have power, and for those who truly mastered the skills taught to them on the island, the summer could be transformational. It could mean the difference between failure and success, between motherhood and . . . well, whatever else one could have. But of course the women couldn't just jump right into carving sigils into candles and working with crystals. They first had to learn the fundamentals, like grounding. So that was what Ursula had focused on that morning, or so Vivian explained. Oona, thankfully (*thankfully* because she didn't trust her new hair would continue to fool her mother if they were trapped together in a room), had been sent to attend the Initiates' lecture. So she, like Shelly, had missed the scene with June, but according to Vivian, only a few minutes into their practice the woman had just started weeping, shaking. Inez had had to lead her from the room. By the time Shelly stopped by the cabin before lunch, June's things were all gone. Her name had been erased from the chalkboard.

"Gosh, what do you think happened?" asked Eight Years, whose name, Oona had learned, was actually Grace. At least five years younger than Oona, she was patient, thoughtful. Sweet, if maybe a little naive. She looked like a 1950s housewife, with her voluptuous hourglass figure and her ringlet curls, and she claimed her life was just about *Leave It to Beaver* perfect: She'd married a kind man who earned a solid living, and she had good relationships with all four of his children. Though they were grown by the time she met them, one even called her Mom. The only thing missing was a baby.

"Maybe some kind of family emergency?" Shelly suggested, taking a sip from her glass of moon tea. Oona knew the recipe by heart: raspberry leaf, lemon balm, ginger, and nettle. It was supposed to help regulate a woman's cycles, maintain healthy blood flow to the womb. "I'm pretty sure I overheard someone saying something about her father."

"Or she just couldn't hack it," said Vivian, smug.

Shelly frowned and Oona wondered if the past twelve hours had caused her to rethink her first impression of Vivian—if maybe, that night at dinner, she'd be able to convince Shelly that it would be better if the two of them ate alone. They could sit at one of the high-tops near the patio on the other side of the cafeteria, far from Vivian and the rest of her gaggle, far from the table of coven witches who had, Oona noticed, now quit with their chatter and were instead quietly surveying the room. Would they recognize her? Oona wondered, as she watched Joyce scan the dining hall. If one of them were to call out her name, what would she do? Deny, deny, deny? Or insist that she was Maggie? If they called for Ursula, would she run?

Oona felt sweat prick at her underarms as, down the table, Vivian grew defensive.

"What?" Vivian asked, looking from Shelly to Grace and back again. "This program isn't for the weak-minded. It's rigorous. Didn't you read all those disclosure forms we had to sign?"

Vivian was once a lawyer, a fact she'd mentioned twice already.

Ignoring Vivian, Shelly spoke to the rest of the table. "Whatever the reason, I hope June will be okay."

"Well of course," the other women murmured in unison.

Grace turned to Oona. "What about your roommate, Maggie?" she whispered. "Have you met her yet?"

"Oh yes," Vivian purred. "Do tell. What's the little princess like?"

"I—" Oona darted her eyes toward the table of coven witches and was alarmed to discover it empty. She swiveled in her seat, hoping that maybe they'd all just gone. But no such luck. Instead, Oona saw Donna standing at the head of a table not too far from hers, chatting. And at the table next door, two of the new witches, who looked like mother and daughter, were asking a group of Mothers if they were enjoying their lunches, settling in okay.

Across the table, Vivian pursed her lips. She was always doing that.

"I don't know," Oona said. "I still haven't seen her. She never came back to the cabin last night."

"Really?" Vivian asked. Oona didn't like how this information seemed to please her. "Do you think we're going to have another dropout on our hands? You ladies could each end up with a private room. Now, wouldn't that be lucky?"

"We're not hoping for that, Vivian," Shelly said.

But Oona wasn't so sure. A private room might be more comfortable. Might be safer. No one to riffle through her things, to discover the cell phone buried at the bottom of her duffel, Jacob's many missed calls. Not to mention the fact that Oona had a bad feeling about Gemma. She'd felt it as soon as she'd seen her in the water: Something was wrong with that girl. Spoiled, Oona thought. Spoiled rotten.

"Maybe you're right," Oona offered. "Maybe she couldn't hack it."

"Maggie," Shelly chided. Then, to the rest of the table, "I asked around, and from what I understand her blood sugar was just low. She fainted while standing on the jetty."

"Likely story," sneered Vivian.

And despite herself, Oona nodded along. She hated to agree with

Vivian, but when she'd woken that morning to find the other bed in her room empty, the covers undisturbed, she'd known enough to guess where Gemma might have spent the night: in the infirmary. And though she'd tried to go back to sleep, in the end Oona hadn't been able to push the image from her mind: Gemma lying in bed with Ursula at her side, holding her hand. She'd tossed and turned before she'd finally given up. To kill the remaining hour before morning meditation, she'd dug her cell out of her duffel. By the time she heard Shelly shuffling around out in the living room, she'd read everything she could find about Gemma Nystrom on her phone.

Well, she'd done that *and* she'd listened to the voicemails Jacob had left her. Just like she'd feared he might, he'd beaten her home. And when he'd realized she was missing, he'd started calling. By the time she'd woken up, he'd left twenty-seven messages on her phone. In the first few he'd sounded worried, but as the night had dragged on—as Oona had slept soundly beside the empty bed of a missing girl—Jacob's voice in the messages had grown more desperate, pleading. He'd sounded terrified, and listening to those voicemails had nearly caused Oona to second-guess her choice. Was she wrong to have left the way she did? Was she being cruel? Well, maybe. But she was doing it for him too—for *them*. And even then, this was only a last resort. After all, she'd tried to talk to Jacob. Countless times, she'd attempted to explain how she felt, that it wasn't just that she was lonely, isolated, friendless; that it wasn't just that she'd felt unfulfilled by her motel job. It was bigger than that. It was existential—a word Oona had discovered the last time she'd tried to google her symptoms, searching for a diagnosis, and had come up short. Like a migratory bird blown off course by a storm, she'd spent every waking hour since being banished from the island trying to reorient herself to a world without Craft. She'd done her best to redefine her idea of home.

But despite her efforts, she'd failed. Portland was not home and it never would be. For a time, Oona had actually given up on the idea of ever feeling whole again. But then she'd gotten pregnant, and the idea had occurred to her: If she became a Mother, then maybe she could found her own coven and, in doing so, finally find her way to a new kind of home.

It was what her mother had done. Sent off on Visitation (a kind of Rumspringa young women in her coven went on to try to get pregnant), Ursula had spent years attempting to become a Mother. Her own mother had left when she was young, so when the rest of her coven began to lose faith in her, it had been her grandmother who'd convinced them to give her more time. Eventually, though, her grandmother died and Ursula was cast out, forbidden to return. To support herself, she'd used the skills her grandmother had taught her and she'd become a midwife in a nearby town. She'd thought that was it for her—the goddesses had found her wanting, and so while she may have had power, she would never be strong enough to practice witchcraft on her own—but then one night, Demeter appeared.

She came to Ursula in a dream and told her to concoct a potion of uterine blood and breast milk, dried placenta. When she next felt her body begin to ovulate, she was to spread this mixture over her womb. Then, when the moon was full, she was to speak her prayer aloud, to describe the child she wished to carry. Oona never forgot the description. Like Ursula, she was supposed to be blue-eyed and blond. She was supposed to be quiet and composed. Obedient and disciplined. Ursula had prayed for a *good* child. Instead, Oona was wild. "Feral," Ursula used to call her. Impatient and nosy and often out of control. Ursula liked to say that she must have failed to follow Demeter's instructions precisely to give birth to such a daughter, but the fact remained that Demeter had followed through. She'd granted Ursula a child, and through that child, the gift of Craft. But even once she was a Mother, Ursula couldn't bear the idea of returning to her old coven, of begging for the scraps of their love. So she started a new coven, on Marrow. And in the early nauseated weeks of her first pregnancy, Oona had comforted herself with the idea that she might do the same. But only nine weeks in, she lost that baby. At eight weeks, she lost the one after that. And on and on, until, afraid of a sixth loss, she finally grew desperate enough to chop off her hair in a gas station bathroom, buy a bottle of cheap dye from a drugstore.

In the note she'd left for Jacob, Oona hadn't told him where she was going, but she had told him about the baby. *You're not thinking clearly*, that's what Jacob had said in the final voicemail he left for her. And maybe he was right. Oona had felt so sure as she'd stood there on the beach the night before, holding her belly, but by lunchtime? She hadn't felt a single flutter all day. She hadn't felt anything, in fact. The fancy organic peanut butter Shelly had spread all over her Ezekiel bread that morning at breakfast hadn't even bothered her. So she had to wonder: What if it was already too late? What if the curse had once again caught up to her?

"Maggie?" Shelly touched Oona's arm. "Are you okay, honey?"

Oona shook herself back to attention. Beside her, Shelly looked concerned. Vivian looked gossip-hungry, and Oona thanked her lucky stars that she'd had the foresight not to reveal the truth about her pregnancy the night before. She couldn't imagine what Vivian might do if she found out that Oona was already expecting. Sitting there in the dining hall, she had a flash of blood and gore. She'd heard horror stories, of course. They all had. About women gone missing, murdered; about babies cut from wombs.

"We were just asking about the rest of the day," Shelly explained. "What's on your schedule?"

While their mornings were spent attending lectures on Craft and learning things like grounding and spell work, the women's afternoons were reserved for personalized treatment. Massage sessions, aromatherapy regimens, essential oil therapies. That afternoon, Grace had a reflexology appointment, while Vivian and Shelly would be undergoing hypnotherapy. Oona dug around in her bag for the folder with her schedule. She'd found it on the coffee table in their common room when they'd gotten back from the beach the night before.

"I have an acupuncture treatment at three," she said, reading from the sheet of paper. "And right after lunch, I have my assessment." She looked up at Shelly. "Do you know what that is?"

"Your physical exam," Shelly said. "I'm pretty sure we all have one at some point this week. Don't we?"

Around the table, the other women bobbed their heads.

Oona turned to search the room for the coven witches, for Joyce in particular, as she'd been the one who'd performed all the checkups (back then, they'd called them checkups) when Oona was young. The last time she'd looked around, Joyce had been seated at a table far from theirs and she'd looked comfortable, sitting beside an older woman with gray streaks in her hair. She'd been nursing a mug of tea, and when the woman started tearing up Joyce had leaned over to rub her back gently. At the time, Oona had thought it was a good sign. Around the dining hall, all the witches had looked like they were deep in conversation, and since lunch was nearly over, Oona had thought that she'd be able to finish her meal undisturbed. But now, when she swiveled to peer over her shoulder, she saw that Joyce had moved to a table only two over. One more and she'd be close enough to reach out and tug Oona's hair. Too close for comfort, in other words. And while for a moment Oona struggled with the urge she felt to be discovered—with her weakness for self-sabotage—her rational side won out.

"Have any of you had your exams yet?" Shelly asked the table.

"Mine's not until Friday," Vivian pouted. "That's late, isn't it? Maybe I need to talk to someone. I certainly don't want to waste an entire week, getting treatment that might not even be suitable for me."

"I don't think you need to worry. They have your medical history," Grace reminded Vivian. Then, to Oona: "I had mine this morning. They took my blood pressure and a few vials of blood. Then they asked me a couple questions. It was pretty simple."

Oona snuck another glance at Joyce and was distressed to realize that she was on the move again.

"Maggie," said Grace gently. "After lunch, I have a reflexology appointment. It's in the building right next to the infirmary. So I could walk with you, if you'd like?"

"Oh," Oona said, distracted. "That's, um. That's really nice, but I . . ." She trailed off as Joyce approached their table. When it looked like she might actually sit down, Oona dropped her eyes and held her breath. But she got lucky: Joyce didn't stop to chat with any of them. At the last second, she swung past them and zeroed in on a woman at the next table over who looked like she was struggling to read her map. Still, Oona thought, it was time to go. "I just remembered, I was going to stop by the cabin before my exam. So I think I'll just head out now."

Shelly nodded at Oona's tray. "But you haven't finished your food."

"That's okay," Oona said. "I'm not that hungry." Then, before any of the others at the table could ask her to wait, she rose, dumped her lunch into the nearest trash can, and headed for the doors.

᙮

As soon as she was outside, Oona breathed a sigh of relief. She was safe, at least for the time being. She could remain hidden as Maggie Jones. But she made it only halfway down the sandy path that led through the woods to the medical buildings before that sense of relief soured, fermented into something closer to resentment, rage. She shouldn't have to pretend to be someone else, Oona thought bitterly as the path's sand gave way to gnarled roots and stone. After all, this place was supposed to belong to her. It was supposed to be her inheritance. If anyone deserved to be there, it was her. But no. While she was forced to sneak away and scuttle through the forest like some kind of vermin, women like Vivian got to take their time finishing lunch, got to complain that the Greek yogurt they'd been served was too tart, that the kimchi wasn't exactly authentic. What had happened to the peanut butter and jelly sandwiches they used to serve, anyway? When had Ursula decided that they were no longer good enough?

She supposed it had probably happened around the same time the Center began accepting girls like Gemma Nystrom. Back when Oona lived on the island, Ursula had had a very specific set of criteria that she required women to meet before she agreed to take them on. Sure, she had still charged a small fee for her services, for room and board and all that, but money hadn't been the only object. Back then, it had been more important to Ursula that she was helping women who reminded her of herself: women who *deserved* to be Mothers. Smart women, brave women, women of faith. Now it appeared that all her standards had gone out the window, because the only thing Gemma Nystrom had to recommend her, at least as far as Oona could tell after researching her online, was her mother's name and money. According to the tabloids, the girl was a mess and a half. Selfish, spoiled, always either drunk or high. Not at all the kind of woman Bare Root had been founded to help, and yet . . .

Oona came to a stop as soon as she recognized the infirmary's yellow door through the trees. She knew that the birthing suites weren't far beyond. A lot had changed about the Center, a whole hell of a lot, including an enormous new—what? Lighthouse?—Oona had spotted back by the dining hall, but the general layout had remained the same. Oona had seen that when she'd studied the map included in her welcome folder. And while she'd forgotten certain things about Bare Root in the years that she'd been gone, the location of the infirmary wasn't one of them. She could probably find her way there even in the dark. She would know it by smell alone, by the way the air seemed to thin out the closer she got to the sacred birthing suites. Anyway, she'd walked that same trail enough as a kid to have memorized it. She'd been running there for every bruise and blister, every beesting and skinned knee since she was five years old. Anything to get Ursula's attention, to get the chance to lie down on a cot's crisp white sheets and feel her mother's hand on her brow.

Now, Oona supposed, Gemma was the one lying swaddled in all that cool cotton. She might even have Oona's favorite quilt tucked around her feet. It was cold in the woods, beneath the thick tree canopy, but picturing Gemma in the infirmary caused Oona's palms to sweat; heat flushed up her neck and into her cheeks. When she was a kid and she got worked up like that, her mother used to say it was the result of bad humors, that the pink in her cheeks was evidence of her bad blood.

On the path, Oona took a few steps closer to the infirmary. The whole of the camp was filled with trees—oaks beside the cook's cabin, copses of hemlock that had sprouted up along the trails—but the infirmary and the birthing suites had been built at the true woods' edge.

Beyond them, until the cliffs, was nothing but forest. As a child, Oona had taken advantage of the forest's darkness, of its leafy density, to spy on the women in the infirmary and in the birthing suites, to spy on her mother, primarily because Ursula had made it clear that Oona was unwelcome in those spaces, especially in the birthing suites. Those rooms were sacred. Without the proper sacraments, no one was allowed to enter, especially not Oona. But of course there is nothing quite so tempting as what has been forbidden. And Oona was a natural spy. Sneaky, reckless. By the time she was six years old, she knew how to walk across pine needles without making a sound.

She never told anyone about the nights she spent in the woods or about what she saw through the infirmary's and birthing suites' back windows. She just took it in. And now, standing so close to that same grove of trees, it all came flooding back. Every anguished wail, every breathless pant, every newborn cry. The wave of jealousy—of yearning—that Oona felt took her by surprise. Like a rogue swell, it nearly toppled her. She never thought she'd dream about one day experiencing such pain. But pain was part of it, she knew. She needed the pain to transform her. Maiden into Mother. That was how it worked.

In order to get to the transformation, though, Oona had to reach full term. And to reach full term, she had to lift the curse. Or at least, she *thought* she did. If she was being completely honest with herself, Oona had to admit that she didn't totally know what she was doing. In fact, there was a chance that she wasn't even cursed. But as sick as it was, she hoped the curse was real because then she would know why she couldn't stay pregnant, and she'd know how to save the baby she was carrying: trick the coven into giving her the protection spell.

Growing up, Joyce had been the one to perform all the checkups, and it occurred to Oona, as she crept ever closer to the infirmary's back window, that perhaps she should have asked Grace if that was still true. If it was, then it would probably be smarter to skip the exam, beg one of the Initiates to perform it later. After all, her disguise wasn't exactly foolproof. So, to be safe, Oona decided to check in again at the windows, just like she'd done as a little girl.

She didn't think it was likely that she'd gotten any taller since the last time she'd slipped between those same pine trees, gripped the window's wooden ledge, and pressed her nose to the glass, but the whole process still felt different, sillier somehow. She nearly turned away, shaking her head at her own childishness, but just then, inside the infirmary, a figure appeared. A short, stout woman came through the doorway to the back room and began making up the examination table. Thankfully she didn't notice Oona, but Oona would have recognized her anywhere. Her small, round wireless glasses, the neat bun she always wore at the nape of her neck: it was Lally, her mother's right hand.

A Green Witch from just outside Galway, Lally had stumbled into Ursula's midwifery practice twenty-nine years earlier and collapsed into her arms. She'd been fleeing her husband, a cruel man who'd beaten her through most of their first month in America. When he took a job as a lobsterman in Portland, Lally seized her opportunity to escape. She got on the first boat she saw and ended up on Marrow still wearing her husband's parting gifts: a busted lip and a swollen eye socket. Ursula let Lally stay with them in their first house on the island, a tumbledown shack near the cliffs on the eastern side. It had no heat in the winter, besides what could be created from the wood-burning stove in the living room, but it was what had come with the position when Ursula had agreed to be the island's resident midwife. While at first Lally's stay was only meant to be temporary, over time her expertise became essential to Ursula's vision for her practice, and it wasn't long before the two women were able to pool their money and buy the campground that the Center had called home since that day.

Lally had known Oona since she was four years old. She had been part aunt, part fairy godmother, and Oona knew that no matter her hair color, there was no chance that Lally wouldn't recognize her once she got her up on the examination table. No, she would have to find another way.

Oona stepped back from the window. Really, she knew, she should go now. Quick, before Lally looked up and noticed her. Or before Joyce walked by and caught her standing in the brush. But to her surprise, Oona found herself reluctant to leave. Of course she'd often thought about her mother in the years that she'd been gone, imagined what she might say or do if she ever returned to the island—get down on her knees and beg forgiveness? Plead with Ursula to commute her sentence to time served?—but in all those years of daydreaming, she'd never had to wonder what she'd do if she ever saw Lally again. For however complicated her love—and it *was* love—for her mother was, her love for Lally was simple. The only thing she wanted to tell Lally was that she was sorry she'd had to leave so abruptly, that she'd missed her, and that she'd thought of her every day she'd been gone.

Despite how badly she wanted to knock at the window, though, Oona knew that she couldn't say those things now. Not while she was supposed to be Maggie. And she needed to keep being Maggie, at least for the weekend. So after a long minute, she finally turned and picked her way back through the brush. Without thinking, she started walking deeper into the woods and then deeper still. She didn't realize where she was going until she came upon the shed.

Back before her mother bought the campground, when the property still belonged to the Girl Scouts, the shed had been used to store equipment for archery. Growing up, Oona used to drag out the heavy hay-filled targets and test her skills with her slingshot by standing first five, then ten, then fifteen paces back. She hadn't thought of herself as lonely at the time, but it was also true that she hadn't had any friends. There were rarely any other children at the Center, and for many years Ursula had forbidden Oona to attend the local school in Port Marrow. The outside world was too dangerous, she said. And if Oona doubted it, all she had to do was look at the Initiates who came through each year. A new batch every summer, but they all looked the same: dirty, hungry, and afraid. They were girls whose parents had kicked them out when they'd turned up pregnant, girls whose boyfriends hit them or who'd gotten addicted to drugs.

They were meant to be a cautionary tale for Oona, but the scare tactic never really worked. Every year, Oona begged to be allowed to enroll in school, and finally, when she turned eleven and the Center really started taking off, Lally helped convince Ursula. The deal was simple: Oona could go, but once class ended she had to come straight back; she wasn't allowed to talk to strangers, especially not tourists from the mainland; and she was not allowed to bring any friends home. No one, absolutely no one, was allowed on Center grounds without Ursula's permission.

That was the year Oona met Daphne, the only other eleven-year-old on the island and the only girl in Port Marrow's one-room schoolhouse who dared speak to Oona on her first day. Everyone else—Jordan Clark, Matilda Johnson, the Roberts brothers—ignored her. Until, that is, they put two and two together and realized why she'd become the new teacher's pet. At that point, she became their favorite target.

It was inevitable in some ways, Oona supposed. Every adult on the island worshipped Ursula. If not because they believed in her power (though most of them did) then because her Center had revived their economy. Still, at the time, it had taken Oona by surprise. She'd never been teased before, never been bullied. The only daughter of the coven's head witch, she'd led a charmed life. Lonely, sure, but protected. In school, though, she'd quickly become a pariah, and for weeks she waited for Daphne to turn on her like the others, but she never did. In fact, far from becoming jealous, when Daphne learned who Oona's mother was, it seemed only to cement their friendship. Much to her brother Jacob's consternation, Daphne was fascinated by Bare Root. Often, she'd beg Oona to sneak her into the Center's classes, introduce her to her mother, but for a long time the closest she got to Ursula was the archery shed.

Located on the very edge of the Center's grounds, the shed had been Oona's first big concession. Though it had made her nervous, she'd agreed that if Daphne could find her way there, then they could hang out inside. Safe, she hoped, from being spotted—by her mother or by Lally, by Joyce or by any other witch. For years, they did nothing more inside the shed than study the herbs Oona pinched from Lally's garden, or practice drawing pentagrams in chalk on the bare plank floors, but not long after they both turned fourteen, Daphne started bringing contraband to the shed: half-drunk handles of cheap vodka, vanilla Camels she stole from her aunt. She claimed she'd read online that these things could be used in the practice of dark magic, and while Oona knew that was bullshit, she never said anything because she loved their afternoons: the two of them lying on the floor of the shed, buzzed on capfuls of sun-warmed vodka, their throats singed from the liquor and from the smoke.

Spotting the mossy peak of the shed's roof through the trees, Oona wondered if Daphne's smuggled goods might still be in there or if someone had cleaned everything out in the years that she'd been gone. She was about to go and check when she saw the door to the shed swing open.

The forest on that part of the island was dense, but since it was only April the leaves were still just buds on the trees, so when the girl stepped out of the shed and into the sun Oona could see the oversize knit cardigan she was wearing, her white leather Mary Janes. She couldn't see her hair, though, due to a dogwood's thin shadow, so for a brief, heart-stopping moment Oona thought it was Daphne, returned. But then the girl pulled a lighter out of her dress pocket, sat down on a nearby log, and started smoking. Daphne had never used a lighter. She'd had a whole collection of matchbooks her father had brought home, mementos from whenever his job as captain of the marine patrol had taken him to the mainland.

Oona debated turning around and giving whomever it was their privacy, but she had a sudden craving for the smell of the smoke from those vanilla Camels. When she emerged into the clearing, the girl on the log looked up. Oona saw defiance chase guilt across her face.

"You're not Holly," Gemma said.

"No," Oona replied, and for a minute she debated turning on her heels and walking back in the direction she'd come. This girl—this rich, spoiled princess—represented everything she resented about the Center and what it'd become, what *she'd* become without it. But as much as she wanted to shun her, Oona had to admit that she was at least a little intrigued too. And not just because, for a brief moment, anyway, Gemma had reminded her so much of Daphne that it had made Oona's chest ache.

"I'm Maggie," Oona lied. "You're Gemma, aren't you?"

"Depends who's asking."

"I think I'm your roommate."

Gemma took a long pull from her cigarette and released the smoke slowly, first through her nostrils and then through her mouth. "Did Holly send you to check up on me?"

"No."

"Then what're you doing here?"

"I could ask you the same question," Oona replied. Though, no-ticeably, she chose not to. Mostly because she didn't care. She didn't want to know why Gemma was sitting there smoking or where she'd slept the night before. She wasn't even curious about the long floral-print dress she was wearing, though it seemed odd for a girl her age, like a costume from *Little House on the Prairie*. But no, Oona wasn't concerned with whatever was or wasn't in fashion for teenagers. All she wanted to know was how Gemma had gotten herself chosen, se-lected by Ursula to be that summer's prized pet. Perhaps, Oona thought, it was because she was already pregnant.

Wondering how far along Gemma was, Oona let her gaze wander down to her belly, but Gemma caught her. "Are you going to tell Joyce on me?" she asked.

"What?" Oona said. "No." She hadn't even considered tattling, though as soon as Gemma mentioned it, she realized that was prob-ably the responsible thing to do. Vivian would have gladly alerted the authorities. And Shelly would have worried if she came upon Gemma alone in the woods. "I used to smoke Camel vanillas," Oona said. "I still love the smell of them." She eyed the spot on the log beside Gemma. "Can I sit?"

Gemma shrugged. "Sure."

So Oona lowered herself slowly. She didn't know exactly what she was doing, but that was hardly new. Ursula had been right about her, it had turned out, from the very beginning: Oona didn't think, she just *did*. She operated on instinct, like some kind of animal.

"You can have one if you want," Gemma offered, begrudging. "But I'll warn you—they're pretty stale." She jerked her chin at the shed behind them. "I just found them in there."

Oona shook her head lightly and said, "I shouldn't." But when

Gemma held the pack toward her she pulled out a single cigarette, brought it to her nose, and inhaled. She could still remember the day Daphne had brought her first pack of Camels to the Center, the way she'd presented the cigarettes along with a small velvet sack she'd stolen from her mother and filled with items she believed might be useful in a ritual or spell: twigs and feathers ransacked from a desecrated petrel nest, a tiny beak Oona guessed had once belonged to an abandoned hatchling, the bottom half of a perfectly creamy petrel egg. Together, the offerings amounted to a bribe Daphne hoped might convince Oona to finally let her spend the night. She was desperate to witness true witchcraft.

Oona had accepted the cigarettes, but she'd never followed through on her end of their bargain. When they'd first met she'd been thrilled at Daphne's interest in the Center—couldn't believe her good luck that she'd managed to find a friend who not only accepted her despite who her mother was but was interested in hearing about life at Bare Root. But as time had gone on, and as Daphne's curiosity had blossomed into something closer to obsession, Oona had found herself more than a little disturbed. Sometimes she'd even wondered—despite all the dazed afternoons they spent spread out across the floor of the shed—whether Daphne was truly her friend or whether she was just using her to get closer to Ursula. Certainly, she wouldn't have been the first. Plenty of Initiates had tried to cozy up to Oona in an attempt to curry favor with her mother. There was Jessica, who'd twice allowed Oona to accompany her on her morning swim. And Maria, who spent more than a month trying to teach Oona Spanish. Well, Oona thought, the joke was on them. Ursula hardly ever paid attention to anything Oona did, unless she was misbehaving. And she certainly never noticed which Initiates were kind to her.

On the log, Gemma pointed toward the cigarette in Oona's hand. "If you light it later," she said, "you better not tell anyone where you got it."

"I won't," Oona assured her. She didn't bother adding that doing so would risk expulsion, but it was true that, in the past at least, Ursula had kicked women out for smoking, just like she'd kicked them out for drinking or for "fraternizing" with men. She didn't even care who the man was—once, she'd sent a woman home for writing a dirty letter to her husband. And while at fourteen Oona might have been willing to incur her mother's wrath (might have even welcomed the attention), now she would sooner swallow the cigarette whole.

Gemma took a drag from her cigarette and exhaled slowly. It was strange, watching her smoke with her hair done up in a braided crown, wearing her long, cult-y dress, but from the way she was holding the cigarette it was clear that she was well practiced in the habit.

"So," Gemma said. "What are you doing out here?"

"I'm supposed to be getting my physical," Oona admitted.

Gemma pointed her thumb over her shoulder. "Infirmary's back that way."

"I know."

Her eyes narrowed as she turned to consider Oona. "You're hiding too."

"Yeah," Oona said. "I guess."

For a moment, the two of them just sat there in silence. Somewhere in the distance, Oona could hear the sound of the sea, wearing away at the cliffside. It was stupid, what she was doing. She was supposed to be lying low, avoiding direct attention. She should stand up and go, she thought, before it was too late.

On the other hand, this could be a good opportunity to find out more about Gemma, to ask the questions that had been pinging around her head since the night before, since she'd watched Holly escort Gemma up the hill.

*Why you and not me?*

The same question she'd once asked Daphne, as she'd knelt down beside her on the cold stone of the cave floor.

One minute passed, and then two, but still Oona stayed silent. She told herself that she just needed to think through her phrasing, make sure she got it right so she wouldn't accidentally reveal too much about herself—but the truth was a bit more complicated; the truth was that she was afraid of just how much Gemma's answer might hurt.

In the end, she decided to start somewhere easy. "How are you liking it here?" she asked. "At Bare Root, I mean. Are you enjoying it so far?"

"Enjoying it?" Gemma rolled her eyes. "You know why I'm here. I know you know. So don't pretend that you haven't heard the rumors, that you didn't spend all night googling me."

"All night?" Oona repeated. "No, I googled you in the morning."

It was a gamble, she knew, teasing Gemma—but luckily it paid off. Gemma gave her half a smirk. "Let me guess: You read that I was some kind of wild child, that I'd lost my mind to alcohol and drugs."

"Something like that," Oona conceded. "So the stories aren't true?"

"No," said Gemma. "Though they might as well be, according to my mom."

"Your mom?"

Gemma nodded. "She thinks only crazy people believe in God. So when she found out that I'd joined a church, she lost it—pulled me out of school and sent me here. Then she leaked all those stories to the press because it's trendy to have a daughter who's suffering from a mental health crisis, but it's embarrassing somehow to have a child who's found God." Gemma blew air out her nose in frustration. "She says it's because she doesn't trust Elijah, but I think she's just jealous. I'm married and she's single, and she hates that."

"Wait," Oona said, as she shook her head to clear it. She'd forgotten how cigarette smoke always left her feeling dizzy. "You're married? Aren't you, like, sixteen?"

Gemma took a long, slow drag and then released another small puff of smoke. "So what? Women have been getting married and having babies at my age for centuries. It's really women like you and Ursula and my mom who are going against God, trying to do what's unnatural by having children long after your bodies say you should be done." She slid her eyes slowly over to Oona. "You know, Mary had Jesus when she was only fourteen."

"I . . ." Oona trailed off. This wasn't at all what she'd expected. Sure, she'd guessed that Gemma's mother had likely been the one who'd sent her to Bare Root, especially after reading all the tabloid articles about rehabs and seventy-two-hour psych holds, but she'd also imagined that once Gemma had met Ursula, she'd come around. Because how could she not? While Oona blamed Daphne for a lot—for the fact that Jacob's parents hated her, for her banishment from the coven, for her many miscarriages—she'd never blamed her for falling under Ursula's spell. Everyone did, it seemed, if given enough time, enough exposure. Even Oona. Maybe especially Oona. It was only her second day on the island and already she could feel the pull of her mother's orbit.

"I don't understand," Oona said, speaking at last. "If you're not here to get clean or to hide from the paparazzi, then why are you here?"

"Because I'm a minor?" Gemma said. Like it was obvious. Like, *duh.* "And because my mom is considering investing."

"Investing in what? In Bare Root?"

"Yeah. She thinks maybe it can be developed into some kind of franchise, or incorporated into her brand, or I don't know. She says Ursula has a gift."

"And you don't believe."

"No, I believe. I just think what she's doing is wrong. It's the devil's work, that's what Elijah says. She's getting her power straight from Satan. And I don't want any of that Satan power used on me."

"But you're already pregnant, aren't you? I mean . . ." Oona glanced down at the swell of Gemma's stomach.

"Yes, I am." Gemma beamed, proud. "I'm five months along."

"So then what would—"

"I overheard them, when my mom first dropped me off. She thinks I'm in a cult and that if I have this baby, keep this baby, then I'll never leave. She thinks it'll keep me tied to the church, to Elijah. But Ursula promised that wouldn't happen. She said she would 'take care of it.' And by *it* she meant my child. She's already tried a few times to convince me to agree to an abortion. Of course I refused, but I know she hasn't given up. No, Elijah and me, we think she's just biding her time. She's planning to use her devil magic against me. I know it. That's why I'm hiding out here."

"What? Here in the woods?"

Gemma nodded.

And Oona knew that she should have felt relief. She'd gotten what she wanted, the answer to her question. She knew now why Ursula had chosen Gemma for special treatment: because money was on the line. Best of all, it sounded like Gemma had no interest in competing for attention—from Ursula or from anyone else. All she wanted was to be left alone, to hide out in the woods. No one was going to prevent Oona, or rather Maggie, from getting whatever help she needed to lift the curse. It was good news all around, and yet rather than feeling comforted, Oona was enraged.

*How fucking dare she?* That was all Oona could think as she sat on that log, staring at Gemma's ridiculous braids. What an ungrateful bitch. She didn't even know how good she had it. What Oona wouldn't have given to be the apple of her mother's eye. What she wouldn't have given to be so effortlessly pregnant, so confident in her ability to bring her baby to term that she would do something like smoke a cigarette. A cigarette! For a second, Oona actually had to stop herself from plucking the still-burning Camel right out from between Gemma's teeth.

Instead, she did the next best thing she could think of: She lied.

Eyeing the cigarette, Oona asked, "Where did you say you found that pack again?"

"In the shed back there," Gemma said, gesturing behind them. "Why? You want another?"

"No." Oona pretended to chuckle. "It's just your talk about the devil got me wondering . . . what do you think that shed is for? I heard some of the witches in this coven practice dark magic, the older ones especially. You know, the Crones. Do you think that shed could be where they store their equipment?"

"Eh," Gemma said. "I think it's just an old shed."

"Are you sure? Because I've heard they use things like cigarettes in their rituals."

"Really?" Gemma looked down at the Camel smoking in her hand.

"You didn't see anything else in there, did you, like alcohol? Because I heard the dark witches like to use alcohol too."

"Well, actually . . ." The quiver in Gemma's voice made Oona only too happy. All of a sudden, Gemma dropped the Camel into the dirt.

She ground it out fast, with the toe of her Mary Jane. "Do you think my baby will be okay?" she asked, once the butt had stopped smoking.

Oona shrugged. "I mean, they do say not to smoke while you're pregnant."

"It was just one, though. It was just one, I swear. I quit as soon as I found out about the baby, but I've been craving them nonstop, so when I found these . . ." She looked down at the pack in her hand. "I figured it was a sign from God, you know, just saying, like, it's okay, you can have one." She looked around, as if someone were out there, watching. The witches, maybe. Or God himself. "I won't do it again, though." She looked up at the sky through the leafless branches. "I promise. I can be good. I'm *going* to be good. A good mother."

"Are you?" asked Oona.

Gemma turned to look at her. Then she burst into tears. Oona's mouth dropped open, in shock. She'd meant to upset her, sure, but she hadn't expected *tears*.

Before Oona could say anything more, though, Gemma took off running. Oona could hear the sounds of her tearing through the woods—the twigs cracking beneath the soles of her shoes, the rustle of the brush as she fought her way back into camp.

For a second, Oona debated chasing after her and apologizing. But in the end, she decided against it. It was just as well, she thought. She wasn't actually sure she had a *sorry* in her. In fact, even despite her tears, she still thought Gemma deserved to be spooked. The girl was a spoiled brat. An ingrate. Not someone who deserved to be at Bare Root. And certainly not someone who deserved to be a Mother. At least, not like Oona did. Oona, who would never have dared to smoke the Camel, no matter how it called to her. Oona, who'd spent the day praying for the return of a nausea that had left her practically bedridden for weeks. *See*, she thought, imagining that maybe Gemma had been right and there was someone out there watching, some higher power capable of granting her deepest wish. Persephone, or Demeter, maybe. Hekate.

*See how I'm willing to suffer? See what I'll sacrifice, what I'll give up?*

Well, none of the goddesses went so far as to appear before her. Not the way Ursula had always claimed they would. But, as if in response to her prayers, suddenly and without warning, Oona felt her stomach seize. Her mouth flooded with sour saliva. Her palms went clammy. For a moment, she felt grateful. Vindicated, even. She was getting what she deserved. Her nausea was returning, which meant that the baby growing inside her was okay.

But just as quickly as it came on, that grateful feeling turned, and an eerie sense of déjà vu took its place. Because she'd had the very same fight before, hadn't she? She'd accused another young mother of failing her child, and only a few weeks later Oona had seen Hekate in the water, had sprinted down the rocky hillside to discover Daphne's body on the shore.

# THREE

It was early in the morning on May 1, Beltane, Oona's third and final day on the island, when she saw a petrel building a nest by the jetty. Or at least, that was what she *thought* she saw. Certainly, the bird looked like a petrel, with its small dark body and the little bits of white near the tips of its wings. But in truth, she'd only caught sight of it for a few seconds before it landed and she lost track of it among the gray and black salt-stained rocks.

Her first instinct, unsurprisingly, was to take off in search of the petrel, but she'd barely made it to her feet before Shelly grabbed hold of her wrist. Curious (suspicious?), Shelly had asked Oona where she was going, and of course, Oona couldn't tell her. There was no possible way she could explain—what? That she'd thought she'd seen a bird she'd come to identify as Daphne's familiar, a sure sign (maybe the only sign) that Oona had been cursed? Shelly might've been more open-minded than Jacob (after all, she'd signed up for the Summer Session), but that didn't mean she'd understand, and it didn't mean she'd believe Oona if she confessed that before every one of her miscarriages she'd not only seen a storm petrel, she'd stumbled across some evidence of its destruction—seen the burrow where it laid its young ravaged, come upon one of its eggs cracked open, turned the corner and discovered two fledglings on the ground with bent necks. And that was in addition to the fact that Oona still needed Shelly, and the rest of the Center, to believe that she was Maggie, at least through the end of the day. So as hard as it was for her to sit back down again wondering what she'd really seen, Oona returned to her yoga mat. Once again she folded her legs beneath her, and once again she doubled at the waist, rounded her back, and stretched into what she hoped was a reasonable approximation of child's pose.

Her plan, at the time, had been to search the rocks after that morning's yoga session ended, but no sooner had they all rolled up their mats than the Initiates began distributing flower crowns. Then the Mothers were all herded into the dining hall for a sparkling matcha breakfast. And after the matcha breakfast came the work of decorating the lodge, stringing marigold and motherwort together into garlands, creating wreaths from the branches of hawthorn trees. Oona hardly had a moment to breathe, let alone time to sneak back to the beach to search the jetty. And while for someone else this lack of confirmation might have been freeing—after all, without proof, she could pretend the sighting had never even occurred—it just added to Oona's growing sense of unease.

As it was, she was worried about Beltane. Or more specifically, she was worried about the protection spell. Bare Root had changed in the years she'd been gone. And not for the better. Ursula had fallen under the sway of some questionable influences—primarily, money and fame. And while Oona wanted to blame Astrid Nystrom, and therefore Gemma, she knew the situation wasn't entirely their fault. Ursula was a grown woman, after all, capable of making her own bad choices. And the other members of the coven—Joyce and Donna and Lally—where had they been, huh? What had they been thinking? How could they have just let Ursula get her way when she came to them with the plans she must have, at some point, presented—plans, for example, to open up their own shop shilling merchandise with the name *Bare Root* stamped all over it: bath salts and incense, crystals and tarot cards.

It wasn't the shop itself that bothered Oona, though. She knew how much it cost to keep the Center up and running. Rather, it was what the shop had come to represent: a general *Glow*-ification of the entire compound. To better appeal to women like Astrid Nystrom, Ursula, Oona thought, had gone soft.

When she was a girl, a visit to Marrow had been far from a vacation. The women who had come to them had struggled—with the lack of heat and the dicey plumbing, with the cold foggy mornings and the wind that howled. But Bare Root hadn't just made them physically uncomfortable, it had also made them spiritually uncomfortable. Back then, Ursula had wanted them to feel afraid. She'd wanted that for Oona too. Because real witchcraft wasn't meant to be a comfort. It wasn't about signs from your dead grandma or daily affirmations. It was about power and control. It was about sacrifice. And so, they'd sacrificed. Most nights, they'd gone to bed hungry. Most mornings, they'd woken up cold. When they'd prayed to their goddesses, they'd knelt with bare knees on hardwood floors, or on stone, or on frozen dirt. When they'd concocted a potion, they'd gathered each ingredient by hand, be it poison ivy or stinging nettle, be it their own red blood. And when they'd celebrated a sabbat, which they'd done even in the off-seasons, they'd kept their goddesses front of mind. They'd made offerings out of everything they possessed: food, jewelry, clothing. It had been years since Oona last sat through a sabbat on Marrow, but she could still remember her final Beltane.

It had been held, as it always was, on May 1. The coven had gathered at the cabin Oona shared with her mother. When night fell they sat on the floor, encircled by a ring of sand pulled from the rocky beach just west of them. At each of their places, a pentagram had been drawn on the hardwood with chalk. The only person who spoke that night was Ursula, as she was the one who led the ritual. When the time came she prayed over her altar, which Oona had moved from Ursula's bedroom to a spot beneath the living room window hours before. It was the only time she'd ever been allowed to touch her mother's sacred instruments, and she'd taken her job seriously, had handled the long taper candles, the bowl of desiccated devil's purse, with utmost care. That last summer, when Ursula had unsheathed her boline to cut through the twine on a bundle of special herbs Lally had gathered for that evening's celebration, Oona had fixed her gaze on the handle of the knife. It was made of mother-of-pearl. Oona had held that knife in just the exact same place earlier, when she'd cleaned it, prepared it for the ritual. So, in a way, it felt like she and her mother had touched hands. And while there had been others there—the Mothers lined up along the far wall, watching, silent; Daphne in the corner, big enough, by then, to need her own chair—for a moment, it had felt like Oona and Ursula were the only two in the room. Just mother and daughter.

That last Beltane had felt blessed, holy. True, Oona had never actually seen Demeter appear, unlike the others in her coven, but she'd sworn she'd felt her presence, heard her breath in the yawning stillness, knelt in the sand before the altar and caught the scent of sun-baked wheat in the air. It had been a difficult night, all in all—long and sometimes painful. At different times she'd felt hungry and bored, stiff and achy, parched and dizzy. But it had all been worth it, Oona thought, because it had worked. By that same time the following year, every single Mother who had been there that evening had not only gotten pregnant, she'd come to cradle a baby safely in her arms.

Well, everyone but Daphne. And what had happened to her wasn't exactly Demeter's fault.

All weekend, Oona had been telling herself that Jacob would forgive her so long as she found a way to receive the Beltane protection spell. But as the days had passed and Oona had come to see what Bare Root was really like now, she'd grown increasingly worried. What if the coven no longer administered the spell? Or worse, what if she didn't receive its blessings in time? If she'd really seen a storm petrel that morning during yoga, then that meant a loss was imminent. So all day she told herself that as soon as the feast was over, she would head down to the beach. She was going to be the first one in line, blessed before the sun even sank below the horizon. Instead, she watched the sky grow dark through the window of her cabin's living room.

It was all Gemma's fault. Though dinner had ended nearly an hour earlier, and Oona and Shelly had been dressed in their ceremonial whites for forty minutes at least, Gemma still hadn't returned. And Shelly was insistent that she and Oona wait for her.

"I want to make sure she's okay," Shelly said, as she paged through her spiral notebook. "She hasn't been home in, like . . . two days."

"Is that what you're writing in that thing?" Oona asked. "You're keeping track of Gemma's comings and goings?"

"No," Shelly scoffed. "Of course not. No, these are just notes from class, so I can keep doing what I'm supposed to be doing after the Summer Session." Shelly closed the notebook and stood up from the couch. She joined Oona at the window. "Don't you think Gemma seemed off at dinner?"

"Gemma's always off," Oona said.

Shelly sighed. "You know what I mean. She seemed quiet. Sad, maybe. I wonder if something happened."

"Like what?"

"I don't know. Something with her mom? With a boyfriend?"

"She doesn't have a boyfriend," said Oona. "She has a *husband*."

Shelly sniffed. "Well, there you go. What is she, sixteen? And she's married? She's in trouble, Maggie. I can feel it."

"I'm sure she's fine," Oona said, though it wasn't true. In fact, that was the only reason Oona had let Shelly convince her to wait: Because once, when Jacob had expressed similar concerns about Daphne, Oona had brushed him off.

"Maybe we should go look for her," Shelly suggested.

"Look for her?" Oona echoed, exasperated. "Where? How? It's already eight thirty, Shelly. If we don't leave soon, we'll be late." She didn't want to make the same mistake that she'd made with Daphne, but she couldn't risk missing out on the protection spell.

In response, Shelly just frowned and checked her watch. "Two more minutes, okay? If she doesn't show within the next two minutes, then we'll leave for the beach. And once we get there, we can find Inez or Holly and report her missing."

"Don't you think that's a little extreme?"

"No," Shelly said, turning, at last, to face Oona. "No, I don't. I mean, we all know the stats on girls like Gemma. Girls *at risk*. And we all saw what happened that first night, when she . . ." Shelly's forehead creased with worry.

"You think she was trying to hurt herself by going in the water?"

"I don't know what to think. But I've known girls like Gemma before, and some of them, when they go missing, you never find them. That's all I'm saying."

Oona shuddered. She knew that what Shelly was saying was true. And as irritating as she found Gemma, she didn't want anything truly bad to happen to her the way it had to Daphne.

Still, when Shelly stepped back from the window and announced, with resignation, "Eight thirty-two," Oona couldn't help but sigh with relief.

"She probably just ate too much at dinner or something," Oona said, as they left the cabin. "She's probably in the infirmary, getting waited on by Holly and Inez."

"Maybe," said Shelly. "I suppose heartburn is a common enough side effect of pregnancy. Is that something you've been struggling with too?"

"Me?"

"You're both, what? Twenty? Twenty-four weeks along?"

A lurch of dizzying fear seized Oona. "No," she said softly. "No, that's not . . . I'm not . . ."

Shelly tutted. "Did you forget I'm an ob-gyn? I've known since the first day I met you."

Feebly, Oona shook her head.

"Don't worry," Shelly told her, as they headed toward the beach. "I won't go blabbing to anyone. Your business is your business, as far as I'm concerned."

"And Gemma, does she—"

"No," Shelly said. "No, she doesn't know. And I won't tell her either. But you know, if *you* decided to tell her, it might help you both. Pregnancy can be lonely. Even lonelier when you're on your own. It might be nice to have someone to talk to who is in a similar position."

Oona thought back to the log in the woods, to the way Gemma had sneered when she'd said that Mary'd been only fourteen when she'd given birth to Jesus. As if Oona might have been able to avoid all her many struggles if only she hadn't gone against the Bible's teachings and waited so long to have a child. Little did she know Oona had been trying for the better part of a decade. And it wasn't her fault that she'd had so many miscarriages. Nor was it God's. It was Daphne's. It was the curse. So no, she wanted to tell Shelly, no, she didn't think it would help to share her news with Gemma because there was nothing similar about their *positions*. Instead, she decided to hold her tongue. It just wouldn't be worth it, she thought. Not when she was leaving tomorrow.

The first thing Shelly did, when they finally made it down to the beach, was go off in search of Holly. And while Oona figured that Shelly probably would have preferred that she look, too, as soon as she saw that some of the other Mothers were already wearing the mark of Beltane, she headed straight for the line she saw snaking through the crowd.

It was selfish, she knew. But though she wanted to help Shelly, to bear witness to her fear the way she'd never done for Jacob, she wanted the protection spell more. "I'll save you a place?" she told Shelly, before they parted. A lame attempt to assuage her own guilt. Still, when Shelly nodded in agreement, Oona felt all the muscles in her neck relax. The tension in her back eased as soon as she joined the end of the line. She'd done it, she thought, as up ahead she watched one of the Mothers kneel before Ursula and Lally. She'd made it: to Beltane, to the beach. And not only was the coven still administering the spell, but she'd arrived in time to receive its blessing.

Somewhere behind her she heard a gull cry and she searched the sky, the dark expanse of water. Had it been a gull or a petrel? she started to wonder. But then she forced herself to turn back around. It didn't matter, she told herself. In only a few minutes, she wouldn't have to worry anymore.

"There you are!" a voice exclaimed. And Oona jumped a little when she felt someone lay their hand on her shoulder, but glancing to her left she saw that it was just Vivian and Grace. They'd both clearly been at the beach for a while already. Each wore the mark of Beltane proudly on her brow.

"Where's Shelly?" Vivian asked. Oona recognized both the necklace and the bracelet she was wearing. She'd seen them for sale in the Bare Root store. Made with citrine and rutilated quartz, the bracelet alone sold for something like four hundred dollars.

"She's looking for Holly," Oona explained. "She wants to report Gemma missing."

"Missing?" Grace asked, in her soft little whisper voice. She tucked a curl of honey-blond hair behind her ear. "That's terrible. What happened?"

"Nothing," said Oona. "She just didn't come back to the cabin after dinner."

"So?" Vivian asked.

And Oona shrugged. It had been hard, but she'd taken great pains all that weekend to keep her opinions about Gemma to herself because she had the sneaking suspicion that Maggie Jones was not the sort of woman who would have shared them. In fact, she was fairly confident that Maggie was a better person than she was in every way. After all, Maggie was the kind of woman who didn't just want a pregnancy, she wanted a baby. She wanted to hold a howling creature in her arms and sing it to sleep.

"I'm saving her a spot," Oona said instead.

"We'll meet up with you after," said Vivian. "We're going to go see if we can't find something to help Grace with her grounding." She pointed to a row of tables where the coven had set up a kind of market, filled with crystals and candles and other things from their shop. All Bare Root TM-ed, of course.

"I'm just not getting any better," Grace explained. "But, gosh, I'm determined to keep trying."

"Good luck," Oona said. And it was only after they'd walked away that she realized she meant it. She didn't approve of the way the coven was hawking their merchandise, trying to make a profit off the celebration of the sabbat, but she knew what it felt like to struggle with Craft. And if there was something on one of those tables that could help, well, she'd probably buy it too. In fact . . .

Oona stepped out of line. The lure of an easy fix was just that powerful. But thankfully, she made it only a few steps before Shelly appeared.

"I found Holly," she said. "She promised she'd go look for Gemma."

"That's good," said Oona, stepping back toward the line. "I saved you a spot."

"Thanks," Shelly said, but she still looked worried.

*It'll be okay*, Oona wanted to say. *They'll find her.* But she knew all too well how cold the comfort of finding someone like Gemma could be. After all, eventually they'd also found Daphne. So instead, Oona remained silent and together she and Shelly watched as the women before them received their benedictions: a sprinkle of morning dew from Lally; and from Ursula, the mark of Beltane, drawn in ash on each Mother's brow.

Soon, it would be Oona's turn. And while she'd been eager to reach the front of the line only minutes earlier, suddenly reality settled in. In order to receive the blessing of the protection spell, she would need to step closer to the light of the bonfire. She was fairly confident that she could make it through the ceremony undetected so long as she kept her head down, but she knew there was no way her mother would fail to recognize her the moment she looked up to have the ashed mark of Beltane drawn across her brow. That's why Oona had worked so hard to avoid her all weekend, why she'd ignored all the special invitations Maggie had received: to join Ursula in the lodge for a private workshop, to swing by her office for a one-on-one after lunch. Because she'd known what would happen as soon as she was found out: She'd be expelled again, sent back to the mainland; charged with fraud or theft; maybe even arrested for trespassing.

Yes, Oona was sure of it. As soon as she stepped forward, her stay on Marrow would be over. There would be no time to say goodbye— to the Center; to the island; to Grace and Vivian and Shelly, women, Oona had to admit, she was beginning to think of as friends.

"Shelly," Oona said, as she turned to—what? Come clean? Confess? Apologize?

But no sooner had Oona spoken her name than Shelly was called up. She knelt in the sand as Lally dipped her fingers into a pearlescent bowl filled with sacred water; she bowed her head to listen to Ursula recite the holy prayer. And though Oona knew she should look away— that if anything, she risked drawing attention to herself prematurely with all her staring—no matter how hard she tried, she couldn't seem to pull back her gaze. How long had it been since her mother had last touched her? she wondered. Surely more than fifteen years.

"Rise, Mother," Ursula commanded, and suddenly Oona's heart began thumping in her ears. Her vision swam.

For a brief moment, she actually thought she might pass out before she even had a chance to receive the spell's blessings, but then Shelly got to her feet. And somehow, when she was summoned closer, Oona managed to stumble forward. Somehow, she kept her eyes open even as Lally sprinkled her head and shoulders with dew, even as Ursula mumbled the incantation. And then it was over. For Oona, it felt like she'd blacked out. One minute she was looking up at her mother, simultaneously praying that she wouldn't be recognized and willing Ursula to open her eyes and claim Oona as her own—and the next minute, she was by the drinks table with Shelly and Grace and Vivian, holding a cool glass bottle of Perrier to her neck.

"Do you feel any different?" Vivian asked, looking from Shelly to Oona.

"What?" Oona replied, dazed. She was still trying to figure out how she'd gotten there—from the fire to the table, from within her mother's orbit to this far-flung, night-chilled spot. She'd been so sure that Ursula would recognize her. Yes, she'd cut her hair, had even dyed it; and yes, it'd been a decade and a half since they'd last stood face-to-face, but still . . . a mother was supposed to know her child anywhere, wasn't she? Blood was supposed to recognize blood. And yet, Ursula had looked at Oona like she was just another Mother. No different from Shelly, or Vivian, or Grace.

"Do you feel any different?" Vivian asked again. "Because I thought we were supposed to feel different. Stronger, maybe. Or more energized? I mean, that *was* the protection spell. Wasn't it?"

"Yes," Shelly replied patiently. "That was the protection spell."

Oona touched her forehead with the tips of her fingers. Had she really received the blessings of the spell? It didn't seem possible, but when she looked she saw that her fingers came away black.

"Maggie," Shelly said, her voice soft with concern. "Are you okay, honey? You look pale."

How could her mother not have known her? Oona wondered. How could she have failed to recognize her widow's peak? Or the scar that split her left eyebrow? It was almost as if she hadn't spent every day of the past fifteen years searching for her daughter's face among the faces of strangers, the same way Oona had sought out Ursula's own.

It was almost as if she hadn't missed her.

"Maggie?"

"I'm fine," Oona said, but even she could hear that her voice sounded weak, warbly. Except no, she would not cry. She'd gotten what she wanted, after all. Hadn't she? She was protected now. Her baby was protected. As soon as she became a Mother, she would come into her power. And once she came into her power, she could form her own coven, her own family.

True, the night hadn't gone the way she'd thought it would, but maybe this was better. Now she would be able to leave on her own terms. And she'd have time to say goodbye. She just needed to pick her moment.

"I'm fine," Oona said again. "I just got a little too close to the fire."

Shelly touched her arm. "Are you sure you don't want to sit down?"

"No," Oona started to say, but then Vivian interrupted her.

"So this protection spell," Vivian began. "How long is it supposed to last, exactly? Because I thought we weren't supposed to see our husbands until we went home at the end of Summer Session. Unless—" Suddenly, she looked panicked. "Are *your* husbands coming to visit before then?"

"I don't think men are allowed at the Center," Grace said softly, as she slipped one hand into the pocket of her robe.

Vivian looked to Shelly for confirmation, but Shelly shook her head. "Don't look at me," she said. "I'm doing this on my own."

Vivian frowned. "Really? I didn't know that. Did we know that?"

"Well, not entirely on my own. I'll have my family for support, and my colleagues."

Vivian pursed her lips and sucked in air through her nose, but before she could say anything else, Oona started talking.

"Babies don't need a father," she said. "I never had one. And look at me. I turned out fine." She laughed, and then she grimaced, and the other women laughed and grimaced too. And for a second, Oona thought, *This is it, this is my moment.* She wasn't going to get a better goodbye, not without confessing the truth, and she still couldn't do that. Not there on the beach, with her mother and Lally just yards away. So best to leave now, go out on a high note; claim she needed a bathroom and then sneak back to the cabin to pack up all her things. The last incoming ferry was probably just then docking, which meant that if she hurried she might be able to catch the final outbound ferry that night.

"I—" Oona said, but before she had a chance to finish her sentence, she heard her cell phone ring. "Sorry," she said, as she began digging through her straw bag, pushing aside her ChapStick and the ginger candies meant to help fight nausea, the Kind bar she'd agreed to hold for Shelly, and the leather pouch of devil's purse she'd kept for the past fifteen years. Her phone seemed to chime louder with each missed ring, but at last she found it.

"Important call?" Vivian asked, as Oona stared down at her screen.

It was Jacob, of course. She'd known it would be. No one else had called her in years—not since she was fired after her second miscarriage and her boss at the motel had stopped calling to let her know her schedule for the week.

"Maggie?" Shelly prompted when Oona just kept staring. "Aren't you going to answer that?"

Startled back into the present, Oona quickly sent the call to voicemail. "No," she said. "No, I'll talk to him later."

"Him?" Vivian asked, nosy as always. "Is that your boyfriend? Husband?"

Oona had always been purposefully vague about whether she had a partner, since she hadn't known Maggie's situation back home. "Just a friend," she said, as she dropped her phone back into her bag. She felt it buzz when Jacob left yet another voicemail. For a moment, she wondered how it was possible that her inbox still had space, but then she remembered that she'd cleaned it out that morning, deleted every one of the nearly fifty messages Jacob had left. She'd listened to the first few when they'd come in, that first morning on the island, but the rest she'd just erased out of hand. She'd figured she'd be home soon enough. And anyway, they all said the same thing: that he was worried, that she was crazy, that he wanted her to come home. But what about what *she* wanted, huh? What about what she *needed*?

"You don't *need* a baby," that's what Jacob would say if she called him back, if she tried to explain. She knew that was what he would say because it was what he'd said countless times before. If Jacob had ever listened to her, if he'd ever understood her (a fact Oona had begun to doubt)—well, he'd long since stopped doing either. Sure, he said he wanted a baby, but he still gave up his old job (and its accompanying medical insurance) to crew for the R/V *Merlin*, then claimed they didn't have the money for IVF. And though he told her he would take the supplements she read about online and ordered for him, though he promised to follow the diet one woman on the message board swore had worked for her, she suspected that he cheated when he was away at sea—that he tossed the chalky pills overboard and drank coffee, that he ate chocolate and salt and chugged beer. Once, she'd considered telling him about the coven she planned to start if she ever got the chance to commune with Demeter, but then she'd found a half-drunk beer can on her makeshift altar. She'd never been able to completely remove the ring stain it'd left behind.

On the beach, Oona's phone began to ring again, so she reached into her bag and turned it off. "Another friend," she lied.

"Someone's popular," said Vivian.

And Oona tried to smile, but the truth was she hadn't had a friend since Daphne. Not unless she counted the women on this beach. She'd been alone since she left Marrow. Well, except for Jacob, and in recent years being alone and being married to Jacob had begun to feel like the same thing. He'd been away at sea for the first four of her five miscarriages. The first two times, she'd had to walk herself to the hospital after work. The next two times, she'd had to call an Uber because the blood loss left her lightheaded and she didn't trust herself to be able to drive their old manual transmission RAV4. The last time, though, that had been the worst one because Jacob should have been home. His boat was docked for the week. But instead, he'd gone to the pub to drink beers with the scientists from the institute. He liked to pretend he was really part of the team, and not just a member of the crew. He'd invited Oona along, too, but she'd decided to stay home because she knew she'd never be able to fake being interested in "Atlantic herring abundance and distribution." And anyway, she wasn't in Portland to make friends. Her time on the mainland wasn't supposed to be a reward, some kind of holiday; it was supposed to be a punishment. She was supposed to suffer until she could figure out a way to make things right again.

But of course, Oona couldn't explain all—or any—of that to the women on the beach. So instead, she just said, "I'll call them back after the ceremony."

And Shelly responded, "That's a good idea. It looks like they'll be starting soon."

She pointed toward the fire, and Oona saw that Ursula and Lally had moved from their earlier positions to stand near the stone altar Oona had actually helped drag onto the beach years before. While the rest of the coven watched, Ursula unfurled an old leather roll. Oona was too far away to smell it, but she remembered its scent: oil and musk.

Ursula had only gotten as far as removing her paten, though, before she was interrupted by Holly's call.

"Wait!" she cried from the hilltop, at the end of the path that wove through the woods. "I've got one more. A straggler!"

It was hard to see from where Oona was standing, but she didn't even have to look to know Holly was pulling Gemma down the hill toward the beach. It was always Gemma. If she wasn't being dragged to her treatment appointments or bullied into attending the group lectures, then someone (usually Holly) was working to track her down, smoke her out. *See,* Oona wanted to say to Shelly, *she was never really missing.* But even Oona had to admit that the first thing she felt upon seeing Gemma was relief.

That relief turned out to be short-lived, though. No sooner had Holly and Gemma reached the circle of light cast by the bonfire than Oona felt her emotions change. Whatever concern she'd had for Gemma was wiped out in an instant. Instead, all she felt was rage.

"What is she wearing?" Oona asked, but no one seemed to hear her.

Grace was too busy examining the crystal she'd bought at the coven's market, and Shelly seemed preoccupied with the question of whether Gemma looked cold.

"Poor thing," she tutted. "I brought a spare jacket. Do you think she wants it?"

"What is she wearing?" Oona asked again.

"I don't know," Vivian said, as she squinted. "Some kind of dress, but it doesn't look like it was made in this century, does it?"

Oona shook her head. "That's not what I meant."

But once again, no one responded. They were all too busy fretting over Gemma. It had been that way for days. Though Oona was confident that Gemma had likely made herself the bane of Holly's existence, as a whole the Mothers tended to be less annoyed by her and more intrigued. Even Vivian, while she had spent their first night down on the beach spreading some pretty nasty gossip, had changed her tune—though unlike the others, she hadn't been seduced by Gemma's money or by her celebrity. Instead, she'd noticed the same thing Oona had noticed: that Ursula had *chosen* Gemma, singled her out for special attention and extra praise. And so she figured that if she got closer to Gemma, she might get more face time with Ursula. Or at least, that was how Oona had overheard her explaining it to Grace.

"It's pink," Oona said. "Her dress. Even though Ursula made it clear that we were all supposed to wear our white robes to the ceremony."

Grace turned until the crystal caught the light from the fire and shone gold. "Maybe it's just the lighting," she said.

"No." Oona bit the inside of her cheek. Hard. "No. It's pink. I can see it. Ursula asked us to wear white, but she's wearing a pink fucking dress."

"Maggie!" Vivian exclaimed, sounding both surprised and pleased to hear Oona swear. "I didn't know you had it in you."

Oona pulled her gaze back from the fire. She'd done a good job, till then, of keeping her temper in check. Because Maggie Jones didn't have a temper. Oona didn't know how, but she knew it to be true. "Sorry," she muttered.

Vivian's eyes narrowed. "You don't like Gemma, do you?"

"What?" Grace said. "Of course she does. Gemma's her roommate."

Oona nodded. "Gemma's my roommate," she echoed, as if that

meant anything at all. Daphne had been her roommate, too, for a little while, and just look what she'd done to *her*.

"You lucky bitch," Vivian said, baring her teeth in something like a smile so Oona would know she was joking. Or at least, half joking. "If Gemma was my roommate . . . well, let's just say I wouldn't be standing around here with you. I'd be over there." She pointed toward the stone altar, where Ursula seemed to be showing Gemma her various instruments. "I'd kill to learn whatever she's teaching her right now."

"I'm sure we'll learn it soon," said Shelly.

"But not from Ursula. And I don't care what anyone says. If you're struggling—I mean *really* struggling—then it's her help you need. There's no substitute. I mean, I told you how I first heard about this place, didn't I?" Vivian glanced around their small circle, and the other women shook their heads. "From my friend Whitney. She was on the board with me at Junior League. And I knew she'd been having trouble. I can't remember who told me. Probably Greer. She always had a big mouth. In any case, when I didn't see Whitney all summer, I just assumed she was in the Hamptons. And when she still wasn't back in the fall, I assumed she'd extended her stay. But then summer came around again and at the Bettencourts' annual gala, who walks in but Whitney, carrying a baby. She'd been to Bare Root, of course. I didn't know it at the time, but she and her husband had been trying for more than decade. They'd undergone every medical procedure money could buy and still . . . nothing. But one summer with Ursula was all it took. And I do mean with Ursula. Whitney spent the whole summer, and then fall, under her special care."

"The fall? I thought they closed to outsiders after the Summer Session," Grace said. "Did she pay extra?"

"I wish!" Vivian exclaimed. "I asked when I called to book my stay, but whoever it was I spoke to claimed that Ursula paid special attention to every Mother at Bare Root. But we all know that's bullshit. I mean, we can see that isn't true, right?"

Oona nodded. She wanted to explain—but of course couldn't—that Ursula picked a favorite every few years. The last summer Oona had been on the island, Ursula had chosen a woman named Sara Cook, had even designed a specialized program for her that she promised would yield results, never mind the fact that Mrs. Cook was, by then, a repeat visitor. It seemed she suffered a loss practically every spring. Oona could still remember her gentle moon face. Her dark, wet eyes. She'd never actually shed any tears, not that Oona had seen, but she could remember watching as her mother consoled her after yet another miscarriage—the way her shoulders had shaken.

By the altar, Ursula wrapped one arm around Gemma's waist, in much the same way she'd done with Mrs. Cook. Only instead of looking comforted, Gemma seemed to shy away. Oona felt her throat constrict in indignation—or was it simple jealousy? All weekend she'd felt like a criminal as she'd hidden from Ursula and Lally, desperate just to remain on the island, at the Center, until she could receive the protection spell. Meanwhile, Gemma was not only signed up for the entire Summer Session, but as Ursula's special project there was a good chance she'd be allowed to return to the island as often as she wanted for the rest of the year.

"It isn't fair," Oona muttered under her breath.

Or at least, she'd intended to mutter it under her breath, but instead Shelly heard her. "What isn't fair?" she asked.

Luckily, Oona was spared having to explain further, because just then the Initiates returned to the beach. She hadn't seen them leave to change into their ceremonial garb, but when Holly and Inez stepped back into the fire's light, they'd shed their traditional lilac robes in favor of white gowns cinched at the waist with coils of gold-threaded rope. On their heads they wore crowns made of flowers and antlers, and in their hands they each carried a wooden koshi chime.

As they ushered the women back to the fire, they swung the chimes gently in the air, cleansing the space around them. "Form a circle," they told the Mothers. And the women complied.

By the fire, Oona stood between Grace and Shelly. On the other side of the circle, she could see Gemma looking unsure: standing there with her arms crossed and her shoulders hunched up around her ears, as if by allowing her to hold her boline Ursula had threatened her rather than honored her. As if—Oona ground her molars at the thought—as if she were *scared*.

The girl didn't know scared, Oona thought bitterly. Not like she did, anyway. No, if anyone deserved to be *scared* of Ursula, it was Oona. But she wasn't. Of course she wasn't. Not anymore.

Not now that she'd gotten what she'd come for.

Not now that she was all set to leave.

She'd been planning to wait for the right moment to say goodbye, but when Holly and Inez put down their chimes and a sudden silence descended upon the circle, Oona decided that she was done waiting around. If Ursula wanted to spend the rest of the night fawning over Gemma, then so be it. Oona didn't have to watch. No, as soon as the ritual got under way and everyone was distracted, she would back out of the circle and sneak off.

"Mothers," Ursula bellowed, her voice reverberating like a struck bell. "We're gathered here today to celebrate the high holiday of Beltane and to welcome in this new season of fertility. Before we can begin, though, I'm going to need you all to help me ground this circle in whatever way you've been practicing these last couple of days.

Whether you use the golden cord method or tree meditation, crystals or rooting, now is the time to put that practice to work. So, please, without letting go of your neighbors' hands, let's all of us begin to ground ourselves and our magic. The earth, as we know, is an abundant and never-ending supply of energy, and grounding is how we draw from that supply. It's how we pull energy up into our bodies so we can do our work. So let's do that now. Let's feel our connection to Mother Earth, feel it in the grit of the sand beneath our feet, feel it in the heat of the fire before us. And with each breath we take, let's pull that energy up, up, up, and into our cores."

Beside Oona, Shelly closed her eyes, but Grace kept hers open. "I don't think it's helping," she said.

"The crystal?" Oona whispered in return.

"I must be doing something wrong. Maybe I'm supposed to hold it differently?"

Oona glanced at Shelly and Vivian, and while they still had their eyes closed like the rest of the circle, she knew she couldn't leave until Grace had hers closed too.

"Forget the crystal," said Oona. "What methods have you tried in class?"

"I've tried everything, it feels like," Grace answered. "But so far nothing's worked."

When she was younger, Oona had also struggled with grounding. Not that she'd had a lot of opportunities to practice, since before a witch was initiated the only rituals she was allowed to attend were the eight sabbats. But still, no matter how many Beltanes she sat through, no matter how many times she celebrated Samhain and Imbolc and Yule, she never got any better at using the methods taught to the Mothers. The golden cord technique always failed her. As did crystal work and rooting. For a long while, she'd thought her case was hopeless, but then one day she'd been swimming in the sea, floating chin up, chest out, held by the waves, and she'd realized that she felt it: the connection to the earth that Ursula had tried to explain.

It wasn't traditional, she knew, but maybe it would also work for Grace. So, "Close your eyes," she told her. And to demonstrate, Oona closed her eyes too. "Imagine you're at sea. Nothing but water for miles around you, nothing but the drift of the tide, the salt sting in your eyes . . ."

Before she knew what was happening, Oona felt some force move through her body. A pulling sensation she recognized, instinctively, as undertow. She was floating, she thought. Floating. Floating.

No, she was being carried away. Pulled from shore, from home. The sea itself was working to swallow her. And for a terrifying moment, she felt her stomach bottom out. The child inside her shuddered, and without thinking she dropped Grace's and Shelly's hands and clutched at her stomach.

When she opened her eyes, Shelly was at her side. "Come," she was saying gently. "Come sit down."

But Oona couldn't. It was bad enough that she'd broken the circle. Thankfully, though, neither Ursula nor Lally had noticed. Oona could see them standing over by the stone altar, busy preparing for the next step of the ritual.

"Good!" Ursula called suddenly, and Oona understood that she'd missed her chance to leave. The circle was now grounded. Quickly, Oona scrambled for Shelly's and Grace's hands. "Now stay where you are," Ursula said. "I'm going to come around behind you and cast the circle with my athame."

From the altar, she selected a long, double-edged knife with a black handle. As she walked the outskirts of the circle, she used the blade to carve a line in the sand. When she was done—when she'd circled the perimeter three times, moving in the direction of the sun—she returned the knife to the altar, closed her eyes, and held up her hands.

"I call on the element of water," she cried, with her face turned up to the sky and the sleeves of her long white robe sunk down beneath her elbows. "I call on the ancestors: the selkies, the mermaids, the undines. Come and join us on this Beltane celebration where the god and goddess unite in sacred marriage and make through their union a more fertile world."

"So mote it be," Lally murmured in response.

And Holly and Inez echoed her. "So mote it be."

"I call on the element of air," Ursula continued, and she moved one of her hands to the large silver pendant she wore around her neck. "I call on the sylphs, the guardians of the watchtowers of the east, of the gentle breeze that softens winter's chill, and the cleansing force of the gale winds, oh ye place of storms and breath of life. We call to you now to aid us in our rites. So mote it be."

"So mote it be," answered Lally, Holly, and Inez.

In the circle, Oona worked to slow her heartbeat. Like Lally had taught her, she breathed in through her nose and out through her mouth, but she couldn't seem to shake her panic. It had been only a moment, but it had felt so real. The smell of the water—silt and salt, old birth and death. And then the pull of the tide, almost like hands on her wrists, on her ankles. Dragging her out, dragging her down.

When Ursula called upon the elements of earth and fire, Oona mumbled along with the rest of the circle, "So mote it be." But she wasn't paying attention. All her focus was fixed on the steady swelling of her lungs and on the movement she felt in her belly—those reassuring flutters—when she breathed up and into her diaphragm. There was no reason, she reminded herself, to be afraid. She was safe. Perfectly safe, standing there in the sand. And as soon as the coven moved on to the next part of the ceremony, she would sneak away to her cabin. She would go back to Portland, to Jacob, and when she came into her power, she'd find a new way to ground herself. She'd never have to feel the undertow again.

At the head of the circle, Ursula turned and retrieved two new items from her altar: a chalice, hardly bigger than two cupped palms, made from a thin, iridescent shell; and a pitcher of rooibos tea.

"This," Ursula explained, as she poured the tea into the chalice, "is meant to symbolize the womb and uterine blood. To bless it, I will call upon the goddess Demeter. Oh, fertile Mother, you who used your sacred uterine bloods to create the world, may you bless all who have gathered here today, all of us who bleed, will bleed, have bled; all of us Maidens, Mothers, and Crones. Draw from our women's mysteries to honor our fertility like we honor yours today and bless this chalice and this tea." With a quick turn to the altar, Ursula retrieved a second ritual knife. Unlike her athame, her boline was single-edged. Its handle, Oona knew, was made of obsidian. With her chest high and her arms still raised, Ursula dipped the tip of the knife's blade into the chalice, then held it up, dripping, in the air.

"So mote it be!" she cried, with a throaty voice.

And the circle echoed her. "So mote it be! So mote it be!"

To complete the ceremony, Ursula tossed two small bouquets of wildflowers and mugwort into the fire: offerings to Demeter. Then she invited the Mothers to join her at the maypole. It was time to raise energy.

Earlier in the day, the women had scrawled their prayers to Demeter on the rainbow of ribbons affixed to the top of the pole. Now, as the musicians began to play, the women were told that they would each need to hunt down their own particular ribbon. Oona found hers right away—a slip of blue silk on which she'd written only

"Mother"—but the others struggled. Vivian had to circle the pole three times before she found her ribbon, while Shelly and Grace both got confused, mistook another Mother's ribbon for their own, and had to be redirected. And Gemma . . . Oona had to bite the inside of her cheek to keep from swearing again. Gemma still hadn't left her spot by the fire. As the introductory song wound down, Holly tried to coax her over to the pole.

"Okay!" Joyce cried. "Is everyone ready?"

Oona saw the women on either side of her nod, so she nodded too. And she *was* ready—ready to be done with the night, with the whole trip. As soon as the dance got going, she could use the chaos to her advantage, sneak off while the others were still circling the pole.

They hadn't practiced the dance before but they'd been shown a video, so they all knew, vaguely, what to do. Still, they got off to a rocky start. They were meant to walk at first, half of them clockwise and the other half counterclockwise, weaving in and out among themselves. But for the first few minutes there was a fair amount of confusion, Mothers bumping into each other, stepping on each other's toes. By the time the musicians finished their first song, though, the Mothers, by and large, had all gotten the hang of it. When Oona looked up, she could see the tops of their ribbons braiding together around the pole. How much longer would she have to continue on? she wondered. Was it safe yet to drop her ribbon and go?

But no sooner had she begun plotting her escape than the band, at Ursula's command, began picking up tempo. The Mothers gathered speed. With women behind her practically stepping on her heels, Oona had no choice but to start moving faster and faster until she was running, panting, dodging the Mothers coming at her, and clinging to her ribbon to stay on her feet. The band continued to play, but after only a minute or two Oona could no longer hear them. Their music was drowned out by the sounds the Mothers made. They cackled and shrieked. They whooped and hollered. They screamed so loud Oona imagined their throats bloodied.

In all her years at Bare Root, Oona had never understood her mother's phrase "raising energy." Not really. Sure, she'd swayed awkwardly to music before, had held and occasionally struck a tambourine. She'd even raised her voice, standing on the beach with Lally beside her in the dead of winter, and shouted till her voice grew hoarse. But it had always felt performative. Disembodied and intellectual. This, though. This felt real. The faster they danced, the more she could feel it: the heat building in her heels, in her fingertips. It was kinetic. Like live wires had replaced her veins.

Across the way, through the blur of bodies, Oona thought she recognized Vivian, her long black hair loosed from its bun. And Grace, only a few steps behind. There were no words to the music, as far as Oona could tell, but Grace had her mouth open like she was singing. No, like she was crying. No. It took a moment, but soon Oona picked her voice out of the cacophony of sound. She was howling. And then it was like a contagion, an ancient hysteria spreading. As Grace's voice carried up the beach, the others started joining in. They were screaming, all of them. Screeching. Shrieking. Oona could feel it in the back of her throat: a talon-like clawing. In her chest, it was like wings were beating against the cage of her ribs. She tried to look behind her, half expecting to see the other women somehow transformed, but instead she got distracted by something she saw move out of the corner of her eye. A bird, she thought, as her gaze followed the thing out over the ocean. A bird with a dark body and white-tipped wings. She tried to keep it in her line of vision, but the dance was too complicated. First she tripped one of the other Mothers, then she lost her grip on her ribbon. Dizzy, she managed to take only a few wobbling steps before she collapsed into the sand.

"Oona?" someone called.

And thinking it was Grace or Shelly, Oona shook her head lightly. If she spoke, she thought, she would be sick. It wasn't possible, was it? A petrel, even after the spell?

"Oona?" the voice called for a second time. "Has anyone seen my wife, Oona?"

*Wife?*

Oona's eyes flew open and there was Jacob: standing, squinting, on the beach. He had one hand visored over his eyes, as if he were staring into the sun rather than into the dark, and he looked worried.

At the sight of him, Oona felt her stomach drop, squeeze. She could taste the acid from the feast's hunter stew at the back of her throat. *Fuck,* she thought. He'd found her. *How* had he found her? But then of course he'd known where she would go. How many times had she woken, flushed and sweaty, with the island's name on her lips? How many nights had she stayed up with the radio as a squall blew in, listening for news of flooding, downed power lines, and destruction at the Center, Marrow fishing boats lost at sea? In many ways, for many years, she'd felt the pull of the island the same way she felt the pull of the tide, the way she imagined storm petrels must feel the draw of their nesting grounds. Her return was nothing more and nothing less than instinct. She supposed it was a testament to their marriage that Jacob knew her so well. And if they'd been alone, Oona might have felt touched. Maybe even flattered. But they weren't alone. And so instead all Oona felt was horror. Nauseating horror. And a desperate need to figure a way out.

Still lying in the sand, Oona surveyed the beach around her. If she crept down to the water, she thought, then walked along the foaming shore, maybe she could make it to the woods undiscovered. And once she reached the woods, then no one would be able to find her until she wanted to be found. More than a decade off-island hadn't changed that. She knew the forest better than anyone. She knew it better than she knew herself.

"Oona?" Over by the fire, Jacob turned a small circle, still searching. And he wouldn't quit searching, she knew, just because he didn't find her on the beach. He would look for her everywhere: in the cabins, the lodge, the dining hall. He would bang on doors with heavy fists and demand to be let in. But if Oona could reach him first, before anyone noticed, then maybe she could convince him that it'd be best to leave. And whatever fight he wanted to have, they could have it on the ferry.

So Oona stood. But before she had a chance to raise her hand or call Jacob's name, her mother stepped away from the Maypole. "Jacob?" Oona heard her ask. Then: "My god, Oona?" Both Jacob and Ursula seemed to spot Oona at the same time and for a moment she felt paralyzed by their attention. She wanted to run and hide. She wanted to lie. She was Maggie. Maggie Jones. Her name was written on the chalkboard in her cabin. One look at Jacob, though, and she knew there would be no point to such a lie. Short hair and a bad dye job wouldn't fool him. Not like they'd fooled her mother. He'd been waking up to her face for fifteen years. And the same way she knew that the gap between his two front teeth was the width of her thumbnail, he knew that the constellation of freckles that bridged her nose took the shape of the stars at night. *Cassiopeia*, he often whispered as he traced his fingertip along her cheekbone.

"Oona?" Ursula said, and her voice had gone hollow, as though she were calling from the bottom of a well. "Is that really you?"

Lally didn't say anything at all, but when Oona nodded she brought her hand up to the base of her throat. Oona couldn't bear to watch her eyes turn glassy, so she started walking up the beach, toward Jacob. Behind her, she could feel the other women at the Maypole slow. Vivian and Grace, Shelly—she didn't have to glance behind her to know that they were watching. Even Gemma. When Oona reached the bonfire, she saw that Gemma was still sitting in the sand, beside the altar, and there was something new in her gaze. Something sharper, more appraising. But Oona didn't have time to think about it, because the moment she stepped into the glowing light of the fire, Jacob rushed to meet her. Before she could even open her mouth to say—what? That she was sorry?—he'd clutched her to his chest. He was scared. When he held her, Oona could feel him shaking. But scared *for* her or scared *of* her, she didn't know. A bit of both, she suspected.

He took her by the shoulders and stepped back just far enough to make out the expression on her face. "Are you okay?" he asked. "Is the baby . . . ?" He looked down at her belly and she nodded, but when he reached for her, for his child, she stepped back.

"Not here," she whispered. The others were still watching. Her mother was still standing somewhere behind her on the beach. God, her mother. Oona couldn't believe she'd been caught right there in front of her mother. Caught wearing a robe nearly two sizes too small. Caught with flowers in her hair. It was pathetic. *She* was pathetic. The prodigal daughter no one wanted to see return. *Don't you have any pride?* Ursula had asked her that last night on the island, when Oona had begged, pleaded with her to let her stay.

"In the car, then," Jacob said.

But as eager as Oona was to get away from the beach, from the awful feeling of all those eyes on her, she knew she couldn't leave. Not yet. "I can't," Oona said. "I need to check the rocks first."

"The rocks?" Jacob's gaze lifted up over the top of her head, and she watched as he took in the jetty: its towering bulk, and the way the waves crashed into its side, all white-capped and frothy. "You can't go climbing on those rocks. You could fall."

"I know," she said. "But I have to."

Only when she turned away, she found he'd taken hold of her wrist.

"Please," she begged.

But he shook his head, and that's when she felt her throat seize up. From somewhere deep inside her, she released a new sound: part whimper, part groan. She knew it would be risky to climb the jetty, but she had to do it. She had to know if the spell had worked. Because the idea of going back to Portland only to lose another baby . . . she couldn't bear it. She couldn't go back to working at a motel, to washing sheets and scrubbing toilets. She never wanted to lay eyes on her pitiful dresser altar again. And remembering the nights she used to spend shut up in their bedroom closet trying fruitlessly to ground herself while Jacob snored in bed on the other side of the accordion doors . . . it made her want to scream. Or sob. Or both. She needed this. *They* needed this. Couldn't he see that?

Couldn't her mother?

*Please*, she thought. *Please.*

*Don't you have any pride?*

Suddenly, a wave of exhaustion swept over Oona. She was so tired of fighting to be understood. So tired of trying to wrangle her unruly body into submission. By the time she realized what she was doing, she had already folded over at the waist, rested her hands on her knees, as if her fatigue had simply felled her.

Instantly, Jacob was back at her side, asking her what was wrong in the same voice he used whenever she locked herself up in the bathroom to cry. *What's wrong, Oona? Tell me. Tell me what's wrong.* But she didn't know what was wrong. She didn't know why her body kept failing to do the one thing that, by nature, it was supposed to be able to do. Unless Daphne . . .

"It's all right, love." She felt Lally's hands on her back before she recognized her gentle brogue. "It's all right. I've got you now."

Jacob stepped away, and Oona swore she could sense his relief. As much as he distrusted her mother's coven, he wanted to be able to hand her over to someone. He wanted, after all these years, not to be the one responsible for soothing her pain.

"It's late," Oona heard Lally say to Jacob. "There won't be another ferry tonight anyway. And Oona needs some rest. So why don't the two of you sleep on it, and you can discuss more in the morning. Yeah?"

With effort, Oona pulled herself back up to standing, and Jacob nodded. "I can stay in town," he said. "But she has to promise not to climb those rocks. Okay?"

"She won't," Lally said. Then, to Oona, "All right, love, come with me."

"Really?" Oona asked. She peered over Lally's shoulder to search for her mother—she couldn't believe that Ursula would really let her stay—but instead she found the beach deserted. Sometime while she'd been busy arguing with Jacob, everyone had gone. The musicians had packed up and left. The other Mothers had returned to their cabins. And Ursula . . .

Lally clucked softly and said, "Don't worry, pet. It's fine. She'll understand your needing to stay till morning."

*Till morning.*

Oona looked off at the path that led through the woods. How was she going to face Gemma and Shelly? she wondered. How was she going to explain why she'd lied and pretended to be Maggie Jones?

Lally patted her hand and said, "I've still got that little cot you slept in as a girl. I can't say it'll be a luxury, but it'll do for now."

"Thank you," Oona said, as she took the hand Lally offered. That squared-off muscular hand, callused from years of work, from pulling life out of the women and out of the dirt.

Oona had missed those hands. She'd missed it all. But that was the trouble, wasn't it? That had always been the trouble for Oona. She loved it here too much. She wanted it too badly: for it all to be real, for it all to be hers.

# FOUR

It had been a gray morning, filled with low-hanging clouds and the kind of cold drizzle that made Oona want to bury herself beneath the heavy, hand-stitched quilt Lally had loaned her. It was the same quilt she'd often borrowed as a child whenever she'd gotten into trouble and fled to Lally for comfort. Oona had been pleased to discover that it still smelled the way she remembered: like salt and sage, and ash from the fire Lally kept burning in her woodstove. It had been a solace, waking up in Lally's cabin again, and all morning Oona had luxuriated in the familiarity, the feeling of coming home. For hours she'd sat by the fire, dressed in one of Lally's old jumpsuits, sipping herbal tea and listening to the pitter-patter of the rain against the single-pane windows, the cottage's cedar shingles. If given a choice, she might never have decided to leave.

But she wasn't given a choice. Ursula called a little before twelve and demanded Lally escort her off the property.

"I'm sorry, love," Lally said when she hung up the phone. "I tried, but it seems she won't forgive you for taking Maggie Jones's place. They've been working together for some time, you see. This was to be Maggie's first summer on the island, but they've been exchanging letters, emails, phone calls for many years. Your mother even sent her some potions through the mail a few weeks back."

"It's okay," Oona said. At least now she understood why her mother had been so eager to meet with Maggie all weekend. "Jacob just texted. He's coming to pick me up." She grabbed her bag and Lally's spare rain jacket, then pressed her lips against Lally's smooth, dry cheek. "Before my ferry leaves, I'll sneak back to get my stuff and say goodbye."

"Good girl." Lally kissed her fingers in a kind of wave, and Oona pushed out into the rain.

Praying the others would all still be in the dining hall for lunch, she crept through the Center like a thief, and by the time she made it to the driveway she saw that Jacob was already there waiting for her, idling in some strange, borrowed old truck. Oona could hear the engine chugging even as she came around the side of the front office. Her stomach cramped lightly as they pulled away.

"I'm sorry," Jacob said, once they hit the main road and the forest swallowed the Center behind them. "I shouldn't have shown up out of the blue like that, I know. I tried to call when the boat docked, but I couldn't reach you and I just—I couldn't wait. I was so worried. About you, about the baby."

Jacob reached across the gearshift to place his palm on her stomach, and Oona felt herself relax into his touch. As sad as she'd been to leave Lally's cabin, she had to admit that it felt good being there in the truck with Jacob. Or maybe not good, exactly, but familiar. And therefore safe.

"How have you been feeling?" he asked. "Last time you were

pretty nauseous. Remember when we were driving down to Portsmouth and we had to pull over into that empty parking lot and—"

Oona smiled. That had been a good day. And memorable, because good days had become a rare event for the two of them in recent years. But that morning, Oona had been grateful for her nausea, grateful that Jacob had the day off from work. So they'd gone for a drive, and along the way they'd allowed themselves to imagine their future, something they used to do all the time but had slowly given up. They both wanted a daughter, they'd decided. A girl with Oona's red hair and Jacob's brown eyes. Jacob had seen a book in a store—*Oceanography for Babies*—that he couldn't wait to buy her. And Oona, she had an illustrated book of herbs. A gift from Lally that she wanted to pass down. At the time, Jacob had looked at her askance, but he'd held his tongue, and Oona could still remember what she'd thought as they'd pulled into that parking lot: *We're going to make it.*

But then, a week later she'd had a bleed. And when she'd set up her dresser altar to appeal to Demeter for answers, Jacob had snuffed out her sigil candles while she was asleep. He denied it, of course, but he'd left behind that half-drunk can of beer.

In the truck, Oona lifted Jacob's hand off her belly. "I think it's too early," she said.

Jacob frowned. "Is everything all right?"

And for a moment Oona debated telling him about the storm petrel. But she knew he wouldn't believe her if she said she was cursed. He probably wouldn't even believe her if she said she'd seen a storm petrel. Instead, he'd tell her it was far more likely that she'd seen a seagull or a swallow. Or maybe he'd claim she hadn't seen a bird at all. He'd tell her that it had to have been a bat. Or some other night creature. A figment of her imagination, some manifestation of her nerves.

"Oona?"

"Everything's fine," she said.

Jacob cleared his throat. "Anyway, it will be nice to eat at Baxter's again. Won't it?"

It wasn't the sort of comment that required a response, so instead Oona turned to look out the window. After Jacob had desecrated her altar, they'd stopped trying for a while. At first, Oona had thought it was her idea, a punishment she was doling out, but then one day Jacob had come home with condoms. And in a voice that made it seem like he was doing her some favor, he'd told her that it would be okay if they never had a child. At the time, Oona hadn't known what to say. She'd been too surprised, too angry. But she'd known, even then, that such an existence would never be enough for her. *He* would never be enough for her. She wanted more.

She wanted to transcend herself, to be transformed through motherhood the way she'd seen her own mother transformed by the magic that ran through her blood. All her life she'd seen Ursula breathe force into the winds that whipped through Marrow, speak strength into the waves that crashed along the shore. Now Oona wanted her own chance to wield such power. She wanted to bear down and pull life from inside her womb. But that just wasn't the sort of thing she could ever hope to put into words, and even if she could, she was sure Jacob would never understand.

"I was thinking maybe we could split a lobster roll. Are you tolerating fish okay? Or does seafood upset your stomach? I know the smell can—"

"I'll be fine, Jacob," Oona said, but just then she felt another cramp. She didn't mean to, but she couldn't stop herself from sucking in a breath.

Jacob tapped the brakes. "What's wrong?" he asked.

"Nothing."

"That didn't sound like nothing."

They had the same bickering argument every time they tried to have sex. The bedroom used to be the one place where Oona had still felt understood, but ever since her first miscarriage Jacob had been cautious around her. Too tender and light-fingered. He treated Oona like she was made of glass. Harder, she would beg. Deeper. Rougher. But Jacob wouldn't—couldn't—give her what she wanted. For weeks after that first miscarriage, he'd hardly been able to touch her. Meanwhile, for her part, Oona had started watching porn. Pregnancy porn. It was gross, she knew, but she couldn't help it. She got off on watching the women run their hands over their bellies, draw their nails along their stretchmarks, and moan like they were feeling the urge to push.

Now, in the truck, Oona remembered one of the women from those videos. A pale brunette, when she'd had a contraction on-screen Oona had touched herself to the sound of her panting. "Oof," she'd groaned. "It hurts."

Oona's own pelvis hurt. Well, ached. But the message boards all said that some aches and pains were to be expected. They were caused by the stretching of the ligaments that supported the uterus, which would need to lengthen as her belly grew.

"Oona?" Jacob asked.

Oona had closed her eyes against the pain. "I'm fine," she said again.

Jacob touched her shoulder. "No, Oona," he said. "We're here."

The Port Marrow boardwalk didn't have much to offer besides the fish market and the ticket kiosk, the marine patrol offices and the ferry dock, but it was home to the only restaurant on the island:

Baxter's Boathouse. Oona had never spent much time inside Baxter's, which was located in a small, dark-shingled building right at the beginning of the boardwalk. Growing up, she and Jacob and Daphne had always gotten their food to go. There hadn't been time to sit and eat, not with Ursula waiting.

No matter how many years passed without incident, Ursula never relaxed her rules. Oona was expected home as soon as school let out. Daphne used to complain, she always wanted to be able to show Oona off, but Jacob never minded. In fact, he'd actually preferred not eating inside. He'd hated the way everyone used to gawk at Oona: the boys and girls from their class, who loved to tease her almost as much as they liked to tease him, the women from his mother's knitting circle, the men who grew up lobstering with his dad and called his father "Cap'n." In some ways, Jacob used to tell her, the adults were worse. They talked about Oona like she was a golden goose, and the hungry way they looked at her . . . it gave him the creeps. For her part, though, Oona would have liked to sit inside. Not to show off or be gawked at, but to spend more time with Jacob and Daphne. Even just an extra hour would have made a big difference to her, especially in those years when she was still dodging her mother's questions about Persephone, still burying her panties in the woods. It had been freeing, back then, to leave the Center, though her longing for freedom had also caused her a fair amount of shame.

Now, though, those feelings of shame were gone. Or at least, they'd been complicated. As Oona followed Jacob into Baxter's, she found herself vacillating between anger and guilt and fear. Al Johnson might've been dead, but what about Mr. Roberts and Mr. Clark? What about their sons, who had spent years terrorizing not just Oona but Jacob, because, as a child, he'd preferred the company of books to that of other boys?

Oona braced herself as the door closed behind them and her eyes adjusted to the restaurant's dim, but they'd gotten lucky, it appeared. The room was empty. There wasn't another soul in sight. No one seated at any of the small laminate tables, no one hunched over the top of the bar. No one even to offer them a menu. So for a while they just stood there, awkward and silent, until Oona lost patience and sidled up to the bar.

"Hello?" she called, toward the back kitchen.

"Hold your horses!" came a call in return.

"We're just gonna sit at the bar, okay?" Oona pulled out one of the stools she realized she recognized from childhood: lacquered wood legs and a red leather seat gone soft with wear, patched in places with duct tape.

Jacob took the stool beside her and said, "I can't believe Jimmy's still here."

"Where else would I be?" Jimmy asked, pushing through the kitchen's swinging doors at the other end of the bar. He didn't smile because he wasn't joking. An ex-lobsterman whose grandfather had opened Baxter's more than a hundred years before, Jimmy never kidded around. "What can I get ya?" he asked, drying his hands on an old dish towel.

"IPA?" Jacob asked.

"We got Budweiser."

"That's fine."

"And for you?" He nodded at Oona.

"Just water, thanks," she said.

Jimmy raised one eyebrow but didn't comment further as he turned to run the sink's tap. When he returned, he was carrying both their drinks and a couple of menus. Single page, double-sided, laminated: the menus were yet another thing about Baxter's that had not changed.

"Unless you already know what you want," Jimmy said. Not quite a question.

"One lobster roll, one vanilla milkshake, and one order of fries," said Jacob.

"We're going to share," Oona explained, when Jimmy looked to her.

"Suit yourself," he replied. Then he turned and headed back to the kitchen.

Oona wanted to tell him that the sharing wasn't her idea. If left to her own devices, she would have ordered differently. But it was bad enough that she was going to have to fight with Jacob about Bare Root. She didn't want to have to argue about their food too.

"So," Jacob said, once they were alone again. "Let's talk."

"All right," sighed Oona.

"Should I start?"

"You always do."

"Oona." Jacob frowned. Already, she was getting scolded.

"What?"

"That isn't fair."

"Okay."

"Okay," Jacob repeated. And for a moment, they sat there in silence. Jacob took a long swig of his beer. "So," he started again. "You left. Without telling me."

"I did," Oona admitted. She resisted the urge to say that she was sorry. Because she wasn't sorry. She was glad she'd left. Glad she'd received the protection spell. And glad, too, for the reprieve of the long weekend. It had been nice spending the past few days doing something other than scrolling the message boards.

"Why?" Jacob asked.

In the bar's sour yellow light, Oona studied his face. Was he serious? she wondered. But he was. Of course he was.

"You know why," she said.

"No, I don't. I really don't. I mean, I know you want a baby, Oona, but to come here? Like this? It's—" He cut himself short.

"Go on. Say it," Oona told him. "Crazy. You think I'm crazy. You think I'm crazy just like they did." She gestured down the length of the empty bar.

"They didn't think you were crazy. They thought you were dangerous."

"Well, maybe I am."

"Oona." Jacob reached to touch the ends of her hair. "What happened wasn't your fault. But this? Changing your name? Dyeing your hair? Running away from home?"

"I wasn't running *from* Portland. I was running *to* Bare Root."

"She didn't invite you, though, did she?"

Oona looked away from him. "No."

"I didn't think so." Jacob sighed and rubbed the heels of his palms into his eyes. "I wish you could find a way to let her go, to let all of this go."

"All of what?"

"You know, the spells and whatnot. The candles. The crystals. That weird pink clamshell. All the junk you keep on the dresser."

"That's my altar."

"You don't need it. That's what I'm trying to tell you. You don't need any of it. You don't need her. You have me."

"She's my family, Jacob."

"No, *I'm* your family. I've been your family for fifteen years. And your mother, she . . ." He shook his head, took another slug of beer. "You know the saying, 'You can't get blood from a stone'? Well, it's true. You can't. You're not gonna get what you want from her, Oona. Her love or her acceptance or whatever—you're not gonna get it."

"I don't care about any of that," Oona lied.

Jacob tipped his head to one side and looked at her skeptically.

"I don't," she insisted.

"Fine." He held up both hands in surrender. "You don't care about that. Fine. All I'm saying is: You don't need *magic*. You never have."

Oona rolled her eyes. He was trying to be cute, referencing the speech that had brought them together, but while the original version had made Oona feel not just accepted but *seen*, the revival had nearly the opposite effect. Frustrated, she gripped her water glass with two hands and focused on the ice inside, melting.

About a year after Oona first met Daphne, the girls started hanging around the docks. Usually, they just sat on the pier, watching the boats come in, but that day Daphne had begun pestering Oona to bring her to Bare Root, so Oona had been forced to explain, for the umpteenth time, that it was against the rules. If they got caught, she said, her mother would do more than just ground her. She would forbid her to ever come back to school. She would use the breach as proof that Port Marrow was just as dangerous as any mainland town, full of all kinds of corruptible influences.

"But there's nothing dangerous about Port Marrow," Daphne had said.

And Oona had just opened her mouth to agree, when suddenly Daphne's brother, Jacob, came tearing around the corner, the Roberts brothers close on his heels.

Back then, Jacob had worn a pair of wire-rimmed glasses and Oona had never seen his face without them, but as he neared she realized that he was holding them in one hand. Not only that, but his clothes were dirty. The cable-knit sweater his mother had made for him looked wet and sandy, and his pants were ripped at the knee.

"What happened?" Oona asked, as Jacob stuttered to a stop. He was red-faced, panting.

The Roberts brothers came to a standstill about three yards away. They weren't quite twins—Dale was older by nine months—but they looked identical. Same big, round head. Same thin, pale lips. Oona hated them. The week before, after learning about the Salem witch trials, they'd snuck up behind her on the jetty and pushed her in. They'd claimed they wanted to see if she really was a witch. "Sink or swim!" they'd chanted.

On the docks, Oona braced herself, squared her stance, but that day the brothers seemed hardly to notice her. Instead, they fixed their beady eyes on Jacob, whom, Oona assumed, they'd found outside the library, returning a tome about marine biology.

Oona hadn't spent much time with Jacob at that point, but she'd seen the way Mrs. Tanaka looked at him whenever he slunk home with his nose bloodied, his eye swollen, a bruise purpling his cheek. Oona knew that look well, had seen it in her own mother's eyes just the week before when she'd lied and said that no, she still hadn't gotten her period. So when the Roberts brothers told her and Daphne to stand aside, Oona shook her head. Ignoring Jacob's pleas, she stood her ground, even as Dale Roberts laughed and asked if she really thought she could stop them. They had, what, fifty pounds on her?

"What are you going to do?" Buck asked. "Turn us into frogs? You're not like your mom. You don't have any power."

"She does too," Daphne said.

But Oona stayed quiet. She knew it wasn't true. She wouldn't come into her own magic for years. In fact, she might never gain access to it if she continued to fail in conjuring Persephone. But of course, she didn't dare admit to that in front of Daphne—Daphne, who memorized every single one of the stories Oona told her of her mother's childhood coven, who hid the drawings she made of pentagrams under her bed, who treated the stinging nettle Oona harvested for her like it was gold. Without magic, without Craft, Oona would be nothing to Daphne, nothing to her mother, nothing at all.

"If you're really a witch," Buck Roberts said, "then prove it."

Oona glanced back at Jacob and saw his nose had started to bleed. He swiped at it with the back of his hand. "It's fine," he said. Then he dug into his pocket and pulled out a crumpled five-dollar bill. Money, Oona knew from Daphne, that he'd earned helping scrub their father's patrol boat. He was saving up to attend some fancy science camp on the mainland, determined to do anything other than work on a boat the way his father did and his father's father before him.

Jacob held out the wrinkled bill. "Just take it," he said.

Oona smacked down his hand. "Put that away."

"Ooo," Daphne jeered. "Now you're gonna get it." She dug into her left pocket and pulled out a miniature glass jar. It looked like the kind the mercantile used to sell sewing pins, but instead Daphne had filled it with petrel feathers, bits of eggshell. She was convinced the birds were special and was always skulking around the beach, trying to raid their nests. "Use this," she told Oona. "And put a hex on 'em. Give them a curse that'll last a thousand years."

"Oh, sure," Oona said, as if it were just that simple—as if she'd ever even *overheard* a hex before. Still, it wasn't in her to back down. So she did the only thing she could think to do—what she often did, though usually only in the privacy of her bedroom: She imitated her mother. With her feet planted firmly on the ground, her legs spread as wide as her shoulders, she closed her eyes and exhaled.

Before Ursula performed a ritual, before she lit a candle or picked up a crystal or began a spell, she always made sure to ground herself first. And while others in their coven preferred more traditional methods—meditation, rooting, chimes—Ursula, Oona knew, always imagined a cave. Dark and cold and still. Once, when she was young, Oona had come upon her mother working and had been surprised to discover that she could actually feel the chill in the air. But the cold Ursula conjured hadn't felt constricting, like Oona might've guessed. It hadn't felt like stepping out into a snowstorm or taking a plunge into an icy lake. Instead, it had been expansive. Ballooning. Her mother called it holding space.

On the docks, Oona did her best imitation of that space holding. She pictured a cave in her mind's eye, the only one she knew: a small cavern at the base of the east-side cliffs where often, as a kid, she'd gone exploring. It flooded during high tide and smelled of salt and algae even when it was dry. As a gust of wind blew across the harbor, Oona worked to catch the smell of the sea on the air. She tuned out all the other noises—the cries of the gulls overhead, the rattling engines of nearby fishing boats—and focused only on the sound of the waves.

At some point, she knew, she was supposed to feel something—though despite asking every witch at the Center, she'd never quite been able to get a handle on what that something would be. A spark, maybe, like when she rubbed her socked feet along the carpet and then shocked herself. Or a gentle rumble, like she could feel when her mother allowed her to ride into town in the Center's truck. But though she kept her eyes closed and her mind focused, her ears tuned and her feet rooted to the wooden dock, nothing happened. There was no spark, no rumble. No telltale whiff of algae. No sudden rush of cold. And after a minute or two, Oona began to feel Daphne growing tense behind her. A few feet ahead, she heard Buck and Dale laugh.

"Use the feathers," Daphne whispered. "Or the shells."

"It's okay, Oona," said Jacob. "It's only five dollars."

But of course it wasn't about the money—it had never been about the money. It was about Daphne and the weight of her gaze. It was about Ursula and the look she'd given her when Oona had asked for yet another package of panties. "What happened to the ones I bought you last month?" her mother had asked. It was about Dale and Buck and their stupid Adam's apples, their too-small yellow teeth. Oona wanted to break her knuckles on their mouths, beat their noses bloody. Even as she stood there, she could feel her hands fisting at her sides.

It wasn't the spark she'd been waiting on, but their laughter did generate something inside her: a kind of electricity. She could feel it moving underneath her skin.

"Shut up," she warned the boys.

But they just laughed louder. So Oona bent her knees, lowered her head. She didn't have a plan. She never had a plan. But later she guessed that if given another ten seconds, she would have charged at them like a bull. Before she could, though, something happened. Overhead, they heard a fizzle, then a crack. They all looked up and the lightbulb in the lamppost right above them exploded. Shards of glass fell all around them like rain.

The boys screamed and ran. Daphne cackled. "I knew it!" she cried. "I knew it! Did you use the feathers? Did they help?"

Oona touched her cheek, and her fingers came away red.

"You're bleeding," Jacob said. He used his sweater's sleeve to dab at her eyebrow, where a shard of glass had cut her.

"You'll tell me how you did that. Won't you?" Daphne asked. "You'll teach me?"

Jacob switched sleeves and Oona looked at him, dazed. "Go get a Band-Aid, Daphne," he told his sister.

But Daphne hesitated. It was as if she didn't trust that Oona would still be there when she returned. "You promise?" she asked Oona, then she waited until Oona nodded.

When they were alone, Jacob pulled his sleeve away from her face and checked the wool to see if the bleeding was slowing any. "Thank you," he said, after he'd stepped back.

"I don't even know what I did," Oona admitted. It wasn't anything she'd have told Daphne, but it seemed safe to share with Jacob. "I wasn't trying to break the lamp."

"Oh, you didn't," Jacob said.

Confused, Oona looked down. There was a piece of glass by her foot and it made a satisfying crunch when she stepped on it.

"No," Jacob said. "I mean, the lamp *is* broken. But you didn't break it. That fuse has been funky for ages. It probably just blew."

Oona didn't know whether to be offended or relieved. "So you don't believe, then?" she asked.

"In witchcraft? No," said Jacob. He unfolded his glasses and worked to bend one of the arms back into place. "But I believe in you."

Oona scoffed, but Jacob just shrugged, like what he'd said wasn't corny.

Like it wasn't the very thing Oona had been waiting her whole life to hear.

Before she knew what she was doing, she stepped forward to kiss him. The blood from her wound mixed on her lips with his saliva, and it felt, to her, like some new kind of ritual, like an invented prayer.

Almost two decades later, the memory of that afternoon no longer moved Oona. Once, it had felt sacred, holy. Now, at best, it just seemed silly. At worst, it filled her with a sense of regret. Who would she be, she wondered, if that lightbulb hadn't exploded, if she hadn't stepped forward to kiss Jacob?

During the first year or two that they lived in Portland, she'd been grateful for her split-second decision, for her impulsiveness. She wouldn't have said she was happy, exactly—after all, she'd been living in exile and they'd been broke, but even despite her dead-end job at the motel, despite their crappy rental in the woods with its leaking roof and its brown well water, despite their ancient RAV4 and the bald tires they couldn't afford to replace—still, at the end of the day, she'd been glad she had Jacob. At night, she'd fallen asleep with her head on his chest. In those early years, he'd been her harbor, her safe place in a storm, and she'd felt like no matter what, she had a partner. They were a team, the two of them. It was Oona and Jacob against the world. Then they'd started trying to get pregnant, and everything changed. Jacob changed. It was a matter of grit, Oona thought. While she was willing to do whatever it took to have a baby, Jacob just gave up. He rolled over and exposed the white of his belly in surrender.

*Coward*, she thought.

"Oona?" He waved a hand in front of her face. She blinked and was surprised to discover that not only had their food come, but Jacob had already finished his half of the lobster roll. The hand he'd used to wave at her was clutching two fat crinkle-cut fries. "Aren't you hungry?"

Oona was afraid to ask what else she'd missed while she'd been lost in memory, but from the look on Jacob's face she guessed that while she'd been busy recalling that day at the docks, their early years in Portland, he'd continued on with his lecture. For a moment, she debated worrying about where they'd ended up, about what she might have inadvertently agreed to just by failing to argue with him, but pretty quickly that worry passed. So she didn't have a partner right now. So what? Now she had something better. Now, she had a plan. She would confirm that there were no petrel nests hidden among the rocks on the jetty. Then, she would board the ferry at four o'clock. And once she got back to Portland, once she had the baby, she would get to work starting her own coven. By this time next year, she'd have a whole new life. *They* would have a whole new life. Because they could be happy again, Oona thought, if only they didn't have to argue anymore about whether to keep trying to get pregnant.

"Here," Jacob said, handing her the uneaten half of their lobster roll. "Take a bite."

Oona reached for the milkshake instead. "Jacob . . ." she started. She wasn't entirely sure what she planned to say—something about her dreams for the new coven, something about how she was doing this for him—but before she could finish her sentence, she was interrupted by the sound of the front door whining open.

By the time she turned to look, a couple, late middle-aged and gray-haired, was already moving toward them. Oona didn't recognize them at first, but then the couple came to stand beside Jacob. The woman said his name, and the sound of her voice—high-pitched, always too chipper—brought everything into focus. It was Mr. and Mrs. Tanaka. Oona hadn't seen them in almost fifteen years, and they'd aged, of course, but it was them, she was sure. Mrs. Tanaka was wearing a hand-knit sweater, just like always. And Mr. Tanaka was wearing his marine patrol jacket, had his hair styled in his signature tight crew cut.

As far as Oona knew, Jacob hadn't initiated contact with his parents since he'd left the island—or, as he would phrase it, since she'd lured him away. Because no matter how many times Oona tried to explain that when she'd called him from that pay phone in Portland she hadn't been thinking, Jacob never believed her. He insisted that she'd known what she was doing when she'd run away from the wilderness program her mother had sent her to. Sure she'd been young, and sure she'd been scared, but she'd never been stupid. When she'd asked him to come to Portland, to join her, she must have known that she was asking him to choose.

And so he'd chosen: Oona over his parents, the life of a seaman over school. He swore he didn't resent her for the way his life had veered off course, but sometimes Oona wondered. Certainly, she knew, his parents blamed her. And that, in and of itself, had cemented their dynamic for the past fifteen years. Anytime the Tanakas (mainly Mrs. Tanaka) wrote or called or, worst of all, showed up at their front door unannounced and started railing against Oona's influence, Jacob defended her. He protected her. Stood between his mother and Oona, his body a shield.

So in Baxter's, Oona turned to Jacob expecting his face to mirror her own confusion. She waited for him to get up and take her hand, to lead her away. But instead, he remained seated. "You're early," he scolded his mom.

"Not by much," she said.

"What's going on?" asked Oona. Because though she couldn't quite piece together what was happening, right away she knew that something was wrong. Why weren't they getting up, storming out? She glanced out the front window to where they'd parked, looking for Jacob's truck, their getaway car, only to realize that she recognized it: The truck was Mr. Tanaka's. He'd had it back when she was a kid.

Warily, she got up from her barstool and started inching backward toward the door.

"Oona, wait," Jacob said. "Just wait a minute, okay? Let me explain."

Oona kept backing up.

"Please." Jacob gestured to her stool. "Sit down. Hear us out."

"*Us?*" Oona repeated in horror.

Jacob sighed and Mrs. Tanaka sniffed, and Oona nearly lost it. She'd done a lot wrong, she knew—with Jacob, with Daphne. But she didn't deserve the sort of treatment she'd suffered at the Tanakas' hands. She didn't deserve to be cast out—barred from the funeral, banished from her coven, exiled to the mainland. After all, she'd only done what she'd done because she was trying to help.

"When you went missing—" Jacob started.

Oona sucked her teeth. "I didn't *go missing*. I left. There's a difference."

"Not to me, there wasn't. I got home from work, and you weren't there. I woke up the next morning, and you weren't in bed beside me. You weren't picking up your phone. You hadn't taken the car. I had no idea what happened to you, Oona."

"I—" Oona opened her mouth, but no more words followed. Standing there, she felt the rising tide of guilt. It was something about the look in Jacob's eyes. She'd scared him. Really scared him. And she hadn't meant to do that. When she'd called the reservations desk at Bare Root, she'd told herself that she was doing what she had to do to save their marriage. Beyond that, she hadn't given him a second thought.

But then, that was the problem, wasn't it? She'd been selfish.

Maybe she was still being selfish.

For a moment, Oona debated finishing her sentence. *I'm sorry, Jacob*—that was what she knew she should say. But when she glanced over at the Tanakas, she saw Mrs. Tanaka shaking her head in disgust, and her shame hardened into anger. She looked back at Jacob and shrugged. "You figured it out."

"Yes," said Jacob. "I did. And when I did, I realized how desperate you must have been to come here. So I called my parents. I figured if you could swallow your pride, then so could I." He took a breath and reached for both her hands. Reluctantly, she turned them over. "They've agreed to help us, Oona."

"Help us . . . how?"

"We have a bit in savings," Mr. Tanaka explained. It was the first time he'd spoken, and Oona was surprised to discover that she'd missed his gravelly voice. After Daphne died, he'd been easier on her than Mrs. Tanaka had. At times, he'd even been kind. Which was why it had hurt more when he'd been the one to stand there beside Mr. Clark and Mr. Roberts, blocking the door to Daphne's service.

"I don't understand," Oona said.

"You can see a doctor," said Jacob. "A fertility doctor. We can finally get some help."

"So long as you agree to give us access to our grandchild," added Mrs. Tanaka.

"Access?" Oona echoed, while at the same time Jacob groaned.

"Mom. Just let me do the talking, okay?"

"We've only asked for a month each summer," Mrs. Tanaka continued. "I think that's more than fair."

"You want . . . my child?" Oona asked.

"For a month in the summer. The rest of the time, of course, they can live with you."

"Oh, can they?" Oona laughed. The whole thing was ridiculous. Oona didn't even want a child, at least not in the way they all assumed. And yet, the idea that she would just hand her baby over to the Tanakas, it was absurd. More than absurd. And after only a few short moments, Oona's laughter began to curdle in her throat. She started coughing, hacking. Jacob had to pat her on the back.

"Are you okay?" he asked.

"Are you kidding?" said Oona. "Am I okay? No, I'm not fucking *okay*, Jacob. I'm barely past my first trimester and you're out here trying to Rumpelstiltskin our child." She turned on the Tanakas. "You're the reason we're in this mess, you know. If it weren't for you, I'd be home still."

"And you're the reason our daughter is dead," said Mrs. Tanaka. "You took both of our children from us, Oona. It's high time you paid us back."

"Jesus, Mom," Jacob said. "We talked about this. It wasn't Oona's fault. I thought you agreed. What happened to Daphne was chemical. If we'd taken her to a doctor, they could have diagnosed her. Postpartum depression."

"Depression?" Mrs. Tanaka repeated, shocked. "Did depression convince Daphne to drink poison? No, that was Oona. And it was Oona who convinced you to quit school, to become a fisherman, risking your life for a job that will never pay. A job you hate!"

"I'm not a fisherman, I work for the university, and I don't hate it," Jacob said, first to his mother and then to Oona. "And even if I did, that was my choice. Not Oona's. Mine." Jacob scrubbed a hand down his face. "You need to let this go, Mom. You need to believe her. There was nothing in that drink but herbs. And Daphne didn't go up to those cliffs until almost a week later."

But Mrs. Tanaka didn't apologize. She just stared Oona down. Cold, calculating.

Before she could think better of it, Oona spit onto the floor by her feet. "Keep your money," she hissed. Then she snatched her coat from the back of her barstool and headed for the door.

"You're being punished!" Mrs. Tanaka called after her. "You're being punished! That's why you can't have a child. Because God knows what you did to Daphne."

"Stop it, Mom," Oona heard Jacob say, but then the door closed behind her and the rest of their conversation was drowned out by the mournful sound of a ferry's horn.

Originally, Oona had thought she'd walk back to Bare Root on her own, but though the rain had eased up some while they'd been inside eating, it was still cold out, and the remaining mist, she knew, would quickly soak through her canvas sneakers if she attempted the trek home. Still, she couldn't quite bring herself to wait for Jacob by the truck that she now knew belonged to his parents. Instead, she started walking toward the beach.

By the time she made it down to the sand, Jacob had caught up with her. "I'm sorry," he said, when he got near. "I swear, I thought they were past all that."

"Past what? Past their daughter's death?"

"No," Jacob sighed. "No, of course not."

"You ambushed me," she said, then she kept walking.

He jogged after her. "Wait a minute, will you?"

"No."

But Jacob had already grabbed hold of her hand. "I'm sorry," he told her. "They were—she was—"

"Awful?"

He nodded. "I never should have gone to them for help. But I was desperate, Oona. I was just as desperate as you were when you left."

Oona tugged her hand free and eyed the water behind Jacob. Any other day she would have continued the fight. In fact, she probably would've found some way to escalate things. She usually did. But the smell of low tide was making her nauseated. All that tangled seaweed, those crab carcasses, those horseshoe shells. "Can we just go?" she asked.

Jacob nodded. "Sure," he told her.

When they reached the truck, he opened her door. And though Oona still hated the idea of driving around in a vehicle owned by the Tanakas, by that point she felt too sick to even suggest walking home.

"How long do you think it will take to pack your things?" Jacob asked, once he'd climbed up into the driver's seat. "I know you have a ticket for the four o'clock ferry, but if you can be quick, I'm pretty sure there's another boat that'll leave in an hour or so."

"It won't take me long," Oona said. "But there's something I have to do first."

"What?"

"I have to go down to the beach at Bare Root. I have to search the jetty."

"Again with the jetty? Why?"

"You won't understand," Oona said.

Jacob stilled, his hands on the wheel. "Does it have something to do with witchcraft? What are you hoping to find?"

Oona didn't have the energy to explain that her hope was that she'd find nothing. "I don't want to fight with you," she said. "I'm tired." And she was. She was so tired. In that moment what she wanted, more than anything, was to be back in Lally's bed, back under her warm, heavy quilt, listening to the fire crackle in her hearth.

"Well, whatever it is, I can promise: You don't need it."

"But I did. I do. I need help."

"Then we'll go to a doctor. Back home, Oona. We'll go see an expert. If you don't want to take my parents' money, then fine. We'll find another way."

For a moment, Oona just stared at him, speechless. "I don't get it," she said at last. "Why now? What's changed? I've been suggesting we see a doctor for years."

Jacob looked down at his hands, still gripping the steering wheel. Over a decade of sun and salt water had caused the skin along his knuckles to crack. "I don't want to lose you over this, Oona."

"And by *this*, you mean our child?"

"Our *theoretical* child." He shook his head. "I know you want a baby. I wanted a baby too. But not at this price. Not at the cost of your health, of our marriage."

Oona felt her jaw set. "I'm willing to do whatever it takes."

"And that scares me," said Jacob, looking over at her for the first time. "Do you understand why that scares me?"

"I need this, okay? *We* need this."

"We?"

"Yes, we. I'm doing this for us, Jacob."

"No." Jacob shook his head again slowly, as if the act pained him. "No, that's not true. And you know it's not true. This is all about you, Oona. This is about what you want. It always has been."

"What's that supposed to mean?"

"I don't regret my choice," Jacob said. "I really don't. But—"

There was always a "but" when Jacob talked about his decision to leave Marrow, invoked his great *sacrifice*.

"But," he said again, "when I chose you, I thought you were choosing me, too, Oona. Over Bare Root, over your mother. I thought our choices meant something."

"You chose," Oona said. "I didn't get that chance. I was kicked out. Banished."

"And whose fault was that? What my mother said back there was horrible, but we both know where she got it from. She's only repeating what your mother told her."

"I know." Oona sighed, and Jacob looked down at the radio, started fiddling with the knobs.

She turned to gaze out the window, at the ferry now floating in its dock, and in the back of her mind she heard Mrs. Tanaka's words again. *Punished.* She'd said Oona was being punished. Well, that was the one point on which she and Mrs. Tanaka agreed. Oona thought she was being punished too. More than that, she thought she deserved it. Not because she'd given Daphne that potion—a concoction made entirely, like Jacob had said, from herbs. But because she'd lied. She'd let Daphne believe that she had power, that she could help her. Because she'd loved too much the way she saw herself through Daphne's eyes: powerful, commanding, a force of nature just like her mother. So she'd agreed to perform the ritual, and five days later, Daphne died.

Sitting in the truck beside Jacob, Oona felt her resolve falter. Maybe he was right, she thought. Maybe she was being selfish. After all, he'd given up everything for her. His family, his home, his education. So didn't she owe him something in return? Couldn't she at least agree to forgo her search of the jetty and take an earlier ferry back?

"Okay," Oona said.

And Jacob turned back to look at her. "Okay?" The hope in his voice made her feel sick. "Okay, like, we can go back to Portland now?"

She nodded, and he cupped her chin in his hand. He leaned forward to kiss her, but before their lips could touch, her gaze snagged on the corner of the windshield. Tucked just behind the wiper's base, she saw a bit of shell. White with a few flecks of brown, like the egg of a storm petrel. When she turned to point it out to Jacob, she felt a jolt of pain up her side. So familiar, it left her cold. "Fuck," she breathed.

"What is it?" Jacob asked her.

Oona closed her eyes. She didn't have it in her to look, but when she reached her hand down between her legs, she felt it—the seat beneath her was wet.

"It's happening again, isn't it?" Jacob asked.

And Oona nodded, gritted her teeth. Her spit tasted sour, and she could feel the acid in her belly swirling.

"What do I do?" he asked, panicked.

"Take me home."

# FIVE

Jacob pulled up to the Center in a cloud of dust, braking so hard and fast they skidded on the clamshell driveway. While Oona sat in the passenger seat clenching her thighs together and praying—muttering the same incantation she'd repeated since they'd left Port Marrow: *please, please, please*—Jacob leapt out of the truck and started sprinting toward the front office.

"Help!" he cried, and Oona could hear the tears in his throat. "Help! Someone, please! It's my wife! She's bleeding!"

He was lucky—they were both lucky: No one was in the front office, but Lally and Joyce had only just left the lodge, so they were able to hear Jacob's desperate cries for help through the woods. They came running. At the sight of them, Oona burst into tears. She'd been able to keep it together for the duration of the drive—hands in fists at her sides, eyes closed against the whipping curves of the road, against her own blood pooling beneath her—but she felt her stoicism dissolve the moment she saw Lally's face.

"It's all right, love," Lally said, as she approached the passenger-side door. "It's all right. We're here now." She looked at Jacob over the hood. "What happened?"

"I don't know. Everything was fine. We were just sitting in the truck, talking, and then suddenly she just looked pale. And . . ." At a loss for words, he gestured helplessly at Oona.

When Joyce eased open her door, Oona turned in her seat. That was a mistake. As soon as she moved, she felt her pain anew. The twisting in her abdomen was like a wringing: a deep and throbbing ache.

"Come to me," Joyce said, and held out her hands, but Oona couldn't do it. Sitting down, she thought, had been acting like a kind of plug. If she got up, she would lose everything.

As if able to read Oona's mind, Lally stepped in front of Joyce. "No," she said. "No, don't try to stand, love. Jacob?"

On the other side of the truck, Jacob twitched to attention, and Oona could see how anxious he was to be told what to do.

"Jacob," Lally said. "Come here. You'll need to carry Oona over to the infirmary."

"No!" Oona wailed. "No! I can't. Please."

"Oona," Lally said. "Oona, stop. Listen. You are not going to lose the baby. But we need to get you lying down so we can see what's going on." She glanced back at Jacob. "Ready?" she asked, and he hurried over.

When he bent to lift her, he whispered, "Everything's going to be okay." But it was an empty promise, and they both knew it. "I'll count to three," Jacob said, and Oona braced herself. "One . . . two . . ."

On three he lifted, and to keep herself from crying out, Oona bit her tongue. So hard, she tasted blood. *Please*, she thought again, as he jogged with her past the front office. *Please, please, please.* There were no other words. There was simply her want: savage, like an animal. And the dank, fecund smell of the woods as Jacob ran.

Inside the infirmary, Lally pointed Jacob to a room at the end of the hall. She instructed him to place Oona on the examination table, and then she told him to leave. He stuttered, "I can't—I won't." But Lally had already made an exception by letting him carry her in. No man, in the history of the Center, had ever been allowed past the front drive. As it was, they would need to spend days cleansing it. Weeks, maybe. Lally wasn't prepared to further bend Ursula's rules.

"This is as far as you go," she told him plainly. "Go back now and wait by the truck. We'll come get you when there's news."

Oona looked at Jacob, expecting him to protest. When he didn't, that's when she really began to feel scared. "I love you," he said, before he left.

As the door closed behind him, Oona turned to Lally. "What are you going to do?"

Joyce was already working to strip off her blood-soaked jumpsuit, pull down her panties. She exposed Oona's bare belly, then told her to spread her legs.

"It looks like you've lost a lot of blood," Joyce said, as Lally squirted gel onto Oona's stomach.

"Have I lost . . . have I lost . . . ?" Oona couldn't seem to get the words out.

"Quiet," Lally told her, as she took a small gray machine out of the far cabinet. She moved what looked like a microphone across Oona's belly.

"Can you hear it?" Oona asked.

"I can't hear anything while you're talking," Lally admonished.

So Oona shut up. *Please*, she thought but did not say. *Please. Please. Please.*

If asked, she would have said that she was praying to Demeter—the Mother—but the truth was both more simple and more complicated than that. When she closed her eyes, when she prayed, Oona saw only one face: her mother's.

As Lally moved the Doppler's wand, the room filled with static. And then—a whoosh. Slow and steady.

"Is that it? Is that the baby?" Oona asked.

Lally frowned, pushed her glasses up her nose, and squinted down at the Doppler, but before she had a chance to answer, Ursula burst into the room.

"She needs your potion, Lally," Ursula declared, pushing up the sleeves of her linen blouse. She tucked the crystal hanging from her neck inside her shirt. "You know the one."

Lally didn't look away from the Doppler.

"And a tincture of dried raspberry leaves and wild yam root too." When Lally still didn't move, Ursula clapped her hands. "Lally!" she barked.

Joyce grabbed a towel from the counter to wipe her hands. "I can go," she offered. "If you tell me where I can find the recipe."

"No," Ursula said. "No. You stay."

With a reluctance that confused Oona, Lally finally looked up and trained her rheumy green eyes on Oona's mother. "Ursula," she said, her voice low.

"Now," Ursula commanded.

"Not her," Oona thought she heard Lally say, but even then she was starting to fade. She didn't know how much blood she'd lost (after her first miscarriage, the doctors told her that she'd experienced a class 2 hemorrhage), but based solely on the numbness she could feel spreading down her limbs, on the dizziness that had washed over her when Jacob had pulled her from the truck, it was a lot. Enough to endanger her life. Still, she wasn't afraid. Not for herself, anyway. No, even as Ursula palpated her belly and her cramps were replaced with a sharp and splintering kind of pain, Oona remained focused solely on the pregnancy.

When her vision began darkening at the edges, she reached for her mother. "I need this," she whispered throatily. But Ursula was busy, distracted. She was pulling geodes from her pockets, lighting candles and placing them strategically all across the floor. So, desperate, Oona grabbed hold of one of Joyce's braids and used what little strength she had left to draw her closer. "I can't lose another one."

Joyce tutted softly. "How many so far?"

Oona's voice broke on the word: "Five."

"Oh, Oona," Joyce started, but she was interrupted by Lally, who had returned with a small glass vial. The potion inside smelled like tobacco and menthol, and something else—something familiar—that Oona could not name.

While Joyce cradled Oona's head, Lally tipped the glass toward her lips. "All of it," Ursula coached. "We need you to drink all of it."

Oona gulped and swallowed, greedy. "Is it working?" she asked when she was done. She tried to lift the sheet covering her. "Am I still bleeding?"

"Patience," said Ursula.

But patience had never been one of Oona's strengths, and as she lay there on the table she began to feel like time was running out for her. There was a storm coming, and the petrels, they were just a sign. A warning. Take care, seek shelter. One day soon, the waters will rise. The winds will howl. And Hekate will ascend from the depths of the sea, from her watery underworld. Already, Oona thought she could feel the pull of the tide, the water churning cold around her ankles. The chill was spreading up her legs.

"It was a shell this time," she told Lally. "Right before I started bleeding, I saw the petrel's shell."

But Lally just laid her warm, rough hand on her forehead, and within seconds, Oona was asleep.

When she first came to, Oona felt groggy and confused. She didn't know where she was. She only knew where she *wasn't*, and she wasn't in the infirmary. Instead, she was in some strange new room, lying in some strange new bed. White iron, she noticed, when she craned her neck to see down to the footboard. There wasn't anything on the white plaster walls to provide context, and across both windows heavy linen curtains had been drawn, so it was dim and hard to see. But there was a rug on the floor by the bed, a pale pink braided oval that Oona thought she recognized, though it took her a moment to realize where she knew it from. When she did, she nearly gasped, she was so surprised. It was hers. It was from her bedroom, or at least it was from the bedroom that had been hers when she was a girl and still living in her mother's cabin.

Lying in bed, Oona rolled onto her side to get a better view and yes, there it was: the faint stain on the rug from when she'd accidentally spilled the mug of tea her mother had left steeping on the kitchen counter, which Oona had stolen because she'd wanted to know how it would taste. Nosy—she'd been such a nosy child. So desperate to be let in on whatever secrets her mother was keeping.

Nothing else about the room was the same—the hardwood floors were so new, Oona was sure she couldn't be in their old cabin—but her mother had kept the rug she'd woven with Lally on Joyce's old, secondhand loom. That had to mean something, she figured. And the fact that she'd woken up there, that had to mean something too. But whether it was a good something or a bad something, she did not know. And for a moment, she felt almost too afraid to find out. Lying there, she debated just sneaking away.

In fact, she was halfway out of bed when Ursula threw open the door and found her. "I wouldn't do that if I were you. You'll pass out and these floors are hard. Real wood."

"Hi, Mom," Oona said, then she braced for Ursula's response. She'd never liked being called Mom. Even as a child, Oona had been asked to call her by her name, but Oona had largely refused because she'd wanted to claim her mother, had wanted everyone to know she belonged to her.

"I'm surprised you're awake," Ursula said. She was holding a cup of something warm, still steaming. The mug looked like it was hand-thrown. "I thought for sure with how much blood you lost, you'd sleep longer."

"Blood?" Oona replied. And that's when she remembered: the cramping, the truck. She ripped back the rest of the bedclothes, but she was clean. "Did it work?" she asked, looking up at her mother. "Did you stop the bleeding?"

Ursula inhaled slowly through her long, narrow nose. "I did."

"And?"

"And we'll just have to wait and see."

"What does that mean?" Oona asked. She'd forgotten just how frustrating she used to find her mother, but already she could feel her patience wearing thin. Why did she always have to be so fucking opaque?

"It means just what you think it means, Oona. It means we'll have to wait and see if the treatment worked."

"But you stopped the bleeding?"

Ursula released one long, disappointed sigh. "Yes," she said. "I stopped the bleeding."

Oona nodded. For a moment, she felt unable to speak. Emotion welled in her throat, and she found herself reaching for her belly. The baby was safe, she thought. *Her* baby. "Thank you," she said at last.

"You're welcome," Ursula replied. And order was restored, at least temporarily. Ursula, the gracious benefactor; and Oona, grateful, like all her mother's devotees. "I should go," Ursula said. "And you should sleep."

"Here?" asked Oona.

"Yes, here," Ursula said. "Where else?"

Oona looked around. "Where are we, exactly?"

"My house," Ursula said proudly.

"This is the cabin?" Oona asked, confused.

"No." Ursula's nose twitched. "No, this is my new house. We only just finished construction, actually. Last October." Oona must have still looked puzzled because Ursula added, "You must have seen it. By the dining hall?"

Oona closed her eyes briefly, trying to remember, and then it came to her. "In the clearing?"

"That's right."

"Oh. I thought that was a lighthouse."

"A lighthouse?" Ursula repeated, irked. Clearly, it was not the compliment she'd been expecting.

"I mean I knew it wasn't really a lighthouse, it was just so . . ." She paused, trying to think of the right words. So big? So white? So circular? "It has a tower?"

"A widow's walk," Ursula corrected, tucking a strand of her long white hair behind her ear. "All the old houses do."

"But it's new."

Ursula sighed. "It's an architectural feature. Forget it. It's probably too complicated for you to understand."

"It's nice," Oona offered lamely. "The house, I mean."

"It's more than nice," Ursula scoffed. "It's home—a sacred home, and not just for me but for our whole coven. We celebrate every sabbat here. We convene around the hearth on every solstice, on every full moon. We—"

"But you're the only one who lives here, right?"

Ursula looked disappointed, as if once again Oona had failed to see her point. "Yes," she said. "I'm the only one who lives here. Me and, well, now you, I guess. For a little while, anyway. Lally thinks it's important that you fully recover before returning to your cabin."

"But . . ." Oona paused. Considered. A smarter woman would keep her mouth shut. What was that saying about gift horses? She wasn't any good at sayings, but Jacob would know. Oona was being allowed to stay, that was what counted. The why shouldn't have mattered. Still, Oona found that she couldn't let it go. "What about Maggie?" she asked. "I mean the real Maggie. Lally said you were upset that I took her place."

"Not took. *Stole*."

"Right," Oona conceded. "Have you heard from her?"

"No," Ursula said, and frowned. "I haven't been able to get ahold of her, which is strange. But since it appears that she isn't coming, and since we can't exactly put you on a ferry in your current state, I suppose you can stay. But only until the baby is born."

"Really?"

"I mean it, Oona. Only until this child is born. Then you have to go. I told you before: You don't belong here. This isn't your home anymore."

"Portland isn't my home, either," Oona said, because apparently she was a glutton for punishment; because just when she'd thought she couldn't be any more shameless, she found a new low.

Ursula looked away, embarrassed—*for* Oona, *by* Oona.

Luckily, they were both saved by Lally, who chose that moment to bustle into the room. "You're awake!" she cried, rubbing her hands together. Oona wasn't sure, but she thought that Lally had changed clothes. Earlier, she'd been wearing a long linen dress that seemed more like something Ursula had chosen than anything Lally would have picked out. But now she looked more like herself again, clad in loose cotton pants and an oversize denim button-down, so worn at the cuffs and at the hem that Oona was pretty sure it was one of the same two denim shirts Lally had been wearing all Oona's life.

"How are you feeling?" she asked.

"Okay," said Oona.

Lally came right up to her bedside and felt her forehead, then leaned over to kiss her on the brow. By the time she'd stepped back again, Ursula was gone. Oona stared at the empty doorway while Lally hefted her heavy doctor's bag up onto the bed. "Do me a favor, love, and pull up your dress a little."

Oona did as she was told. "What am I wearing?" she asked, as she tugged the hem of her nightgown up over her stomach.

"One of our new birthing gowns. We give them to all the Mothers now. Well, all them that give birth here."

Oona rubbed the hem between her fingers. The fabric was incredibly soft.

"They call it *modal*," Lally said. "It comes with a matching robe. I'm sure yours is around here somewhere. Now, this may be just a wee bit uncomfortable," she warned Oona, before she began pressing the pads of her fingers into the soft flesh below her rib cage. "Any pain?" she asked, as she continued to palpate. Oona shook her head no. It was a lie, but one she felt compelled to tell, just in case Ursula was still out in the hallway, listening. Oona knew there was no faster way to turn her mother against her than to appear weak.

Ursula had never been a soft touch. If anything, vulnerability made her angry. Oona could still remember how much she'd hated it whenever her daughter would pretend to be sick. Of course, Oona only ever did it to try to steal back some of her mother's attention— from the Initiates, who liked to sit in a circle at her feet; from the Mothers with their never-ending sob stories; from the local women, who, it seemed to Oona, got pregnant four, five, six times over, just to get a chance to be treated by the famous Marrow "witch." Whenever Oona had complained of a headache, or a stomachache, or a full-body chill, Ursula had accused her of being manipulative, of being selfish. There were women out there, she used to say, who *actually* needed her help. So instead of her mother, it was Lally who had often indulged Oona, who had pressed cool washcloths to her face, run her fingertips down Oona's arms and legs, and massaged her small, tight muscles.

Once more under Lally's care, Oona felt the childish longing to be soothed, coddled, but she resisted. Instead, when Lally was done pressing her stethoscope against her belly, she sat up.

"Do you know how far along you are?" Lally asked.

"I think around twenty weeks," said Oona. "Why? Can you not find the heartbeat?"

"No, but don't you worry. Sometimes you can't at this stage, not without a Doppler." Lally helped Oona pull down her nightdress. "You know, it's funny, if she hadn't lost her most recent pregnancy, Maggie Jones would have been about twenty weeks along by now too."

"She had a loss?" Oona asked. "Recently?"

Lally nodded, sadly. "Just a few weeks ago. She rang us up, saying she was done, but somehow your mother convinced her to keep trying."

"Is it bad that I was doing her treatments?" Oona shook her head. "I mean, I know it was bad, it was wrong, but is that why . . ."

"No," said Lally. "No, nothing you did caused your bleed, love. I promise. If anything, those treatments might have been a help. After all, Maggie Jones is dealing with a similar issue. She's suffered multiple losses over the last few years."

Oona released the breath she'd been holding. "Okay. That's good, I guess. Or not good, but you know. At least the massages and the acupuncture and everything were meant for someone like—" Oona didn't finish her sentence. She was going to say "someone like me," when she'd realized that of course that wasn't true. They might have both been pregnant, they might've even been the exact same number of weeks along, but that didn't mean that Oona was anything like Maggie. At the very least, she knew there was one big difference: Maggie Jones could afford Bare Root.

At the foot of the bed, Lally had been packing away all her various instruments, but when Oona stopped talking mid-sentence, she paused. "What's wrong?" she asked.

"I can't pay," said Oona. "Mom told me I could stay until the baby's born, but I don't—we don't—there isn't any money."

"Oh, I'm sure Ursula isn't expecting you to pay."

Oona gave Lally a pointed look.

"I can cover you," said Lally.

"I can't ask you to do that."

"You want to stay, don't you?"

Oona nodded. "I *need* to stay, but if Jacob found out I'd borrowed money from you . . ."

Lally nibbled at her bottom lip, like she often did when she was thinking. Then: "I have an idea. You'll work off the debt."

"I will?"

"With me. The girl we hired to help me in the greenhouse walked out about a month ago, so we've been planning to bring in someone new anyway. And you already know the work. You used to have such a talent for the garden."

Oona pretended to consider the offer, though there really wasn't much to think about. She would've spent the summer cleaning up osprey shit if it meant that she got to stay on Marrow. "When can I start?" she asked.

"Not for a week, at least. Joyce told me about your other losses, so to be safe, you'll need to be on bed rest for a wee bit."

"Okay," Oona said.

Lally snapped closed her doctor's bag—bulky black leather, it looked like something from another era. "How many were there?" she asked.

"Five," said Oona, and this time she kept her voice steady.

"And have you gone to a doctor? Do they know what's wrong?"

Oona shook her head. "They say it's just bad luck."

Lally patted the blanket tucked around Oona's feet. "I'm sure they're right, love."

"No," Oona said. "They just don't understand." The curse had been a theory before, but now she was sure: Daphne was after her babies. If she didn't get help, there would soon be another bird, another ransacked nest, another cracked egg, another dead fledgling. And then, of course, another bleed. Oona had thought the protection spell would be enough to keep her safe, but for some reason the spell had failed her. Now she needed to figure out why, which meant she needed to tell someone the truth about what was happening.

"Oona," Lally said, because Oona had been quiet for too long and it'd become clear that she was hiding something. "Tell me."

"It's pretty bad."

"Tell me," Lally insisted.

So Oona took a deep breath. She'd never actually voiced her theory about a curse to anyone. "I keep seeing storm petrels before I bleed."

"Storm petrels?"

"Birds. Sometimes I see them, and sometimes I see their babies. Or what's left of their babies. I see damaged nests and cracked eggs, young with their necks snapped or their wings broken."

"Even today?"

Oona nodded.

"That *is* strange," Lally allowed.

"They're a sign," Oona said. "From Daphne."

"Daphne?"

"She's cursed me from the underworld. She wants me to suffer the way she's suffered, because I fucked up the ritual."

Lally sat down at the foot of the bed. "I don't understand."

"I performed a ritual," Oona said. "Don't you remember? I asked Hekate to bring Daphne down to the underworld. At first, I didn't think it worked, because nothing happened. But then . . ."

"Then she died," Lally finished.

"Then Hekate came for her," Oona clarified. "She was supposed to be able to come back, only she didn't. So I must have done something wrong. And now she's trapped down there, and she's pissed. She blames me."

"What ritual did you perform?"

"I can't remember, but I found it in one of Mom's books."

"Which book?"

"I don't know. Just one of the books she had by her altar."

"Okay." Lally began chewing on her lip again. "I won't bother lecturing you about how those books were off-limits for a reason."

"Please don't," said Oona.

"Just know that even if the ritual you performed did work, Hekate doesn't hold women hostage. Daphne isn't trapped in the underworld. You are not to blame for her death, Oona," Lally said gently.

But Oona insisted, "Yes, I am."

She was convinced that everything that had happened with Daphne could be traced back to one afternoon. Usually, in the shed, they only drank a couple capfuls of vodka each, but that day they'd gotten a little reckless and after a while the liquor had loosened Oona's tongue. Though she'd intentionally refrained from telling Daphne about Persephone and the secret of her buried panties, once she started divulging, she found it difficult to stop. She told Daphne everything she knew about the Maiden, the Mother, and the Crone; all she knew about what it would take for her to one day come into her power. And for a full week after, she regretted what she'd done. She stayed up late at night listening for the plink of clamshells against her window, searching the woods for the telltale sign of a flashlight's beam. In recent months, Daphne had only increased her badgering, and Oona worried that what she'd told her might inspire Daphne to do something outrageous. After all, she'd seen the way Daphne had looked at her that day in the shed, the way her eyes had seemed to glow in the dim.

But to Oona's surprise, nothing happened. Nothing obvious, anyway. There was a boy who'd shown up to spend the summer with his uncle. He was around their age, and though Oona didn't think he was anything to write home about, he was new to the island, and there was nothing like new for the girls their age. Oona didn't get to spend much time in town with school out of session, but on the rare occasion when she convinced Lally to let her run an errand, she overheard three different girls waxing poetic about the birthmark he had on the back of his neck. A stork's kiss. So sexy.

Oona, of course, was already taken. She and Jacob had started dating not long after their first kiss. But it had given her a strange kind of secondhand pride to see the way the new boy drooled over Daphne. And it had been nice, going to the beach for a double date when Oona could sneak out. There'd even been talk about the four of them meeting up one day on the mainland. But after the boy left, Daphne never mentioned him again. "It was just a summer fling," she said, whenever Oona asked if she was sad or lonely. "Not everyone falls in love after just one kiss."

At the time, Oona had laughed the way she'd known Daphne wanted her to laugh, but deep down, she'd felt nervous. She'd known that something was up. And two months later, when Daphne confessed that she was pregnant, Oona hadn't felt shock or pity. She'd felt satisfaction. *Ah*, she'd thought. *Now it all makes sense.*

They'd fought about it, she and Daphne. Oona had accused Daphne of getting knocked up on purpose, so Ursula would let her join her coven. She'd accused her of not actually wanting her child. And then, even though she'd promised to help, she'd screwed up the ritual.

So of course she was being punished, she thought. She deserved it.

"Please, Lally," Oona said now. "You have to believe me, you have to *help* me. If you don't, no one will. And I'll never be able to carry this baby to term. I'll never be able to come into my power. I'll never be able to set things right again."

"Oh, Oona."

"Please," she begged.

Lally sighed, resigned. "Okay, love. Okay. I will help you. Of course I will. What is it you need me to do?"

"I don't know. I came here for the Beltane protection spell because I thought it would be enough to keep the baby safe. But it wasn't. I received the spell's blessing last night, and today I still had a bleed."

Lally frowned. "That's not good," she said.

"I know," said Oona.

"Have you tried counteracting the ritual?"

"No. Is that something you could do?"

"Ah," said Lally. "Would that I could, love. But since you're the one who performed the original ritual, you would have to be the one to perform the counter-ritual as well. Close the circle, so to speak."

"But I can't," Oona protested. "I never saw Persephone. I don't have any power."

"Well," said Lally, with an arch to one eyebrow. "It seems that isn't true. If you summoned Hekate . . ."

"You mean . . . ?"

Lally nodded, and for a moment, despite herself and the circumstances, Oona felt proud. "Hekate is a very dark, very powerful goddess, Oona. In order to get her to come to you when you called, you must have been drawing from some powerful reserves yourself."

"I guess," Oona hedged.

"I know," said Lally.

"But what if I can't do it again? It's been almost fifteen years. And I don't even know what I did the first time."

"I'll help you," Lally said. "When you're ready, we'll track down the book and I'll help you. But for now, just try to rest. You should be safe for a while. The potion I gave you should protect the baby until you go into labor." She pulled the bedsheets up to Oona's chin, patted her cheek. "We can talk more later, okay? Sleep now."

"Okay," Oona said, because while her conversation with Lally hadn't completely reassured her, it *had* drained her, and as soon as she lay back against the pillows she could feel the promise of sleep beckoning.

When Oona woke again a few hours later, Jacob was standing by the door. Leaned up against the frame with his hands in his pockets, he looked like he'd been waiting there awhile. For a minute, Oona watched him as his gaze roved around her room, taking in the bare white walls, the iron daybed, the corner chair that Oona hadn't even noticed before. Its seat was the color of heavy cream, and its arms and legs looked like they'd been fashioned out of driftwood. It was nothing like the thrift store furniture Oona had grown up around.

"Hey," Jacob said, when he noticed that she'd woken. He moved to crouch by her bedside. "How are you feeling?"

"I'm okay."

"And the—" Jacob's gaze flicked down to her belly. She noticed that he hesitated to say "baby." "Lally told me she thought everything was still . . . ?"

"For now," Oona said.

"Good. That's good. Right?"

"Yes," said Oona. "We got lucky. My mother was nearby."

"Your mom? I thought it was Lally who—"

"It was both of them, Jacob."

Jacob stood, his brows knit together. Unlike Lally and Ursula, he hadn't yet changed his clothes. Oona could still see the bloodstains on his khaki pants, and on the sleeves of his fleece jacket. The toes of his work boots were covered in the clamshell drive's dust. "How?"

"How what?"

"How did they stop the bleeding?"

"Lally gave me something."

"What kind of something?" Jacob asked.

Oona debated how to respond. She should tell the truth, she knew. Admit that Lally had given her a potion, used Craftwork. But she was tired—too tired for another fight. So instead, she lied. "Medicine of some sort," she said. "I don't know what kind, exactly."

"Medicine," Jacob repeated, nodding. "Medicine, that's good."

"They're midwives, you know. So they know what they're doing."

"I'm sure they think they do, but they're not doctors, Oona. And you should have been seen by a doctor. Someone with expertise, training. Someone with a medical degree."

"Jacob," Oona said. She didn't know how long she'd been out, but she still didn't feel up to this. "Please. Don't do this. This is good, remember?"

He sucked in a breath, then exhaled slowly. "You're right," he said. "You're right. Whatever happened, I'm grateful." Still looking down at Oona, Jacob rolled his shoulders, passed his fingers through his hair. "So," he said. "Now what? Is Lally going to send you home with more of that medicine or . . . ?"

Oona looked away. She thought she'd be used to it by now—the feeling of disappointing him—but when she spoke next, even she could hear the sorry in her voice. "I'm not going back to Portland right now," she said. "My mother, she said I could stay. And Lally said I could work off the cost of the session, once I'm cleared from bedrest. I want to have the baby here."

"Here?" Jacob repeated, shocked.

Oona nodded. Her plan had been to go back to Portland after Beltane, but that was because she'd never thought staying would be even a remote possibility. Now that it'd been put on the table, now that her mother and Lally had offered . . .

"And what about me?" Jacob asked. "I can't just stay here, Oona. I have a job back home. It was hard enough getting the time off to come here for a few days."

"I know," she said. "So you should go. I'll let you know when it's time."

He looked down at her, skeptical.

"Look, I know you wish they were doctors with fancy degrees, but how many doctors have I seen, Jacob? How many ER waiting rooms have I sat in while I nearly bled out? No one else has ever been able to save my babies. *Our* babies. And whatever medicine Lally gave me, it worked."

Jacob turned away and began to pace. It was dark in the room, thanks to the heavy linen curtains, but when Jacob moved across the window a stray beam of light illuminated his face, and Oona was struck by just how much he looked like his father. They had the same deep-set eyes, the same square jaw. "I can't just leave you here," he said.

"Yes, you can," said Oona. "I'll be okay. I'll be with my mother."

Jacob cut his eyes at her. "That's exactly my point."

"Please," Oona said, more out of habit than anything. Because it was what she always said. Please take this pill. Please put down that beer. Please eat this sweet potato, and this avocado wedge, and this ginseng. She didn't know why she kept trying. He never listened. Never heard her. Not really.

"Okay."

"It's not just my mother, either. Or Lally. They have ways to help me here. There are nutritionists on staff, and chiropractors. I'll be getting acupuncture and reflexology. There are studies on the benefits of acupuncture. I can send them to you."

"Oona. I already said okay. If you think the midwives here can help, then okay."

"Really?"

He nodded. "But I want to be here for the birth. I don't give a fuck about the rules," he said, casting his eyes back at the door. "I'm going to be there."

"Of course you will. It'll be fine. I'll talk to her."

"And you'll call me?" Jacob prompted. "Or I'll call you. Every day."

"Every day," Oona promised.

Jacob bent to kiss her forehead just as Ursula appeared at the open door. "She needs to sleep," she said, without looking at Oona.

Jacob stiffened.

"He was just leaving," Oona said.

"Good. I'll walk him out."

"Just give us a minute."

"I don't have a minute," Ursula said. "There's a class waiting. Mothers who came here the right way, who applied year after year, who paid for their room and board, who—"

"Okay," Oona cut her off. "I get it. He's going. Right, Jacob?" She begged him with her eyes: to keep his word and let her stay, to *listen*.

It took him a moment, but in the end Jacob agreed. He kissed Oona one final time, then he promised to call her later. Ursula followed him out onto the porch.

From her place in bed, Oona heard the key turn in the front door's lock, and she knew she was alone again. Or not quite alone, she supposed. Because there was the baby. The little fish swimming inside her. She was surprised to find herself comforted by the idea and wondered if her mother had felt the same way.

When Oona was a girl, Ursula had insisted that power did not run through her blood; but once, they had shared the same blood, hadn't they? Once, they had been not two, but one. So it wasn't crazy to think that Oona could still come into her inheritance. It wasn't crazy to think that she might prove Ursula wrong, that she might still turn out to be her mother's daughter, that one day—one day soon— she might belong.

# SIX

It was still early when Oona woke. There were hours yet till sunrise, but when she heard her mother banging around in the kitchen she knew she had no chance of falling back to sleep. Later that day she was supposed to return to the cabin she shared with Gemma and Shelly. The night before, she'd packed up all her things: her pajamas and her phone charger, her toothbrush and the robe Lally had given her. There wasn't much, given that she'd been there for three weeks, but then again she hadn't been allowed to do much other than lie in bed and scroll the miscarriage message boards, tiptoe to the bathroom to check and recheck for fresh blood.

It had been strange being there in her mother's house. Ursula hadn't exactly coddled her, but she had checked in more than Oona remembered her doing when she was sick as a child. And though she'd never stayed long, when Oona had asked about the brown blood she'd found one day when she wiped, Ursula had reassured her, promised her that she was safe. Other than that, they didn't really talk.

Mostly, Ursula worked. But even when she was home, Oona got the feeling that she was avoiding her. She'd had the same feeling often when she was young. On more than one occasion, she'd asked Lally why her mother had gone to such lengths to conceive her—all that praying to Demeter, all those rituals and spells—since it seemed obvious to Oona that she didn't actually want to be a mother. Now, Oona supposed, she understood. Though she did catch herself thinking more about the baby, imagining its tiny hands and feet, picturing what it might look like: a girl with Jacob's long lashes, a boy with her copper curls.

She didn't let herself indulge in daydreaming too much, though, because she knew she had more important things to do. She had to find the book she'd used for Daphne's ritual.

When Lally had first agreed to help her, she'd made it clear that they wouldn't be able to do anything without the book. So as soon as Oona's restrictions were scaled back from twenty-four-hour bed rest to pelvic rest and light activity only, she began to search. By the end of her three-week stay, she'd gone through every book her mother kept on the crisp, white shelves in her living room. She'd dug around under the beds and in all the dresser drawers. She'd even riffled through the contents of her mother's closet, pushed aside her dress whites and the spare Initiate robes. But no matter where she looked, she always came up empty-handed. "Just ask her," Lally said, because she didn't know the agony of Ursula's withering stare.

For years, Oona had schemed and plotted in hopes of getting even a fraction of the attention Ursula had given her those past three weeks, which wasn't saying much. But now she'd been spoiled. And she dreaded doing anything that might jeopardize their newfound . . . well, it wasn't quite intimacy, but it was something. It was more, anyway, than what they'd had those past fifteen years. So despite Lally's urging, she'd hesitated. Day after day, she'd made up some new excuse for why she hadn't asked. And now it was moving day and Ursula was up early, which could mean only one thing: Someone in town had gone into labor.

It was dark out still, the kind of wet-ink dark that meant dawn wasn't even on the horizon, but as soon as Oona heard her mother's kettle whistle, she knew that she was about to run out of time. If she didn't get up now, walk into the kitchen, and ask about the ritual, then she might never bring it up. Once she left her mother's house, it wouldn't be so easy. Ursula was busy and rarely, if ever, alone. No, Oona thought as she threw back the covers, the time to ask was now. "Now or never," she muttered—recited—as she stood and fumbled for her robe.

Her sense of urgency propelled her down the hallway, but she faltered once she reached the kitchen, and her mother, who was sitting at the white marble island, looked up.

"Something wrong?" Ursula asked. She was nursing a cup of coffee. Black and bitter, Oona knew.

"No," Oona said, but since that was all she said, Ursula kept staring. She looked so long that Oona began to feel uncomfortable and started pulling at her robe, tightening the sash, making sure her belly was covered.

"I have a patient," Ursula said at last. She was wearing a necklace Oona recognized from the gift shop: a small piece of green malachite strung on a twenty-four-karat-gold chain. In the shop, a placard said malachite was known as the "midwife stone" and that it could help with labor. The necklace sold for $350 in the store.

"A patient," Oona repeated. "Right. I figured."

"With the last one, she labored for three days. So I may be gone awhile. If you need anything, you know, there's Lally."

"I'm moving back into my cabin today."

"Oh, right," Ursula said. "I forgot. Well that simplifies things, doesn't it?"

"I guess," Oona said. She tried not to let her mother's casual dismissal hurt her feelings. She didn't know what more she could have expected.

Ursula drained her cup and then stood. "I better get going. Mrs. Gallagher lives way out past Port Marrow, and I'm sure the driving will be slow. This time of year, there's always fog."

"I remember," said Oona. Because of course she did. When she was young, they used to make the drive together—back before the Initiates, and the Mothers, and the Nystrom money; back when the coven was just the three of them: Oona, Ursula, and Lally.

Once Ursula was done rinsing her cup in the sink, she turned to Oona, and for a moment she looked so expectant that Oona actually thought she was about to invite her along. She was still half thinking through what kind of excuse she'd give Lally, who had promised to come by that morning to help her move, when she realized that actually all Ursula wanted was for her to step aside. She was blocking the way to the front door.

As soon as she'd shuffled over, her mother brushed past her. She made it all the way to the end of the hall before Oona got up the nerve to chase her down.

"Wait!" she called from the steps of the porch.

"What is it?" Ursula asked, one hand already resting on her car's open door. A new car, Oona realized. A white Lexus. New house. New car. She supposed Gemma had been telling the truth. Astrid Nystrom really was investing. "I'm going to be late."

"I need to find something," Oona said.

"Can't this wait until I'm back?"

"It's a book."

"What kind of book?"

"A spell book."

Ursula corrected her. "You mean a grimoire. Why do you need to find a grimoire?"

"Because . . ." Oona said, but then she trailed off. She'd imagined this conversation with her mother countless times over the past three weeks while she'd been laid up in bed, alternately googling *pregnancy brown blood* and doomscrolling, but in her head Oona had never had to explain. There was a part of her, she realized then, that had assumed her mother already knew—about the ritual, about Hekate. She wasn't sure how, but when Oona was growing up, Ursula had always seemed to know when Oona had done something she wasn't supposed to, so she'd just figured her mother knew about the ritual too. And though she wasn't exactly sure how witchcraft worked, she had a hard time imagining that Ursula didn't somehow *feel* when others nearby performed a spell or a ritual. Like how dogs could hear certain high-pitched whistles. Or how some people could feel a shift in bariatric pressure right before a storm.

"Oona," Ursula prompted, "I don't have time for this. Just tell me what's going on."

"I'm cursed," Oona blurted. Then she braced herself for her mother's response. She expected Ursula to condemn her, to tell her simply that if that was so, then she was sure it was Oona's own fault—a punishment she'd well earned with pride and ego, for messing around with Craft she did not understand. If her mother had said any of that, Oona would have been forced to agree. After all, it was what she believed: that she was being punished. Instead, Ursula laughed.

"You're not cursed," she said, dismissive.

"I am," Oona insisted.

"No, you're not." Ursula shook her head lightly, as if Oona were playing some kind of joke on her, then she climbed into the driver's seat of her car.

Oona raced down the porch steps and managed to grab hold of the door's edge before Ursula closed it. "You don't understand. When I performed that ritual for Daphne, I summoned Hekate."

"Oona," Ursula said, and Oona could tell from her tone that she was quickly running out of patience. "Listen to me: You are not cursed. I don't know what was in that potion you gave Daphne—that *sludge*—but whatever it was, that's what killed her. Not the ritual. And certainly not Hekate." She frowned slightly, out of pity, maybe, or from distaste. "It's like I told you back then: You'd need power in order to commune with a goddess, and you just didn't inherit any. I know you don't like hearing that, but it's true."

"But what if it's not?" Oona asked. "True, I mean. What if I do have power?"

"You don't," Ursula said. "Believe me. Have I ever lied to you? There is no curse, okay?"

She sounded concerningly like Jacob, and Oona shuddered.

Ursula shifted into drive. "Oona?" she said, and she nodded at Oona's fingers still wrapped around the door. "You're making me late."

"I've looked everywhere," Oona said. "For the book. But I can't find it. It'd been on your altar that last summer. Do you know where it could be?"

Ursula's gaze flicked down toward the clock on the dashboard and she sighed. "I moved most of my books to my office. If I give you permission to go look there, will you take your hand off the car door?"

Oona nodded.

"Fine." She turned to rummage through the bag she'd tossed onto the passenger seat. When she turned back, she was holding a single key. "All the books are on the shelves, okay? So I don't want to come back to find any filing cabinets broken into. Our clients' financial records are confidential, understood? No prying."

"I'm not sixteen anymore, Mom."

"No prying. I mean it."

"All right. I promise," Oona said. She plucked the key from her mother's fingers, then stepped back from the car.

As she watched Ursula pull away, her taillights growing dim in the rising fog, Oona thought about how she should really finish packing. There would be plenty of time to search the office later, after she was all moved in. Hell, she could even enlist Lally's help. Two sets of eyes would be better than one. And yet . . . despite her promise to her mother, Oona felt an overwhelming desire to go alone. Not to pry, she told herself. She had no interest in violating the privacy of the other Mothers. But because as nice as it had been living again under the same roof as her mom, it had also been deeply unsatisfying, in a way Oona struggled to explain—to Jacob, when he'd called; even to herself.

For years, she'd believed there was something essential about her mother that she'd failed to understand because she'd left the island when she was still practically a child. But after three weeks of living just down the hall, she still felt no closer to any real kind of knowledge. Sure, she now knew the scent of her mother's favorite perfume and her preference for tea in the evenings. But those things didn't add up to much. Certainly, they didn't add up to a whole person. And that's what Oona wanted to know: Who was her mother, really? Who had she been back then, and who was she now? It might have been naive, but she hoped that Ursula's office might give her better insight. It had been messy when she was a girl. And messy meant lived-in. More lived-in than Ursula's house, which was so white and sparse it was nearly sterile. Though Oona had searched it top to bottom, she hadn't found so much as a throw pillow out of place, let alone anything truly telling.

She left a note for Lally taped to the outside of the front door, explaining that she'd gone to Ursula's office, then she set off across the grounds. It was the most exercise she'd gotten in three weeks, and it felt good to stretch her legs again, move her muscles. A little nerveracking, maybe, but good.

Nearly every building on the Bare Root campus had been renovated in some way since the last time Oona had lived on Marrow. Two structures, though, remained the same: Lally's greenhouse and Ursula's office.

The greenhouse Oona understood. No doubt Lally had objected to any kind of replacement. But Oona might've guessed that the office would've been one of the first to get redone, run-down as it was. When she arrived, though, she saw that it still contained the same old filing cabinets. Bulky, rusted things, painted the color of dirty seafoam. Even the desk was unchanged. Oona had been inside her mother's office only once that she could remember—with Daphne—but she recognized the desk: its many nooks and crannies, its tiered sets of drawers. Seeing it, she felt the urge to pull out each one and sift through it. She wanted to crawl down under the desktop and carve her initials into the soft wood. Instead, she simply sat down in her mother's chair and placed her hands on the armrests, the way she imagined Ursula might do.

When she'd asked about the book, Oona had deliberately left out one detail. She wasn't totally sure, but she guessed that the book she'd borrowed—stolen, her mother would correct her—hadn't been just any old grimoire. She guessed it was a Crone's textbook, a manual meant only for those who'd been approved to practice dark Craft. It was the way Lally had talked about Hekate. Of course Oona had known that she was the goddess of the Crone, but somehow she hadn't put two and two together earlier. She hadn't realized that if she'd invoked Hekate in her ritual, then that meant the ritual she'd performed had been dark. If she *had* explained, it might've saved her some time. Three of the four walls in Ursula's office were lined with bookshelves, and it seemed likely that there was some sort of order to the way in which the books were stored—like with like, and so on. But because Oona hadn't told her mother what sort of book she was after, she was left wondering where to start her search.

When she'd gone through the books in her mother's house, she'd read each page carefully, searching for Hekate's name—one of the only things she remembered about the ritual. That, and the fact that it included a recipe for a potion, though it was true that after so many years she'd forgotten the potion's name. There had been mugwort in it, she was pretty sure. And maybe aster. She couldn't remember much about the rest, other than that she'd gotten everything she'd used from Lally's reserves.

At first, Oona intended to go through the books in the office just as meticulously, but after only the first shelf, she grew impatient. She started skimming, licking the pad of her thumb to flip past each starchy page. All it took was a quick glance at one or two spells and she could tell whether a book was a Crone's textbook. There were no dark Craft books in that first bookcase, nor in the second. In fact, there were no dark Craft books in the office at all. Oona was exhausted by the time she finished with the final shelf—all that bending down and squatting, all that balancing on her tiptoes—and she still had nothing to show for her efforts.

Feeling defeated, she almost decided to give up—trudge back across the campus to Lally and admit she'd neglected to tell her mother her suspicions about the book's true nature. First, though, she needed to rest. So she sat down again in Ursula's chair and gripped the armrests where she saw the leather was darkest—stained, she imagined, by the oil from her mother's hands. It wasn't how power worked, she knew, but she liked imagining that she could feel some trace of her mother's energy. It had been the same when she was a girl and had been allowed to hold Ursula's boline. At the time it had felt like something had been conferred—some knowledge, some charge.

Sitting in her mother's chair, Oona looked out across the office: at the dust coating the tops of the filing cabinets; at the blinds, hanging broken across the windows. The desk looked like it could use a good coat of stain and polish. One half had been discolored by the sun. And the carpet . . . goose bumps rose along her arms. She guessed that it hadn't been cleaned in years. Decades, maybe.

Honestly, Oona had a hard time believing her mother worked there. The room was so scuzzy, so unkempt. So unlike Ursula, who had never been anything other than exacting. Borderline rigid. Well, maybe not so borderline.

The last time Oona had been inside the office, she'd noticed the stacks of paper on the floor, the filing cabinet drawers so full they were nearly bursting. But she hadn't thought much about it at the time because she'd been so focused on Daphne. Plus, that was fifteen years ago. The office had been old then, sure, but everything had been old back then, before the Nystrom money. Now the office stuck out like a sore thumb. What was she waiting for? Oona wondered as she leaned forward to better examine the desk's tiered cubbies.

Her mother had forbidden her to pry, but looking in the cubbies didn't feel like prying, open as they were. If there'd been a piece of paper left on the desktop, Oona wouldn't have hesitated to read it over, so she figured the cubbies were fair game. Maybe there would be an invoice that would explain why her mother still hadn't demoed the whole building—some outlandish figure that she wasn't prepared to tackle until the rest of the Nystrom investment came through. But no, in the first cubby there was nothing but a roll of stamps and some blank envelopes. In the second, only a few routine bills: one for heat and one for electricity, invoices for a couple shipments from the mainland.

Below the cubbies were two small drawers, which Oona supposed should have been off-limits, but she pulled them out anyway. She didn't expect to find much, and she didn't: just a handful of pens and pencils, a sleeve of staples, a hard ball of rubber bands. She was just about to give up, quit stalling, and go find Lally, when she noticed something funny about the second drawer. Like the first, it was long and narrow, but it seemed shallower, and it was empty, which Oona found strange. No pen caps, no stray paper clips. She swiped her finger across the bottom. No dust, at all. She jiggled the drawer in place and heard something knock against wood. It was hollow, she realized. The drawer had a false bottom.

Now this, she thought, the knob still in her hand, would almost certainly be considered prying. She'd promised not to dig into any of the financial records, but she couldn't imagine that whatever her mother kept hidden inside her desk drawer was a patient file. Before she could get the drawer off its track, though—tug it out and turn it over—she heard the front door whine open and then the sound of footsteps in the hall.

"Lally?" Oona called, but no one answered. Suddenly, the footsteps stopped. Oona froze, sitting there at the desk. For a minute, maybe longer, she didn't move, hardly breathed. It made no sense; after all, she had permission to be there, her mother had given her the key, but still she felt like she'd been caught breaking in, that she was in the middle of some kind of standoff. And then, just as quickly as they'd stopped, the footsteps started up again. Only this time it sounded like whoever was out in the hall had turned around. And they weren't walking anymore, they were running. Sprinting out of the building.

Oona shoved the desk drawer back into place and leapt up from her mother's chair. She ran to the window and pulled back the dusty blinds, but for a long time the bit of path she could see stayed empty. Shelly was the only person who walked by.

Oona was still at the window when she heard Lally call her name. After giving the desk a final once-over, she crossed the office to pose before a bookshelf, fixed a frown on her face.

"Did you find it?" Lally asked, once she reached the office. She was breathing hard, and even from across the room Oona could see the broken capillaries in her perpetually rosy cheeks. The walk across camp had clearly been taxing for her. And it was true that the heat probably didn't help. Three weeks could make a big difference when it came to the weather on Marrow. While Oona had been on bed rest, locked away in her mother's house, spring had finally arrived, and though the new buildings all had central air, Ursula's office had only one small, rusty metal fan to cool it, and Oona hadn't even thought to turn it on.

Now she blotted at the sweat on her upper lip and shook her head. "It's not here," she told Lally, and the frown she wore deepened. The mystery of the footsteps had momentarily distracted her, but she remembered: She hadn't found the book.

"It'll turn up," said Lally.

"What if it doesn't?"

Lally clucked softly. "It will."

But that was not an answer that comforted Oona, and she spent the rest of the day with her own words echoing in her head. What would happen if she couldn't find the book?

Later that afternoon, after they'd finished moving Oona's stuff back into her cabin, after she'd gone to lunch and apologized to Shelly, Vivian, and Grace, Oona decided to call Jacob. When she'd first told him that they would speak every day, she'd thought she would regret the promise, but she was surprised to find that she was actually looking forward to the call. It had been a long time since she'd felt heard by Jacob, but for the past few weeks he'd really listened on their calls. When she'd told him about the spotting, he'd looked up her symptoms and assured her they were normal. When she'd confessed to googling, he'd laughed along with her and then encouraged her to cut it out. He'd told her to trust her mother. He'd actually said that: *Trust your mother.* Oona had nearly asked him to repeat himself, she'd been so caught off guard.

She dialed his number walking back from the dining hall, but he didn't pick up. Usually, that meant he was either down at the docks prepping the boat for another trip or at the institute helping one of the scientists log their research. It was just as well, Oona thought, looking at her phone. Her battery was nearly dead.

Still, she wanted to try again. Up until that point, she'd been careful about what she told him. He thought she was there because the Bare Root witches were accomplished midwives, and she'd let him think that because it was easier than admitting the truth.

She'd never told Jacob about the curse, because if she told him about the curse, then she would have to tell him about the ritual, about how she'd led Daphne down the cliffs to the sea cave, about the potion she'd given her to drink and the way Daphne's eyes had fluttered just before she'd fallen asleep. *Fallen asleep or passed out?* she'd often imagined Jacob asking, and in the past that had been enough to make her lose her nerve.

But now things were different. Or at least, she hoped they were. Jacob was listening to her. And if he could find it in himself to listen—really listen—then she thought it was her responsibility to tell the truth.

So when she got back to the cabin, she hurried to her room, planning to grab her charger, but she stopped short when she realized she wasn't alone. Gemma was there, curled up on her bed, facing the wall. At first Oona assumed she was asleep, but after a moment she heard the telltale sound of sniffles and debated sneaking back out of the room. Her three weeks at her mother's house had softened her, though. No one could take her place as her mother's daughter, and it was embarrassing, really, to think she'd ever been jealous of this pathetic, sniveling girl.

Looking down at Gemma, Oona suddenly felt overcome with a sense of déjà vu so intense, the only thing she'd ever felt like it was the moment she'd come upon Gemma in the woods. She'd been there before, she thought. She'd stood there in that same room staring at that same narrow back as it trembled, listened to that same girl's stuttering breaths.

And in a way, she had. Only back then, both the room and the back had belonged to Daphne. Oona could still remember it. Daphne had been about twelve weeks along, and while at first she'd felt great—ecstatic, even—by week nine, morning sickness had set in and it had quickly become debilitating. She couldn't keep anything down, couldn't get out of bed, could hardly lift her head off her pillow without getting dizzy. Their teacher had asked Oona to stop by after school, to deliver Daphne's missed assignments, but when she went upstairs, Daphne couldn't even sit up enough to meet her eye.

"This was a mistake," Daphne'd groaned. "I think I need to tell my mother. She would send me to the mainland to get it taken care of, but maybe that wouldn't be so bad. I have a great-aunt down in Boston. Mom's always threatening to send me to her. But Boston might be okay. I could finish school there. Maybe even go to college? I could leave this godforsaken island once and for all."

"An abortion, you mean?" Oona had asked.

And from her bed, Daphne had nodded, pink-cheeked and tearful.

In the moment, Oona said nothing, but now she had to wonder if she'd missed her chance. If she'd just agreed with Daphne that day, then maybe her friend would still be alive. And in fact, she *had* agreed with her. Or at least, she had at first. As soon as Daphne had said she'd made a mistake, Oona had started nodding—*yes*, she should get an abortion; *yes*, she should tell her mother—but she'd stopped when Daphne started sketching out her future on the mainland. She hadn't wanted her to leave. It was that simple, that selfish. She hadn't wanted to be left behind.

In her bedroom with Gemma, Oona cleared her throat. Once, she'd climbed into bed and curled up beside Daphne; offered up, as comfort, her own steady heartbeat, her even breath. But she couldn't quite stomach the idea of getting that close to Gemma. So "Hey," she said instead, from a safe distance. "Are you okay?"

"I'm fine." Gemma sniffed.

"Did something happen?"

"Please just leave me alone."

"Okay," Oona said, but she didn't leave, and eventually Gemma pushed herself up to sitting.

"What are you doing?" she asked. "Why are you still standing there?"

"Because I'm worried," Oona said, which wasn't exactly a lie because seeing Gemma's puffy face had inspired some concern. Without her usual braids, she looked younger. She looked like what she was: a child. "Are you sure you can't tell me what happened?"

"You don't want to know."

Oona nodded. This was almost certainly true. But . . . "I'll go if you tell me."

"It's about your mom."

"My mom?"

"Ursula?"

"Right," said Oona, though somehow she hadn't realized that of course it wouldn't just be Shelly and Grace and Vivian who knew. The whole Center was probably aware now of her real identity. "What did she do?"

"She poisoned Elijah against me."

"Elijah?"

"My husband? She told my mom to sic her lawyers on him, told her to say that if he didn't stop contacting me, she would sue."

"On what grounds?"

"Statutory rape," Gemma spit, disgusted.

"But you're married."

"Not in the eyes of the court. I was too young to get a license without a parent's or guardian's permission. And there was no way my mom was going to give me permission. She thinks Elijah runs a cult."

Oona lowered herself onto her bed. "Does he?"

"No, of course not," Gemma snorted. "My mom just doesn't understand. She thinks faith of any kind is a form of brainwashing."

"But she believes in my mother?"

"I know. It doesn't make any sense. But no one else would give her the kind of guarantees she wanted. All the other programs and centers talked about consent, about a mother's, even a teenage mother's, parental rights. Ursula didn't mention any of that stuff. She just promised she'd take care of it, swore that I wouldn't leave here with any ties to Elijah or his church. My mother thinks she's heaven-sent, but I know the truth. What kind of person makes a promise like that? Only someone who's making bargains with the devil. Only someone who's messing around with some dangerous stuff. Don't you think?"

"I do," Oona said, and the sincerity in her voice seemed to surprise them both.

Gemma even smiled a little, rubbed at her running nose with the back of her hand. "Was she always like this?" she asked. "I mean, so controlling? Like, when you were a kid?"

"My mother?"

"Yeah."

Oona shrugged. The answer was yes, of course.

Ursula used to remind her all the time that she couldn't trust anyone in the outside world. And then one day, she just stopped. She sided with Daphne, with the Tanakas. To keep the coven safe, she cast Oona out. Put her on a boat and shipped her off to the very place she'd always warned her was perilous.

Oona could have confessed all this to Gemma. It might have—as Shelly had once argued—brought them together. But in the end Oona decided against it. Gemma wanted it too much. Oona could see it in her big brown eyes, all shimmery still with tears. Doll eyes. She wanted them to be the same, when they weren't. However right or wrong she was, Gemma's mother was doing what she thought she had to do to save her. She was trying to bring her home. Meanwhile, Oona had had to sneak back onto the island. On the beach, she'd stood face-to-face with her mother and Ursula hadn't even recognized her, hadn't so much as blinked.

A gnawing feeling took hold in Oona's belly. She could taste the bitterness of envy on her tongue. "How do you know Ursula's the one behind the lawsuit?" she asked. "I mean, if the lawyers were sent by your mother . . ."

Gemma leaned back against the wall and moved her hands down to cup her stomach, the hard round ball Oona could see even though she was sitting down. "Elijah told me," she said. "Ursula confiscated my phone when I got here, but for a while I had a burner she didn't know about. Then some snitch here reported on me, told her they'd seen me going live on Instagram so I must still have a phone." She narrowed her eyes at Oona. "Was that you?"

"No," Oona said. She waited for Gemma to say more, to doubt her, but she didn't.

"Anyway, I couldn't call Elijah for a while. But finally I convinced one of the Mothers to let me borrow her phone. I called him this morning. I thought he'd be happy to hear from me. Instead, he hung up, like, two seconds into the call. All he told me was that Ursula had called a week before and said that if he didn't end things with me, he'd be getting served papers. At first, he ignored her, but then two days later a lawyer knocked on the door of his church. If he didn't agree to cut off all contact, they were going to go to the police and accuse him of statutory rape."

"So he decided to end things? Just like that?"

"What else could he do? He'd lose his church, his flock. He's a man of God, Oona. He can't just abandon them."

"Instead he's abandoning you. And you think Ursula's the bad guy in this situation? Sounds like she did you a favor."

Gemma sucked her teeth. "Some favor," she sneered.

Oona clenched her jaw. The girl didn't know how good she had it. How lucky she was. In the early days of Oona's banishment, before she ran away from wilderness school, she'd spent a lot of time lying awake at night, listening to the wolves howling in the distance, trying to figure out if there was some secret explanation for what her mother had done. She'd wanted, desperately, to believe that Ursula hadn't really betrayed her, that instead she'd lied to the Tanakas to protect Oona, somehow.

Of course, in the end she'd been forced to accept the truth, and now she realized just how foolish she'd been for hoping, how pathetic, how sad. Because this was what it looked like when Ursula tried to protect someone. It looked like a lawyer with a cease-and-desist letter, it looked like a rape charge.

Sitting on her bed, Oona took a deep breath. She exhaled slowly, purposefully, as if she could expel the anger she felt brewing inside her, like it was some kind of bad humor. But it didn't help. She still felt angry. No, she felt jealous. She felt whiny and petulant, like an overgrown child. But it wasn't fair. Gemma had everything, just like Daphne'd had. She had her own mother to love her and Oona's besides. She had a husband back on the mainland, who, odds had it, was not actually a cult leader. And she'd had such an easy pregnancy, with no need for late-night doomscrolling, no threatened miscarriages, no bleeds at all.

Appearing totally unaware of the shift in the room, Gemma pulled up her shirt to expose the small swell of her belly. Oona nearly choked when she saw her smooth, blemish-free skin. She didn't have a single stretch mark.

"How is that possible?" Oona accidentally said out loud.

"What?" Gemma asked.

But Oona just shook her head. It was more than just the way her body looked, she thought as Gemma continued rubbing her belly. It was more than just her perky breasts and her long, lean limbs. It was the way she took her pregnancy for granted, so entirely unaware that her body could ever do anything to betray her trust.

For a moment, rage burned through Oona. She had the sudden urge to lash out. To rip Gemma's hands from her stomach, to hiss, or scream, or shout.

But no. Oona knew all too well what dangers could follow when she let her jealousy get the best of her. She was capable of so much more than making Gemma cry like she had in the woods. Just look at what she'd done to Daphne!

So before she could do anything she would regret, Oona said the first thing that came to mind—"I have to pee"—then she stumbled out of the room.

Calling Jacob from the cabin was no longer an option, so instead she headed for the dining hall. Lunch was long since over and dinner wasn't scheduled for a few hours, so she hoped it would be empty. Luckily, it was.

Her hands shook as she dialed Jacob's number. Suddenly, she felt desperate to hear his voice. He didn't pick up until the fourth ring, though—so long, Oona began to worry the call might go to voicemail. When he said hello, she felt relief course through her blood.

In the background, she could hear the sound of gulls.

"Are you down at the docks?" she asked. Not because she needed to know—it was obvious from the gulls' screeching—but because she didn't know how else to begin. She couldn't just start off talking about the cave. He would think she'd lost it. And maybe she *had* lost it. But if she had, then it was even more important that he not know.

"We're leaving tomorrow before dawn. Professor Harrigan heard there's a school of herring up past Bar Harbor."

"How long will you be gone?"

It was the sort of question she'd often asked him in the past—when are you leaving, where are you going, when are you coming home—and asking it again brought on a kind of homesickness that surprised her.

"Trip should take about a week," Jacob said. "I'll try to call, but we'll probably be out of range for most of it."

At first Oona felt the nervous trill of anticipated loneliness, but then she remembered: She wasn't at home. There would be more for her, in the coming days, than the message boards and dark, empty windows. There would be meals with Shelly and the others, classes with Lally and Joyce. There would be yoga and Pilates and Reiki and acupuncture.

And Gemma, she remembered. There would be Gemma sleeping next to her in her bed, her snoring light enough to remind Oona that her breath could be snuffed out.

"Jacob." Oona interrupted her husband's monologue about the captain's various strategies for their upcoming voyage. "I need to talk to you about Daphne."

"What about Daphne?" Right away, Oona could hear the suspicion in his voice.

"Do you remember what you said to me, the day we found her?"

"Oona."

"Do you remember what you said?"

On the other end of the line came a beat of staticky silence.

Oona continued pressing. "You told me it wasn't my fault. But you don't know what I did. In the cave. I never told you about the ritual."

"What ritual?"

"I just wanted to help." Oona was sitting on the floor of the dining hall, tethered to the nearest outlet. Her voice echoed in the empty, cavernous room. "No," she corrected herself, because hearing her own lie reverberate made her nervous. "No, that isn't true. Or it's not the whole truth. I *did* want to help, but I also wanted to impress my mother. I wanted to prove that I *had* inherited her gifts."

"You mean . . ."

"Craft, yes. So I performed a ritual. I summoned Hekate, Jacob." Oona swallowed the sob that was rising in her throat. "Jacob, it *is* my fault. Daphne's death, the miscarriages. All of it."

When she was done, she held her breath, waiting for his response, but for a long time he didn't speak. There was just the sound of the gulls on the other end of the phone, and an engine turning over. Then, finally, he said the word *please*.

"Please tell me that this isn't why you decided to stay on Marrow. Please tell me you're there because your mother is a good midwife."

"You want me to lie?"

"Jesus Christ." Jacob sighed, and there was a ruffling noise that told Oona he was running his hand through his hair, like he often did when he was frustrated—with the situation, with her. "What do you want me to say, Oona? Huh? Why did you even call me?"

"Because you deserve to know the truth."

Jacob pushed air out his nose. Oona could hear it through the phone. "I can't do this right now," he said. "Professor Harrigan's waiting on me. We're still down here preparing the boat. I'm at work, Oona. You realize that, right?"

"I know."

"We can't both just spend the summer playing pretend. One of us has to make money to pay our bills, pay our rent. Unless that stipend Lally's giving you covers more than just your stay at camp."

"That's not fair," said Oona.

"None of this is fair," Jacob agreed.

And for a while, neither of them said anything more. The silence on the line seemed to swell, pulse, like the moment between a crack of lightning and the roll of thunder. For a second, Oona was sure that whatever was said next would be the end to everything, a truth so devastating, they would never recover. And she panicked. She ended the call without so much as a goodbye.

# SEVEN

According to the schedule included in Oona's welcome folder, the first day of June was supposed to begin with a class on invocation. Unfortunately, though, as the Mothers had been told earlier that morning at yoga, Ursula had been called away. So instead, about an hour or so before lunch, Oona joined Shelly and Grace and Vivian at the lodge to listen to the Initiates run through a lecture on altar creation and maintenance that Oona was pretty sure they'd already given just a few days before. Still, in the beginning, she tried to pay attention. She listened as Holly explained the purpose of an altar, and as Inez detailed all the various options for altar placement inside a home, but after only a few minutes her thoughts began drifting. And it didn't take long before Oona found herself running through the mental checklist she always seemed to be running through in those days: ideas for where she could find the book she'd used to perform Daphne's ritual.

She was nervous, that was the thing. Not quite desperate yet, but definitely worried. Because by that point, she'd spent nearly every day of the past week searching for the book and she still hadn't found it. After her mother's office, she'd looked through all the books in the Center's so-called library, really more of a shack where Mothers left behind their beach reads. Then, when that had turned up nothing, she'd started approaching the other coven members, asking to look through their things. Most had been nice about it, though some of the members had resented the intrusion. Carol, whose teenaged daughter, Alice, was the only Maiden at the Center that summer, had been particularly unwelcoming. Lally said it was because she was worried that Oona's return to the island would somehow jeopardize her daughter's ability to become a full-fledged member one day.

"We didn't take it," Carol had insisted, as she'd shadowed Oona around their cabin. In the bedroom, Oona had come upon Alice reading a magazine. Tall and thin, with her brown hair styled in a pixie cut, Alice had looked up when Oona asked her if she'd seen the book, but she didn't respond. "She can't talk," her mother had explained. And the way she'd said it—so dismissive, so curt—made Oona wonder if her daughter's muteness embarrassed her.

Later, Oona told Lally that she hadn't meant to offend them or accuse them of thievery. "I just thought maybe they'd borrowed the book and had forgotten to return it," she said. "But it wasn't there."

Nor was it in any of the other witches' cabins. It wasn't in the dining hall or the lodge or Lally's greenhouse, either. Of course, almost fifteen years had passed since the last time Oona had seen the grimoire, so it wasn't inconceivable that it was gone, but every other book she remembered from her mother's collection was still there—most, granted, in her home or office, but some she'd spotted on the other witches' shelves, and one she'd even discovered tucked away behind a potted jacaranda in the greenhouse. So Oona assumed—well, she hoped—that the book she needed would turn up too. She just had to think of some new places to look. But it was hard to concentrate with Holly droning on about altars. And harder still to think over the noise from the storm.

It was supposed to make landfall that afternoon. Though they'd barely spoken since their fight, Jacob had called the night before to warn her. "You can't go outside," he'd told her. "I mean it, Oona. Remember, you have the baby to think about now." Selfish. He'd basically accused her of being selfish, a bad mother already, all because she'd once told him that she felt more herself during a storm: the pelting rain, the whipping winds, the destruction. But just because she used to sneak down to the beach during storms when she was younger, risking tidal surges and rogue waves to search the sand for fulgurite, that didn't mean she would do so now. She was going to be a mother soon, for fuck's sake. Lower- *and* uppercase *M*. And while it was true that one had mattered more to her than the other when she'd first arrived on the island, in recent weeks that had begun to change. Ever since her threatened miscarriage, Oona had spent more time thinking about the baby, imagining the good, warm weight of them in her arms, daydreaming about the snuffles of their sleep. She'd even started keeping a list of names. On the phone, she could have told Jacob all of this—the bit about the list would have almost certainly won him over, softened him to her again—but she wasn't sure if she wanted him to soften. Anger could be good for him, good for *them*, she thought. Not that Jacob seemed angry, necessarily. More like disappointed.

At the front of the room, Holly and Inez had draped a long driftwood bench with a white linen tablecloth. Usually, Inez explained, she preferred red (her own altar to Ate was wrapped in crimson satin), but they had designed this altar to appeal to Amphitrite, goddess of the sea. So along with the driftwood and the froth-colored linen, they had arranged on their altar an assortment of objects that looked like they'd been pulled from the ocean: wave-worn stones and freshly combed gull feathers, a glass jar filled with chalky white clamshells, and a ceramic incense stand glazed with dye made from kelp. Even the cauldron looked like it had been crafted from sea-foam, and the salt in the white marble mortar was so coarse, one could imagine it had been collected that very morning in the bay with a sieve.

"You could also include charms, if you wanted," Holly said, "or a small glass of tea. Some witches like crystals, while others prefer bowls of herbs. It's a personal choice. The only thing that matters is that whatever is on your altar should help you channel your magic, help you connect with your goddess. So when you craft your altar, you want to keep in mind not only your own preferences but what might speak to her. Offerings are good: tea, like I said. Or sweets. Cakes, cookies, candies. Some goddesses, I hear, go gaga for fruit, while others prefer more savory snacks. Like jerky, maybe. Or even potato chips."

Vivian leaned over Shelly to whisper to Oona. "She isn't at a birth, is she?"

On Oona's other side, Grace leaned closer. "Who?"

"Ursula," Shelly said, eyes still locked on her notebook, where she seemed to be recording every single thing Holly and Inez said. "Now hush, all of you."

"Her *mother*," Vivian clarified. Then, to Oona, "You know where she really is, don't you?"

When Oona had first sat down to explain to the three of them why she'd lied and told them her name was Maggie, it was Vivian's reaction she'd feared the most. Not that she would have cared if the woman had refused to ever speak to her again—they were not friends, after all; a fact she'd reminded herself of more than once—but she'd worried that Vivian could make her life there at Bare Root uncomfortable. She could turn the others against her, and yes, of course, Oona would be fine on her own. She'd always been fine on her own—back in Portland, on Marrow before Daphne. Things were simpler that way. But she had to live with Shelly, so she preferred that things not be unpleasant.

Well, they'd still turned out to be unpleasant, but in a different way. Far from being upset, Shelly and Grace had been happy for her. They'd heard Jacob screaming, they'd seen the blood, and they didn't care much that she was now going by Oona rather than Maggie. Vivian, for her part, had been impressed. Oona had thought she'd be jealous, resentful, but the news seemed only to motivate her. It was like Oona had replaced Gemma, become Vivian's ticket to success. The way Vivian saw it, any time she spent with Oona—stretching beside her at morning yoga or sitting next to her at lunch—got her that much closer to Ursula and her orbit. So for more than a week, Oona had had a new best friend, a shadow she couldn't seem to shake.

All day, every day, Vivian pumped her for information. She was worse than Shelly had been back when they'd first arrived. Vivian was convinced that Oona knew more than she let on, which wasn't usually true, though in this case she was right. The Mothers had been told that Ursula had a birth to attend to, but Oona had seen her mother's calendar in her office when she was poking around. Ursula was on the mainland, yes. But she wasn't at a birth. She was at a meeting with Astrid Nystrom—to talk about her investment, Oona assumed.

Up by the altar, Inez was holding a white soapstone knife. A boline. "This knife," she was explaining, "is used mainly for cutting herbs and for carving, not for directing magic. So it must be kept very sharp. And it must be cleansed and consecrated before its first use. Does anyone know the most effective way to cleanse a boline?"

On the floor of the workshop, a trio of women raised their hands, including Vivian, who, when called upon, informed the rest of the group that the best thing to do when you acquired a new boline was to wrap the knife in a layer of cloth and then bury it in the dirt for a full moon cycle, allowing the charge of the earth to purify the tool.

"Very good," Inez said begrudgingly. She didn't like Vivian. Oona wasn't sure Inez liked any of them besides Ursula, and maybe Holly. "Now what about storage? Does anyone know the proper way to store the knife?"

Bored, Oona turned away from the altar. The rain hadn't yet started when she'd left her cabin, but now she could hear it tapping against the skylights overhead, and when she looked, she could see that a mass of dark gray clouds had begun to gather, thick as smoke. Once, it would have sent a thrill running up her spine, but now all she could think about was how hard it would be to continue looking for the book in the rain. Not that she knew where to look next. Unless . . .

"Oona?"

She only pulled her gaze back from the skylights when she heard her name. It was Holly. "I'm sure you know all about the proper care of a boline knife, Oona," she said. "Perhaps you could enlighten your classmates?"

If it was anyone else, Oona would have suspected them of trying to chastise her for not paying attention, but Holly had never been anything but kind. A happy little Girl Scout. So Oona knew that she wasn't trying to trick her, she was trying to give her an opportunity to show off. Only Oona didn't want to show off. She just wanted to be left alone, to think. The germ of an idea had occurred to her, but it hadn't had the chance to fully form. Something about Holly, about Inez . . .

"I think Vivian knows," Oona said, distracted.

Vivian didn't wait for Holly to direct the question to her, she just blurted out the answer. "It's best to store a boline wrapped in leather and kept with your other magical instruments."

"Very good, Vivian," Holly said.

Oona tried to think. She'd nearly come up with another place to look, and if she didn't remember it now, she was pretty sure her idea would be lost forever. So what was it? Did she need to check the equipment storage closet? No, she'd already looked there. The classrooms? No. She'd searched them too. The Mothers were all sitting on the ground, atop tasseled cushions. As she racked her memory, Oona toyed with the tassel nearest her left foot. If only she was able to sit in a proper chair, maybe she'd be able to remember. She didn't know how Holly or Inez could stand teaching so many classes from the ground. Didn't their tailbones ever ache like hers did? Didn't their calves ever cramp up? When they woke each morning in their cabins, didn't they— Wait, their cabins. She'd combed through the cabins of practically every other person at the Center besides the Initiates, and if anyone would have borrowed the book, chances were high it was one of them.

Oona was just about to stand up, claim she wasn't feeling well, and use the rest of the lecture to search their cabins—she was already half-plotting how she could convince Lally to give her copies of their keys—when the door to the lodge blew open and a woman stumbled in, followed by a gust of wind and rain.

For a moment, Oona thought it was Hekate again, come for her. That's how pale the woman's skin was, how wild and windswept her hair. But of course it wasn't the sea witch. It was Gemma. Or at least some version of Gemma. Though not, Oona had to admit, a version she'd ever met before. Gone were her braids and her starched white collar, gone were her floral print dress and her white Mary Janes. Oona didn't know if Gemma had secretly brought this new clothing with her, or if she'd stolen it from the other women at the Center, but either way, the result was the same: She looked like herself again. Or like the Gemma Nystrom Oona had seen pictures of back when she'd first googled her. Ripped black leggings and scuffed white sneakers, dirty hair hanging lank over her eyes, and a sweatshirt so double extra-large that its sleeves draped far past the tips of her fingers. So big, in fact, that from behind, she almost looked like she was wearing an Initiate's robe.

"Gemma?" Grace asked, and it felt to Oona like she'd vocalized the question they were all thinking: *Gemma, is that really you?*

But Gemma didn't so much as glance in Grace's direction. She kept her head down as she picked her way across the room.

"So nice of you to join us," Inez said, sarcastic as always.

Holly said nothing. For a moment, she just frowned at Gemma, concerned. Then, once the room settled again, she continued with her lesson. Holding up the cauldron, she asked, "Who can tell me what this is for?"

When no one else raised their hand, Oona moved to do so. With the baby, with the bleed, there was no way Holly would question her when she said she needed to go lie down.

But the second she moved her arm, Shelly took hold of her elbow. "Do you know what happened to her?" she asked.

"What happened to who?"

Shelly flicked her eyes at Gemma. "To *her.*"

"Who said something happened?" whispered Oona.

In response, even Vivian clucked her tongue. It was obvious something had happened—something, presumably, not good. But the way Oona saw it, Gemma was owed some *not good*. Her pregnancy had been far too easy.

"Do you think we should say something?" Shelly asked. "I think we should say something."

"No," said Oona.

Up at the front of the room, Holly had put down the cauldron and was now holding aloft a mortar and pestle, asking the Mothers if they'd ever used one. But of course, they had. By June, the women were too advanced for this lesson. Not only did they know how to use a mortar and pestle, most had become adept at drying herbs. They had books, sourced by Lally, that explained which plants were best for eating and which were best for grinding, which could be boiled in a cauldron and which should be placed at the base of a candle before the wick was lit. Still, the women were patient with Holly and Inez. Or at least, most of them were. Vivian couldn't seem to keep from shouting out answers prematurely, while over in the corner Gemma seemed to have promptly fallen asleep.

As the rain drummed against the skylights overhead, Oona turned her mind back to her plan. Now there were only thirty minutes left in class, which wasn't really enough time to track down Lally, convince her to give her the keys to the Initiate cabins, and search. So she would have to go another time. Knowing Lally, she would probably insist that Oona ask permission, the way she'd done with the coven members, and with Holly that would probably go over fine, but with Inez? Oona watched as Inez played with the lighter she would use to light the taper candles at the end of the lecture. Inez, she guessed, would put up a fight. She prayed to Ate, after all, goddess of reckless-ness and ruin. She draped her altar in red silk.

Oona hadn't known her long, but she knew that Inez didn't suffer fools. It was just about the only thing she had in common with Ursula, who had almost certainly designed the example altar on display. Ur-sula had always selected white tablecloths for her altars and loved working with shells. Oona's mother believed that she could read the patterns present on the opalescent inside of mussel and clam shells, much the way other witches could read tea leaves. In fact, that was the method she'd used to test Daphne when she'd shown up at the Center that last winter, looking like a wannabe Initiate at the end of her pilgrimage to the island, hoping for the chance to don a purple robe.

The day Daphne had first told Oona about the baby, she'd sworn her to secrecy, and at the time Oona had been happy enough to agree, but as the months had dragged on—as Daphne's morning sickness had passed and she'd returned to school, dressed in larger and larger sweaters—that promise had become increasingly difficult to keep. Oona didn't give a damn about Mr. and Mrs. Tanaka, but she hated keeping the secret from Jacob. For the first time in her life, she felt bad about lying. Still, when he asked, she kept her mouth shut because she assumed it was just a matter of time. Daphne's secret *did* have an expiration date. So for months, Oona was patient. And in January, she thought that patience had finally been rewarded when, yet again, Daphne failed to show up for school. Curious—well, nosy—Oona offered to drop off Daphne's missed schoolwork on her way home, but when she arrived at the Tanakas', Daphne wasn't there. So she left the papers on her bed and continued back to the Center.

Once home, she went by her mother's office, intending to knock three times on her door the way she always did to signal her return. Only when she entered the building she found that the hallway wasn't empty. Daphne was there, standing just outside her mother's door.

Oona practically ran down the length of the hall. Gripping Daphne's arm, she hissed, "What are you doing here?"

Daphne tried to shrug her off. "I came to see your mom."

"You're not allowed to be here," Oona whispered.

She tried tugging, but Daphne stood her ground. "I want her to be the one to deliver my baby," Daphne said.

"Are you crazy?"

"What? She's a midwife, isn't she? She helps women in Port Marrow."

"That's not the point." Oona eyed the door to her mother's office and lowered her voice. "You have to come with me. Now. She can't find you here. Like this. Please."

But Daphne shook her head. "I've been asking you to bring me here for years and you always find some reason to say no. But you can't say no now. I belong here. I belong here more than you. I'm a mother."

"Not yet," Oona growled.

Daphne folded her arms. "Soon."

If it were anyone else, Oona would have turned and left them there. *Your funeral*, she wanted to say. Except it wouldn't be Daphne's funeral. It would be Oona's. She was the one Ursula would blame. So she tried again. "You can come back tomorrow, okay? Just give me a chance to speak to her first."

"You've had six years," Daphne said.

And then there was no more time for debate. Ursula's door swung open and a woman stepped out into the hall. Petite, with a round face and shoulder-length black hair, Mrs. Cook had long been a fixture at the Center. Every summer, it seemed, she returned, asking to try some new treatment plan she'd read about on the internet, begging Lally to make a potion from a new kind of flower or herb.

When Daphne had first started wearing her oversize sweaters, Oona had teased her. But by January, she no longer noticed whether Daphne was wearing her own clothing or a navy fisherman crewneck she'd borrowed from her dad. When Daphne stepped to the side to let Mrs. Cook pass, though, Oona realized that despite the sweater's slimming vertical pattern, she could see the outline of Daphne's growing belly. And Mrs. Cook seemed to see it too. Or at least she stared at Daphne a long while without speaking. Then, without warning, she burst into tears. She fled down the hall and out the doors.

"Sara?" Ursula called from inside her office. "Is something wrong? What happened?"

Daphne glanced at her, worried, but it never occurred to Oona to run after Mrs. Cook. Even if she'd caught up to her, she wouldn't have known what to say. She never knew what to say to the repeat visitors. And this was Mrs. Cook's sixth visit to the Center. She was likely running out of time to have a child.

"Sara?" Oona heard her mother stand up from her chair, and once again, she reached for Daphne's wrist. She gripped her so hard her nails dug into her skin. *Please*, she begged her with her eyes, but Daphne was stubborn, had always been stubborn. As if to cement her decision, she took another step closer to the door. And that's how they were standing when Ursula found them: Daphne practically at the threshold and Oona one step behind, her fingers still latched around Daphne's wrist.

For a moment, Ursula didn't say anything—she just glared at Daphne as she tucked a loose strand of her long white hair behind her ear. Slowly, though, her gaze moved past Daphne to land on Oona. "Lally insists you're bright," she said, her tone clipped. "But sometimes, I wonder. How many times have I told you that outsiders are not permitted on Center grounds?"

"I know but—"

"And yet, here one stands. Here, outside my office, my inner sanctum, one of the most sacred places in all of Bare Root."

*Sacred?* Oona thought. She knew the birthing suites were sacred, but the office? Since when? Still, bright or not, she knew better than to voice that question.

Instead, Daphne spoke up. She said, "I came on my own."

"Well," Ursula said, still without so much as a glance at Daphne. "Then you must know the way out."

"No, wait, please," Daphne said, as Ursula turned and began walking back to her desk. For a brief moment, Daphne hesitated in the doorway, but then she did something Oona had never dared to do: Without waiting for permission, she stepped inside. "I'm pregnant."

That got Ursula's attention. Only a few feet from her desk, she stopped walking. Then, slowly, she turned back around. For the first time, she looked at Daphne. Really looked at her. Her dark blue eyes moved up the length of Daphne's body, tick by tick. But instead of saying anything to the girl, Ursula called for Oona. "Why didn't you tell me?" she asked, once Oona crept in from the hall.

Oona didn't know what to say. It hadn't occurred to her that her mother would be interested in school gossip.

Before she could think of an explanation, Daphne started talking again. "I asked her not to tell anyone," she said. "No one knows. Not my parents, not my brother."

"The baby's father?" Ursula asked, as she returned to her desk chair. Daphne shook her head. "No."

Ursula tapped her nails against her desktop, thinking. Her gaze drifted away from Oona and seemed to settle somewhere at the far end of the hall, on the doors Mrs. Cook had, only moments before, pushed open. Oona watched as her mother appeared to arrive at a decision. When she gestured to the chairs set out for Mothers on the other side of her desk, Daphne sat down eagerly, but Oona remained wary. She didn't sit until Ursula invited her a second time—until she insisted.

Once they were all settled, Ursula turned to Daphne. Leaning forward, she folded her hands over her desk, braided together her long, slender fingers. "So," she said, and Oona felt her stomach clench. This was always how their conversations began when she was in trouble. "Daphne, tell me why you're here."

"I'm here because I want you to be my midwife."

"You want me to deliver your baby?"

Daphne bobbed her head, up and down. "I'm your biggest fan."

"My what?" Ursula chuckled, as if no one had ever said such a thing to her before. The phoniness made Oona nauseated. Or maybe it wasn't the phoniness, maybe it was the fact that Daphne's flattery was working. Ursula was warming to her. Oona could see it happening, right there before her eyes.

"I admire you so much," Daphne continued. "I always have. You can ask Oona. I've been begging her to bring me here for years. It's not her fault I came today, though. Really. She told me I wasn't allowed. But I had to come. I had to at least ask. Will you deliver my baby?"

Leaning back in her chair, Ursula let out a single, short breath. A sigh—of what? Disappointment? Regret? "I wish I could," she said. "But right now I'm not taking on any new patients from Port Marrow. I just don't have the time. I have too many obligations here, at the Center, and it's a long drive into town."

Reluctantly, Daphne nodded. She dropped her eyes. And for a moment, Oona thought maybe that would be the end of it.

But then Ursula sat forward and said, "Unless . . ."

Daphne perked up again. "Unless?" she repeated, hopefully.

"You *could* give birth here."

"Yes!" Daphne practically squealed.

Ursula frowned, shook her head lightly. "No, no. That wouldn't work. Your parents wouldn't like it."

"Then I won't tell them," said Daphne. "I won't tell them anything. I won't even tell them about the baby!"

Ursula raised a single eyebrow and glanced down at Daphne's belly. "Pretty soon they'll be able to figure it out for themselves. Although maybe, if you were to—" She cut herself off. "No, that would be risking too much. You're still young. A minor."

"But I'm not," said Daphne. "Or I won't be. I turn eighteen next week."

"You do?"

"Yes."

"Well, then. I suppose if you wanted, you *could* move in here."

"Here?" asked Daphne.

"Here?" repeated Oona, who had been watching the conversation play out with a mounting sense of dread. Surely, her mother wasn't suggesting what she thought she was suggesting. Daphne might soon be eighteen, but that didn't mean her parents wouldn't notice if she just went missing. And what was Oona supposed to say when Jacob asked her where his sister was? Was she just supposed to continue lying to him forever?

"I'll do it," said Daphne.

Ursula sat back. "Are you sure? You would keep this baby a secret from the father, from your family? You would leave your home to live here?"

"Yes," said Daphne solemnly.

"Why?"

If she'd been smarter, more patient, Oona would have let Daphne speak for herself. She might very well have put her foot in her mouth, misstepped or misspoke, and convinced Ursula to rethink her offer. But lack of patience had always been Oona's Achilles' heel. Before Daphne could so much as open her mouth, Oona blurted, "She wants to join the coven."

She thought this would turn her mother against Daphne, make

her suspicious of her motives the way it had made Oona suspicious of Daphne's entire pregnancy. But instead, Ursula smiled. If you could call it a smile. Oona had never been entirely convinced that *smile* was the best descriptor for the expression that sometimes lit her mother's face when she bested Lally at a game of chess. She never gloated when she announced her checkmate, but her lips always curled in the exact same way the moment Lally took her hand off her piece, solidifying her fatal mistake.

"Is that true?" Ursula asked Daphne. "You want to join our coven?"

"Yes," said Daphne sheepishly. It was the first time Oona had ever seen her look shy.

"Do you have power? Have you ever been tested?"

Daphne glanced accusingly at Oona. "I didn't know there was a test."

"It's supposed to be for Initiates," Oona said, defensive. "Or for older witches."

Without offering more information, Ursula stood and crossed the room. When she returned, she was carrying a bowl of shells. Oona thought she recognized it, though the last time she'd seen the bowl it had been on her mother's altar.

Daphne eyed the bowl, apprehensive. "Do I have to close my eyes?"

"No," said Ursula. "Just pick a shell. Whatever shell calls to you."

After some deliberation, Daphne reached into the bowl. Oona resisted the urge to lean in closer so she could see. As much as she hated to admit it, she knew that she wouldn't be able to tell much from Daphne's choice. She didn't have her mother's gift for shell reading.

In the end, Daphne chose a mussel shell. Oona held her breath while Ursula ran her fingertip around the shell's inky blue edge, and then down into the trough of its pearlescent hollow.

"What does it say?" Daphne asked. If it were anyone else, the desperation in her voice would have embarrassed Oona. All that naked wanting. But as it was, Oona found that she'd inched her way right up to the edge of her seat.

Ursula smiled. A real smile this time. Or, rather, a more traditional one, since Oona had the sneaking suspicion that her mother's other smile was actually more genuine. "You can stay."

Daphne gasped. "Does that mean . . . do I have . . . I can join the coven?"

"It means there is hope," Ursula said. "With the right training, the proper sacraments . . ."

Oona felt her whole chest seize. Her heart *hurt*.

On the other side of her desk, Ursula stood. "Now, I'm afraid we don't have any spare cabin beds at the moment, but you can bunk with Oona in her room. I'm sure she won't mind."

Oona opened her mouth and then closed it, silent. She felt like a fish yanked from the sea. Dying. She felt like she was dying. "Let me pick one," she said to her mother. "Let me pick a shell."

Ursula sighed.

"Please," Oona said. She lunged forward and managed to pluck out a pink-bellied clamshell just before her mother moved the basket out of reach. She held it up to the light. "What does it say?"

Ursula pushed up the sleeve of her wool sweater and looked down at her watch. "I've got to go. I'm teaching a class in ten minutes. But if you're sure you can keep this secret"—she nodded at Daphne's stomach—"then you are welcome here."

"I can. I will. I promise."

"Good." Ursula escorted the girls out of her office and down the hall. Outside, she made sure to lock the doors to the building, then she left them. Daphne said something about going back into town to

get her stuff, but Oona was barely listening. It was hard to hear anything over the roaring in her ears. Was it the sound of her blood moving in her veins, or had she started screaming? It was surprisingly
hard to tell. Certainly, she felt like screaming. Every muscle in her
body ached, and her throat felt raw, ravaged. She even thought she
could taste blood.

Without saying a single word, she grabbed Daphne's hand and
ripped away the shell she'd chosen, held it up to compare it to her
own. But no matter how she squinted or how she turned Daphne's
shell, she couldn't see what made it special, what made her mother
decree that, for Daphne, there was hope. *What about me?* she wanted
to ask, but by the time she looked around again, she was alone. Her
mother off to teach her class. And Daphne . . . Daphne off to collect
her things so she could move to Bare Root and take Oona's place in
the coven's rites and rituals, in her mother's classes, in Oona's own
damn bed.

While Oona'd been busy thinking about Daphne and her shell,
Holly had moved on to lecturing about candle placement.
Apparently, it wasn't an exact science but there *was* an art to it. Or so
Holly claimed. As best Oona could remember, an altar was meant to
have four tall taper candles, one placed in each corner to represent the
four winds. In addition, a white goddess candle was often placed in
the very center of the altar. This candle was lit first—followed by the
north, south, east, and west, and then any other specific spell candles
a witch might currently be using, be they inscribed with a rune or a
prayer.

From the floor beneath the altar, Inez pulled out an old wooden milk crate filled with different kinds of candles. "Who would like to volunteer to come up to the altar and show us where these candles go?" As she scanned the room, her eyes slid right over Vivian's up-thrust hand and then seemed to settle on Gemma, who was, at least, awake again. "Gemma?" she asked.

But Gemma shook her head slowly. She seemed to be in some kind of pain, gritting her jaw and massaging her temples.

Holly opened her mouth to speak, but Inez cut her off. "Gemma," she said sharply. "That wasn't really a question. We've been over this: You are expected to participate in class. So please come up here and place these candles on the altar."

Oona hated to admit it, but she knew Inez would never dare speak to another Mother that way. It almost made her want to stand up and say something—almost.

Reluctantly, and with some effort, Gemma rose. She looked shaky as she walked up to the altar, but Inez didn't stop her. She just waited, with her arms crossed. Then, once Gemma was before her, she pushed the box of candles toward her. "Let's start with the candles representing the four winds. Can you pull those out?"

Gemma stared, unmoving. It was difficult for Oona to see, so far back, but it looked like she was swallowing hard. Oona thought she could see her throat working.

Inez sighed. "Fine," she said. "Just point. Point and I'll pull them out."

But still, Gemma didn't raise her hand. She just stood there until the room went quiet around her, until there was nothing left but the muted sounds of the storm. Then, at last, her fingers twitched, and she brought both hands up to her temples. "My head," she moaned, then suddenly she vomited—all over the altar and onto the floor.

"Oh!" cried Holly, as she rushed toward Gemma.

Inez stepped back, appalled.

"Something's wrong," Holly said. "Inez, you need to go find Lally." Then, when Inez still didn't move: "Now!"

The wind howled as Inez pushed out into the storm. Another Mother had to force the door closed behind her. Meanwhile, up by the altar, Holly helped Gemma back down to the floor. She laid her on her side, and Gemma curled up into the fetal position and started crying. "My head," she wailed. It was the only thing she could say, despite the many questions being lobbed at her—by Holly and by the other Mothers, who, after Inez left, rushed to gather around her.

"When did you first start feeling sick, honey?" Shelly asked kindly.

"Rank the pain you're feeling," demanded Vivian.

"Just hold on," Holly said gently. "Lally is going to be here any minute and then we'll get you feeling as good as new."

Oona was the only Mother who didn't get up to kneel at Gemma's side. So the girl was sick, so what? It was about time she suffered from something.

Hell, even Daphne had been sick for the first trimester, and had then fallen ill again when she hit seven months. She'd been living at Bare Root for more than five weeks by that point—sitting in Oona's chair at their dining room table, sleeping in Oona's bed while Oona slept on a pallet on the floor. At first, Oona had told herself that it would be nice to have Daphne sharing her room, like a kind of extended sleepover, but the pleasure had worn off after about a week. It was replaced by a seething jealousy. A refrain circled in Oona's head: *This isn't fair.* It wasn't fair that Oona was being made to lie to Jacob, that she had to claim Daphne was just staying over for fun. It wasn't fair that Daphne got to attend all the coven's sacred rites and rituals even though she wasn't a member yet. And it definitely wasn't fair that on the day Daphne got sick, Oona came home to find her mother perched at the end of her bed, massaging her swollen calves just the same way Oona had always begged her to.

Inside the workshop, Oona heard Lally call out even before she got the door open. "I'm here!" she cried, as Inez trailed her into the room. "I'm here!"

"I think it's her head," Holly explained.

"I'm an ob-gyn," said Shelly. "I'm happy to help, if I can."

Oona stared pointedly up at the skylights, though she'd long since stopped paying attention to the storm. It had been the same with Daphne, she remembered. At Ursula's instruction, Oona'd strapped an ice pack to Daphne's head. But it hadn't been a simple pregnancy headache, like they'd thought at first. Or dehydration. It had been something more complicated, only Oona couldn't remember what.

Sneaking a peek at the women all clustered around Gemma, Oona debated asking Shelly, but she really didn't want to get involved. She didn't want to have to explain to the others who Daphne was or what had happened to her. And anyway, she thought, Lally would figure it out.

"We're going to have to carry her to the infirmary," Lally announced to the Initiates. "Holly, you'll hold her under her arms, and, Inez, you'll get her feet. Ready? One, two, three. Someone get the door!"

Grace popped up to help and the rest of the Mothers all rushed to the window. For a few minutes, they watched Inez and Holly carry Gemma across the grounds. Then, once they were out of sight, the Mothers began to gather their things.

"It's nearly lunch, anyway," Vivian said, as she pulled on her rain slicker. She turned toward Oona. "Are you hungry? Should we go get something to eat?"

"Sure," Oona said, but then she remembered her plan: the Initiate cabins. She wouldn't be able to get keys from Lally, but she could at least walk by, test the doors. "Actually, you know what, I think I forgot something at the cabin. My . . . my phone. So I'll meet you there."

"I'll save you a seat," Vivian promised, then she and Shelly and Grace followed the others out into the rain.

Oona hung back, pretending to need extra time to put on her raincoat. She fumbled with the snaps until she could no longer see the yellow of Shelly's slicker out the window, then she pulled up her hood and stepped out into the storm.

It was raining harder than she'd expected, and the wind had certainly picked up in both strength and speed. Overhead, it looked like the trees were being bent in half. Oona could hear their creaking, the violent crack of a branch snapping off. This was why Jacob had told her to stay inside, she thought, as she hurried through the forest. And wouldn't it be just like her to fuck up and prove him right? Well, she would just need to move quickly, then. The Initiate cabins weren't that far away. Only a little past the infirmary and the birthing suites.

She would be there in a matter of minutes, she told herself, as up ahead the infirmary came into view. And she would have been, if only she hadn't noticed the infirmary door hanging open and heard a scream so long and wailful she had to stop to wonder if what she'd heard had been a person or the wind.

Then she heard it again, undeniably human, and an image flashed in her mind.

*Daphne.*

She had howled like that too, Oona remembered. About an hour after Oona had returned home and found Ursula massaging her legs, Daphne had taken a turn for the worse. She'd thrown up, just like

190

Gemma had. Yellow bile all over Oona's gingham comforter. And the whole while they'd waited in the infirmary for Lally to run tests, she'd clutched her head and moaned.

In the rain, a shiver worked its way down Oona's body as she stepped closer to the infirmary door. It'd been nearly thirty minutes since Holly and Inez had carted Gemma away. Surely, by now, they'd gotten things under control. Probably the medicine they'd given her just hadn't kicked in yet. And anyway, what was the likelihood that she had the same thing Daphne'd had?

There was no need for Oona to go inside. No one had asked for her assistance. She had more important things to do. And yet . . .

Before she really knew what she was doing, Oona had pushed her way through the infirmary doors, marched down the hall, and come to a stop outside Gemma's sickroom. Through the open doorway, she could see Lally inside. She was checking Gemma's blood pressure. Oona held her breath as Lally squeezed and squeezed and then squinted. Though Oona was dripping puddles onto the floor, she didn't take off her coat until she saw Lally shake her head. "No better," she said to Holly and Inez.

"Still?" Oona asked from the hall.

Lally stepped away from Gemma's bed. "Oona? What are you doing here?"

"I came to see what's wrong with her."

"You know I can't tell you that. Patient confidentiality," Lally said, then she turned toward Holly and Inez. "Can you two sit with her a moment? I want to try ringing Ursula again."

"Of course," Holly said, and she reached for Gemma's hand.

Inez said nothing. Oona noticed that though she was inside the sickroom, she was standing as far away from Gemma as she could get.

At first Oona assumed it was because she didn't like Gemma, but upon closer inspection, she realized it was because Inez was scared.

"Go back to your cabin," Lally told Oona, as she brushed past on her way to the office.

For a moment, Oona debated obeying her command. Or at least, she debated continuing to the Initiate cabins. With Holly and Inez occupied, she might even have time to do more than just test the locks. If she found a way inside, she could begin searching. But instead, she stayed. Though she couldn't remember the name of the condition Daphne had suffered from, she felt sure that she would recognize it if she heard it spoken aloud. And she needed to know that whatever Gemma had, it was different; that the haunted feeling she'd been struggling with all session—it was just in her head. Gemma wasn't some kind of shadow Daphne, dragged out of the underworld to torture her. She was just a girl. A spoiled girl who deserved whatever bad luck had befallen her, who had probably even brought it on herself by smoking moldy shed cigarettes.

Careful not to let her damp shoes squeak on the linoleum, Oona crept down the hall. She paused outside the door of the office, where she could hear Lally leaving her mother a message on the phone.

"Her blood pressure is really quite high," Lally said. "And we've seen evidence of protein in her urine. We're suspecting preeclampsia."

Preeclampsia. That was the name. Just like she'd thought she would, Oona recognized it instantly. For a moment, she felt victorious. But quickly that sated feeling was replaced with dread. What did it mean? she wondered. What were the odds?

"We've already done all I can think of," Lally said into the phone. "We even gave her a mixture of dandelion leaves and hawthorn berries, but so far nothing's changed. If she doesn't improve soon, we'll have to medevac her, and you know the hospital will insist on notifying her next of kin. I don't know if you want to warn Mrs. Nystrom, to try to get ahead of this news or . . ."

Oona couldn't be sure they'd tried the same combination on Daphne, but she remembered that whatever they'd tried, it hadn't worked. Daphne had declined rapidly, confounding them for hours. For a while, they'd even thought they might have to send her to a hospital on the mainland, but then, sometime in the wee hours of the morning, they'd stumbled upon a potion. Or, more specifically, *Lally* had stumbled upon a potion. Oona remembered that part because it had seemed to piss her mother off—that it had been Lally, not Ursula, who had saved the day. So even though Oona couldn't remember the name of the potion—couldn't recall a single ingredient—she felt sure that Lally would. All she needed to do was remind her, then she could be on her way, confident that whatever was going on—be it supernatural or not, the work of Hekate or just sheer coincidence—Oona would not be to blame. Not again. Not this time.

She waited until Lally hung up the phone, then she stepped into the office. "Do you remember my friend Daphne?" she asked.

"Oona," Lally said, surprised. "What are you still doing here?"

"Daphne had preeclampsia too. And, at first, nothing you gave her helped. She just kept getting sicker and sicker."

"Were you eavesdropping just now?" Lally asked. "What did I tell you about patient confidentiality?"

"You found a potion," Oona said. "For Daphne. You found a potion that saved her. Have you tried that potion on Gemma?"

"I don't know which potion you mean. We've tried dandelion leaves and hawthorn berries and—"

"No, it was a *potion*. Not just herbs. It involved some kind of spell. You don't remember?"

Lally removed her glasses and rubbed at the bridge of her nose, like she often did when she was stressed, or tired. "Oona, love, it's been fifteen years."

"But . . ." Oona started, only there was no but. It had been fifteen years and Lally didn't remember any more than Oona remembered the name of the book she'd stolen off her mother's altar. If only she was the type to keep a diary, if only she was the sort to write things down . . .

Oona said as much to Lally, then she turned back for the hallway, but she managed to take only a few steps before she heard Lally exclaim, "The file room!"

"What?" Oona asked, confused.

"The file room!" Lally said again, then she bustled past her, and Oona had to hurry to follow her down the hall.

When she finally caught up, she found Lally in a small, dark room just off the building's foyer. "I know it's got to be here somewhere," she heard Lally mutter, as she yanked at what sounded like a filing cabinet drawer.

Oona felt around for a light switch, then blinked rapidly when light flooded the room.

"Here we are!" Lally crowed, triumphant, as she pulled a thick file from one of the cabinet's bottom drawers. She carried it to the wooden table in the center of the room, and then flipped back the cover.

Oona spun in a small circle. "Since when has the infirmary had a file room?"

"Since always," answered Lally, distracted. She was paging through the file's contents. "Where did you think we kept all our patients' information?"

"I don't know." Oona frowned. "I guess I never thought about it before." When Lally sniffed, Oona stepped up behind her to try to read over her shoulder. There was a strange symbol on the file's tab.

It almost looked like a ladder with an X drawn over the rungs. "Is that Daphne's file? What does it say?"

Without answering, Lally thumbed through a few more pages. Intake forms, blood results, patient history. Oona tried to read alongside her, but Lally turned the pages too quickly.

"It really should be here," she mumbled. "If we gave her a treatment, it should be here."

"Then where is it?"

Lally wrinkled her nose. "Hold on. I'm still looking. I'm still . . . Here it is!"

"Really?" Oona leaned closer to try to get a better look, but Lally had already plucked the page from the file and was taking it with her into the hallway. A bigger woman, Lally didn't usually move that quickly, but Oona found she had to jog a little to keep up. "Where are we going?" she asked.

"The greenhouse, of course. We'll be needing milk thistle and cramp bark and—" Lally stopped short about a yard past the door to Gemma's sickroom. "What am I on about? I can't leave." She turned to Oona. "You'll have to be the one to do it, love."

"Me?"

Lally folded the paper in half, then in half again, and tucked it into the front pocket of Oona's slicker. "I can't be leaving the infirmary until your mother returns. If Gemma were to take a turn . . . I can't leave Holly and Inez alone with her."

"Well, then call for one of the other coven members! Call for Joyce or Donna or even Alice. One of them should be able to do it."

Lally sucked her teeth softly. "Joyce and Donna are in town, performing exams."

"Alice, then."

"Alice is only a Maiden. She isn't allowed to practice Craft. And anyway, I don't think she actually has much power."

"How do you know?" Oona asked, thinking again of her mother's shell test.

"I just know," Lally said. "The same way I know that you can do this."

Oona touched her rain jacket's pocket. "But I'm not even a Maiden, let alone a Mother. I've never been initiated, I never saw Persephone."

"But you summoned Hekate, didn't you?"

"I guess."

"It shouldn't have been possible, and yet it happened. You made contact. So you must have power. And while normally I'd be recommending that you follow the rules, that you go through the proper sacraments before you begin practicing Craft, there just isn't time for that now. Gemma needs you."

"But what if I hurt her? You said when I communed with Hekate, I used dark Craft. So what if the potion I make turns to poison? What if my mother was right about whatever it was I gave Daphne that day?"

"Do you want to hurt Gemma?"

Oona thought about it. "No." She'd wanted Gemma to suffer, yes, but only from a bout of late-term morning sickness, food poisoning, a stomach bug. She hadn't wanted anything truly bad to happen to her any more than she'd wanted Daphne to jump from those cliffs.

"You're a good person, Oona. Or mostly good, anyway. And you've got your mother's blood running through you. That's all you need. So go. We can't be wasting time like this, gabbing. You'll find all the ingredients you need in the storeroom. I keep dried milk thistle in a jar on the top shelf in the cabinet, and cramp bark in a tub down below."

Before Oona could protest again, Lally shooed her into the foyer, opened the door, and gently pushed her out into the storm. "Be careful, love!" she called. Then she closed the door again, firmly. And for a moment, Oona just stood there in the rain.

She could go back to her cabin, she told herself—hole up like she'd told Jacob she would. She didn't have to risk doing more harm than good, like she had with Daphne. But even as she comforted herself with these alternate scenarios, these escape routes, Oona admitted that she knew the truth: Lally was right. She was Gemma's only hope. She'd known it since she'd first remembered Daphne's illness, maybe since the day she'd come upon Gemma in the woods. So for the second time that day, she ignored the promise she'd made to Jacob, and she walked on despite the storm.

In the greenhouse, Oona found the ingredients quickly. Both the milk thistle and the cramp bark were exactly where Lally'd said they'd be, and thankfully the other components were easy to locate too. The only one Oona had any trouble with was the bloodstone, but eventually she found it tucked in a drawer beside a rose crystal and one made of citrine. So just ten minutes after she left the infirmary, Oona had all the makings of Lally's potion assembled on her enamel worktable. She even got a kettle of charged water set to boiling. But of course it wasn't simply a matter of steeping the right herbs in the right water for a few minutes. She wasn't brewing tea. She was making a potion, and potions required spells.

Oona knew how to do the prep work—how to cleanse the space and draw the circle, how to ground herself and raise energy—but she'd never cast a spell before. Not on purpose. Not without another witch's help. But then she *did* have help, she reminded herself, smoothing out the paper before her. She wasn't winging it, like she'd done with Daphne, she was following Lally's instructions, which said to first add two cups of boiling water to a jam jar, as if she really were making tea. Next, she was to sprinkle in the herbs: one tablespoon of dried milk thistle, three tablespoons of dried nettle, one teaspoon of dried cramp bark, and six tablespoons of dried raspberry leaves. Holding the nettle, Oona felt something in her chest tighten. In all likelihood, she had foraged for that very herb only days before while helping Lally, pulled it from the ground with her own two hands. But was that a good sign, she wondered, or a bad omen?

For a moment she hesitated adding the nettle, but eventually she was able to shake off her doubts. All she had to do was follow the instructions exactly as they were written—no ad-libbing, no making anything up. Each time she added a new ingredient, she had to speak four words over the brew: *infuse, imbue, impart, immerse*. She had to speak this incantation twice for the nettle and the raspberry leaves, and three times each for the cramp bark and the milk thistle. Then, at the very end, she added the bloodstone.

"Steep for fifteen minutes," Oona read aloud from the sheet of paper. "Then strain and serve."

While the potion steeped, she searched the larder for a cheese-cloth, which she found stored in a box under a chair. It would be nice to sit, Oona thought, as she ran her hand over her swollen belly. She'd been so focused on Gemma, and on the potion, that she hadn't real-ized just how badly her feet hurt, how much her back ached, but when she checked her phone, she saw there wasn't time. Her alarm was set to go off in thirteen seconds. So instead, she got the cheesecloth ready, then she poured the tonic from the jam jar into a bowl, and then from the bowl back into the jam jar. When she was done, she screwed on the jar's lid. It was ready, whatever it was that she'd con-cocted. The only question remaining was: Would it work?

⌘

Oona rushed back to the infirmary, and this time she didn't bother waiting by the door to the sickroom, she just entered, brandishing the jam jar. Lally plucked it from her hands.

"Did it go all right?" she asked.

Holly was looking at them both, perplexed, but Lally didn't explain. Oona could tell from Inez's face that in the time she'd been gone Gemma had gotten worse.

"I followed the instructions," Oona offered without confidence.

Lally nodded. "Then I'm sure it's right."

"I hope so," Oona said. Certainly, she wanted it to be right. Gemma *needed* it to be right, but still, when Lally unscrewed the lid and tipped the jar toward Gemma's lips, Oona had to fight back the urge to knock it away from her, to call out, "Poison!"

In just a few minutes, Gemma had drained the jar. Then there was nothing more to do but wait.

"It may take a few hours for us to see results," Lally cautioned.

"I'm staying," Oona countered, though Lally hadn't actually suggested that she go.

Oona was supposed to talk to Jacob that night, to confirm that she'd made it through the storm safely, but standing there at the foot of Gemma's bed she felt prepared to miss the call, prepared even to face the brunt of Jacob's wrath—well, more like irritation since Jacob never seemed capable of true anger; no, anger was Oona's sole domain. Still, she felt both ready and willing to let him down. This was more important, she thought. Not Gemma, though of course her health was important. But by *this*, Oona meant something more. Something bigger. Something to do with figuring out what had really happened to Daphne. Something to do with the question of whether the spell had worked. It felt like she was on the precipice of having her lifelong question answered: Did she have power? Was she a witch?

Oona got so lost in her own thoughts that she almost missed the moment Gemma stirred. But Lally didn't. As soon as Gemma's fingers twitched, she was out of her chair and reaching for the cuff. Squeeze, squeeze, squeeze. Oona couldn't watch. For a second, she felt like she had on the beach at the base of the cliffs, standing frozen on the sand as Jacob splashed out into the surf, as he dragged Daphne onto shore, as he pumped his fists against her chest—and then . . .

"Progress," Lally concluded.

"Really?" Inez and Oona asked at the same time.

"Not much, but enough. We won't need to medevac her. At least, not right now." With that, Lally took a deep breath in and then released it slowly. "I'm going to see if I can't reach Ursula," she said to Holly. "To let her know." On her way out of the room, she cupped Oona's face. "Good work, love."

"I just followed the instructions," said Oona. It would have been unseemly to take credit, especially in front of Holly and Inez.

But later, on her walk home from the infirmary, with the storm all but passed, Oona let herself indulge in the unseemly—glory in all her most self-aggrandizing thoughts. Despite what her mother had always said, she *did* have power, she *was* a witch. A dark witch, maybe, but a witch all the same, which meant that not only was she skilled enough to make a potion—for Gemma, for Daphne—but she was capable of performing rituals, of communing with goddesses, of summoning Hekate.

She had her mother's blood running through her. And so would her daughter, she realized, as she stopped in front of her cabin door. She reached for her belly. *A girl*, she thought for the first time. No doctor had ever confirmed the baby's sex, but suddenly she was sure of it. Maiden, Mother, Crone. Three generations of Walker women. The three faces of the witch. It was so perfect, it felt nearly fated. Predestined.

One day soon, she thought, she was going to have everything she'd ever wanted.

"*We* are going to have everything we ever wanted," she whispered to her belly as she walked.

# EIGHT

It was a quiet ride into town, and Oona felt grateful. With anyone else, she knew, she would have been forced to make conversation—to listen to Lally complain about her arthritis or hear Joyce wax on about her new love for pottery. But with Alice, Oona got to stare silently out the window, to let her gaze soften as the pine trees that ran along either side of the car began to blur. She would use the time to think, she'd decided even before Alice had pressed the ignition, shifted the Jeep into drive.

When Ursula had first told Oona she needed her help, asked her to meet the ferry in town to pick up a bunch of medical supplies she'd ordered from the mainland, Oona had been thrilled. More than thrilled, she'd felt *honored*. This, she'd thought, was what she'd been waiting for. Finally, she was being treated as a true member of her mother's coven, and all because she'd saved the Nystrom deal. Sure, she'd also saved Gemma's life, but that didn't matter nearly as much to her mother, and Oona knew it. No, the important thing was that

Ursula hadn't had to tell Astrid Nystrom that she'd failed her daughter right at the very moment that Mrs. Nystrom was handing over yet another large check. The idea was to franchise, Ursula had told Oona the next morning when she'd summoned her to her office and sat her down on the other side of her heavy wooden desk. If everything went according to plan, by the following year they would have a second location in Palm Springs, then a third in Napa Valley, a fourth somewhere in Connecticut. The list went on and on.

"Lally told me what happened," Ursula said. "I didn't believe her at first. I thought, power? No, not *my* Oona. But she told me that without your help, the whole deal would have fallen through. So it looks like I was wrong about you. When I first laid eyes on you down at the beach, realized who you really were, I thought I was being punished. That night, I prayed to my goddesses. I begged them for their mercy, apologized for whatever I'd done to turn them against me. But now I see: Your return is actually a blessing, not a curse. The goddesses sent you here to help me realize my vision for this coven, for Bare Root. You are here for a reason. Do you feel it too?"

Eagerly, Oona nodded. Not necessarily because she felt goddess-sent, but because she'd finally gotten what she wanted. Her mother had admitted that she had power.

Of course, if she'd thought about it longer, she might have had questions—about her mother's vision, yes, but also about the reason she'd returned to the island: the baby, the girl (she was now convinced) who was right at that moment kicking at her bladder. Or at least, Oona assumed it was the baby's fault that she suddenly had to pee. In truth, she hadn't felt any actual kicks—hadn't felt the baby at all, really, since her bleed. But that had more to do with the placement of her placenta, she figured. She'd done a lot of googling and according to the mothers online, if the placenta grew between the baby and the front of her stomach, it could make it almost impossible for her to feel anything going on inside her womb. Still, she'd been meaning to ask her mother about it, to get some confirmation, because though she'd originally only thought about the pregnancy as a means to an end, ever since her threatened miscarriage she'd begun feeling differently. More protective, more attached. In the end, though, she'd decided it wasn't the right time. Whatever was happening between them, she didn't want to fuck it up.

Later, she was glad she'd remained patient. Because just before the phone rang and her mother abruptly ended their conversation, she invited Oona to join the coven for breakfast the following morning down on the beach. Soon, Oona was eating all her meals with the coven. She even started attending rites and rituals again, when her mother hosted them in her home. And two weeks after saving Gemma's life, on the day she officially entered her twenty-sixth week of pregnancy, Oona was asked to perform a bit of coven business on her own.

Well, not entirely on her own. Technically, she was driving down to meet the ferry with Alice. Originally Carol was supposed to go, but then she threw out her back and Ursula said Alice couldn't go alone. After all, the girl didn't speak. She might be able to drive the Jeep there and confirm they'd been given everything in their order, but she wouldn't be able to tell the crew who she was or where she'd parked, she wouldn't be able to ask them to load up the trunk. Oona didn't know if any of that was necessarily true. Alice was nineteen years old. She might have been mute, but surely she'd found other ways to communicate. Oona didn't bother saying any of that to Ursula, though. She was just happy to have been asked, happy to accompany Alice— to, as Ursula put it, chaperone the trip.

Yes, Oona thought as on one side of the road the trees gave way to the expanse of the ocean, the water's surface surprisingly clear and still, the past couple of weeks had been a dream come true for her. The meals, the rituals, walking back to her cabin and so casually saying that she was "headed home." Even the fact that she was right then sitting in the passenger seat of the very same Jeep that had met her at the docks back in April. But despite all the moments of joy the past two weeks had brought her, there had been moments of real worry too. Sometimes it felt like swimming in the ocean: For a long while, the water would feel so good, so warm, and then suddenly, she'd stop paddling and her feet would sink down and the water there would be so different, such a shock of cold. Because all the work she'd been doing—for her mother, for the coven—hadn't left her with much time to look for the book.

In the weeks since Gemma had collapsed, Oona had managed to search the entirety of Holly's quarters but, no surprise, it hadn't been there. Nor had it been in the cabin where Inez was staying. Now Oona was out of ideas. Only she couldn't be out of ideas because her due date was fast approaching. The potion Lally had given her when she was miscarrying would protect her only until she gave birth, then she'd be at Daphne's mercy. No, then her *daughter* would be at Daphne's mercy. So before that happened, she needed to come up with some new places to look. The grimoire had to be somewhere, she thought, tucked away in some forgotten cabinet. Or maybe locked up in that one false-bottom drawer? Oona didn't think it likely, but she *was* curious about the drawer, just like she'd once been curious about all her mother's hiding places. When she was younger that curiosity had often gotten her into trouble, but now she was hoping it might finally pay off. Where else had she gone snooping as a kid?

There was the shed, of course, Oona thought, but she couldn't imagine the book was there. She was the only one who'd ever spent any time in that shed. Well, she and Daphne. And Gemma, Oona supposed. But if the book was there, Oona felt pretty sure Gemma would have found it. And if Gemma had found it, then she almost certainly would have said something when Oona told her the shed was where Crones practiced their dark Craft. Still, Oona supposed, she could try looking. And in the kitchen too. And in the cellar. Hell, she thought, she might as well search the barn, which the coven had converted into a garage in recent years. It would be easy enough to take a quick look around once they got back to the Center. Her job that day, as Ursula had explained it, was simply to act as a liaison between Alice and the ferry crew. Once they got back to Bare Root, the others would take care of the unloading.

It wasn't much of a plan, Oona thought as up ahead Port Marrow came into view, but it was better than nothing. And it wasn't impossible that in one of those places she might stumble upon the book. Maybe it was even in one of the other Jeeps. The Center basically had a small fleet of them. Someone could have accidentally left it behind in a trunk or lost it under a seat. It wasn't likely, but Oona tried to tell herself that there was a chance. She tried to fight down the doubt she could feel rising inside her—the panic that clawed at her throat. *Breathe*, she told herself, as Alice pulled into the parking lot just north of the ferry dock, but when she opened her car door the smell of diesel in the air nearly caused her to choke.

"What now?" she gasped between coughs, when Alice came around the other side of the car.

In response, Alice gestured to a small wooden bridge that ran over the canal separating the docks from the parking lot. Oona had to resist the urge to roll her eyes. She hadn't meant to ask how they would get to the boat. She'd spent years walking across the bridge's rotting planks, standing on the lowest rung of its railings to peer down into the cloudy, brackish water below. She meant, when would it be time for her to complete her task? Oona wanted desperately to prove herself. She wanted to be useful. No, not just useful—essential. But neither her mother nor Carol had given them much direction before they'd left. Probably because Alice had already run this same errand a hundred times. Still, Oona resented having to trail after her like a child.

It was petty, not to mention physically taxing given how big Oona was getting, but she jogged a little as they crossed the parking lot to ensure that she would be the first one to cross the bridge. Then she kept up the pace all the way down the length of the pier. By the time they reached the ferry, she was panting hard and sweating. Alice didn't wait when Oona stopped to catch her breath. She just marched past the passenger gangway down to the stern of the boat, walked up the wide unloading ramp, and disappeared inside the ferry. Oona had seen her mother do the same thing countless times when she was young, but somehow she'd imagined that the practice had changed. She was surprised to see that it was all still so informal.

When Oona finally caught up to Alice, she found her standing outside the metal gate at the rear of the empty car hold. Clearly, the ferry had arrived some time ago. The passengers were all departed, the cars (if the boat had carried any) long since driven away. Oona glanced back toward the pier and saw the stack of cargo containers waiting, she now realized, to be loaded. She wondered if they were late.

"Where is everyone?" Oona asked, but Alice didn't even acknowledge that she'd spoken.

Oona gritted her teeth. The girl was mute, not deaf. She knew Alice had heard her. And though it was true that Oona wasn't fluent in sign language, she did know some. Alice could at least try.

"Have you spoken to someone?" Oona asked instead. A yes-or-no question would surely work better. Oona waited, but Alice neither nodded nor shook her head.

"Fine," Oona snapped. If Alice wouldn't communicate with her, then she'd just have to find somebody who would. She checked the pier again. Next to the stack of shipping containers was a forklift. No driver yet, but it was only a matter of time.

She turned to walk toward the forklift, but then a man appeared on the other side of the gate. Young and too whippet-thin to be of much use, he looked like he hadn't showered in more than a week.

Without bothering to say anything to Oona, Alice hurried toward him. She started signing, rapid-fire, as soon as he pushed open the gate. But when she finished, he didn't respond. He just stared at her, a blank look on his face. Then slowly his gaze shifted, settled on Oona. "What do you want?" he asked.

"Me?" Oona said, surprised.

Alice snorted in frustration and stepped in front of Oona. Once again she started signing, but this time she also mouthed the words. Oona watched as she explained that they were there on behalf of Ursula Walker, on behalf of Bare Root Fertility Center. A shipment had come in for them that morning and they were there to claim it. They just needed help getting the boxes loaded into the car.

The man blinked, slow and stubborn. "I don't speak retard," he said. Then he turned like he was planning to walk away, to leave them there to uselessly rattle at the gate.

Oona didn't think before she acted. Just reached forward and grabbed him by the wrist, snatched the clipboard he was holding out of his hands. Then she turned it over to Alice.

For a moment, Alice looked at her, perplexed.

"There's a pencil tucked in at the top," Oona prompted, thinking maybe Alice didn't get what Oona meant for her to do.

Alice used her fingers to tap at the side of her head, then she brought her hand down suddenly, dismissively. Oona didn't need to be fluent in sign language to understand that Alice had signed something irritated like *I know.*

She released the pencil from its trap, turned over the paper attached to the clipboard, and started writing. When she was done, she handed the board back to Oona, who passed it to the ferryman.

"I don't—" he started to say, but Oona cut him off by squinting at the name tag on his work shirt.

"Joey, is it?" she said. "Just trying to figure out who we have to thank for helping us, since I know my mother will ask."

"Your mother?" he repeated.

"Yes. I'm Oona Walker."

The ferryman—Joey—folded his arms across his chest. He seemed to be weighing his next move, trying to calculate just how much trouble he could get into with his bosses if he told them to fuck off. In the end, though, while he did sigh dramatically, he also turned and walked back into the hold.

When he reemerged, he was pushing a dolly stacked high with cardboard boxes and carrying the thin metal clipboard clamped between his teeth. Alice took the clipboard from his mouth when he unlocked the gate, and Oona watched as her eyes scanned a new piece of paper. For a minute or two she bobbed her head, then something changed. She frowned and squinted. Started pointing—first at the piece of paper, and then at the tower of boxes.

"What's wrong?" Oona asked.

Alice ignored her. She kept gesturing at the boxes.

"They're all there," Joey said. "I checked."

Alice shook her head. She squatted down before the dolly and pointed at the bottommost box's label.

"What's going on?" Oona tried again.

Distracted, Alice scribbled something nearly illegible on the back of the order form and shoved it at Oona.

"We're missing a box," she read. "Wait. We're missing a box?"

*Yes*, nodded Alice.

"No," said Joey.

Again Alice squatted down on her knees, and though he squatted beside her, for a second it seemed like Joey was going to keep fighting. Instead, he took a breath. He rubbed his chin, scratching at his stubble with dirty nails. Then, with another loud sigh, he climbed back to his feet.

"Come on," he told Alice, and he pushed open the gate.

"Wait here," Alice mouthed to Oona.

Like she was a kid. *I'm going to be a Mother soon*, Oona wanted to say. Instead, she pointed down at her belly. "Where else would I go?"

While Alice followed Joey into the hold, Oona wandered back toward the ramp. It was silly, she knew, but she felt disappointed. She'd really wanted to be able to prove herself useful on their trip, but the truth was that Alice didn't need her. In fact she was so self-sufficient that Oona almost had to wonder why her mother had bothered sending her, almost had to suspect Ursula of giving her busywork. But no. That couldn't be. After all, Ursula had called her goddess-sent, told her she'd returned *for a reason*.

It was embarrassing how much that had meant to Oona, and as she stood there by the ramp she felt her cheeks burn with shame. Or maybe it was the heat. The fact that she'd practically raced Alice to the boat. She'd feel better, she thought, if she could sit for a minute.

Down on the docks, she saw a bench. She was just about to lumber down the gangway toward it when something caught her eye. Before she really knew what she was looking for, she'd turned around to scan the boardwalk.

A hat. A dark green hat she recognized instantly, though it took her brain a moment to catch up, to realize who the hat belonged to and what it meant that she was seeing that hat moving down the pier.

Jacob.

When she'd first left for Marrow, she'd stolen that hat and packed it in her duffel bag. But in the days after her threatened miscarriage, she'd given it back. Because she'd felt bad—about the theft, about leaving. Because she'd wanted to thank him for hearing her. And because, well, he'd needed it. He hadn't slept, hadn't showered, hadn't changed clothes. With the hat, at least, he'd been able to hide his greasy, unkempt hair.

At the time, she'd felt good about returning the hat. Benevolent, generous. Now she felt like ripping it off Jacob's head and throwing it into the sea.

What was he doing there? He was supposed to be . . . well, honestly, Oona didn't know where he was supposed to be—at home? On a research trip? It'd been a few days since she'd last checked in. But wherever he was supposed to be, she knew it wasn't on Marrow. So what was going on?

Another woman might've turned back around to stew or scheme, but not Oona. Suddenly, all her aches and pains were forgotten. Her swollen ankles, her throbbing heels. She could no longer even feel the heat. Without so much as a cursory thought for Alice and their missing box, she started power walking down the gangway.

By the time she made it to the pier, Jacob and his hat were nowhere to be found, but she didn't let that stop her. She knew what she'd seen. So she scoured the boardwalk until she found him: walking up the steps from the beach.

"What are you doing here?" she barked from the top of the crumbling cement staircase.

Jacob looked up. But though Oona expected to see him startle, sure she'd be catching him off guard, instead he threw up his hands. When he spoke, exasperation edged his voice. "Finally! I've been looking for you everywhere. I went by the Center but of course no one would tell me where you'd gone. *She's out* was all they'd say. Ridiculous. I'm your husband. Your emergency contact. And they can't tell me anything more than *she's out?*"

"What are you talking about?"

"I'm talking about you, Oona. Feels like I'm always talking about you these days."

When Oona failed to respond quickly enough, Jacob raised one reproving eyebrow. "I got your voicemail," he said.

"I didn't call you," Oona replied, defensive.

"Not on purpose," he agreed. "But you must have butt-dialed me or something because you left me a message and I heard you. I heard you, Oona."

It was like a reflex for her: the guilt, the shame. "Heard me doing what?"

"Praying," said Jacob.

Relief coursed through her. Followed quickly by indignant rage. "You heard me . . . praying?"

Jacob nodded slowly, sagely. Smugly, Oona thought. As if he was sure he'd bested her, that now she would understand: He'd had no choice but to sneak back onto the island, to skulk around the harbor, to stalk her. She'd forced his hand.

"So what?" Oona said.

"So what?" Jacob echoed, baffled. "So I had to come check on you, Oona. I had to ask Professor Harrigan for another week off. I mean, I had to find out what the hell was going on! You told me that you only came back because the women here are accomplished midwives. You swore it had nothing to do with your mom. And I believed you because we agreed. For years, we agreed: She's a liar. But then you called me last month talking about rituals and Hekate, talking about power, and I got nervous. Then I heard your voicemail and I got scared. After everything she did, after everything she took from us, everything *I* gave up to take your side over hers. How can you trust her again? How can you believe in her? In Craft?"

"Everything *you* gave up?" Oona repeated.

"I lost my whole family, Oona. Not just my sister. My parents too. Because I told them that Ursula was a fraud. Because I chose *you*."

"Well maybe you shouldn't have," she said bitterly.

"Maybe," said Jacob, "but it's too late now. What's done is done."

Oona's gaze slipped down to the stairs, to the stone disintegrating beneath her feet. It was the first time she'd ever heard him admit to any kind of regret, and she was surprised by how much the admission hurt her.

Sensing an opening, he stepped closer and reached for both her hands. "Look," he said, his voice softer now. Sweeter. "What happened last month was awful. And I know the others have been just as hard. You think Lally's medicine is what saved the baby so I won't argue with you. And who knows, maybe you're right. There have been studies about different kinds of herbs, about Eastern medicine. I won't rule out the possibility. But you're six months along now, more. And I looked it up. If you went into labor tomorrow, the baby would live. Or at least it would if we were back in Portland, near a real hospital. Here?" Jacob looked around, as if he couldn't quite believe where it was the two of them were standing. "Here, I don't know."

Oona stared at his hands, cupped around hers. "You want me to come back," she said, still struggling to come to terms with the fact that he'd returned to Marrow.

Jacob nodded. "I want you to come *home*. And I want us both to put this place behind us. Once and for all. We don't need it, Oona. We don't need this island and we don't need witchcraft. We have each other."

"And that's enough for you?" Oona asked. "*I'm* enough for you?"

"Yes," said Jacob. "You are. The real you. You and this baby." He moved his hands down to her belly and smiled.

Oona stepped back. "What if this is the real me, though?" she asked. "What if I really am a witch? What if everything I told you on the phone is true—about the ritual, about Hekate?"

Jacob raised his eyebrow again, and she saw a smile tug at one corner of his lips.

He thought she was a joke. The fucker.

"I saved Gemma, you know."

"Who?"

"Gemma Nystrom. She had preeclampsia. Her blood pressure was through the roof. But I made a potion and it cured her."

"Oona."

"She's alive because of me."

Jacob shook his head in disbelief. Or was it disappointment? In the moment, it was hard for Oona to tell, or to judge if the difference even mattered. Either way, it was clear that he wasn't going to be supportive, that he didn't want to hear any more about the "real" her. He thought he knew her, thought he loved her, but the woman he loved was just a shell. She'd been hollow, empty, all those years. But now? Now she was flesh and blood and sinew. She was flexing muscles and pumping lungs. She felt alive for the first time in a long time and it made her sad that Jacob didn't see that.

If she was honest, it broke her heart.

"I didn't come here to talk about Gemma," said Jacob.

Oona thought, *You shouldn't have come here at all*. And she would've said as much—after the way he'd shaken his head at her, after the way he'd told her, "What's done is done," she wanted to hurt him the same way she'd been hurt—but instead, she echoed Jacob and whispered, "Gemma."

Jacob sighed. "What did I just say?"

But Oona wasn't focused on Jacob anymore, because just over his shoulder she'd spotted Gemma, climbing the ferry's passenger gangway. "What on earth . . . ?" she muttered, and she started moving toward the ferry.

"Hey!" Jacob jogged after her. "Where are you going? We're having a conversation here."

Oona paused. Briefly, she dragged her gaze back to him. This was the moment when she usually gave in, when she capitulated to whatever it was Jacob wanted because he'd invoked his great sacrifice again. But something about seeing Gemma had broken the spell. "Are we?" she asked. "Because it sounded more like a lecture to me. I've tried to tell you who I am, how I feel, but you don't want to listen. You just want to tell me what to believe."

Oona glanced back at Gemma just in time to see her step aboard the ferry. While she supposed there was a chance Gemma's trip was sanctioned, most likely, she knew, the girl was running away. Running *toward* Elijah.

A part of Oona wanted to pretend she hadn't seen Gemma, wanted to just let her go. In the first few days after she'd prepared the potion, she'd thought that things might change between them, but though Lally had told Gemma what had happened—what Oona had done for her—Gemma never so much as offered up a simple thanks. *Thanks for saving my life, Oona. Thanks for helping me even though I've been such a brat.*

"Oona." Jacob waved a hand in front of her face in an attempt to draw her attention back to their so-called conversation.

If she returned to arguing with Jacob, no one would ever know. She would not get blamed for letting Gemma escape. That would be someone else's problem—Holly's, most likely. Or Inez's. Still . . .

Oona's eyes flicked back toward the stern of the ferry, to the ramp where, she imagined, Alice was still waiting for their missing box. If she did nothing, then her mother would never know that she was capable of more than just riding shotgun while Alice performed actual coven business. If she stopped Gemma, then maybe she could finally prove that she was worthy of all their trust.

"I have to go," Oona said.

"Go?" Jacob repeated, bewildered. "What do you mean, go? I bought us tickets for the ferry."

Oona winced. "Am I really that predictable, then?"

"What?"

"You were so sure your guilt trip would work, that I'd cave."

"Oona."

"I know you think a hospital would be better, but you're forgetting one thing: We don't have insurance, so we can't afford a hospital. If anything were to go wrong, we'd be on our own. And I'm tired of being on my own. So you can do whatever you want, but I'm staying, Jacob." And with that, she walked away.

∽

Inside the ferry's cabin, Oona found Gemma sitting on a jump seat, tucked away in a spot so small it was nearly invisible from the gangway's ramp. If Oona hadn't known about the jump seats—hadn't chosen them herself to stay hidden—she probably would have missed her. Instead, it was the first place she looked.

Tapping Gemma on the shoulder, she said, "I found you."

Gemma startled before she turned around. "What are you doing here?" she asked.

"I was running an errand in town when I saw you boarding. You're not supposed to be here, are you?"

Gemma shrugged. Near the bow of the ferry, an older couple, tourists, struggled with their luggage. Across the aisle a group of local women were taking their seats. Judging by the canvas tote bags they carried, Oona guessed they were headed to the mainland to do some shopping. There was a Walmart in Scarborough, not too far outside town.

"I don't want to make a scene," Oona said. "But you need to come with me. You know that, don't you?"

Gemma stuck her thumb in her mouth and began nibbling at her nail. It had been a mistake, Oona realized, to mention the possibility of a scene. Now Gemma knew what she had to do to get Oona to back down. Already she could see her scheming. But instead of stomping her feet and swearing, Gemma simply turned in her seat to better face Oona.

"Please," she said. "Don't make me leave."

It was the expression on her face, even more than the words she spoke, that surprised Oona. She looked genuinely afraid.

"Why—" Oona started to ask, but the ship's horn interrupted her.

There was no time for a longer conversation. The ferry would be leaving soon. "Come on," Oona said, taking Gemma's wrist. "We have to go."

Gemma shook her head and refused to stand. Her gaze settled on Oona's swollen belly. "You can't make me," she said.

Oona didn't want to admit that Gemma was right, but it'd been hard enough for her to climb up the gangway's ramp on her own. She would never be able to drag Gemma back down it.

The horn sounded again, and Oona looked around the cabin. There had to be something she could do, someone she could ask for help, a crew member or—

Oona glanced down the aisle, toward the stern of the ship, and spotted a man wearing a marine patrol uniform. She recognized the dark green pants and khaki jacket right away. "Excuse me," she called, as she hurried toward him. "Excuse me, sir, I need your help."

To get the officer's attention, Oona touched his elbow. She nearly gasped aloud when he turned around. It was Jacob's father.

"Oona," Mr. Tanaka said, surprised.

Oona glanced back at Gemma. For a second, she considered just letting her go. Anything not to have to ask Mr. Tanaka for help.

But it was too late. He followed her gaze. "What's going on?" he asked. "Does she need medical assistance?"

"No," Oona said. "It's nothing like that. She's running away."

He frowned, quizzical.

"She's supposed to stay at Bare Root for the summer, but she's trying to leave. I need to bring her back, but she won't come with me. She's only sixteen."

"Ah," Mr. Tanaka said. "I see." He checked his watch. It was clear he didn't want to get mixed up in their situation any more than Oona wanted him to. "I have a dentist appointment on the mainland in a couple hours," he said. Oona tried to look disappointed, though secretly she thrilled at the news. *Oh well*, she thought. She'd tried! "But," he continued, and Oona's heart sank. "If the situation is really as you say and I don't ask to check the girl's ID, well . . ." He trailed off, seeming to continue his debate in silence. "All right," he sighed. "Let's see." Brushing past Oona, Mr. Tanaka approached Gemma. "Miss," he said. "You're going to need to come with me."

Gemma tried to look innocent. "Me?"

"That's right. I've received a report that you're a minor, leaving the island without permission. So I'm going to need to see your ID."

The ferry horn sounded one final time, and Mr. Tanaka held out his hand to Gemma. "Let's get this sorted down on the pier."

B ack on the docks, Gemma turned over her ID, and when Mr. Tanaka saw that she was indeed sixteen, he offered to let her call a parent or guardian to confirm she had permission to travel to the mainland. When she declined, he pulled out his keys.

"Come on," he said. "I'll give you a ride."

"You don't have to do that," Oona interjected. "We have a car."

"You sure about that?" Mr. Tanaka asked, raising a single dubious eyebrow.

"Yes," Oona said, but as she scanned the pier for Alice she realized that with the ferry now departed, she and Gemma and Mr. Tanaka were alone. All the local fishermen were already out on the water, and the few men who worked for the ferry line had waited only as long as it took to see off the boat, then they'd turned and headed down the pier to Baxter's. Even Jacob had left.

"We were missing a box," Oona tried to explain, but the truth was obvious. Alice had ditched her. The parking lot was deserted save for Mr. Tanaka's truck.

On the other side of the lot's bridge, Mr. Tanaka jingled his keys in his palm. "Last chance," he said.

Reluctantly, Oona nodded. With each step, her sense of regret grew. She should have just let Gemma leave, she thought miserably as Mr. Tanaka took Gemma's backpack from her and threw it into his truck bed.

"Need help?" he asked.

"No, thanks," said Oona.

By the passenger-side door, Gemma held out her hand.

"Step here," Mr. Tanaka coached, and she placed one foot on the kick step while he gave her a boost from behind.

Meanwhile, Oona struggled to climb into the back seat. Her lower back ached, and she could feel the strain of her awkward movements in her pelvis, but she'd go into premature labor before she asked for help.

"Nothing new about the Center's entrance, I assume?" Mr. Tanaka said, as he pulled out of the lot and headed toward the main road. "I haven't been there since . . . well, you know. But it's still a straight shot from here. Right?"

"That's right," Oona said.

In the silence that followed, she studied Mr. Tanaka's face in the rearview mirror. The last time she'd been in a car with him he'd been driving his patrol vehicle. She'd met him at the gate to the Center to help direct him to the cliffs. Daphne had died the week before, and Mr. Tanaka had asked to see the bluff she'd jumped from. Jacob had thought it was all too morbid, but Oona had understood.

Back then, they hadn't talked on the drive to the cliffs. When Oona had to give directions, she pointed. When they hit the end of the sandy road, she used hand gestures to explain that they would have to walk the rest of the way. Mr. Tanaka had thrown the car into park, but though Oona opened her door, he didn't turn off the engine. For a long while he just sat there, both hands on the wheel. Then he raised his eyes and met hers in the rearview mirror. "I know everyone says it was a blessing in disguise, Daphne losing the baby. They said she was too young to become a parent anyway. But I think she would have been a good mother, if the baby had lived."

"I think so too," said Oona. It was the same thing she'd told Daphne a month earlier, when she'd found her weeping outside her mother's office. As soon as Daphne had brought up the baby, Ursula had shut her down. She'd called the stillbirth a "blessing in disguise," just like Mr. Tanaka said. For Daphne's sake, Oona had pretended to be shocked, but she'd always known her mother could be mercenary.

Parked at the edge of the forest, Mr. Tanaka turned around in his seat. "I need to ask you a question," he said.

"Okay," said Oona.

"Before she did what she did, Daphne was saying some strange things. She was struggling, even before you gave her that potion. I think you know that."

Oona nodded.

"She thought the baby had lived. She thought she'd heard it cry."

Again, Oona nodded.

"She said—" Mr. Tanaka shook his head a little, as if he could hardly believe the rest of his own sentence. "She said the baby had been taken by a witch. She said the stillborn child was a changeling."

"A changeling," Oona echoed. She felt Mr. Tanaka searching her face.

"Is that—could she—is there any chance that she saw what she thought she saw?"

"Do you mean . . ." Oona asked, frowning. "Are you asking if changelings are real?"

Mr. Tanaka grimaced. "Yes, I guess that is what I'm asking."

"No," said Oona.

"No?"

"No. Changelings are not real."

Still turned around in his seat, Mr. Tanaka let out the breath he'd been holding. Oona couldn't tell if he was disappointed or relieved. "And what about what your mother told us about the potion?" he asked. "Was that true? Was this really your fault somehow?"

"The potion?" Oona asked, confused.

"Ursula said you gave something to Daphne, something that made her sick, messed with her head. You were jealous, she said. Because Daphne appeared to have inherited some kind of power, and now that she'd become a mother, she was going to be invited to join the coven. But is that true? Is that really what happened, Oona?"

Oona frowned as she tried to wrap her mind around what Mr. Tanaka was telling her. She knew that the night before her mother had gone into town to visit Daphne's parents, but she'd told Oona that she was just going to pay her respects. Now it appeared that she'd done quite a bit more than that. She'd blamed Oona for everything.

For a second, Oona felt betrayed. But then she looked at Mr. Tanaka—took in his red-rimmed eyes, his five-day-old beard—and nodded. She'd told him yes, it was her fault. Not because she'd poisoned Daphne—she knew she hadn't—but because she'd seen Hekate in the water, bearing Daphne's body through the surf. Because she'd told Daphne that if she followed Hekate down to the underworld, she'd be able to return with her baby. But more than a week had passed, and Daphne hadn't come back. Neither had her child.

"I'm sorry," Oona said, tears in her throat.

Mr. Tanaka turned back around to face the steering wheel. "Get out," he told her, without anger.

Oona scurried from the car. She darted into the woods, but instead of running back to Bare Root she hid behind a tree and watched Mr. Tanaka, watched as he beat at his car horn, as he laid his head on the wheel and screamed. For over an hour she watched him grieve, stood there behind that tree until her legs started shaking and her own trapped wail began burning in her throat. She wanted to turn away, to run home, but she couldn't. Because her mother was right: She'd caused this.

Of course, had she known the extent of what her mother had told the Tanakas—how she'd begged them to spare the Center and not press charges; promised, in exchange, to send Oona away to a school for troubled youth—she might not have punished herself by bearing witness. Instead, she might have granted herself a little more grace. She might have even chosen not to confess. Because while it was true that the potion she'd given Daphne had made her sick, it hadn't killed her. It wasn't the potion that had led Daphne to jump from the cliffs.

Sitting in the back seat of Mr. Tanaka's truck on the drive home from the pier, Oona couldn't help but think about that day in the woods, by the cliffs. He'd given her a chance, Oona realized, and for the first time she recognized how strange that was. No one else had ever bothered to ask her what had happened. Most just believed Ursula. And even Jacob, though he'd defended her, had never wanted to hear her side of things. He'd diagnosed Daphne the second they'd discovered her body. Postpartum depression. He'd read about it in a book. But Mr. Tanaka had tried to give her the benefit of the doubt.

"So," Mr. Tanaka said, glancing over the gearshift at Gemma. "Tell me: Why were you trying to run away?"

"It doesn't matter," Gemma said, sulking. She was slouched against the doorframe, her forehead resting on the window's glass.

"Okay," Mr. Tanaka said.

Gemma looked at him sideways. "You won't believe me anyway. No one does. *She* definitely doesn't." Gemma tossed a glance over her shoulder, toward the back seat.

"Okay," Mr. Tanaka said again.

This was a side of him Oona had forgotten. He was stern, yes. Intimidating. But he'd always been patient, even when she and Jacob and Daphne were kids. Patient while Jacob spouted off facts about blue whales and orcas. Patient when Daphne asked him to be her guinea pig so she could test out a new, homemade spell. He'd been patient, even, with Oona, the few times her mother had been called away for a birth and she'd had dinner with the Tanakas, embarrassing herself by shoveling forkfuls of spaghetti into her mouth before the rest of the family finished saying grace.

"It's Ursula," Gemma said, pushing herself up straighter. "I think she's trying to hurt my baby."

In the back seat, Oona sucked her teeth. "Oh, please," she said. "My mother's not a *threat*. If she was trying to hurt your baby, then why did she help you when you nearly miscarried the other week?"

"She didn't," Gemma said. "You did."

"Yeah, and I still haven't gotten a *thanks*."

"Have you talked to your parent or guardian about your concerns?" asked Mr. Tanaka.

Gemma snorted. "My mom is the one who sent me here."

"Because she's trying to protect you," Oona said. "Just like Ursula. Even if Elijah isn't running some kind of cult, he's still a grown-ass man who *married* a teenager."

Gemma whipped around in her seat. "For your information, I haven't spoken to Elijah since last month. He's a good man and I love him, so I'm going to keep him out of trouble. I was leaving to do this on my own."

"Do what?" Oona asked, indignant. For a moment, she forgot about Mr. Tanaka sitting in the front seat. "Have a baby?"

"Yes," Gemma said. "Have a baby. Ursula said I wouldn't be able to do it, but she's wrong. She doesn't think I'll be a good mother. She told me so when I was in the infirmary for a follow-up last week. She said she was glad I'd recovered, but it was a shame I hadn't lost the baby. It would have been hard, she said, but it would've been a blessing in disguise, because I'm too young to have a child, too immature and selfish. But she doesn't know me. I'm neither of those things. Not anymore, anyway. I'm going to be better. This baby is going to get the best of me."

"I'm sure you'll do great," Mr. Tanaka said after a long pause.

Oona said nothing. Suddenly, she didn't want to argue anymore. For a mile or two, she stared out her window, watching the forest around them thicken as they approached the Center grounds. But as the truck's tires hit the clamshell drive she felt the itchy weight of someone's gaze, and when she looked up at the rearview mirror she locked eyes with Mr. Tanaka. So, she thought, he'd heard it too. *A blessing in disguise.*

It was a common enough saying. And in Gemma's case, Ursula probably wasn't even wrong. Oona didn't care what Gemma said—sooner or later she was going to go back to Elijah. And how was that right or good?

Feeling defensive, Oona turned back to her window and refused to look anywhere else again until the truck came to a stop. Not waiting for Gemma, she flung open her door and clambered out. "Thanks for the ride," she shouted.

"I'm sorry we made you miss your appointment," Gemma said.

"That's okay," Mr. Tanaka said. "I've always hated the dentist."

Gemma smiled, and Mr. Tanaka held up one hand as a goodbye. "If you ever need anything," he started to say, but Oona cut him off by slamming Gemma's door closed.

"You need to stop lying," Oona said, once the truck had pulled away. "And I need to go find my mother. Tell her I brought you home."

"Go ahead," Gemma said. "Go tell her what a good little girl you've been. It won't make a difference, though. I hope you know that. I hope you know it won't make her love you. I've already tried that route. I've been the good girl, I've been the bad girl. I've been every kind of daughter I could be. But I'm done being someone's daughter. I'm ready to be someone's mother." Gemma looked down at Oona's belly. "Maybe it's time you did the same."

Oona opened her mouth to argue, but Gemma turned away. Without another word, she walked off in the direction of the cabin, and Oona was left standing alone on the clamshell drive.

In the distance, she could see the Jeep parked over by the converted garage. Holly and Inez were helping with the unloading, while Alice stood consulting the order sheet nearby. She could go over and help, Oona thought, and pretend she'd never been ditched. Or she could head straight for her mother's office and explain where she'd been. It was the smarter move, she knew. Her mother would be proud to hear she'd prevented yet another Gemma-related disaster. And on the off chance that Alice planned to rat her out, it'd be better if Oona beat her to the punch. Still, when Holly waved, Oona found herself walking toward her, lifting her own hand. She could always go see her mother after they finished unloading, she figured. For the time being, Gemma wasn't going anywhere.

# NINE

This job looks good on you, love," Lally told Oona one morning, in mid-July. Class was just about to start, and the other students were filtering into the greenhouse. From her chair in Lally's small, windowless storeroom, Oona could see them parading single-file through the dark interior—where Lally kept all the plants that thrived in shade: foxglove, lungwort, hellebore—and out into the conservatory's bright light.

"Nothing looks good on me right now," Oona said, gesturing to her belly. "I'm as big as a house."

Lally tutted. "I'm being serious," she said. "These last few weeks, I've seen the spark come back into your eyes. I look at you now and I think: There she is; there's my Oona; there's the girl I know and love."

Though Lally had offered Oona the role of her assistant back in May, it took some time before she began trusting her with anything more important than what Oona had not-so-lovingly dubbed her "game of fetch." *Pass me the fireweed, love, would you? Pop back to the larder and see if we don't have any more dried chamomile?* Oona hadn't minded, not really. The job was paying for her stay at Bare Root, so she was smart enough to know not to complain. Still, she'd gotten excited when, not long after she successfully put together the potion for Gemma, Lally finally started asking her for real help.

First she sent her to the woods, alone, to forage for stinging nettle, then she sent her to the beach to search for devil's purse. By July, Oona was even helping Lally run her classes. Inez wasn't thrilled about that particular development, but no one else seemed to mind. Shelly and Grace were happy for her, and Vivian acted like she was the one who'd been promoted. She'd been craving a VIP experience since the day she'd stepped foot on the island, and at long last she'd managed to finagle one: In class (and sometimes even out of it) she treated Oona like her own personal TA. She insisted they sit side by side in every workshop, and on days when they practiced brewing herbal remedies, she made Oona review and approve her every step. At home, in their cabin, Oona often complained about it to Shelly, but secretly she liked being relied upon.

"I feel good here," Oona said to Lally, smiling.

"And in Portland?"

Oona shook her head. "I wish I didn't have to go back."

"Do you? Have to, I mean?"

"Well, I can't stay here. Mom made that very clear. Once this baby is born . . ." Again, Oona reached for her stomach. She was doing that more and more each day. Stroking, rubbing, caressing. When she thought about the future, when she imagined returning to Portland to found her own coven, she pictured doing so with a baby in her arms. She was going to be a good mother, she'd decided. A better mother than Ursula, anyway.

"Do you want me to talk to her?" Lally asked. She and Oona had finished all the prep work for class early, so for the past thirty minutes they'd been sitting in Lally's larder, sipping chilled mint tea. Now Lally rose from her stool, collected her cup and Oona's, too, and brought them to the sink in the corner.

"It wouldn't make a difference," Oona said, rising from her own stool.

"I'm not so sure about that," said Lally, as she passed Oona a spare apron.

Oona turned so Lally could tie it. She'd never thought there was even a remote possibility that her mother would let her join the Bare Root coven. She'd thought that if she wanted Craft in her life, she would have to form a coven of her own.

Behind her, Lally fussed with her apron strings. When she'd first offered her the job, Oona hadn't thought she really needed an assistant. She'd assumed that Lally had just taken pity on her and come up with the idea on the spot. But over the course of the past few weeks, she'd found herself studying Lally's hands: her slow-moving fingers, her swollen knuckles. Some days, like on the day they'd first scavenged for stinging nettle, it had seemed that even gripping a pair of shears caused Lally pain.

When at last Lally finished with her bow, Oona turned back around. "You really think you could convince Mom to let me stay here?"

"I do. But you don't need to be deciding right here and now. Give it some thought, yeah? I know you have a whole life back in Portland. And there's Jacob to consider too."

"Right," Oona sighed. "Jacob."

She hadn't spoken to him since their fight. He called often, at least twice a day, but she always sent him straight to voicemail, left all his texts on "Read." At some point, she knew, she would have to talk to him again, but she was still too angry. More than that, she was still too hurt. That moment when Lally had looked at her and said *There's the girl I know and love*? That's what she wanted from Jacob. She wanted to feel seen.

For a moment, Oona debated explaining the situation to Lally, but before she could make up her mind Vivian appeared at the storeroom door. "There you are," she said, as if she didn't regularly come to retrieve them on the days they lingered, chatting, for an extra minute. "I'm at the first table on the left."

"I'll be right there," Oona said, and she scanned the room, looking for the storeroom keys. Along with mint tea, the larder was also where Lally kept all her most dangerous ingredients—hemlock and belladonna, oleander and white snakeroot—so they never left it unlocked, even when they were just going to another part of the greenhouse.

"Go on," Lally said, plucking the keys from her apron pocket. "I'll close up."

The lesson plan for the day was to create a tonic for pain relief. It had been Oona's idea. Inspired by her own aching calves and sciatic nerve twinges, she'd remembered a draught Lally used to give her when she was little. Comprising a handful of feverfew leaves, a pinch of devil's claw, and a strip of white willow bark, it wasn't a simple concoction, exactly, but neither was it an especially complicated one.

Earlier that morning, she and Lally had pulled out all the tools the Mothers would need to produce the tonic. At each work station, they'd laid out a set of silver measuring spoons, a granite mortar and pestle, and a small iron cauldron complete with a Bunsen burner. At the beginning of the summer, Lally had prepared the ingredients as well, but a few weeks back she'd determined that the Mothers were ready to begin practicing both herb identification and preparation. Some days that meant she took the class out to her garden; other days it meant she led them into the woods. That morning it meant that before being set loose in the greenhouse, the Mothers had all been given a copy of *Cunningham's Encyclopedia of Magical Herbs.* They were supposed to use it to identify each of the plants mentioned in the brew.

"I found white willow!" Vivian announced, only a few minutes after Lally finished explaining the assignment. The rest of the Mothers were all still sitting at their tables, studying their textbooks, when Vivian marched up with the bark in hand. "I won't tell you where I found it, though," she said to Grace and Shelly. "So don't bother asking."

"Already?" Grace replied, as Vivian placed her piece of bark on the table.

"Keep an eye on this," she instructed Oona, then she left to find the next herb on the list.

Grace wobbled off her stool. "Come on, Shelly. I guess we better start looking."

"Looking?" Shelly repeated, without glancing up.

"Yeah," Grace said. "We've got to find the bark and the feverfew and the rest of it. I think I have a pretty good idea where the devil's claw might be."

Shelly nodded, but she didn't move. She was turning the pages of her book, but it was clear that she wasn't actually studying the material. She was just staring off into space.

"Shelly?" Grace asked.

"Do you need help?" Oona offered. She pushed back from her

own table and nearly tripped on a jasmine vine. During the offseason, that part of the conservatory was primarily used for storing climbing plants—lobelia and dichondra, clematis and moonflower—but during the busy season, the Summer Session, those plants were all moved to the sides of the room. Or at least, their pots were. It could be difficult to contain the actual plants' serpentine growth.

"Shelly," Oona said, once she'd regained her footing.

She placed her hand on Shelly's upper back, and at last Shelly blinked. "What's wrong?" she asked, turning toward Oona. "Are you okay, honey?"

"I'm fine," Oona said, though the truth was that she did feel sick. It was a combination of the humidity level in the conservatory and the room's jungle smell—loamy, like blood and wet earth. "What about you?" Oona asked. "Are you tired? You were zoning out there pretty hard."

"I found devil's claw!" they heard Vivian crow from the next room over.

Shelly smiled at Oona. "I'm okay," she said, but she didn't turn her attention back to her book. Instead, her gaze slid off to the left and seemed to land on another table of Mothers: two women who looked like they could have been Shelly's cousins. They had the same thick dark lashes, the same aquiline nose. Well, maybe that was the problem, thought Oona. Maybe Shelly was homesick.

She hadn't noticed anything was wrong at first, but a few weeks earlier she'd caught Shelly loitering outside the infirmary, pacing and chewing on her nails. And not long after, she'd seen her sprint out of the lodge. At the time, she'd assumed Shelly had gotten bad news. Though the Center didn't do a ton of testing, they did make exceptions. Especially if a Mother requested it, which Oona thought Shelly, being a doctor, was likely to do.

Vivian wasn't concerned—she thought maybe Shelly was just growing impatient with the Center's practices—but Grace worried she might be depressed. For her part, Oona didn't know what to believe. Shelly didn't seem sad, necessarily, but she did seem different— almost as if she'd given up.

"Where's Gemma?" Shelly asked, before Oona could return to her seat.

Gemma was the only person at the Center Shelly still seemed to care about. She asked after her countless times each day. It had seemed normal at first. Gemma *was* their roommate, so it only made sense that Shelly would sometimes wonder where she was. But ever since Oona had told Shelly what happened in Port Marrow—described how Gemma had tried to run away—Shelly's curiosity had blossomed into something closer to fixation. She searched for her in the dining hall each morning at breakfast, checked for her in the room she shared with Oona every night. Vivian guessed it was because Shelly's mothering instincts were kicking in, but Oona didn't think that made much sense. After all, Oona was the only one of them sure to become a mother. So if anyone had instincts kicking in, shouldn't it have been her?

Still, she supposed it was nice the way Shelly worried. She liked imagining that if she started acting funny, Shelly would fuss over her the same way—that she would notice if Oona stopped showing up for meals or woke up one day more short-tempered than usual, all the things she had once relied upon Jacob to note. Without him around, it was comforting to feel like someone was watching out for her. In her better moments, the knowledge actually helped Oona feel more at peace with her decision to trade Portland for Bare Root. *See?* she argued with Jacob in her head. *Isn't this better for us both?* She'd found the community, the *sisterhood*, that she'd been searching for, and he'd been granted a summer's reprieve, time away from being her sole caretaker, her keeper.

If only she'd found that same sisterhood among her mother's coven, rather than just with her new friends. But unlike Grace and Shelly and Vivian, the other witches in her mother's coven didn't seem to like Oona very much, let alone care enough about her to worry over her skipping meals. Lally loved her, sure. And Joyce tolerated her. But Donna didn't seem remotely interested in getting to know her as an adult. Meanwhile, Carol flat-out resented her existence, and Alice refused to even look her in the eye.

"I found feverfew!" Vivian cried, as she hurried up to Shelly and Grace's table. "I can start working on the tonic now, Oona, right?"

Stepping away from Grace and Shelly, Oona turned to examine the flower Vivian had brought her. She held her hand out for the clipping, and then brought the blossom to her nose. "Sweet," she said. "So not feverfew. Sorry."

Vivian frowned and picked up her copy of Cunningham's encyclopedia. Clearly irritated, she turned each page with force. "Look," she said, when she'd found the entry for feverfew. She tapped the page with one long fingernail. "Look. It's right here."

Oona smirked. It was wrong, she knew, but she couldn't help but take some delight in getting to correct Vivian. She loved the fact that she didn't even have to scan the page. "This," she said, trying and failing to keep the smugness out of her voice, "is chamomile. It's a kind of daisy, just like feverfew, so they look very similar. They both have yellow centers and white petals, but feverfew has a flat top. And it smells bitter. Here"—she held the flower back out to Vivian—"smell."

Reluctantly, Vivian sniffed. Her frowned deepened. "Sweet," she admitted.

Oona reached for Vivian's book. Under each hand-drawn illustration of an herb or flower, there was a description and list of possible uses. She was flipping quickly, searching for chamomile, intending to show Vivian the difference, when her eye caught on the image of a flower that looked familiar. She thought she recognized its spiky leaves, its long stem. But it wasn't basket flower, like she'd thought at first. It was milk thistle. The same flower she'd used, albeit dried and ground up, in the medicine she'd made for Gemma.

Suddenly an idea occurred to her—an idea so simple, so obvious, she wondered why she hadn't thought of it before. If Lally had written down the ingredients for the potion they'd used to treat Daphne's preeclampsia, then maybe she'd also written down something about the potion that Oona had made Daphne drink inside the cave. After all, it was Lally Oona had run to when Daphne woke up dizzy with a splitting headache, when she puked halfway through their hike back up the cliffs. Surely, when presented with a sick patient, Lally would have asked exactly what Daphne had ingested, and surely Oona would have remembered the ingredients at the time.

It wasn't as good as finding the book itself, but it was a start, Oona thought. If Lally had written down the complete list of ingredients in the potion, then maybe that would help narrow down the list of possible draughts. And that, in turn, might lead them to the ritual.

Still, after so much disappointment, Oona was afraid to be wrong. More than that, she was impatient. She didn't want to wait for class to be over to ask Lally to check Daphne's file. So without bothering to find the entry for chamomile, Oona closed Vivian's book. "Bitter," she said, distracted. "You want bitter. It'll be in the same area you found this, though." She handed the chamomile flower back to Vivian, then turned and walked toward the front of the room, to where Lally was sitting at her own table, yea-ing or naying the other Mothers' finds.

Oona managed to wait until Lally finished explaining the differences between cat's claw and devil's claw to an older Mother, though she supposed she didn't do a very good job of disguising her sense of urgency, because when Lally was done she asked, "Is something wrong?"

"I have a headache," Oona said, which wasn't even a lie. "I think I need a glass of water."

"You should go to the dining hall, then. The water there is better, it's filtered."

Oona nodded. This, of course, she already knew. "I'll be right back," she said.

"Do you want me to go with you?" Lally offered.

"No, thanks. I'll be all right."

Lally pursed her lips, and her gaze ran the length of Oona's body. She was inspecting her for any other signs of distress. "You're sure?"

"I'll be back in fifteen minutes."

"Okay, then," Lally said, and she turned her attention to the next Mother in line.

O  utside, Oona followed the path to the dining hall only as far as could be seen from the greenhouse. She cut back through the woods as soon as she'd rounded the bend.

Her mother was away, she knew. There had been an announcement at breakfast: Ursula wouldn't be giving her usual afternoon lecture because she needed to visit a patient in town. Virgie Clark, who had a child just a few years younger than Oona, was somehow pregnant again and expecting twins. Oona wasn't sure when her mother would be back, but she figured she had at least an hour, and she didn't think it would take even half that long to break in. She knew where Lally hid the spare keys to the infirmary—under a loose shingle in the side of the building, five rows from the bottom—and she knew in which cabinet Daphne's file was stored. All she had to do was be quick with her snooping, and she'd always been good at that. Even seven months pregnant, she made sure to step lightly up the front steps and down the hall. She eased the file room door open so it wouldn't whine or squeak, and instead of turning on the lights, she used her phone's flashlight. Within a few minutes she was seated at the table in the center of the file room, reading about Daphne's mid-pregnancy height and weight, the results of her first urine test at the Center, and her experiences with carpal tunnel syndrome.

Of course, she could have flipped right to the back of the file. If Lally had recorded any notes about the day Oona had brought in Daphne, that's where they would be. But despite her eagerness, and the time crunch she was under, Oona still found herself reading each page slowly, line by line. She wasn't sure why, but in recent weeks every time she experienced a new symptom she found herself wondering if, when *she* was pregnant, Daphne had felt the same thing.

At the time, Oona had been so jealous of Daphne's pregnancy—of the way it brought her closer to Ursula and the coven—that she hadn't bothered to ask Daphne much about how it felt. Assuming Oona was right and Daphne had gotten knocked up on purpose, in hopes that becoming a mother would allow her access to Bare Root, then it seemed entirely possible that she had harbored some of the same fears that Oona was now struggling with. Maybe she'd even asked herself the same questions, once upon a time. Questions like: *I think I want this, but can I really do it?* Questions like: *Am I too greedy, too selfish, too broken to be the kind of mother I want to be?*

Did all mothers-to-be feel so unsure of themselves? Oona wanted to ask Daphne. Did they all worry about their motivations? Their values? Their sense of morality? Did they all feel a dark pulse in their blood?

Had Daphne?

Well, if she had, then there was no record of it. Oona read through every page in the file, but there were no mentions of Daphne confessing to feeling nervous, no notes about her expressing any anxieties or fears. Disappointed, Oona flipped back to the beginning of the file, intending to read through it one more time, closely, but she got only halfway through the first page before she remembered the real reason she'd broken in. She turned back to the final page and was relieved to see handwriting she recognized instantly as Lally's. In an entry dated August 1, Lally had recorded Daphne's temperature (*99.6— elevated, perhaps, but not quite a fever*); the presentation of her pupils (*dilated, black*); and a list of symptoms (*headache, nausea, dizziness*). Oona felt her own heart rate kick up as she read. *More*, she thought. *I need more.* And then there it was: a final note scrawled at the bottom. *Patient ingested . . .*

Before she could read any further, Oona closed her eyes. She'd found it. At last, the recipe for the potion. Or had it been poison? She took a deep breath. Either way, it was time to find out.

She opened her eyes again and continued reading. *Patient ingested a mixture of mugwort and aster, valerian root, and asphodel.*

With a sigh of relief, Oona sat back in her chair. Herbs. Simple herbs. Just like she'd always claimed. Potion, not poison.

"Valerian root, mugwort, aster, and . . ." Oona peered back at the file to remind herself of the final ingredient, but when she scanned the page she noticed that Lally's August 1 memo was not the only late addition to Daphne's report. There was another note, dated not long after the birth. A record of the baby's death, added by Ursula, Oona assumed, given the tight nature of the script. But what was strange was not the final diagnosis—stillbirth—it was what came before. A documentation of the baby's vitals, written in pencil, by Lally. For a long moment, Oona studied the specifics on the page, the measurements of the baby's heart rate and muscle tone, the success of her respiratory efforts, the color of her skin.

Instinctively, she understood what it meant, but it was hard to believe, hard to really wrap her head around—though the truth was there, written plain as day. Daphne had been right. The baby *had* lived, at least for a few minutes. Long enough for Lally to listen to her heartbeat, anyway. And long enough for everyone in the room to hear her cry.

Daphne had heard her daughter cry.

And Ursula had lied about it—to Daphne, to Oona, to the Tanakas. She'd insisted—all those long months while Daphne raged—that the baby had been stillborn. She'd even marked it down in her file, though the record above clearly stated otherwise.

Why?

Lost in her thoughts, Oona held the pages in her hands until she heard footsteps in the hallway. She tried to hide the file, but Lally appeared in the doorway before she could.

"Oh," Oona breathed, relieved. "It's just you. I thought you were my mom."

"What are you doing in here?" Lally asked. "You told me you'd be back. *Fifteen minutes*, you said."

Oona swallowed the guilt she felt like a knot in her throat. "Has it been much longer than that?" she asked, knowing that if Lally was there, searching, time must have gotten away from her.

"It's been more than an hour," Lally said. "Class let out, and I started feeling worried. But how did you get in?"

Oona pulled the spare key from her pocket and Lally clucked softly. "Your mother always said you were sneaky."

Oona shrugged. "I couldn't wait."

"Your head hurt that badly, did it?" Lally looked concerned.

"No, my head's okay."

"What was so urgent, then?" Lally asked, and Oona watched as her gaze began to rove around the room.

"This," Oona said, holding up the file.

Behind her glasses, Lally squinted, then reached to turn on the room's overhead light. "What is that?" she asked as they both blinked, waiting for their eyes to adjust.

"Daphne's file. I don't know why I didn't think of it before. I came to you after Daphne got sick. And you gave her something to make her feel better. So I thought, maybe, you'd written it down."

Lally stepped closer, eyeing the file in Oona's hands. "And did I?" she asked, hopefully.

Oona couldn't keep the smile from her face when she said, "You did." Opening the file again, she turned to the final page and read out the list of ingredients. "Apparently, whatever I gave her had valerian root in it. And mugwort and aster."

"Mugwort and aster . . ." Lally repeated, as she pulled out the chair next to Oona.

"And asphodel," Oona added, once she'd sat down. She pushed the folder toward Lally. "See?"

But Lally didn't move to pull the file any closer. She just stared at it for a long moment, as if she were suddenly afraid the pages might burst into flames. "Asphodel?" she said. "Are you quite sure?"

"Yes," Oona said, though looking at Lally's face nearly caused her to doubt her memory. It might've just been a trick of the light, but she thought Lally looked pale. "Is that bad?"

"No," Lally said, though she didn't sound entirely convincing. "But it is uncommon. They say asphodel was the flower Persephone was picking before Hades kidnapped her, so it's typically only used in rituals pertaining to the underworld."

"Well . . ." Oona said, and Lally's face fell.

"Oh, Oona. What did you do?"

"Nothing," Oona said, defensive. But of course they both knew that wasn't true.

They were told that the baby, as her file said, had been stillborn, but Daphne had sworn that she'd heard her daughter cry, sworn that she'd gazed into her wet brown eyes, sworn that she'd held her to her breast and felt her suckle. And that belief, it quickly drove her mad. For weeks, she didn't eat, didn't sleep. She hardly spoke, except to call out for her daughter. Jacob and Oona took turns holding vigils outside her bedroom door. On Jacob's days, he mostly just sat on the floor, reading aloud from the book he'd found about postpartum depression. But Oona wasn't as patient. She'd begged Daphne to tell her how she could help. For a long time, though, Daphne insisted there wasn't anything she could do. It was only Ursula—Ursula was the one who'd taken her daughter, so Ursula was the one who would know how to get her back. As May bled into June and Daphne finally rose from bed, she started making daily pilgrimages to the Center. Every day, when Oona got home from school, she would find Daphne there, camped outside the doors to the infirmary. "Where is she?" she would scream, whenever either Ursula or Lally passed. But for their parts, neither Ursula nor Lally ever rebuked her. Though she disturbed the other Mothers, they never called her parents or the cops. "She's grieving," Lally would say, whenever Oona expressed her disbelief. "Just give her time. It'll pass."

But it didn't pass. Instead, it transformed. After Jacob graduated and school let out, Daphne shifted her focus from Ursula to Oona. "If your mother won't help me," she said, "then maybe you will. You have powers. I know you do. You can help me find my baby."

"Find her where?" Oona had asked, as gently as she could. "She's gone, Daphne."

"No, she's not. I know she's not."

"She is," Oona insisted. And then she said the four words she would learn to regret most. "She's in the underworld."

"How do you know?"

"Because that's where we all go when we die."

"Then I'll go there."

"Daphne."

"I'll bring her back."

"You can't."

"You'll help me. I know you will. Please, Oona."

*But I don't have powers. But I haven't inherited my mother's magic. But no goddess has ever appeared to me.* These were just some of the excuses Oona should have given Daphne, confessions that she should have made. Only she didn't.

That night, while Ursula was out teaching a class on childbirth, Oona snuck into her bedroom. There were hundreds of books on the shelves—the displacement of which Ursula might not have noticed easily—but for whatever reason Oona felt herself drawn to the book already open on her mother's altar. It seemed to carry with it the smell of the sea. Though maybe Daphne's shell was to blame for that. Oona noticed that the mussel shell she'd chosen from her mother's basket was still present on the altar, as were a few of the other Mothers' things: a charm from a bracelet Oona could remember one of them wearing, a birth announcement card Ursula had been sent in the mail, a stack of Mrs. Cook's medical records.

Since it was the first time she'd ever gotten her hands on a grimoire, Oona was tempted to go slow, to hold the leather cover up to her nose and inhale its briny perfume, to fan through the age-worn edges of the long-grain cardstock, but she knew she didn't have much time. So instead, she skimmed, searching for any mention of the underworld. When she found a ritual she thought might work, she copied its directions onto her hand.

They waited until the night of August 1 because the book said the ritual needed to be performed during a full moon—and because August 1 was Lughnasadh, another of the eight sabbats, so Oona knew that Ursula would be preoccupied, performing her own ritual with the Mothers down at the beach. They chose the cave at the base of the cliffs because even before she'd figured out her grounding practice, Oona had known that she felt most powerful by the sea. And despite all her doubts, she was still hoping that the ritual might work, that she might really be able to help Daphne.

She hadn't anticipated the cold. Late summer, but there was a storm brewing on the horizon, set to make landfall later that night, so the water was all churned up, the waves white-capped and frothy; and the rock that made up the cave's walls, ceiling, and floor had likely never seen sun, so it was icy beneath the thin soles of their sandals. When Oona spread a blanket out for Daphne to lie down on, she shivered from the chill.

Around the blanket, per the ritual's instructions, Oona lit the candles she'd stolen from her mother's stash. Outside, they could hear the storm approaching, the thunder's roll and rumble, the waves' roaring crash. Oona gave Daphne the potion she'd put together in the greenhouse only a few hours earlier—a concoction meant to bring on a sleep so deep it looked like death. She watched while Daphne chugged it down, then gagged.

"You have to drink all of it," Oona reminded her. "Then lie back and place these on your eyes." She handed Daphne the only coins she'd been able to dig up—a tarnished penny and a dented quarter. "Don't fight it," she coached, when the potion took hold and Daphne thrashed.

It was only once she was sure Daphne was asleep—asleep and not dead; she knew because she'd checked—that Oona attempted to ground herself and cast her circle, call in her ancestors and raise energy. Then she spoke the words she'd copied first onto her hand and then later onto a piece of paper. Not that she really knew what she was saying. She hadn't spent much time studying the spell. She'd just written it down, then subbed in Daphne's name and her missing baby. She prayed to Hekate, because that was what the ritual said to do. She asked her to lead Daphne to the underworld to bring back her daughter, much the same way she'd once led Demeter to retrieve Persephone. Then she waited for Daphne to wake up.

Looking back, Oona didn't know exactly what she'd expected would happen—she hadn't had a good idea of what it would look like if the ritual actually worked. Had she really thought she would look down and find Daphne lying on the floor of the cave with a baby beside her? No, she supposed she hadn't. But she'd thought, at least, the ritual might bring Daphne some kind of peace. She'd hoped, perhaps, that in the underworld, Daphne would be reunited with her daughter, that she would finally get the chance to say goodbye. When Daphne woke, though, she didn't look contented. She looked despondent. She woke frantic, gasping, like Oona had been holding her underwater all that time.

"It didn't work." That was the first thing she said, and Oona felt her heart sink.

"Are you sure? What happened? What did you see?"

"Nothing. Just nothing. I didn't make it. She didn't take me. Hekate. She didn't take me to the underworld."

"I'm sorry," Oona said, but it wasn't enough and they both knew it. Still, it was the only thing she could think to say. So she repeated it: when Daphne tried to stand and ended up down on her knees, her head aching; when they hiked back up the cliffs and Daphne had to stumble off into the brush to puke; when she ended up back in an infirmary bed with an IV because Oona finally confessed to Lally, and later her mother, about the potion but not the ritual. "I'm sorry. I'm so sorry."

"It's okay. It's not your fault. We'll try again." That's what Daphne had said.

But in the end, there hadn't been time. Before Oona could return to Ursula's book, before she could attempt another spell or potion, Hekate had come for Daphne. She'd lured her out into the sea.

In the file room, Oona looked at Lally. "The ritual," she said. "I asked Hekate to bring Daphne to the underworld, just like she brought Demeter."

Lally nodded, once and slowly, as if the movement caused her pain. "I think I know the book," she said. "Come with me."

Oona resisted asking Lally any questions as she followed her across the Center grounds, but when they came to a stop outside the Bare Root office building, she hesitated. "Mom's office?" she asked. "No. The book isn't in there. I already looked."

"Not everywhere," Lally said cryptically. Then she pushed open the front door.

By the time Oona caught up with her again, Lally had already entered Ursula's office. For a moment, Oona considered whether she could get away with waiting out in the hall. Her mother would be back soon, after all. And if she found them in her office, snooping, there'd be hell to pay. She'd probably even kick Oona out.

It didn't take long, though, before her curiosity got the better of her. Through the open door, she heard the telltale sound of a desk drawer being opened and right away she thought of the mysterious false-bottom drawer.

"What's in there?" she asked, when she stepped inside the room.

Lally already had the drawer pulled out, the wooden slat laid atop the desktop, and she was digging through whatever Ursula kept in the secret space underneath.

"It's like a kind of safe," Lally explained. "We keep instruments of dark magic in here, things that could be dangerous if they fell into the wrong hands."

"Not much of a safe, if you can just break in," said Oona.

Lally looked up, her gaze newly sharp. "You can't be telling her I'm showing you," she said. "You understand that, don't you, love?"

"Wait, what?" Oona asked. She glanced behind her, nervous suddenly.

"Oona," Lally sighed. She pinched the bridge of her nose with two fingers. "Love, if I'm right about which book you used, and I think I am, then all of this"—she gestured around herself—"all of this is my fault."

"What do you mean?"

"A few days before you performed your ritual, your mother asked me to draw up a potion. It's called the Lazarus Draught."

"So?" Oona asked.

"So," said Lally, "it was from a book that normally we keep under lock and key. I must have put it back on her altar by mistake, instead of returning it to this drawer."

Oona stepped toward the desk and attempted to peer into the exposed drawer. "The book is in there?" she asked.

"Yes," said Lally. Then, "Do you want to see?"

In response, Oona moved around the desk to stand by Lally's side.

"This," said Lally, removing a small sackcloth bag, "is bone dust. And these"—she held up a jar—"are baby teeth. This is a culture from Mamie Cadden's ergot," she said, lifting another small, sealed jar from the drawer, "and this is a cutting of the rope used to hang the midwife Margaret Jones in 1648."

"In Salem?" Oona asked.

Lally shook her head. "Charlestown. Boston." Pulling out two small, straw-bodied dolls, she continued. "Have you ever seen these before? These are called poppets. You can use them to direct your Craft." Lally held one of the dolls out toward Oona. "Do you want to touch?"

With a small shudder, Oona shook her head. Truth be told, she was tempted. She could feel the power of all those talismans in the air. A reverberation, like a plucked string. But she didn't dare. "And the book?" she asked instead.

Lally turned her attention back to the drawer. "We keep the grimoires down at the bottom," she said, as she removed what looked like a rusted railroad spike and a blood-flecked handkerchief, a stack of yellowed tarot cards and a slim red notebook, with a hand-drawn rune on the cover that Oona thought she recognized but could not name. It looked like a gate, maybe, or a ladder.

"Here," Lally said, removing a sheaf of half-burnt papers. "Take these, will you? But keep them together."

Oona turned and placed the stack on top of a nearby cabinet, then she returned to the desk. There was something about the symbol on the notebook that had snagged her attention. While Lally continued searching, it came to her: Daphne's file. She'd seen the same symbol drawn on the tab of Daphne's file in the infirmary.

"Hey, Lally," Oona said. "Do you know what this symbol means?"

Lally looked up, confused. "What symbol?" she asked.

Oona pointed and Lally seemed to still. The muscles around her mouth tightened. "Oh, I'm sure I don't know," she said carefully. "Part of your mother's coding system, no doubt."

"Coding system?" Oona repeated, as she reached for the notebook. "Coding for what?"

"For the Mothers," Lally said, plucking up the notebook before Oona could lay hands on it. "We've had all kinds of different systems over the years, to keep track of who had what complications during pregnancy or during labor. I'm not sure what it's doing here, though. It's meant to be kept in the file room." Lally returned the notebook to the drawer. "I'll have to tell Ursula it's been misplaced. Anyway, it doesn't matter. I've already found what it is we need."

"Really?" Oona asked. "Are you sure?"

"I'm sure," said Lally.

And once Lally placed the book on the desktop, Oona was sure too. It was something about the smell of the book. The chill in the air around it. The way just looking at it brought the taste of salt to her tongue. In that moment, she could remember it clearly: how she'd knelt before her mother's altar, how it had felt to scrawl the ritual's directions onto her palm.

"It was toward the end," she said, as Lally began turning pages.

"I think I know the one. Was it . . . ?" Lally passed her the book, using her pointer finger to indicate a ritual, handwritten in ink, on one of the book's final pages.

*Blessed Hekate, Great Mother, to You I pray,*

*I honor You as the Gatekeeper of the Underworld*
*As She who resides at the Threshold,*
*As She who guards the Doorway,*
*As She who holds the Keys.*

*O, Torch Bearer,*
*Lead me the way You once led fair Demeter.*
*Guide me in my search for my child.*
*Grant me safe passage,*
*And bring me safe return.*

*Hail Hekate, Queen of the Witches,*
*On the night of this full moon, I offer to You*
*Like Demeter before me,*
*My sacred blood,*
*My womb.*

*Hail Hekate, Queen of the Underworld,*
*Who heard Persephone when no one else did.*
*Hail Hekate, Queen of the Middle World,*
*Who guided the maiden back to the earth*
*Creating the seasons.*
*Hail Hekate, Queen of the Upper World,*
*Return to me as the wheel of the year turns.*
*As You guided Persephone,*
*Deliver me from darkness.*

*Hail Hekate.*
*Hail Hekate.*
*Hail Hekate.*

When she was done reading, Oona sat and stared at the page for a long time. There it was, in black and white: the reason why she kept miscarrying. Because, like Demeter before her, she'd offered up to Hekate her sacred blood, her womb.

So it wasn't Daphne's curse, then, but Hekate's.

"Fuck," she heard herself breathe.

Lally took the book and spun it around so she could read it. "And this is what you recited, word for word. You're sure?"

"I asked her to help Daphne, not me, but otherwise, yes. I think so."

"This is bad, Oona," she said, as if Oona didn't already know.

"I thought it was Daphne," Oona said, still stunned. "I thought she was punishing me for screwing up the ritual. For failing to bring back her baby."

"I'm sorry, love," Lally said, and at first Oona thought she was trying to console her, but then she continued. "There isn't any counter-ritual for this."

"What?"

"This ritual, it isn't really a ritual. It's more like a deal. You struck a bargain with Hekate. You offered her something in exchange for a favor. And did she do as you asked? Did she lead Daphne to the underworld?"

Reluctantly, Oona nodded. "She took her," she said. Because *led* sounded too gentle, even fifteen years later. There had been nothing gentle about Daphne's fall, or about the way the surf had pummeled her soft body.

Lally tapped the open book. "The only way to get Hekate to change the terms of your deal, Oona, is for you to suggest a new arrangement."

"A new arrangement?"

"You need to get her to agree to renegotiate your deal. You need to offer her something else."

"Like what?"

"I can't tell you that, love. But it has to be something important, something of equal value."

"Something as important as my fertility?" Oona asked, incredulous.

"Yes," Lally said.

# TEN

Oona was exhausted. It had been a long day, preceded by a long week. The night before, she'd stayed up past midnight working on her potion, and that morning she'd awoken at four to start again. She knew she needed to rest. Everything hurt: her knees, her back, her hips; even her wrists felt tired. But she didn't have time to take a break. Oona had always known that she would be protected by Lally's spell only until she went into labor, but now apparently she didn't even have that long. After they'd found the book, Lally had told her that if she hoped to commune with Hekate, she would need to perform the ritual during a full moon, and the next full moon was set to occur on the night of Lughnasadh, which was only ten days away. They had to be ready by then.

Of course, that meant Oona had to figure out what kind of sacrifice she planned to offer up in exchange for her fertility, but it also meant that she had to prepare the same potion she'd given to Daphne, the so-called Lazarus Draught.

The recipe for the potion had been written in Lally's grimoire on the page opposite the ritual. Like Lally had noted in Daphne's file, it called for a concoction of mugwort and aster, valerian root and dried asphodel. Luckily, Lally had all the ingredients they would need there in the greenhouse. Along with the asphodel, which she'd become something of an expert at cultivating—she'd learned it grew best in a gravel pot—Lally also grew whole troughs of mugwort and aster, and had planted row after row of valerian in the woods. But as Oona soon learned, producing the Lazarus Draught wasn't nearly as simple as preparing Gemma's medicine had been. The valerian had to be harvested, dried, and turned into an oil. The mugwort had to be steeped and the aster had to be steamed. And the asphodel was the most complicated of all. Once the flower heads had been successfully dried out, Oona would need to extract a seed with careful precision and then split it open with what looked to her like a surgical knife.

Every day for the past week she had practiced the seed extraction with Lally, but each time something had gone wrong: she'd moved too quickly or too slowly; she'd been too careful or not careful enough. Earlier that week, her hand had slipped and she'd accidentally butchered the head she was working on. It had taken a few days to prepare another, but by noon on the last Friday in July they were ready to try again.

"Easy," Lally warned her, as she approached the new flower head with a set of tweezers. They were in the greenhouse, bent over the same enamel-top table Oona had sat at with Vivian only days before. It was a hot day, even for late July, and as the sun beat down on them through the glass overhead, Oona could feel a bead of sweat dripping down the back of her neck, rolling between her shoulder blades. Putting down the tweezers, she rubbed her palms dry on her apron front.

"Are you okay, love?" Lally asked. She was sweating too. Every few minutes, she had to push her glasses back up the bridge of her nose, use a handkerchief to mop her hairline. "If you need to take a break . . ."

Oona shook her head and picked up the tweezers again. Best as she could remember, she hadn't bothered to extract a single seed last time, she'd just thrown the flower in whole. No wonder Daphne had gotten so sick. She couldn't afford to be so careless this time. There was too much at stake. Her Craft, of course. And also her unborn child. Her daughter. "What if I can't do this?" she asked, tweezers poised in midair above the flower head.

"Just go easy," Lally said again, so Oona worked to relax her mind. *Easy.* She'd never been easy in her life, but she supposed that was the point, wasn't it? To be a mother, she needed to be different. She needed to be better. Patient, generous, kind.

"Easy," she whispered, then she sucked in a breath and exhaled slowly. As she approached the flower head, her hand began to shake. At the very last second, she squeezed her eyes closed, and when she opened them she saw it: clasped between the two prongs of her tweezers, a single seed.

Lally hissed with pleasure and ushered Oona toward the other end of the table, where they already had a magnifying glass set up. "Just one long incision," she said, handing Oona a sharpened scalpel.

Before she could hesitate again, Oona cut into the seed.

"That's it!" Lally exclaimed. "That's it. You've done it."

Dropping the tweezers onto the tabletop, Oona realized that for the past few minutes she'd forgotten to breathe. She could feel her pulse beating in her ears. "You're sure?" she asked. "I'm done?"

"Well, there's still the valerian root to add, but you're done with the asphodel as soon as you add that seed to the mixture."

For a moment, Oona stared down at her work. When she'd first discovered the ingredients for the potion listed in Daphne's file she'd felt hopeful, maybe even a little proud, but in the week since, she'd begun to despair again. In so many ways, this process felt like a test—like a crucible she needed to pass in order to prove herself worthy of motherhood and its gift of Craft—and for weeks, months, years now, she'd felt like she was failing: failing to conceive, failing to keep her babies alive, failing to deliver them, healthy and whole and wailing, into the world. But now . . . now here was her potion, nearly complete.

Reaching for her belly, Oona half expected to feel some wriggle of movement, some acknowledgment of what she'd just managed to pull off, but like usual she felt nothing. Still, it didn't sour her mood. She was relieved, yes, and optimistic for the first time in weeks, but more than that, she felt powerful. She felt like the kind of woman who could actually drink from this potion to summon Hekate; the kind of mother who would lay down her life, at least for a few moments, for her child. She felt like Demeter. She felt like Daphne.

While Lally watched, she added the seed to her glass jar, where the rest of her potion was already steeping. In the next room, she had the valerian root curing in alcohol. It would be ready by the following morning and then she would need only to strain it. For now, though, there was nothing left to do.

She could rest.

As if able to read Oona's mind, Lally put a hand on her shoulder. "Go home, love," she said. "Get off your feet. Take a nap."

"I might just do that," Oona said, as she removed her apron and handed it to Lally. Technically, it should have been her job to do the cleaning up. She was the assistant, after all. But her heels were throbbing, and her swollen ankles pulsed. She could practically hear the siren call of her little bed waiting for her. "You're sure you don't mind?" she asked.

"I'm sure," Lally said, then she shooed Oona out of the conservatory and down the long dim hall to the greenhouse's front door.

"Thank you," Oona said before she stepped out into the light again, into the heat of the day.

As she made her way across the Center grounds, Oona had only one thing on her mind: sleep. Already she could feel herself drifting, her limbs going slack.

Too slack.

She tripped over a tree root just as the path she was following opened up onto the infirmary. She hadn't realized it at first, but she'd gone the wrong way. She needed to turn around.

"Let go of me!" a woman shrieked, and Oona stopped mid-pivot.

As it was, she knew she would have only about an hour to nap before someone came to fetch her for lunch, so she was tempted to ignore whatever she'd heard, but before she even had a chance to make a decision one way or the other, she heard the same voice again.

"I said *let go*!" the woman cried. And then there were the unmistakable sounds of a scuffle.

Oona resigned herself to getting involved. With a sigh, she headed toward the infirmary, imagining she would need to break up some kind of fight. In the past, she'd witnessed Mothers squabbling over all kinds of so-called injustices: the way the Initiates played favorites during classes, all the various treatments—Reiki, acupuncture, massage; once, she'd even seen a Mother rip out a chunk of another Mother's hair because she claimed that during the Beltane ceremony Ursula had spent longer with her fingers pressed to that Mother's brow.

So when she pulled open the infirmary doors, Oona wasn't surprised to discover two women locked in battle. She wasn't even particularly surprised to see that one of those two women was Vivian. No, what surprised her was recognizing Shelly, which she was only able to do once the two women finally stumbled apart. Never in a million years would she have expected to find Shelly caught up in a catfight. Vivian, sure. She could've guessed Vivian fought dirty. But Shelly? No. Never. No way. Shelly was too sensible, too mature. And yet . . . there she was: her locs tousled, a sheen of sweat glazing both her forehead and her chest.

"What's going on?" Oona asked, stunned.

Vivian held up one of her arms, displaying two red, raised scratch marks running down the length of her forearm. Haughtily, she declared, "I'm going to sue."

Oona looked at Shelly in disbelief and waited for an explanation.

Instead, it was Grace who spoke up. Oona hadn't even realized she was there, hidden among the shadows. "We were looking for bug spray when we caught her."

"When *I* caught her," Vivian corrected.

"Caught who?" Oona asked. "Doing what?"

"Caught Shelly." Vivian pointed dramatically across the infirmary's small foyer. "She'd broken into the file room and was poking around."

"The file . . ." Oona glanced down the hall. She was so sleep-deprived, she felt like she was underwater, but then memories began to surface like air bubbles. The footsteps in the hall outside her mother's office, Shelly pacing in front of the infirmary. Oona looked at Shelly.

"It's not what you think," Shelly said.

"I'm not sure *what* to think," said Oona. "But that doesn't matter. I'm going to get my mother."

"No!" Shelly cried.

"Watch out!" Vivian called. She lifted her injured arm again. "When I told her I was going to report her, this is what she did."

"I'm sorry," Shelly said, looking at Vivian's arm and wincing. She looked genuinely remorseful. "I didn't mean to hurt you, Vivian. I just—I can't get sent home yet."

"Yet?" Oona asked.

Shelly pinched her lips shut.

Grace turned toward Oona. "I tried asking," she said in her breathy voice, "but she won't tell us why she's here."

"I don't care why she's here," Vivian said. "She broke the rules, and Ursula needs to be alerted."

Suddenly, Vivian's eyes tracked up over Oona's shoulder, and when she whipped around, Oona found Alice standing in the door-way, frowning. Like Oona, she'd likely been drawn over by all the noise.

"What do you think, Alice?" asked Grace.

In response, Alice said nothing. She never did. At least, not in the traditional sense. But still, all three women waited for her verdict.

Vivian lost her patience first. "She's never going to answer you," she said. "She doesn't talk. There's something wrong with her."

"There's nothing *wrong* with her," Oona snapped. She didn't know why it bothered her so much when people dismissed Alice. Maybe it had something to do with the expression she'd seen on Carol's face, the wincing embarrassment she'd heard in her voice when she'd told Oona that Alice was mute. After all, Oona had been that girl, too, hadn't she? The perpetual disappointment.

Alice stared at Oona for a long while, a thoughtful pinch to her brows. Then she gestured at Shelly.

"I can't," Shelly said plaintively. "You won't believe me."

"Try us," said Grace.

"Come on, Shelly," Oona said. "If you don't tell us what you were doing in the file room then I'll have to tell my mother. And I really don't want to tell my mother."

"But—" Vivian started.

"Vivian," Grace said, her voice all gentle admonishment.

Reluctantly, Vivian settled. And for a moment, all four of them were quiet. Oona watched as Shelly struggled with what to do. Then, at last, she spoke. "I was looking for a file," she said.

"Whose file?" Oona pressed.

"My sister's."

"Why? Was she a patient?"

"No." Shelly worried the skin just under her chin, squeezing it between her thumb and forefinger. "Or, I don't know. She might've been. That's what I've been trying to figure out. When she got pregnant, my sister was only sixteen. Our parents kicked her out, and a few months later she went missing. I was only a little girl at the time so it's hard for me to remember everything that happened back then, but one of her friends swears that one day, when they were hanging around by the soup kitchen, a woman approached them saying she ran a fertility clinic and liked to do pro bono work. She offered my sister free room and board, free prenatal care, free everything. All she had to do was follow her back to the island where she worked."

"And you think that island was Marrow?" asked Oona.

"Where else?" Shelly said.

"Well, have you found anything to suggest she was actually here?"

Vivian asked. Oona noticed she sounded a little defensive, as if Shelly's story had made her regret trying to report her and threatening to sue.

"No," said Shelly sadly.

Grace tutted her commiseration.

"You don't remember any program like that, do you, Oona?" Shelly asked.

Oona frowned. "The only girls I can remember my mother ever letting stay here like that were Initiates." *And Daphne*, Oona thought but did not say. "My mother must have records of past Initiates though. Have you asked her?"

"She checked her list. No Tracy."

"Tracy . . ." Oona repeated, hoping the name might jog a memory of some kind.

"Wait a second," Vivian interrupted. "Does that mean you didn't come here for treatment? You're only here to find your sister?"

Shelly cringed. "I know it was wrong. I took a spot that could have gone to a woman who really needed to be here and I'm sorry for that. Really. But there wasn't any other way. Trust me, I tried. I begged Ursula to meet with me. I told her I just had a few questions. I assured her I wouldn't take up too much of her time. But she refused. Flat-out refused. For years! Eventually, I got desperate. I was convinced Tracy had been here. But now . . ." Shelly exhaled, and her shoulders sunk. "I'm sorry I lied to you," she said, and her eyes moved across the foyer from Vivian to Oona to Grace.

"That's okay," Grace said. "We understand, Shelly. Actually." She closed her eyes. "I have a secret too."

"You do?" Shelly asked.

"You do?" echoed Vivian, with decidedly more disbelief.

"I'm not here for treatment, either," Grace confessed.

"Why are you here, then?" asked Oona.

"Well, technically I guess I *am* here for treatment, but I'm hoping it doesn't work. I don't actually want a baby. I'm—oh gosh, I'm still on the pill."

"What?" Vivian asked. "What do you mean, you're still on the pill? I thought you said you and your husband had been trying for years. Eight years, you told us."

"We have. . . ." Grace said.

"He doesn't know," finished Oona.

"I just haven't found a way to tell him," Grace said. "So I—"

"You lied," Vivian said accusingly.

Grace nodded. Guilty, she hung her head.

From her position by the doors, Oona watched Vivian for her reaction, nervous. But surprisingly, Vivian didn't say anything at first. She didn't snap or shout or threaten to report Grace to Ursula. She just stayed quiet for a long while. Then, at last, her gaze swung over to Alice. "What are you going to do?"

Oona was surprised by the concern she heard in Vivian's voice. Only minutes earlier she'd been threatening to run to Ursula herself. Now she was . . . what? Hoping for leniency?

Alice screwed up her brow and seemed to weigh her options. She studied all four of them, but Oona most of all. In fact, she stared so long Oona began to feel nervous. Sweat pricked at her underarms.

"Alice?" she prompted. "You won't tell, will you?"

"No."

Oona sighed with relief. She was so distracted by the feeling of having been spared, pardoned, that at first it didn't register that Alice hadn't simply shaken her head. She hadn't mouthed the word *no*. She'd spoken. "Alice!" she gasped.

Alice grimaced. "And that's my secret," she said. "I'm not actually mute. Not anymore. But I haven't told my mother, because she'll just credit Ursula, and I know it has nothing to do with her. It was leaving the last coven we were a part of; it was leaving High Priest Ambrose."

"You belonged to another coven before this one?" Oona asked.

"And to another one before that. My mother thought Bare Root would be different because it was a coven led by a woman . . ." Alice met Oona's eye. "You're the only one here who's ever shown me any respect."

"I'm sure that's not true," Oona said. But she wasn't sure. After all, she'd seen the way the rest of the coven looked at Alice, the way her own mother seemed to wince every time she had to explain that Alice was mute. Was that shame, Oona wondered, or regret?

She was on the verge of asking why Alice didn't just give up the act, when Vivian spoke. "I lied too," she whispered.

Shelly turned toward her. "What did you say?"

"I lied too," Vivian repeated, louder this time. She took a breath. "Albert isn't waiting for me in our penthouse on the Upper East Side. He's in Sing Sing. Tax evasion. And I'm not rich, at least not anymore. I'm broke. I sold everything I had to come here. The apartment, my jewelry, the furs. My parents have passed. I'm an only child. And I'll be lucky if Albert gets out before we're seventy. My whole family is gone. So if this doesn't work . . ." Vivian hiccupped, and it wasn't until then that Oona realized she was crying. She hadn't even known Vivian was capable of tears.

"Oh, honey," Shelly said, and when she opened her arms Vivian stepped into her hug. Like a little girl, she laid her head on Shelly's shoulder, snuffled into her collarbone. Grace rushed across the foyer to wrap her arms around them both. And then it was just Oona standing there on her own, watching, hesitant. Oona and Alice.

"What about you?" Shelly asked.

"What about me?" Oona countered.

Shelly sucked her teeth. "Come on. We've all seen you scurrying off to the greenhouse. You've spent more time there than you have at home this week. What's going on?"

Oona bit the corner of her bottom lip. Somehow it had never occurred to her that the others might notice her comings and goings, and now she felt foolish for having failed to come up with some kind of cover story. Because she definitely couldn't tell them the truth. They would think she was crazy, just like Jacob did. They would think she was evil.

"It's nothing," said Oona. "I just needed a little extra help."

"With what?" Vivian asked.

"A potion," Oona answered honestly. She hoped that might be enough, but the others just stared, waiting for her to elaborate.

When she didn't, they looked disappointed. Vivian looked angry. She shook her head in disgust.

"You'll think I've lost it," said Oona.

"What did we just say to Shelly?" Grace asked. "Try us."

Oona gnawed on that same corner of her lip. She could refuse, she knew. It was likely the smarter option, the *safer* option. But she could sense that if she walked away, there would be no going back. They would freeze her out. "The potion is called the Lazarus Draught," she said at last. "I need it to reach Hekate."

"The goddess of witchcraft?" asked Vivian.

She nodded.

"Why do you want to reach her?"

"Because I need to renegotiate our bargain."

"Your bargain?" echoed Shelly.

Oona swallowed. This was where she'd lost Jacob, the first time she'd explained what she'd done. And she knew the women before her were different from Jacob. They were there at Bare Root, after all. But it was one thing to spend the summer playing with crystals and experimenting with Reiki; it was another thing entirely to ask them to believe her when she said she'd accidentally given away her fertility and the only way she could reclaim it was by putting herself into an asphodel-induced semicoma.

"Try us," Alice said softly.

So Oona told them—about Daphne and her stillbirth, about the ritual and the cave. She even told them what Lally had said she would need to do on Lughnasadh: offer Hekate something of greater value to her than her child.

When she was done, she held her breath and waited for them to laugh at her, but surprisingly, no one did. Instead, Shelly opened her arms again, and Grace and Vivian and Alice did, too, and then the four of them just waited until Oona shuffled forward and let herself be enveloped in their embrace.

L ater, on the walk back to her cabin, Oona felt a warmth radiating through her body, and she was pretty sure it wasn't due to the sun. Her friends' response to her confession had surprised her in the best kind of way, and for the first time in a long time she felt understood and supported. She felt *seen*. Was this how her mother felt all the time? she wondered. Was this how Lally and Joyce felt? Donna? Because if this was what it felt like to be part of a coven, Oona wasn't sure how she was going to give it up. And she *would* have to give it up, at least temporarily, if she remained committed to her original plan. At the end of the Summer Session, she was supposed to return to Portland, to found her own coven somewhere closer to home. But founding her own coven would take time. Years, maybe. Possibly decades. She'd been young when her mother had first moved them to Bare Root, but she remembered the early days, when it had been just her and Ursula and Lally. They'd been lonely, she knew. And Oona would be lonely too. Hell, she'd been lonely for years, living out in the woods with Jacob. She just hadn't realized how lonely until now.

As she rounded a bend in the path and her cabin came into view, Oona felt her heart clutch. *Home*, she thought. But before she could follow that train of thought any further, her gaze snagged on a man pacing in front of the cabin's door.

It was Jacob.

Oona could hardly believe her eyes. She'd been clear, she thought, the last time she'd seen him. And if she hadn't been, then surely the many times she'd sent him straight to voicemail should've driven the message home. She wanted space. She *needed* space. And yet there he was: once again ignoring her wishes, once again refusing to do as she'd asked.

"What are you doing here?" she hissed, as soon as she was within earshot. She unlocked the door to her cabin and shoved him inside. "Are you trying to get me kicked out? You know men aren't allowed on Bare Root grounds."

"I know," Jacob said. He held up his hands like *Don't shoot*, but Oona wasn't feeling particularly violent; she just felt tired. Exhausted by the idea of having the same conversation. Again.

"What are you doing here?" she repeated, after she'd checked her bedroom for Gemma to make sure she and Jacob were really alone.

"I had to come," he said. "You stopped picking up my calls. You've been leaving all my texts on 'Read.'" He scratched at a patch of what looked like three-day-old stubble. Clearly he hadn't been sleeping, and there was a part of Oona that felt guilty seeing him looking so rough.

For a moment, she felt the urge to put her arms around him. Instead, she walked into the living room and sat down on the couch.

Jacob followed. "I need to talk to you about something," he said, as he settled onto the opposite end of the sofa. "I want us to go back to Portland."

Oona sighed. "Haven't we already had this conversation?"

"Ideally, we'd catch one of the ferries leaving tonight, but if you need more time we could probably still make it so long as we catch the 9:06 tomorrow morning."

"Make it? Make what?" Oona asked.

"Our appointment," he said. "With Dr. Berry."

"At Maine Medical Center?"

"That's right."

Oona felt her brows knit together, and though she tried, she couldn't quite keep the skepticism from her voice. "You're saying you got me an appointment? With Dr. Berry? Tomorrow?"

"Tomorrow at noon," Jacob replied. Then he frowned. "I thought you'd be excited. You've been talking about Dr. Berry for years."

That much was true. Oona had become a Dr. Berry devotee after discovering her name on one of the message boards. According to a handful of other local "survivors," Dr. Berry was single-handedly responsible for delivering their children safely into the world. For a long while Oona had been desperate to add her name to the wait list, but Jacob had always said they couldn't afford it.

"I don't understand," she said from the couch. "How? I told you, I won't take money from your parents."

"I know."

"Then how?"

Jacob exhaled slowly and ran a hand through his unkempt hair. For the first time Oona noticed that he was starting to go gray at the temples. When had that happened? she wondered. Over the summer, or before? "Dr. Berry said we couldn't waste any more time. When I told her about our history of losses, she said she needed to see you right away. She couldn't believe you'd gone this long without proper medical care."

"But I have been getting care," Oona said. "From the midwives."

"I said *proper* care. You know, like from a doctor?"

"My mother and Lally have done more for me than any doctor ever has."

"I know you think that, but they don't have medical degrees. And as grateful as you may be for the herbs Lally gave you, they've also made mistakes. Serious mistakes. Just look at Daphne."

Oona shook her head gently. "That isn't fair. They had nothing to do with what happened to Daphne. My mother barely even saw her after her delivery."

"And that's exactly my point. If she was a real doctor then she would have known that Daphne was vulnerable. She would have seen the signs, she would have realized that she was sick. And she would have been able to help her."

"How many times do I have to tell you? What happened was my fault. I performed the ritual. I invoked Hekate."

"Oh, Oona, come on. She was suffering from postpartum depression. On top of that, she'd lost her child."

"Had she?" Oona asked.

"What?"

"Had she? Do we know that for sure? Because Daphne swore up, down, and sideways—"

Immediately, Oona thought about the file. Daphne's file. And what she'd seen there. The telltale slant of Lally's script. She hadn't told Jacob what she'd discovered. Why hadn't she?

At the other end of the sofa, Jacob got to his feet. His patience was running out; Oona could sense it. He always got this way when she pushed him too far: antsy, restless. Back in Portland, he used to pace up and down the hallway each time they fought about trying again. "Just come and meet with the doctor, okay? It'll only take a few hours. And if you don't like her, then we can see somebody else. The lady at the insurance company said—"

"Insurance? What insurance?"

"I got a new job," he said. "One that comes with benefits."

"Where? Doing what?"

Jacob blinked. Suddenly, he looked sheepish.

"Doing what?" Oona asked again.

"Okay, listen. I didn't have a lot of options. Not if I wanted to get us qualified for coverage fast. Most places make you wait three months after they hire you—"

"Doing what, Jacob?"

"I'm working for my dad."

"Your *dad*? But how?" And it was only then that Oona realized she'd made a mistake. She'd assumed that Jacob had gone home after their last conversation, but instead, she now saw, he'd stayed in town. "You've been living with them," she said in horror. "Haven't you?"

"I've been *staying* with them," Jacob clarified.

Now it was Oona's turn to stand up, Oona's turn to shake her head. "I can't believe this," she muttered. "Did you not hear the way they spoke to me at Baxter's?"

"I know, but listen—"

"Your mom basically told us that she's planning to kidnap our child!"

Jacob snorted. "She isn't going to *kidnap our child*," he said. "She only asked to be allowed to see the baby."

"That is not at all what she said. Don't try to gaslight me. I was there. I heard her."

"Okay, okay." Once again, Jacob held up his hands. "Look, we've all said things we regret. Haven't we? At least they're trying. My dad got me the job, no strings attached."

Oona rolled her eyes.

"I'd really like it if you would try too," he said. "I'd like us all to put our differences aside, before the baby comes."

"Our *differences*? Are you serious?"

"Yes, I'm serious. Is that really too much to ask? They're my family, Oona."

"And Ursula is *my* family."

"It's not the same."

"Of course it is." Oona closed her eyes. "I'm not going back to Portland with you, Jacob. Not right now, anyway. I'm going to have the baby here, on Marrow. With my family."

"Oona."

"The answer is no."

"No?" Jacob scoffed. "That's it? Just *no*? After everything I—"

Oona cut him off. "Yeah, yeah, *after everything you sacrificed*. I know the speech. Spare me," she said, and then she clapped a hand over her mouth.

The two of them stared at each other in shock.

She'd never before said anything like that. Usually when he invoked his sacrifice, she just gave up, gave in. But something about learning he'd been staying with his parents had emboldened her.

"Oona . . ." Jacob started, but then he trailed off.

And for a long moment neither of them said anything more, until eventually the silence that hung between them began to feel like a presence in the room, like a shadow stood upright.

Jacob cleared his throat, but before he could try again, Oona said, "I think you should go now."

Mutely, he nodded, and she followed him to the door on the far side of the room.

At the threshold, he paused and pressed his lips to her cheek. "I love you," he said.

"I know," said Oona. But it was only after he'd gone that she realized she hadn't said *I love you too*.

And that was when she understood what she had to do. For years now she'd thought that she could never leave her marriage, because doing so would mean that she and Jacob would both end up alone. But now it seemed that Jacob had reconciled with his parents. And Oona? Well, of course there were no guarantees, but if she wanted to discover who she was once she came into her power; if she wanted to join her mother's coven and experience the kind of kinship she'd found with Shelly and Vivian, Alice and Grace; if she wanted to one day meet her child (her daughter!)—then she would have to take a chance. To join a new family, she would have to leave behind the only other family she'd ever known. She would have to sacrifice her marriage.

# ELEVEN

Lally had told her not to think of it like an audition, but to Oona's mind that's exactly what it was. Originally, the plan had been for her to perform the ritual in private, with only Lally there to serve as a guide, but when her mother had gotten wind of what she had planned, not long after Lally attempted to convince her to let Oona remain on the island, she'd insisted that she and the rest of the coven be allowed to observe. It would be a simple matter of bearing witness, Ursula said, just like it would be for any other member of the coven, but Oona didn't buy that explanation. She thought they wanted proof. Proof that she really did have power, proof that she could actually wield her Craft. After all, it was one thing to throw together a potion like she had for Gemma. It would be another thing entirely if she were able to summon the goddess of witchcraft herself.

The Center's Lughnasadh celebration was set to begin not long after sunset, which meant that Oona really should have been back at the cabin with Shelly, changing into her ceremonial whites. Instead, she was in the greenhouse, running through her ritual. She knew she couldn't afford to mess it up. And for some reason, no matter how many times she practiced, she kept tripping over the same line.

"O, Torch Bearer, lead me the way You once led fair Demeter. Guide me in . . ." Standing there in the conservatory, Oona trailed off. Guide her in what?

She reached for Lally's grimoire. "Guide me in my search for my child." Why couldn't she remember that one fucking line?

If she were able to talk to Jacob about it, she knew what he would say. *It's a mental block.* Jacob was big on mental blocks, and he thought Oona had a lot of them. It had been a thing between them in the past. He thought she needed therapy, but it was obvious to Oona that he just wanted there to be someone else whose job it was to listen to her problems. He was always trying to outsource his caretaking.

Well, he'd be free of her soon enough, wouldn't he?

And then he'd be grateful. He'd practically admitted as much at the docks, when Oona suggested that perhaps he'd made a mistake in choosing her over his family and he'd said, *Maybe, but it's too late now.*

Only it wasn't too late. They could still make other choices. *She* could still make another choice—for herself, for them both.

So really, it was a favor she was doing him, she thought, as she stood there at the table. It was a kindness, a gift, a—

Oona cut herself off mid-rant. She'd been doing that a lot lately—attempting to justify her decision—ever since their last big fight. But no one had asked her to justify it. Not Shelly, not Grace, not Alice. Certainly not Vivian. As for Lally, when Oona had told her what she planned to offer up to Hekate in exchange for her baby, Lally had said simply, "Okay."

Outside, a roll of thunder sounded. It wouldn't be long, Oona thought, until the rain began. Traditionally, the Lughnasadh feast was held down on the beach, but that day the weather report called for a storm, so Ursula had relocated the whole affair to the lodge. Well, everything but Oona's ritual, which would still need to happen at the base of the cliffs, in the cave. Lally had insisted on that. To renegotiate her bargain with Hekate, Oona would need to return to the same place where they'd originally made their deal. Never mind the fact that she hadn't allowed herself to get within a mile of those cliffs since the day she'd seen Hekate in the water, since the day they'd discovered Daphne on the shore. And never mind the realities of Oona's current condition: her unwieldly eight-months-pregnant belly, her swollen ankles and aching back. "You'll do what needs to be done," Lally had said, when Oona asked how she would make it down the cliffside. And Oona had agreed because there was no other option. She needed the ritual to work. For her baby, yes, and for herself. Because now that she'd made her decision, she couldn't imagine returning to the mainland. But if she failed to impress her mother and the rest of the coven, then she'd have no other choice. The next day, she'd have to get on a ferry bound for Portland. For along with commemorating the traditional start of the harvest season and celebrating labor in all its forms, Lughnasadh also marked the last day of the Summer Session. Tomorrow, the Mothers would all have to go.

In the greenhouse, she turned her attention back to the grimoire in front of her and began reading, but it took her only a minute to realize that she'd accidentally turned to the wrong page. Rather than an invocation meant to call upon Hekate, she was looking at some kind of spell. A charm, she thought, though it could have just as easily been a hex, knowing the sort of dark magic the book was otherwise concerned with. Either way, Oona had no plans to read further.

Though she was tempted—as she'd been by all the book's entries—she knew there wasn't time. She was running late enough as it was. Only when she reached forward to turn the page, something caught her eye: a symbol, like a ladder with an X drawn over it. The same symbol that she'd seen written on Daphne's file.

Oona knew there was no reason to read further. Lally had already told her that the symbol was part of a coding system, having to do with the Mothers' medical records. So whatever the symbol's origins were, they didn't matter. And anyway, glancing out the window, she could see that it was nearly dark. The feast would be starting soon. And worse, it looked like the storm was drawing closer. Outside, the wind was kicking up. Oona could see, silhouetted against the dusky sky, the branches of the oak trees bowing and swaying. She should use what little time she had left to finish her practice, to get changed. But though she pinched the corner of the page to turn it, her hand didn't move. Her eyes skimmed until they landed on a single word: *changeling*.

She was reading a changeling spell.

For a moment, Oona thought she might be sick. Her vision darkened and her head swam. In fear of falling, she clutched at the table. But after only a few seconds, the feeling passed. Still, she pulled over a nearby stool and lowered herself onto it, just to be careful. For a count of sixty, she focused on her breath. In, out. In, out.

It didn't mean anything, she told herself. She should just ignore it. Turn the page and swallow the bile stinging the back of her throat. She should stuff the book into her backpack and leave to get dressed for the ceremony. But despite knowing what she *should* do, Oona found it impossible to rise from the stool. She hadn't thought of the exact pitch of Daphne's wails in months—years, maybe—but now those weeks of sitting outside her bedroom door came rushing back.

It was as if she'd held vigil, listening to her friend weep, just that very afternoon. That was how clearly she could remember the way Daphne'd sounded—her voice thin and shredded—as she'd insisted that her baby was alive, that she'd been taken from her, stolen. What if Daphne had been right? After all, she'd been right when she'd said that she'd heard her daughter cry.

Oona massaged her temples. She felt crazy for even wondering if what Daphne had said might be true. But then again, everything Oona had done that summer had been a little crazy. More than a little, Jacob would say. And if she could believe that the only way to save her unborn child was to lure Hekate up from the underworld, to sacrifice her marriage, then why couldn't she believe that changelings were real?

If there was even the slightest chance that Daphne's daughter hadn't died but had been stolen, then Oona needed to know.

She was running out of time, but Oona packed up the book and the rest of what she would need to perform the ritual, and then she fled the greenhouse. At first, she didn't know even where she was going, but she'd figured it out by the time she reached the path: her mother's office, the false-bottom drawer.

I n her rush to get across campus, Oona had neglected to think about how she'd actually get inside her mother's office, so she was relieved to discover, when she arrived, that the door was unlocked. Whether it was luck, or fate, or some manifestation of her burgeoning power, Oona didn't know, but she didn't spend too much time questioning it. Once she confirmed that the office was empty—her mother likely down at the lodge, overseeing the production of all the traditional

Lughnasadh decorations: the garlands made from wheat and bilber-ries, the dried corncob centerpieces, the bouquets of chrysanthemum and marigold—she stepped inside and closed the door behind her.

It was difficult to see in the dark, but Oona knew better than to draw attention to what she was doing, so she made sure to leave the lights off. Instead, she waited for her eyes to adjust, then she crept toward the desk. In the dark, she felt for the drawer, pulling it off its track before setting it soundlessly on the desktop. She hadn't seen how Lally had removed the false bottom, so it took a few attempts before she figured out the latch, but eventually she prized the wooden slat free.

Her cell phone had a flashlight, but she was afraid to use it be-cause there wasn't much that was more suspicious-looking than the beam of a flashlight moving around an otherwise dark room. She re-membered the notebook was different than the other books, though, its leather less worn. So when her fingertips brushed the spine of a book that felt surprisingly smooth, she brought it over to the window, where she could just make out the symbol on its cover in the light of the rising moon.

This was it, she thought, as she held the book in her hands. Some-how she knew—somehow she'd *always* known, since she'd first dis-covered the drawer—that this was where she would uncover the truth, if she wanted it. All she had to do was look inside the book and she would know whatever it was her mother wanted to keep secret, whatever she'd been hiding from Oona—not just for the summer, but all her life.

Sucking in a deep breath, Oona stepped closer to the window, but instead of cracking open the book, she paused. She was so close to getting everything she'd ever wanted. If the ritual went well, then by next summer she could be in the lodge, working right there alongside her mother. She could be a full-fledged member of the coven. And she could be still, if she turned around right then and walked back to her cabin, if she chose to forget about the symbol and the book and the changeling spell.

But she couldn't. She knew she couldn't—not any more than she could forget the sound of Daphne crying, or the way Mr. Tanaka had looked at her when she'd told him that what had happened to his daughter was all her fault.

She had to know if she'd told him the truth that day.

So she opened the book and she turned to the last page, assuming it would hold the quickest answers. At first it seemed like she'd made a mistake, wasted her time. The book appeared to be nothing more than a collection of records. All three of the columns that dominated the page had been hand-drawn, and Oona recognized her mother's script—so tiny and compact. But as her eyes scanned the page, she discovered no answers, only more questions. While one of the columns held a list of dates, the other two, she saw, were filled with names. Women's names—Betsy, Eliza, Margot, Anna. In each row, beside each date, there were two names. But none Oona recognized. At least not until she looked down at the very bottom of the page, not until she saw a row with Gemma Nystrom's name written in one column, and in the other, a name that looked like *Maggie Jones*, only it had been crossed out. Replaced. There was a new name penciled in beside it: *Oona Walker*.

For a moment, Oona just stood there by the window, confused. Outside, she could hear the festivities beginning: the faint sound of music and every now and then a peal of screeching laughter. Pretty soon, she knew, her presence would be missed. But the lists of names, they didn't make sense. At first, she thought that perhaps they were simply a record of those who had attended that summer's session, but then she remembered that she hadn't known any of the other names. There was no mention of Shelly, or Grace, or Vivian, no matter how far back she turned. And Oona turned back pretty far. Soon, she was looking at entries from five years ago, if the dates were to be believed. Then ten. Then fifteen. Then—

In the air, Oona's hand stilled above a page. At last, she recognized another name, though immediately she wished she hadn't. But no matter how many times she blinked and rubbed her eyes, the name didn't change. Her mother had clearly written *Daphne Tanaka* in the same far left column where she'd written *Gemma Nystrom* on the book's last page. While in the column where Oona's own name had appeared, Ursula had scrawled another name Oona knew, though it took her a beat longer to place it: *Sara Cook*. Mrs. Cook. The woman she'd seen weeping outside her mother's office the day she came home to find Daphne in the hall.

But what was the link? Oona wondered. What was the connection between Mrs. Cook and Daphne? Too stunned to think clearly, Oona lifted her eyes from the page and stared out the window. In the distance, she could see fairy lights twinkling and the flickering of the torches that always lined the path during the Lughnasadh feast. Mrs. Cook had come to the Center every summer for years. She'd been desperate to have a child, but no matter what Ursula had done for her, she'd returned the next summer still empty-handed, looking more and more haggard as the years wore on. Until, Oona remembered, that last summer—the summer when Daphne'd had her baby. That year, Ursula had designed a special program for Mrs. Cook, a treatment plan she'd promised would finally work. And it had, or so Oona had assumed, since at the end of that Summer Session Mrs. Cook had left the island looking like she'd been transformed. Oona could still remember her waving goodbye from the back seat of the truck before

Lally drove her to the ferry. In fact, she remembered it distinctly because, at the time, she'd been confused. Upon first glance, she'd mistaken Mrs. Cook for Daphne, who was also set to be discharged that very day. Before then, Oona had never realized how similar the two looked, but it was true that they had the same almond eyes, the same button nose. Aside from Daphne's freckles, and Mrs. Cook's perfect cheekbones, from a few yards away they looked like they could be kin.

And suddenly Oona knew what sort of record she was holding. Still, just to be sure, she ran her finger down the column of dates. Sure enough, she saw it was May 12 that connected Daphne to Mrs. Cook. May 12—the day Daphne's daughter was born.

Feeling sick again, and unsteady, Oona sank down to the floor. How many times had her mother done this? How long ago did it start?

Frantic, Oona flipped to the front of the book and searched for the very first entry. And that's when she saw her mother's name. Written in the same column as Mrs. Cook's, beside a date Oona recognized instantly. Her birthday.

# TWELVE

For a long time, Oona didn't move from her spot on the floor beneath the window in Ursula's office. It was like she'd forgotten how—how to bend her joints, how to flex her muscles. Ursula was not her mother. Not the mother who'd given birth to her, anyhow. She hadn't spoken her into being, hadn't willed her into existence, hadn't done any of the miraculous things she'd claimed she'd done to bring Oona into the world. Instead, she'd stolen her. Though from who, Oona didn't know. Some woman named Nora, according to the record. Some woman—or, more probably, some girl. A girl like Shelly's sister, Tracy, whose name Oona had also discovered in the notebook. Someone young and vulnerable. Someone desperate and alone. Just thinking about it left Oona feeling dizzy—so nauseated that suddenly she felt the need to push up from the floor and stumble down the hall to the bathroom.

By the time she reached the toilet, she'd broken into a cold sweat. But before she had a chance to kneel on the hard tile floor and bring up the bile she could feel burning in her stomach, she felt a gush of something warm and wet between her legs. Panicked, she dropped down onto the toilet seat and worked to peel off her leggings. She was expecting blood—she knew that when she lost her mucus plug, it would likely be gory—but she thought that if it were her mucus plug (or worse, her water breaking), the blood would be viscous, gluey and wet. Instead, what she found when she pulled down her panties stole her breath. Goose bumps stippled her arms and the room seemed to swing away from her like a door pushed open. The blood—it was dark and filled with clots thick as curd. For a moment, Oona froze, flooded by an awful underwater feeling. She put her hands on her knees and waited for the dizziness to pass.

Once she could catch her breath, Oona stuffed a wad of toilet paper between her legs and stood. Only seconds earlier, as she'd sat slumped beneath the window, she'd been considering marching out to the lodge. She'd wanted to confront her mother with the book. She'd wanted to demand answers.

But now . . . now it felt like there wasn't time. Her baby was coming, and she still needed to complete the ritual.

For a second, she debated hiking out to the cliffs, but she didn't think she'd be able to make it down to the cave on her own. She'd started cramping. So she settled on a different plan. She would go to the infirmary first. If she could just make it there, then Holly or Inez or whoever was working that night's shift would be able to give her something. There were medicines, she knew, that could slow down labor's progress, and she wouldn't need long. An hour, maybe two. Just enough time to find Lally and get down the cliff face; just enough time to summon Hekate and renegotiate their deal. So before she could talk herself out of it, Oona pulled up her pants, grabbed the notebook and her backpack from the office, and rushed out of the building.

The woods, Oona noticed, seemed darker than they had only a half hour before. But perhaps that was because this time she was running away from the lodge—away from the warm glow of its lights—rather than toward it. Or perhaps it was because she'd lost the moon. The storm that Ursula had been so concerned about had finally arrived. Overhead, the clouds were swirling. Oona could see them through the trees. And the wind, as she ran, began to whip, cold and briny. She could feel the grit of the salt in the air as it hit her cheeks. *Please*, she thought, as she veered off the path, aiming to cut through the forest to reach the infirmary quicker. *Please. Please. Please.* Beneath her feet, she could hear twigs cracking like bird bones. She could picture the petrels again, dislodged from their nests. "Almost there," she whispered—to herself, to her belly. The cramping that she'd initially felt in her abdomen was now radiating around to her back. "Just hold on. We're almost there."

When Oona emerged from the woods and caught sight of the infirmary, she nearly cried out in relief. She didn't dare reach down to feel between her legs—she was too afraid to find the wad of toilet paper soaked through, her pants soiled—so she just kept moving. Step by step until she reached the front door.

"Hello?" she called, because there was a light on in the office at the end of the long hallway. "Hello? Holly? Inez? Anybody! I need help!"

But though she waited for the sound of footsteps, she heard nothing, and after a moment she realized, with horror, that she'd done the wrong thing, run in the wrong direction. The infirmary was empty. Everyone was at the lodge.

"Oh god, no," she moaned, reaching for the wall because suddenly she was unsure whether her legs would hold her.

She didn't think she had it in her to make it all the way back to the lodge. Nor was she sure that she had the time. She still hadn't felt between her legs, but when she looked down she could see the trail she'd left all along the wood floor, the droplets dark as oil. For all she knew, it might already be too late.

That's when she noticed the light again. At first, she'd assumed it'd been left on in the office, but on second glance she realized that it was coming from the same examination room where Lally had brought her, months earlier. Suddenly, she had an idea: Before she ventured back out into the woods, into the storm, she would first make sure that the baby was not in distress. True, she had never been trained to use the Doppler, but she'd watched Lally and it hadn't looked that hard. She was sure she could figure it out. So with one hand still pressed up against the wall, she staggered down the hall toward the light.

The last time she'd been inside that room, Oona had watched Lally retrieve the Doppler from the far cabinet, but when she looked she found the cabinet empty. Instead, she discovered the Doppler lying on a rolling tray beside the examination table, its probe disconnected from its base. The tube of gel was there, too, so, as delicately as she could, Oona climbed up to sit on the table. Then she pulled up her shirt and rolled down her leggings, just like Joyce had done for her that day.

After squeezing a hefty amount of the gel onto her stomach, Oona lifted the Doppler and pressed the probe against her skin. She didn't mean to, but her eyes closed as soon as she heard the static on the speaker, then the low whoosh of fluid moving around in her abdomen. Once again the words came back to her, unbidden: *please, please.* But she stopped mumbling when she realized she didn't know who she was praying to anymore. To Demeter? To Hekate? To Ursula?

Lying flat on the table, Oona moved the probe over her belly as slowly as she could bear. For a long while there was only static, but then she heard it. Or at least, she thought she heard it. Slow and steady. It sounded the same as it had the day Lally had checked. But when she looked down at the Doppler, she saw that the heartbeat she'd measured wasn't fast enough to be her baby's. No, she quickly realized, at only eighty-four beats per minute, the heartbeat she was hearing must be her own. So she moved the probe—left, right, lower, higher. And then she moved it again. But she couldn't find the baby's heartbeat. Every time she thought she'd caught it, it just turned out to be her own. How had this been so easy for Lally? Oona wondered. How had she been able to tell the difference between her heartbeat and her baby's, when they sounded so much alike? When they—

But that's when Oona realized: The two heartbeats, they weren't supposed to sound the same. Compared to the mother's, the baby's heartbeat was supposed to be fast, a gallop.

In that moment, a new panic came over Oona. A realization so painful, it felt like a kind of death. There was no other heartbeat. There never had been. At least, not for a long while. Ursula and Lally had lied to her—that day with the Doppler, and when Oona had woken up in her childhood bed. The truth was that she'd lost the baby. And suddenly, it all made sense: why Ursula had refused her many requests for a follow-up ultrasound, why she'd never felt the baby move. And yet . . .

Dropping the Doppler back onto the tray, Oona brought her hands down to her belly, still round and hard beneath her palms. How could she look so pregnant, *feel* so pregnant, if there was nothing?

How could there be nothing inside her?

Where had her baby gone?

Like a tide rising inside her chest, Oona could feel a scream shuddering up her ribs. How could this happen? How could her mother do this to her?

But of course, Ursula wasn't her mother. And that was the trick, wasn't it? The answer to all the questions that were flooding Oona's mind, the questions that had dogged her since childhood, the questions that had both driven her from the island *and* called her to return. With Ursula, she'd always felt less loved—less loved than the members of her coven, less loved than the Initiates, less loved than the Mothers. Now she finally understood.

But what she didn't understand was why. Why take her all those years ago, if Ursula was never really interested in becoming a mother? Why spend the summer deceiving her into believing in a hysterical pregnancy, if the truth was that she'd miscarried months before?

Dizzy, Oona climbed down from the table, stood there on jellied legs, and looked around the room. When she'd had her miscarriages she'd known what to do with all the adrenaline coursing through her body, but now? Now there was nothing she could do. Whether she prayed to Hekate, Demeter, or Ursula, it wouldn't matter. Whether it took her minutes or hours to seek medical attention, the result would be the same. There was no one out there who could help her. No one to save her baby. No baby, even, to be saved.

Still, her legs trembled and her hands twitched to move. So she did the only thing she could think to do. She dialed Jacob's number. Three times in a row her call failed. Cursing, Oona blamed the storm. When her fourth attempt ended in a dial tone, she reached into her memory and called the Tanakas' landline.

"Hello?"

Oona had braced herself for the possibility that Mrs. Tanaka would be the one to answer, so when she heard a male voice on the other end of the line, she sighed with relief. "Jacob," she breathed.

"I'm afraid not," the voice answered.

Oona stiffened. "Mr. Tanaka?"

"Oona?" Mr. Tanaka asked.

"I'm looking for Jacob," she explained. "Is he there?"

"Oona?" Mr. Tanaka repeated. "I can barely hear you. Where are you?"

"I'm looking for Jacob!" she shouted.

"Jacob's gone back to Portland," Mr. Tanaka said. "He told us you asked him to go back."

"Right. Yes. I did. I just . . ." She trailed off. She couldn't quite believe that Jacob had really done as she'd asked him. Was it possible something she'd said had finally sunk in?

"Have you tried his cell?" Mr. Tanaka asked.

"I can't get through."

"Must be this storm," he said.

"Yeah," Oona agreed. She was stalling, she knew, but she couldn't seem to bring herself to end the phone call.

On the other end of the line, Mr. Tanaka cleared his throat. "Oona?" he said, after another moment's staticky silence. "Oona? Are you still there?"

"Yes," she said softly. "I'm here."

"Is something wrong? Is it the baby?"

She swallowed. She shook her head. *No*, she planned to tell him. *No, there's nothing wrong.* But when she opened her mouth, her voice caught in her throat. She choked.

Mr. Tanaka didn't wait for her to try to say more. "Where are you?" he asked.

"The infirmary," she managed, her voice a croaky whisper.

"Don't move," Mr. Tanaka told her. "I'm on my way."

After he hung up, Oona spent a moment just listening to the dial tone. She couldn't seem to decide on her next move. So she just stood there with her ear pressed to her phone. She stared off into space and let her gaze drift out of focus. Patiently, she waited to regain control of her limbs.

After a minute or two, she could feel her fingers again and she put the phone down. When she pulled herself back to attention, she realized she was looking at the tray. Beside the Doppler and the gel Oona had left uncapped, there was a file open. A file with a symbol on the tab.

She'd been in such a rush before, such a blind panic, that she hadn't noticed the room was in a state of disarray. Now, though, as she turned in a small circle, she took it in. Not only had the lights been left on, but the countertop beneath the cabinet where the Doppler was usually kept was strewn with what looked like used instruments: a speculum, a thermometer, a stethoscope. There was a puddle of water by the door, and the table where Oona had been sitting only moments earlier was missing its sanitary paper. When she looked, she saw it lying on the floor, half-crumpled and stained with blood.

Clearly, something had happened. For some other Mother, something had gone terribly wrong. But it had nothing to do with Oona. Or so she tried to convince herself as she adjusted her clothing and walked the four steps toward the door. But she couldn't leave. And it was all because of that file.

She had to know who it belonged to. Once she did, then, she told herself, she could go.

Though the symbol was visible, a loose piece of paper from the file obscured the name until Oona moved it. "Gemma Nystrom," she read aloud. She should have known. Maybe she even *had* known. Maybe that was why she'd tried to leave without looking. Who else would have that symbol on their file but the only other Mother at the Center whose name Oona had seen recorded in her mother's book?

*The book*, Oona thought. She'd left it on the ground by the door beside her backpack, but now she retrieved it, laid it on top of the examination table, and flipped to the last page. It was just as she remembered: There was her name, and there was Gemma's. The only thing missing from the entry was the date.

Suddenly everything that had confused her about that summer seemed to shift into focus. Her phony pregnancy, her mother's decision to let her remain on Marrow, even the way she'd entertained Oona's request to join the coven—none of it was real, and none of it was about Oona. Instead, it was all about Gemma. Or really, it was all about Ursula. So she could deliver on the promise she'd made to Gemma's mother to *take care* of Gemma's supposedly unwanted pregnancy. Somewhere along the way, Ursula had come up with a kill-two-birds-with-one-stone plan.

Oona looked down at the book on the table, at the room around her. The missing date, the way Gemma's file had been left open, the bloody paper and the puddle on the floor . . .

Gemma had gone into labor. Oona didn't know why it'd taken her so long to put two and two together, but now it was clear. She must have complained of pain or experienced early contractions and, eager not to disrupt the festivities, Holly and Inez had probably brought her to the infirmary for a quick check. But upon examining her further, they must have realized that Gemma wasn't faking and rushed her straight to the birthing suites.

For a second, Oona felt her heart clutch. It was the same lonely, jealous feeling that always seized her when she heard about another birth. But just as quickly as it came on, it was replaced by the chilling realization that if Gemma was in labor, then that meant she was in trouble—that today's was the date Ursula intended to write down in her book.

When Daphne had gone into labor, she'd asked Oona to stay with her. She'd wanted her to be in the room when she gave birth. But Ursula had said no. She'd claimed she needed Oona to stand guard. The birthing process was sacred, she'd said, and so it was important that Oona made sure no one interrupted. And because she'd wanted to be good for once, because she'd wanted to be like Daphne—Daphne, who Ursula was always praising for being so dutiful and well-behaved—Oona had agreed. For hours, she'd sat on the birthing suites' steps, just like she'd been instructed, pretending that it gave her no joy at all to think of Daphne calling for her inside. In some ways, it had felt like a fitting punishment for all that Daphne had taken from her those last few months. And at the same time, it had also—perversely, shamefully—made Oona feel loved. After everything, she was still the one Daphne wanted standing there beside her, still the one she wanted holding her hand.

When Mrs. Cook had arrived, it had taken Oona a few moments to recognize her. At first, she just looked like another member of her mother's coven, dressed as she was in what appeared to be one of Ursula's old robes. Oona had been sitting on the topmost step, elbows on her knees, but she stood when she saw a figure emerge from the forest. Imagining it was Joyce or one of the other senior coven witches, she got a rush thinking she was going to be able to turn them away. But when it had turned out instead to be Mrs. Cook, Oona had frozen. Of course she'd known what she was supposed to do. But as much as she'd feared disappointing her mother, she'd really wanted to see that summer's chosen one get taken down a peg, which she surely would if Ursula discovered her in the birthing suites. Oona hadn't even realized how badly she wanted to hear her mother tear into Mrs. Cook until she saw her in that robe.

And so instead of calling out to Mrs. Cook, instead of chasing after her or attempting to flag her down, Oona just watched as she scurried around the corner of the building. From her place on the steps, she listened to the side door creak open and then closed.

When she'd walked out of the greenhouse, Oona had wanted to know if she'd been honest with Mr. Tanaka that day she'd driven him to the cliffs. She'd wanted to know if what had happened to Daphne was her fault. Well, now she knew.

And she knew, too, just what she had to do.

She'd failed Daphne, but there was still time to help Gemma.

# THIRTEEN

As soon as Oona opened the door, she realized that the storm they'd been waiting on all afternoon had arrived while she was inside the infirmary. Overhead the sky had turned dark, purple as a bruise, and in the distance she could hear the rolling of thunder. With a crack, lighting broke across the sky.

When she saw how powerful the wind had become, the way it was moving through the forest like a wave, shaking the pine trees' branches and causing their trunks to bow, she was tempted to wait—for the storm to die down, for Mr. Tanaka to arrive. But then she heard a woman scream, and she knew there wasn't time. She couldn't let what had happened to Daphne happen to Gemma. She couldn't let Ursula add any more names to her book. So with one final glance back toward the road, Oona stepped out from under the building's small overhang.

She started calling Lally's name even before she reached the top of the birthing suites' front steps. "Lally!" she cried, as she pounded on the door. "Lally!"

She couldn't bring herself to call out *Mom*.

"Let me in!" she shouted.

It took a few minutes, but eventually the door swung open and Lally's face appeared in the gap. "Oona? What are you doing here?"

"I need to come in."

"You can't," Lally said, though not unkindly. "Oona, love, you know the rules. The birthing suites are sacred."

"Bullshit," Oona snarled, and Lally blinked, taken aback.

Oona hadn't realized just how angry she was, but now her rage seemed to boil inside her. With each beat of her heart, she could feel it pulsing through her veins like blood. "Move," she said. A warning.

Lally stumbled backward as if pushed, and Oona didn't wait for any further invitation; she just barged past her.

Despite the grandiose name, the birthing suites contained only two patient rooms, and since there was no one else in labor, the door to Gemma's room had been left open. Before Lally could stop her, Oona stepped inside. By Gemma's bed, Ursula was holding an IV bag.

"Get away from her," Oona barked.

Ursula turned. "Oona?" she asked, sounding confused. "What are you doing here?" She glanced down at Oona's hands. "Is that blood?"

"Get away from her," Oona repeated.

On the bed, Gemma hardly seemed to register Oona's presence. She faced her, but her eyes were glazed over like she'd gone deep inside herself . . . or was in some kind of stupor.

"What is that?" Oona demanded, gesturing to the IV bag. In the weeks after Daphne lost her daughter, she'd spent hours complaining to Oona about "the fog." She'd sworn her baby had lived—that she'd heard her cry, that she'd looked down and seen her dark eyes blinking—but she hadn't been able to remember much else about that day. At the time, Oona had assumed it was just another symptom of labor, something to do with the rush of hormones or the loss of blood. But now, seeing that IV bag, she wondered if perhaps the fog was something more dangerous.

"Just fluids," Ursula said, as she finished connecting the bag to Gemma's IV line.

"I don't believe you."

Ursula looked at her, perplexed. "What's going on?" she asked. "If you're not hurt, then why aren't you at the lodge? And where is Lally?"

"I know everything," Oona said. "I know what you did to Daphne, what you're trying to do to *her*." She pointed at Gemma. Her eyes were just about closed, but her mouth was still open, drool strung between her lips.

"Is this about your ritual?" Ursula's gaze ticked up over Oona's head to where a clock hung on the wall. "You know, you don't need to wait for me and Lally. You can start without us. You have the potion, you have the grimoire, you have everything you need."

"Stop it," Oona growled. "Stop it. Just stop it."

"I'll ask Joyce to go with you. She can report back to the rest of the coven. She can tell us if you succeed, and then—"

"Shut up!"

On the bed, Gemma moaned, and Ursula hung the IV bag on a pole. "Lally?" she called.

Dutifully, Lally appeared in the doorway, as if all this time she'd just been standing out in the hall, waiting to be summoned.

"Lally," Ursula said. "Take Oona into the other room and look her over, will you? I don't know if she has a fever or what, but she isn't making sense. You didn't take the potion already, did you, Oona?"

Lally held out one arm, ready to wrap it around Oona's shoulders, ready to lead her away. But Oona refused. "There's nothing wrong with me," she said.

Ursula gestured to the puddle on the floor. "Are you *bleeding*?"

"Oh, goodness, love." Lally tutted. "Come now. Come with me. Let's check on the baby."

"The baby?" Oona repeated, but the word caught in her throat. Lally winced. And whatever remaining doubts Oona had, whatever kernel of hope she'd been nurturing that this was all just some big misunderstanding and that Lally would be able to walk her into the next room, pull out the ultrasound machine, and prove that her baby was still nestled safe inside her, a second heartbeat behind her ribs—all of that vanished the moment she saw Lally's face. "There is no baby," Oona said. "I'm not pregnant."

"What are you talking about?" Ursula said. "Of course you are. Just look at you. Lally?"

Reluctantly, Lally held out her arm again, but Oona stepped backward, out of reach. She looked at Gemma. She was still breathing, but her skin looked waxy and pale. "No," she said. "No, I won't leave her. I won't leave Daphne."

"Daphne?" Ursula echoed. "See, you are ill. Please, just go with Lally, okay? She'll help you."

Oona shook her head. She didn't trust Lally's *help*. She'd just give her whatever Ursula had given Gemma, whatever they'd given Oona the day she'd started miscarrying. She wheeled on Lally. "How could you do this to me?" she asked.

Tears welled in Lally's eyes. "Not *to* you, love. *For* you."

Oona swallowed a bitter bark of a laugh.

"It's true," Lally insisted. "We were just trying to help. Both you *and* Gemma. We thought—"

Ursula cut her off. "That's enough."

But it was too late. As the wind rattled the front door, Oona stepped toward Lally. "How exactly were you trying to help Gemma?" she asked. "And what about the others? How were you helping them?" Once she'd understood what sort of records Ursula's notebook contained, she'd realized that some of the names listed were familiar to her. Initiates she remembered from childhood. Minnie, who always wore her hair in two braids. Maria, who'd taught Oona a little Spanish. Jessica, who used to start every day with an icy swim. "What about Minnie and Jessica? What about Maria? Where are they? What happened to them?"

"Lally," Ursula warned. "It's time for Oona to go. She's clearly not well. If she won't consent to an exam, then at least take her back to her cabin. Give her something to sleep."

Preemptively, Oona stuck up her hands. She would fight—punch, scratch, bite—if either one of them dared to get near her. But Lally didn't attempt to move any closer. In fact, she appeared not to register Ursula's instructions at all. "I didn't know about the others," she said softly. "I didn't know about Daphne until after. I promise."

Oona shook her head. "I don't believe you," she said. Because of course Lally had known, and of course she'd gone along with it. Nearly thirty years ago, Lally had washed up on the island's shores. She'd been beaten, bruised, broken. She'd been abandoned, and Ursula had given her a family and a home. For Ursula, Oona knew, there wasn't anything Lally wouldn't do. And Oona resented being told otherwise. She resented being lied to.

Frustrated, Oona bent down to dig through her backpack, searching for her mother's book. When she found it, she turned to the last page before Daphne's entry. "You're telling me you didn't know about Maisy Deckard, who apparently lost her baby on July 29, 2007? Or

Imani Williams, who you claimed had a stillbirth in May of 2005? According to your records, you gave her baby to Juniper Scott. Just like you gave Juanita Alvarez's baby to Octavia Gomez. And Francesca Miller's baby to Sadie Bishop. You're telling me you didn't know about any of that? Come on, Lally."

"I swear to you, Oona," Lally said. "I didn't know. It was only after you brought Daphne to me and told me you'd given her the Lazarus Draught that I got suspicious. I started thinking about how your mother had asked me to make that same potion just a few days before, how she'd been asking me to make it for years. So I confronted her. And that's when I learned the truth."

Oona scoffed but said nothing. The whole time she'd been reading, she hadn't dared to look up, in case she lost her nerve. But now she locked eyes with her mother.

"Where did you get that?" Ursula asked. Her voice was cold, accusing, as if the book in Oona's hands were nothing more than proof that, once again, she'd been caught snooping. "That doesn't belong to you."

Oona kept reading. "You gave Mitzi Brown's baby to Amanda Watkins on June 23, 1998. And Tracy Moore's baby to Michelle Jackson on April 25, 1997."

Ursula pressed her lips together. "You need to give that back."

"No," Lally interjected, with a sidelong glance at Ursula. "No, Oona. Keep going."

Oona closed the book, then opened it again to the very first page. "Don't you dare," Ursula warned.

Oona didn't even have to look down. As soon as she'd read the book's first entry, she knew she would never forget it as long as she lived. "Nora Reilly lost her baby on March 18, 1990. Instead, her daughter was raised by another woman: Ursula Walker."

"Oh, Ursula," Lally gasped. "What did you do?"

"Nothing," Ursula snapped.

"She stole me," Oona answered. "She kidnapped me, just like she kidnapped all the children in this book."

"Kidnapped?" Ursula scoffed. "Please."

On the bed, Gemma began to stir.

"What would you call it, then?" Oona asked. Somewhere in the back of her mind, she was aware that whatever was going on with Gemma was likely more important, but in that moment it was like everything else in the room had ceased to exist. There was just her, her mother, and the book. There was just the promise of the truth, pressurizing the air like the storm. "Who was she?" Oona asked. "Who was Nora Reilly? Tell me."

Gemma grunted and rolled over, moaning.

"Lally," Ursula said, shoving the sleeves of her linen dress up past her elbows. "I need another syringe."

But Lally didn't move. She just stood there, stunned.

"Tell me who my mother was," Oona insisted.

Gemma grappled for the bed rails. "It hurts," she groaned. "It hurts."

"Lally!" Ursula barked.

Oona stepped closer. "Tell me who my mother was!" she cried.

And Ursula, who had so far managed to maintain her composure, finally cracked. "*I* am your mother!" she roared. "I am your mother, Oona. Me! Nora Reilly was no one. She was nothing. She was just some girl."

"*Some girl?*" Oona repeated, galled, horror-struck.

"Yes. Some girl. Some girl from Lubec."

"The town where you grew up?"

Ursula marched over to the row of cabinets that ran along the far wall and began searching through them, squinting to read vial labels and nudging aside boxes of surgical gloves.

"No," Lally said, stirring to attention finally. "No, not in there. In the drawer." She crossed the room and tugged open the drawer closest to Gemma's bed, retrieving a vial and a syringe.

Gemma rattled the bed rails and unleashed an animal howl, while Ursula jabbed the needle into the top of the vial. She turned the whole thing upside down to extract what she needed.

"How did you know her?" Oona asked, once Ursula finished administering the shot, and Gemma dropped back onto her pillow.

"I didn't," Ursula said, her eyes still trained on Gemma. "She was a patient of mine. At the midwifery practice I inherited from my grandmother. Nora was one of the girls who came to see me. One of the local wharf rats."

"She was what?"

Ursula sniffed. "A drug addict, Oona. And a whore. I told her that, given her history, she'd need to go to the hospital to deliver, but she knew that if she did they would test her and she'd go to jail. So she came to me instead. She showed up on my doorstep in the middle of a goddamn nor'easter. Bled all over my rug, my sheets. Soaked the mattress. And then, when it was all over, she refused to mother. Refused to even look at the baby she'd birthed." Ursula glanced back at Oona, to make sure she was listening. "She wanted nothing to do with you, Oona. Do you understand? I tried to get her to hold you, but she refused. Just lay there with her eyes closed."

"Maybe she was tired."

Ursula chuckled cruelly. "She wasn't *tired*. She was strung out. Or going through withdrawal. She was a junkie, thinking only about her next fix. If I'd left you with her, you'd be dead. No doubt about it. She would've abandoned you. It might've taken a month or a year or five years, I don't know, but she would've done it. She would've abandoned you the same way my mother abandoned me. Because that's what addicts do."

"You mean your mother was an—"

"She was *undeserving*, Oona. That's what she was. She had everything a woman could want: a coven, a child, Craft. And she threw it all away so she could live life in the 'real world.' Well, you've lived in the real world now, haven't you? So you understand the mistake she made."

Oona shook her head. "Just because your mother left you—"

"She wouldn't even feed you, Oona! For hours and hours you screamed to be fed till I thought I'd lose my mind. But Nora? No. Nothing. Eventually, I had to do it myself."

"Are you saying you . . . you nursed me?"

Ursula paused, and for a brief moment, it looked like her eyes softened. "Yes," she said. "I did."

Oona wanted to leave it at that. She wanted to turn on her heels and walk out of the room, follow the trail she'd taken through the woods back to her mother's house and crawl into her childhood bed. She wanted to pull the covers up over her head and fall asleep in a cocoon of blankets so soft and warm that in her dreams she might mistake them for a womb.

When she blinked herself back into the moment, she realized Ursula was watching her. "Listen to me," Ursula said, stepping away from Gemma's bed and closing the distance between them. She reached up to tuck a loose strand of hair behind Oona's ear. "Listen to me," she purred. "I may not have given birth to you, but I am still your mother. Have I not loved you the way a mother would? Have I not given of my body? My blood? Have I not begged, bartered, and stolen for you, the way Demeter did for Persephone? Is that not what I'm trying to do right now? I'm trying to work miracles for you, Oona. I'm trying to give you the very thing you want most in the world. Don't you want to be a mother?"

Tears clotted at the back of Oona's throat. "You know I do."

"Then just give me that book and go back to the lodge and we can forget this ever happened. You'll be a mama by the time the sun comes up."

"A mama," Oona sighed, as if the very word held magic. And in a way, it did. For what was Ursula promising besides a kind of magical solution? All Oona had to do was walk away. All she had to do was lie down and close her eyes and when she opened them, she'd have everything she'd ever wanted. What could be more magical than that?

Over on the bed, Gemma groaned. Oona looked up. According to the monitor, her heart rate—and her baby's heart rate—was holding steady, but she still looked pale. She was clutching two big fistfuls of her bedsheets and trembling. What was in that IV bag? Oona wondered.

Inching closer, Ursula dropped her voice to a whisper. "Listen, she'll be fine. More than fine. You'll be doing her a favor, really. A kindness. You'll be sparing her the same way I spared Nora, from a life that would only break her heart. And her daughter—*your* daughter—she'll be saved."

"Saved from what?" asked Oona, half-mesmerized by Ursula's gentle tone.

"From a girl who is too young, too selfish, to be her mother. They're all the same, you see. These girls. Gemma. Nora. My own mother . . ."

"Daphne?" asked Oona.

"Yes," whispered Ursula. "Daphne too."

Oona nodded, thinking. She supposed it was true. Daphne *had* been selfish. But then again, so was Oona. Sure, she'd masqueraded as a mother willing to do anything for her child, to scale a cliff face or drink poison. But none of that had been about the baby. It'd been about Craft. If anything, it should be a mark against her that she'd been considering performing that ritual. She'd been willing to put her child at risk to get what she wanted, and what was more selfish than that? At least Daphne had wanted to be a mother. It may have been about the coven for her, too, at first, but by the end? There was no doubt in Oona's mind that Daphne's grief had been about losing her daughter.

"Daphne wanted to be a mother," Oona said quietly. "She didn't consider herself *spared*."

"She would have, though," Ursula insisted. "If she'd just given it a little more time. But she was impatient, that girl. Impulsive. And just look at what she did—to you, to me, to her family. Now, *that* was selfish."

"What did she do to you?"

"She almost cost me this business," Ursula said. "If I hadn't convinced her parents not to sue, I would've lost everything."

"You mean, if you hadn't convinced them to blame me."

Ursula frowned. "You gave her that potion, Oona. You know, you're far from blameless here, my dear."

"You told her her baby was stillborn. I was just trying to help bring her back."

"Back from where?" Ursula asked.

"From the underworld," answered Lally.

Oona had forgotten she was there, standing only a few feet away, listening.

"Those girls were only down in that cave because of a lie *you* told them, Ursula." Lally looked at Oona. "I tried to tell her, love. We could have avoided a lot of tragedy if we'd just told everyone the truth. Because what we did? It was for the best. You see that now, don't you? The babies got mothers who were ready to become mothers. The adoptive mothers got what they most wanted in the world. And the girls, they got something too: They got a second chance, an opportunity to escape their circumstances and make something of themselves, the way I did."

"You're saying the adoptive mothers, they didn't know? Maggie Jones didn't know?"

"Maggie?" Lally asked, confused.

But Ursula didn't look confused. She looked caught. Guilty. "I don't know what you're talking about," she said airily.

"Before I showed up, you were planning to give Gemma's baby to Maggie Jones. Weren't you?"

"No," said Lally. "No, this was just for you, Oona. We did this because we love you."

Oona bit her lip. For a moment she didn't trust herself to speak. Was it true? she wondered. Was it all because they loved her? It was certainly the version of the story she wanted to believe. She turned to Ursula for confirmation. "Mom?"

But she never got to hear Ursula's reply, because just then a figure appeared in the open doorway.

"Captain Tanaka," said Lally. "We didn't hear you come in. Is something wrong? Is it Mrs. Potter? Is she in labor?"

Oona turned to watch Mr. Tanaka enter the room. "You found

me," she breathed as he got closer. But to her surprise he walked right past her, didn't stop until he reached Gemma's bedside.

"Unless it's an emergency," said Ursula, "I'm afraid we've got our hands full at the moment. So if you could please wait out in the hall."

"Oh, I've *been* waiting," said Mr. Tanaka. "I've been out in that hall for a while now." He reached into the pocket of his marine patrol jacket and pulled out a set of handcuffs. "Ursula Walker, I'm placing you under arrest. Turn around and put your hands behind your back."

"W-What?" Ursula stammered. She stepped backward, away from him. "What are you talking about? You can't just barge in here, Captain Tanaka. This is a medical facility. We're in the middle of a delivery."

"Yes," he said. "I can see that." He looked down at Gemma and concern knitted his brow. She was conscious again, but just barely. "Are you okay?" he asked.

"No, she's not *okay*," said Ursula. "She's in labor!"

"What was your name again? Gemma? Are you okay, Gemma? Have they hurt you?"

Slowly, as if the effort pained her, Gemma shook her head.

Mr. Tanaka turned his attention back to Ursula. "Hands," he said, as he motioned for her to turn around.

"On what charge?" Ursula asked, her voice pitched high in disbelief.

"Kidnapping," said Mr. Tanaka. "Aggravated kidnapping, I assume. I'll let the DA handle the specifics once they listen to your confession. I got it all on tape. Everything you said just now."

"My confession," Ursula chuckled. "Please." But Oona noticed her face looked pinched. Her laughter sounded hollow.

"Your hands," said Mr. Tanaka. "Don't make me use force."

"Force, John? Really?"

"Turn around."

With a great indignant sigh, Ursula did as she was told, and Mr. Tanaka clasped the cuffs around her wrists.

Lally didn't wait to be asked. As soon as he looked at her, she offered him her back, and he bound her wrists too.

"Now what?" Ursula asked, impatient. She flicked her eyes at Gemma. "What are you going to do about her? Is she just supposed to deliver on her own?"

"The coast guard are on their way," he said. Then, almost to himself, "But it may be a while longer before they get here. Thirty minutes, maybe more." He looked at Oona. "Do you think she'll be okay?" His gaze dropped down to her belly. "And what about you? Are you hurt?"

"No, I'm fine," Oona said. A lie, but she didn't think she could bear telling Mr. Tanaka the truth—speaking the words aloud. It was all still too fresh, too painful. If she told anyone, she would need to tell Jacob first.

"Is there anyone who could watch over her until the Coasties get here? Could you?"

"Me?" asked Oona.

"It's that or we all wait here together," Mr. Tanaka said. He used the pads of his thumb and forefinger to rub at his hairline. Oona had been so focused on herself, on her own feelings of exhaustion, that she hadn't realized how tired Mr. Tanaka looked. No, not just tired. Distraught. And of course he was. He'd just learned that Daphne had been telling the truth about her daughter. He'd just learned that he had a grandchild out there somewhere.

To spare him the pain of spending any more time in that room, Oona told him she'd be fine to wait with Gemma. If there was an emergency, she could always call Shelly. Shelly was an ob-gyn, Oona assured Mr. Tanaka. So if anything happened, she would know what to do.

"Good," said Mr. Tanaka, and he started guiding both Ursula and Lally toward the door.

He'd just reached for the knob when Oona cried out, "Wait!"

Everyone turned but Ursula.

"It'll be okay, love," Lally said gently. "You can let us go."

But Oona couldn't. Not yet. Not before she heard the answer to the question she'd asked her mother right before Mr. Tanaka interrupted them. She spoke to Ursula's back. "Was it true, what Lally said?" she asked. "Did you really do it for me?"

For a long moment, Ursula didn't move. She didn't speak. She was quiet so long Oona began to wonder if in fact she'd even heard the question. But then, at last, she turned, and Oona read the answer in her eyes.

"I do love you, Oona," Ursula said. "I always have. Since the very first day I called you mine, since I spoke you into being."

"No," Oona said. "Stop. You didn't *speak me into being*. You didn't *will me into existence*. There was nothing magical about it."

"Wasn't there?" Ursula asked. "The day you were born, when I offered you my breast, I felt my milk let down. I saw it bead on my nipples, tiny white pearls. I still can't explain that. Not even after all these years. Can you?"

Mr. Tanaka didn't give Oona time to respond. He pushed open the door and took hold of Ursula's elbow. "The coast guard will be here soon," he reminded her. "And Jacob's on the ferry. He's probably about an hour out by now."

"You reached him?" Oona asked, surprised. "And he's coming?"

Mr. Tanaka nodded. "He's on his way."

And then they were gone. Oona watched as the door swung closed behind them. She listened to their steps echo down the hall. *One hour*, she thought. She had one hour to decide how she was going to tell Jacob. One hour before it all became real—the truth about her mother, about Daphne, about her own baby.

Suddenly, Oona felt desperate to leave the room. To run. Her calves itched and she felt the muscles in her throat tighten. Sweat broke out across her back and underneath her arms. Queasy, she eyed the door, the windows. What she needed was air. Fresh air.

"Gemma," she said, "I'm just going to step out for a minute. I'll be right back, okay?" She didn't know if this was actually true, if she would really return or if she'd decide to wait for the coast guard outside by the building's entrance. "Gemma?" she repeated. "Did you hear me? I'm going outside."

When she didn't respond, Oona figured she was sleeping. It was important to rest during labor, she knew. But she didn't want Gemma to wake up alone and confused, to do something stupid, so she shook her shoulder gently. "Hey," she said, and suddenly Gemma's eyes flew open.

"The baby," she whispered. "The baby's coming."

"Right now?" Oona asked. "Are you sure?" She swung around to look at the door, and at the clock hanging above it. If Mr. Tanaka was right, then the Coasties were still twenty minutes out. Quickly, Oona dug through her bag and pulled out her phone, but it wasn't until the call failed that she remembered the storm.

"Fuck," she breathed.

"Where's my mom?" Gemma asked from her bed. "I want my mom. They said she'd be here."

"Oh," said Oona, as she tried again to reach Shelly. "Oh, um, I don't know. Maybe she's on her way?"

"I need her now!" Gemma's voice was thin with panic. "I need my mom now. It hurts. It really hurts."

"Okay," Oona said, more to herself than to Gemma. She stepped back over to the bed and patted—well, not quite Gemma's arm, but the sheets. "Okay. Look, my phone's not working. So I'm just going to have to go find Shelly. Somehow. Maybe she's still at the lodge. But I'll be right—"

"No!" Gemma grabbed hold of Oona's shirt and wouldn't let go. "No! Don't leave me!"

"Gemma, I need to get Shelly."

"No! You can't. You can't leave me. I need you. I need her. I need my mom." And Gemma started to cry. For a moment Oona just stood there watching her. Gemma's voice was in her head. *I need my mom now.* Well, she needed her mom too. Why had she told Mr. Tanaka she could keep Gemma safe until the coast guard arrived? She didn't know how to deliver a baby. The closest she'd ever gotten to a birth was spying through the window, sitting on the steps listening to Daphne labor inside. *Oona,* she'd cried. *Oona, I need you.* But Oona had refused to leave her post. She'd just listened to Daphne call for her over and over, hoping that her mother might soon call for her the same way. *Oona, I need you.*

On the bed Gemma rasped her name, and Oona blinked herself back into the room.

"Okay," Oona said, stepping up to the bed. "Listen. I know you wish your mom was here to help you. Believe me, I do too. But I'm what you've got. I'm *all* you've got. So spread your legs and let me see what's going on." Oona pulled Gemma's left knee toward her own chest. "Yep, that's the head," she said. "Okay. So what you're experiencing right now is called the ring of fire, which means it's time to push." Shoving aside the stack of blankets at the foot of the bed,

Oona did her best to climb up onto the mattress. It was hard to maneuver around her own belly, but when Gemma spread her legs again, Oona got up onto her knees. "On the next contraction, I want you to take a deep breath and then give it all you got, okay? And push from your bottom."

With a weak nod, Gemma sank back against the sheets. Only seconds later she was up again, curling over the dome of her stomach, screaming in pain.

"That's it!" Oona cried. "That's it! You're doing it!"

Gemma bared her teeth like a dog and growled.

"Good," Oona coached. "Good."

As the pain crested, Gemma stopped pushing, but the muscles that had tensed all down her arms and her back didn't seem to relax. And as another contraction seized her, Oona watched as Gemma transformed—as she became something both more and less than human. A goddess in bodily form. It was just as Oona had once imagined for herself: When Gemma bore down, she could see the power rippling through her. For a moment, she was enraptured, bearing witness to true magic, true ritual: the sacrificial offering of the body, the blood. Had Oona ever loved anything enough to rend herself in two?

But of course she had. She'd loved her mother that much. She'd loved Craft and the coven. She'd wanted it all so badly, she'd been willing to drink poison. And Ursula, she was going to—what? Watch? Watch as Oona risked her life for nothing?

As if unable to help it, Oona inched closer to Gemma. Closer and then closer still. Until she could feel the heat coming off her body, until she could smell the sweat on her skin. It wasn't fair, she thought, as Gemma grunted, panted. This was supposed to be *her* birth.

Her baby.

"One more big push," Oona said. "Next contraction. Okay?"

Gemma said nothing, but seconds later she grabbed hold of the bed railings and pushed until she was red in the face, until the skin around her lips turned white and sweat broke out along her hairline, until—

"She's here!" Oona cried. And suddenly the room was filled with the sound of a baby's wailing. Oona looked around for something she could use to clamp and cut the cord. "It's a girl," she said, as she struggled off the bed. "You have a daughter." She glanced up at Gemma, expecting to see her sitting there with her arms extended, reaching for her child. Instead, her eyes were closed.

Well, Oona told herself, she'd always heard that labor was exhausting.

While Gemma rested, Oona went to work wrapping the baby. When she was done, she lifted the bundle and carried it back to the bed. "Here's your daughter," she said, but Gemma didn't stir. Didn't even open her eyes. "Come on," Oona said, as the baby started whimpering. She shook Gemma's shoulder. "Come on. Get up. You need to feed her. She's hungry."

Nothing.

"You're not dying, are you?" Oona asked. She pulled back the sheets to check for signs of a hemorrhage but saw no evidence of fresh blood. Gemma still needed to deliver the placenta, of course, but she hoped the coast guard would be there by then. "No, you're fine. You're just tired, but you can sleep later. Right now, you need to take this baby. You need to feed her."

In her arms, the baby cried harder, her little voice ragged in Oona's ear.

"Gemma," Oona tried one more time, but before she could finish her sentence a spasm of pain shot through her, forcing her to double over at the waist. She let out a soft grunt and looked down, as if expecting to be able to identify the source of her suffering. Instead, all she saw was a new puddle of blood on the floor.

"Fuck," she breathed as another cramp worked through her, leaving her short of breath. It was like a kind of wringing. Every muscle in her body ached. Even her breasts felt tender. "Gemma," she hissed.

The baby screamed, and when Oona looked down she saw that the little girl had somehow pulled her arms free from the blanket. Her hands were fisted up by her chin and she'd gouged a scratch into her left cheek. The mark was red and raised, like a welt.

Oona carried the baby back to the foot of the bed. "Shit," she muttered, as she attempted to redo the swaddle. "Shit. Shit. Shit."

She didn't know how long a newborn could go without eating, but it was clear the infant was hungry. On the bed, she arched her back and wailed.

"Okay, okay," Oona cooed, as she lifted the baby. Cradling her in one arm, she began searching the cabinets for formula, but she didn't find any. The coast guard would probably be there soon, but would they have formula on them? Somehow, Oona doubted that it was part of a standard-issue paramedic kit.

Her first instinct was to head to the greenhouse, to find Lally and ask her what to do, and it hurt when she remembered she couldn't do that.

She was sure there had to be formula somewhere at the Center, but for the life of her she couldn't think where it might be stored. The infirmary? The kitchen? If Gemma would just wake up, Oona could go and check, but she didn't dare take the baby out into the storm.

As she paced back and forth, she studied Gemma. Was this how Nora had looked? Peaceful, even despite her daughter's desperate wailing? Had she just lain there like fucking Sleeping Beauty while

Ursula sweated through her clothes trying to figure out what to do, how to keep alive such a tiny, fragile little bird?

Suddenly, a thought occurred to Oona. A terrible, niggling little thought. The same kind of thought that had, all those months before, driven her to board a ferry bound for Marrow.

She looked down at the baby in her arms. Her underarms itched and her breasts tingled. Her nipples stung. She didn't know if her mother had been telling the truth when she'd said she nursed her, but still, Oona unhooked her bra. She lifted her shirt hem and brought the baby to her chest, then she held her breath until she latched. And she waited. Any minute, she thought, she might feel it: the hormone rush of her milk coming in. She'd read on the blogs that for some women it came with a sense of sudden euphoria, while for others it brought on nausea and tears. Either way, Oona thought, she would recognize it. Just like she'd once recognized Hekate in the water by the cliffs.

*O, Torch Bearer,* she thought. *Lead me the way You once led fair Demeter.*

The baby suckled, snorted. Was that it? Oona thought.

Was that the taste of salt on her lips? The brine of low tide in the air? Power. Craft. Witching. Magic. Was that it?

Suddenly, Oona felt the urge to take the baby and run. How far could she get, she wondered, in her condition? How long could she survive, hiding in the woods?

What her mother had done was wrong. Of course it was wrong. But this was wrong too. This screaming, starving baby. Her empty, aching womb. And Gemma, just lying there, refusing to open her eyes, to see her child. This wasn't what motherhood was supposed to look like.

Standing there, Oona started to plot and scheme. She knew the woods better than anybody. She could feed the baby with her body, the same body that had failed her so many times before. It would be wrong, but Oona would find a way to make it right in the way she raised her daughter, in the love she showed her child. She would do things so differently than her mother had.

But then the baby made a soft snuffling noise and Oona lost herself for a moment watching her tiny fists tense and release. She didn't look up again until she heard the sound of the front door opening. Out the window, she could see lights flashing, and behind her a trio of voices sounded in the hall.

"This way!" Oona heard one of the Coasties call.

Soon the room was full of them. They rushed toward Gemma so quickly, they didn't even seem to notice Oona at first. She backed up toward the door. This was her last chance, she thought. For motherhood, for magic, for a family.

Then one of the Coasties spotted her. The woman. Of course it was the woman. "Is that . . ." she started, as concern twitched across her face.

"She was hungry," Oona explained.

"Right," the woman said gently. Too gently. And Oona thought, *She knows*. She could see it in the careful way the woman moved, in the way her gaze never once shifted from the baby. She was treating Oona like she was an animal in danger of spooking; like she was feral, wild. Which was exactly how Oona felt. "Can I take a look at her?" she asked.

For a long moment, Oona didn't respond. She just gazed down at the baby she was cradling.

"Ma'am?" the Coastie asked.

Oona looked up. She took in the soft folds of flesh around the guardsman's middle, her sagging breasts. A mother.

"She still needs to deliver the placenta," Oona said, nodding at Gemma. "And you should check the contents of that IV bag. I think they gave her something. A sedative, maybe."

"Larry," the woman said without turning, and one of the other two Coasties unhooked Gemma's IV. "Now," said the woman, stepping closer.

"Okay," said Oona, but still she didn't move.

In the end, the woman had to pry the baby from her grip. Using her pinky as a hook, she unlatched the infant. Then she took her to the bed to confirm her lungs were clear, listen for her pulse.

Oona took her breast into her hand and massaged it the way she'd read she was supposed to—in her book about pregnancy and new-born care, on the blogs—then she waited to see a drop of milk appear, but nothing happened. She was completely dry.

The Coastie glanced back at her. "Don't worry," she said. "It's normal. You're only, what? Thirty-two, thirty-four weeks along?"

"I'm not pregnant," Oona said, her voice hollow.

The woman frowned, clearly confused, but she didn't get a chance to ask any follow-up questions because just then the baby began to cry again, and Oona saw her window. While the Coasties were all distracted, she turned and walked out of the room.

Outside again, Oona discovered that the storm had passed. The sky was clear. The wind had died down to nothing more than a light breeze. There was no sign of Jacob yet, but if Mr. Tanaka said he was coming, then Oona was sure he was on his way.

There was so much she needed to do. She needed to find Shelly and tell her what she'd learned about Tracy. She needed to bring

Ursula's book to Mr. Tanaka so he could use it as evidence. She needed to re-clasp her bra.

Had she really tried to nurse Gemma's baby?

Jesus Christ, what was wrong with her?

Oona scrubbed a hand down her face. Through the trees, she could just make out the moon, hanging low over the eastern cliffs. Her mother had lied about so much—about Daphne and her baby, about the Center and the coven, about Oona's own pregnancy. But she hadn't lied about the way motherhood granted a woman access to power. Oona had seen it happen in that room. She'd seen Gemma transform. And she'd felt it herself when the Coasties had come for the baby. She'd felt more powerful in that moment than she ever had before. Rabid. Vicious. A creature both fanged and clawed.

Even standing there on the steps, she could feel it humming through her body: a desperate, reckless kind of energy. She wanted her baby back. Gemma's baby. The baby her body couldn't accept was not hers.

She wanted all the babies she'd lost. She ached for them.

For the first time, Oona understood what had driven Daphne to the cliffs, and she wanted to follow in her footsteps, trail her ghost through the woods. She still had the potion she'd concocted in her backpack—the poison—and she wanted to drink it. She wanted to lie down on the cold, stone floor of the cave and wait for Hekate.

*O, Torch Bearer.*

But of course it wouldn't work. She knew that now.

And, she realized suddenly, so had Daphne.

She hadn't gone to the cliffs because she'd been lured there by Hekate. She'd gone because she'd been transformed the same way Oona had been transformed, but she hadn't known what to make of her new teeth and talons, so she'd torn herself apart.

Yes, the truth was obvious now: Oona hadn't been cursed—not by Daphne and not by Hekate. She might've been haunted, but only by her own guilt.

In the distance, she heard the sound of the ferry's horn. Jacob. It was time to go meet him at the docks, time to tell him the truth. And not just the truth about her mother or about the baby, but the truth about herself.

She wanted to follow Daphne, and he needed to know that. He needed to know that she'd had similar thoughts back in Portland too. She'd told herself that her return to Marrow was a homecoming, but really it was an escape. She'd fled Portland looking for answers, hoping the coven would be a solution, hoping motherhood would be a salve. She'd wanted her mother to save her, she'd wanted magic to save her. But instead she'd learned that her mother wasn't her mother and there was no magic in this world.

She'd become a thing with teeth, claws, feathers. And now there was no going back. If she wanted to survive she was going to have to find a way to protect herself from herself, the way Daphne never had.

She was going to have to leave Marrow, leave the siren call of the cliffside. She was going to leave and never look back.

# EPILOGUE

*Three months later*

It was cold up by the bow, and windier than Oona'd thought it'd be when she'd bypassed the cabin in favor of the so-called sundeck, but she'd missed the smell of the sea. For the past month, she'd been on the road, driving through landlocked state after landlocked state. After a lifetime spent living within the same ten-mile radius, it had been a much-needed adventure. But this—this felt like going home.

Clutching the chilled metal railing with both hands, Oona pulled in a deep breath. If he'd been there, Jacob would have told her to be careful, reminded her to watch out for rogue swells. Ursula would have chastised her for acting like a child. But Oona was on her own, which meant she was allowed to be a little reckless. There was no one there to insist she keep both feet on the ground, no one to prevent her from leaning over the railing in hopes that she might be able to see the island through the mist.

Jacob was back in Portland, and Ursula and Lally were at the women's correctional center in Windham, awaiting their trials. Or at least that's where Oona assumed they were, since that was where Mr. Tanaka had told her they'd be sent. After he'd turned Ursula and Lally over to the FBI, he'd come back to Bare Root to pick up Oona and Jacob. Oona had wanted him to drive them straight to the docks, but it had been too late by the time she'd finished explaining (confessing?) to Jacob. The ferries had all stopped running. So instead, they'd had to spend the night at Jacob's parents' place.

The next morning, Oona went back to the Center to collect her things. She looked for Shelly and Grace and Vivian, but she couldn't find them amid the chaos. There were too many people milling about—marine patrol and FBI and local detectives; families who'd come to collect their Mothers; even Astrid Nystrom's people, who'd arrived late the night before, not long after Gemma and the baby were airlifted to a hospital in Portland. Oona packed her duffel under the watchful eye of both a junior agent and a member of Astrid's team, and though she tried to ask for news—of Gemma, of the baby; *her* baby, she couldn't help but think—the only response she received was a request to sign an NDA.

In the end, she and Jacob left without much fanfare. Mr. Tanaka drove them to the ferry, and though the case had already been turned over to the FBI, he promised he would do his best to notify Oona of any developments. "From what I hear, they're going to try to locate everyone they can—all the birth mothers, all the children. They'll make connections, if they're desired. And it's not that I doubt their ability to do the work, but these things can move slowly. So you might want to find a lawyer, someone who can help keep the pressure on while they track her down."

"Who?" Oona asked.

"Your mother."

*My mother's in jail,* Oona thought. Then she realized that he meant Nora Reilly. "I'll do that," she said.

But she did not.

In fact, once she got back to Portland Oona didn't do much of anything. Jacob took a leave of absence from work, theoretically so they could spend some time together, grieve together, but Oona just wanted to be alone. She loved Jacob, as she reassured him every time he asked, but being in the same room with him was borderline unbearable. The way he watched her, *monitored* her, made her want to peel off her own skin. And then there was the guilt. Jacob didn't try to make her feel bad—as he'd explained many times, he deeply regretted all the years he'd used his sacrifice as a kind of cudgel; he'd never done so out of malice, just out of fear—but that was the worst part. He didn't have to try. The "I told you so" was evident on his face: as he watched her pack up her dresser altar, when he found a collection of taper candles forgotten in a closet and asked if she wanted him to throw them out. He'd never asked for acknowledgment, or for an apology, but Oona could tell he was waiting, expectant, and it was that tension that made her want to rip out her own hair.

After a week she begged him to return to work, and then she started walking. She spent a month circling the city, watching her belly deflate and marveling at how strange it felt to be alone again. Not just alone on her walks, but alone inside her own body. She left early each morning and often didn't return until well after sundown.

She was unhappy, that was the thing. In fact, she felt much the same way she had before she'd left for Bare Root. Only now she couldn't blame the curse. So instead, she walked.

She followed the same loop every day—past the cemetery, up toward the library, and then down around to the wharfs—but she barely paid attention. The point wasn't to go anywhere specific; the point was to keep moving. Because when she'd left Marrow, she'd promised she'd find a way to protect herself *from* herself, and this was the only way she could think of to ensure she didn't go back on her word.

"So you really just walk the whole time?" Jacob asked her one night, after she'd crawled into bed beside him. "You never go into any stores or restaurants? You never talk to anyone?"

"No," she'd told him, which was initially the truth. However, by October she had begun to linger at one of the stops along her route: the soup kitchen on Congress Street.

Though she'd never actually gone with Ursula on any of her recruiting trips, she'd learned through the Bare Root Reddit board that St. Vincent de Paul was where Ursula used to go. Jessica, Maria, Minnie—Ursula had met them all on Congress Street. Or so the posters on the message board had claimed. Oona had found the board late one night when she couldn't sleep, and while most of the posters were conspiracy theorists, true crime–obsessed cyber-sleuths with too much time on their hands, some of the posts were disturbingly accurate and verified by Mr. Tanaka after the fact.

Like the story about Maggie Jones. A few weeks after Oona got back to Portland, someone posted on the message board that Maggie had died by suicide on the morning she was supposed to fly to Maine. At the same time Oona was sailing across Casco Bay, claiming Maggie's name as her own on the docks in Port Marrow, Maggie's husband was coming home from a business trip, walking into his bedroom to find his wife.

They said it was the potion Ursula had sent her, but Oona knew that wasn't true. It was just an easy answer, and people loved easy answers. They loved having a villain to blame.

And then there was Shelly's sister, Tracy. Another victim lured away from St. Vincent de Paul. Oona read on the message board that Tracy had OD'd. Apparently, a Jane Doe had washed up on the beach in Port Marrow back in 1997. When no one came to identify the body, the town had had her cremated, but the police had held on to her effects.

After Oona confirmed the story with Mr. Tanaka, she called Shelly. They'd stayed in touch, she and Shelly, and Grace and Vivian too. They were all on a group text that felt, in some lovely ways, like the coven Oona had once imagined they'd all belong to. Shelly was back in San Francisco. When Oona called her, she was at work. Oona had never been to Shelly's clinic, but she liked picturing her in scrubs, a stethoscope draped around her neck. Maybe if Shelly had been her doctor, Oona would have actually gotten medical treatment for her recurrent miscarriages; maybe she never would have gone back to Bare Root.

While the phone rang, Oona braced herself for Shelly's response. She expected tears, maybe even keening. But it turned out that the FBI had reached Shelly first. She already knew about her sister's death, and while it had saddened her, it had also brought her a strange kind of peace. She'd made plans to return to Marrow to collect Tracy's belongings. She'd also made plans to visit Grace down in Connecticut, because the FBI had told her something Mr. Tanaka had not revealed: In addition to Tracy, they'd also located Shelly's nephew. He was living in a small town by the beach. His mother had passed, his adoptive mother (his kidnapper?). So there was no need for Shelly to debate pressing charges. She could go out there and meet him, with no extra baggage to weigh her down.

On the phone, Shelly asked Oona if she wanted to come. They could all stay at Grace's, she said. It would be fun. But Oona demurred. She said there wouldn't be enough room, what with Alice all but living there. It was a convenient excuse, but it was also true.

When the Center got raided, Alice and Carol fled like the rest of the coven, but while Carol decided to follow Joyce and Donna to another coven just beginning to put down roots on the Gulf Coast, Alice had decided she'd had enough. She showed up at Grace's front door and Grace took her in gladly. It was nice, Grace wrote in their group chat, for her husband to have a child in the house again. Not that Alice was a child, exactly. She was nineteen. But while Grace's husband had accepted her decision to stop trying for a baby, it was obvious how much pleasure he got from helping Alice study for her GED.

In the group chat, Vivian told Grace that one day soon she would need to convince Alice to apply for college. She claimed Alice's selective mutism wouldn't be an issue and said that if any school rejected her for it, then she could sue.

Vivian was all about threatening to sue now that she was working as a lawyer again. Her old job had refused to take her back—it'd been more than a decade since she'd gotten married and quit—but she'd found a firm in Astoria willing to take a chance on her. So she'd moved to Queens. And while her new place was small—nothing compared to her old penthouse—it was an easy commute to her office, and more important, it was close to a good public school.

Vivian's final transfer had failed, but not long after, she'd registered to become a foster parent. Nothing was for sure, but fostering to adopt was on the table and Vivian was hopeful. She was only half kidding when she asked the other women on the group chat to cast a spell for her.

Oona had never specifically asked the others about their relationships to Craft, but she herself had largely given it up. It just hurt too much, she'd told Alice, who had understood. On a FaceTime call with Grace, Oona had thought she'd spotted an altar in the background, but it didn't look like the candles were new, and the offerings of flowers and herbs appeared to be dried up, dusty. Shelly, certainly, no longer believed, but then again she'd never really believed. She'd only come to Marrow to find Tracy. So though Oona'd never asked, it appeared that aside from Vivian's tongue-in-cheek request, they'd all abandoned Craft. In fact, there was only one Mother from that Summer Session who still seemed committed, though sometimes Oona wondered if what she was seeing was real. It was just so unlikely, so surprising. But the way Gemma wrote about motherhood on Instagram, the language she used to describe postpartum healing and breastfeeding, well, it was uncanny. She sounded just like Ursula. It gave Oona the chills every time she scrolled through her feed.

Oona had Gemma's number—she'd convinced Astrid's lackey to give it to her while she'd packed—but she hadn't yet reached out. Instead, she watched Gemma's life unfold online. On Instagram and in the tabloids. From what she'd read, Ursula had been right about one thing: Elijah *was* running a cult. Well, Oona had thought cynically, it often takes one to know one, doesn't it?

Gemma seemed happy, though. And so did Daisy, her daughter. Maybe she was the reason Oona couldn't bring herself to call. From the pictures, it looked like she had red hair, just like Oona, and the way the sun caught her green eyes made Oona's sternum ache. So though she'd twice opened up a new text message and started typing, though she'd once gone so far as to dial her number and listen to the line ring, Oona had never followed through, never actually made contact.

It was the same story with Lally and her mom. They'd tried to reach out, Lally more than Ursula, but Oona kept dodging their calls. It was just too painful. And anyway, what was there to say? If she told them that there were nights, especially after she learned about Maggie, when she cried so hard she hyperventilated and ended up passed out on the floor, Lally would just apologize again and Ursula would get defensive. And the same thing would happen if she told them that sometimes she got so angry she could do nothing but scream—into her pillow, inside the shower, at Jacob. So instead, she followed their case through the message boards. And once a week, she spoke to Mr. Tanaka.

He wasn't on the case anymore, since it'd gone federal, but he stayed in touch with the agents while they worked to track down his grandchild, and he told Oona what he could. He called every Friday afternoon—to inform her when their bails were set, to let her know when they'd received their court dates. Sometimes there was nothing new, but he still called. Every week at four p.m., like clockwork. So at three p.m., Oona's stomach always started hurting, but the pain usually went away once she finally heard the phone ring. On the last Friday in October, though, Mr. Tanaka didn't call. Not at four, or at five, or at six, or at seven. By the time she finally gave in and dialed his number, Oona felt like she couldn't breathe.

"I have news," Mr. Tanaka said, by way of greeting. He didn't even bother with hello. "They found her. Nora Reilly."

For a moment, the hearing cut out in Oona's left ear and a high-pitched ringing took its place. By the time it faded, Mr. Tanaka was reading an address, giving her the name of a social worker who would soon be reaching out.

"Oona?" he said, when she failed to respond. "Are you there?"

"I'm here."

"She's been looking for you, Oona. The agent I spoke with wanted me to tell you that. Apparently, she's been trying to find you for years."

"Oh," she said.

Her insufficient response clearly left Mr. Tanaka feeling uncomfortable. He cleared his throat. "Do you want me to call Jacob?" he asked.

330

"No," she said. "No, I'll be fine. Thanks." Then she ended the call.

For a long while, she just stared at her phone. She'd returned home early from her walk that day because Jacob was out at the pub and the house was empty. Through the kitchen window, she could see that the sun had set hours before. It wouldn't be smart to go outside. The long walk into town would be dark and treacherous, not to mention freezing cold. But Oona felt like she had no other choice. After what Mr. Tanaka had told her, she couldn't just sit there on her couch. No, she had to move. So she started walking: past the cemetery, up toward the library, and down around to the wharfs. She ended up at St. Vincent de Paul. There was a girl there who she'd taken to studying (stalking?). Fifteen, maybe sixteen, she seemed familiar, though Oona could never quite decide who she reminded her of: Daphne, Gemma, herself.

Earlier that day, the girl had asked Oona for money, told her she was trying to get a prescription for mifepristone but she didn't quite have enough. At the time, Oona had explained that she wasn't back to work yet, but as she stood there on the sidewalk before the church she spotted a patch of pennyroyal growing wild in the side lawn and she realized there was still a way she could help the girl.

The last time she'd seen her, the girl had been headed toward her car, a beat-up old sedan she'd parked about halfway down Congress. Oona was relieved to discover that it was still there. Though it looked like the girl was asleep inside, she knocked on the driver's-side window. And when the girl stirred but didn't sit up, she knocked again.

"What do you want?" the girl called out finally. Oona expected her to be groggy, but instead she just sounded annoyed.

Oona held up the bouquet of pennyroyal, and the girl cracked her window.

"Whatever you're selling," the girl said, "I don't want it."

She started to roll her window back up, but Oona stuck her hand inside the crack. "Wait," she said. "Do you remember me? A few hours ago, you told me you were trying to get mifepristone."

For a moment, the girl studied Oona, then she took her hand off the window control. "Right," she said. "Yeah. Well, don't worry about it. I got the script."

"Oh," Oona said. "I thought . . . never mind." She stared at the bouquet of pennyroyal in her hand. "Guess you won't need this, then."

"What is that?"

"Pennyroyal. It's an herb."

The girl looked at her askance.

"It can help end a pregnancy," Oona explained, but the girl still looked dubious. "You won't need it, though, if you've already taken the pill."

The girl shifted in her seat. "I haven't," she said.

"Haven't what?"

"Taken it."

"Oh," Oona said again. "Do you want—?" She held up the pennyroyal, but the girl shook her head, so Oona turned to go.

It was just as well, she thought. Better, maybe. After all, that pennyroyal had been growing wild. Who knew what pesticides it'd been sprayed with, what chemicals it'd absorbed from the soil? Really, offering it to the girl hadn't been a very good idea. No, Oona just needed to go home. Take a sleeping pill, maybe. And wait for Jacob to return.

She was halfway down the block when she heard a car door open.

"Is there an herb that can help with nausea?" the girl asked.

"Nausea?" Oona repeated, turning back around.

The girl opened her mouth and then closed it. "No, forget it," she said. "I don't know what I was thinking. I can't just start eating random plants off the side of the road. I don't even know you." She reached for the door's handle.

Oona stepped toward her. "Ginger," she blurted. "Ginger can help."

The girl scoffed. "Yeah, I've tried that. Ginger candies. Ginger tea. I want to keep the baby, but I can't work if I can't quit puking. And I can't quit puking."

She moved her fingers to the base of her throat, and for a minute Oona was transported back to Marrow, back to the woods surrounding the old archery shed. *Why you and not me?* she'd thought once, about Gemma. It was the same thought she'd had about every pregnant woman she'd met since she'd first experienced a loss. In some way or another, she'd spent her whole life asking that question. *Why you and not me? Why am I not deserving too?* But of course the truth was that motherhood wasn't something you *deserved*. It wasn't a title bestowed upon a woman, like Bare Root made it seem. Motherhood was choice. It was action. It was Daphne jumping from a cliff to try to reach her child in the underworld. It was Gemma sneaking onto that ferry to raise her baby on her own. And in the beginning, before everything went so wrong, it was Lally filling her garden with juniper and feverfew and motherwort, searching the forest for stinging nettle and pulling laminaria from the sea. By caretaking the way she had, Lally had been motherhood embodied. And that was what Oona wanted too. Even if she couldn't *be* a mother, she could still *mother*. Just like she had with Gemma. Because for whatever reason— herbology, magic—the potion she'd given Gemma had worked.

Oona took another step closer to the car, and there, by a drainage grate, she saw peppermint growing. It could be good for nausea, she thought, if made into a tea, so she picked first one stalk and then another. And then, before she had a chance to second-guess herself, she cupped the stalks inside her hands.

"What're you doing?" the girl asked.

But Oona didn't respond until she was done whispering the incantation. Her version might not have been perfect, but she thought it was probably pretty close. After all, she'd spent a lot of time that summer working with Lally on healing spells.

"Here," Oona said, approaching the girl. "I know you don't know me, and I know this probably seems really weird, but this will help. Just ask for a cup of hot water and let it steep for ten minutes. Drink all of it."

The girl took the stalks from Oona, holding one leafy stem in each of her hands.

Oona dug her phone out of her back pocket. "Do you have a cell?"

The girl nodded, though she still looked suspicious.

"Take down this number. It's for a friend of mine. She works at Planned Parenthood out in San Francisco, but she's from Portland and she can help you. She can help you with, well, whatever you choose."

Oona rattled off Shelly's number, and while it was possible she was just pretending, it looked like the girl added Shelly's contact info to her phone. "Thanks," she said. "And thanks for—" She held up the stalks.

"Peppermint," Oona offered.

"Right," the girl said. "Okay. Thanks for the peppermint, then."

"I'm Oona. I live out on Willow Glen, if you, you know, if you need more or something. I know a little about plants."

The girl nodded. "Okay."

∽

It was late by the time she made it home, but Jacob hadn't returned. Any minute, she knew, his car would pull into the driveway. But until then, the house was hers, and everything was still as she'd left it. Her sweater hanging off the back of the chair in the dining room, her cup of tea on the floor by the couch. And her notebook sitting on the kitchen counter, with Nora Reilly's address scribbled somewhere inside.

When she'd left Marrow, Oona had thought she'd known what she had to do, but turning her back on the island, on Craft, on Ursula—none of it had been enough. She'd still felt like she was in mourning for some unlived version of her life.

And maybe she was. But for the first time, it occurred to her that the life she was meant to lead . . . it wasn't at Bare Root. Maybe it wasn't even in Portland, despite how good it had felt to help that girl.

Suddenly, Oona plucked the notebook off the counter and turned to the page where she'd written Nora's address. Washington state. Bainbridge Island.

She ran to her bedroom closet. Shoving aside the box filled with crystals and taper candles, she pulled out her duffel. By the time Jacob got home, she was ready to go. She already had Nora's address plugged into her GPS. The drive would take her forty-seven hours without stops. But she planned to stop—anywhere and everywhere she saw something growing that she could harvest. She wanted to create her own larder, like Lally had once done.

"And that's not something you can do here?" Jacob asked.

When he'd returned from the pub, he'd found her standing in the driveway, waiting. This time, at least, she was determined to say goodbye.

"You know I might not be here when you get back," he warned her. "Professor Harrigan just offered to let me come along on his next expedition. If you leave now, Oona, I might just go."

She nodded gently. "I think you should."

He blinked. "Really?"

"You deserve to go, Jacob. You gave up so much for me," she said. "Too much, maybe."

"Maybe," Jacob choked. When he spoke, she could see the narrow gap between his two front teeth, and for a second she felt her resolve falter. Was it really possible she'd never fit her thumbnail inside that gap again?

But she couldn't stay. She'd been wrong about so much—about her mother, about Daphne, about Bare Root—but she'd been right in thinking that she and Jacob needed a break. They needed time to figure out who they were, and what they wanted, on their own. They needed time to forgive each other and themselves.

So instead, when she pressed her lips to his cheek, she tried to memorize the way he smelled—like salt and brine, like the sour musk of low tide. The kind of scent she could feel in her solar plexus.

Then she turned and climbed into her car.

She thought of that moment often as she made her way across the country, as she spent her days with no one but the radio for company and her nights sleeping alone in her car. But when the ferry she'd boarded in Seattle finally approached Eagle Harbor and the port came into view, she knew that she'd made the right choice. Like a petrel returning to its nesting grounds, Oona could feel the draw of the island, of Nora—the draw of home.

# ACKNOWLEDGMENTS

Thank you to everyone who believed in me and in this novel.

To my brilliant agent, Marya Spence, whose enthusiasm for my work gave me permission to finally take my writing seriously. And to Mackenzie Williams.

To my team at Putnam: Kate Dresser, Lindsay Sagnette, Tarini Sipahimalani, Ashley Hewlett, Jazmin Miller, and Shina Patel. Thank you for your cheerleading, for your handholding, for your faith.

To Gaby Mongelli, for first taking a gamble on me.

To Kristina Moore, for your hard work and vision.

To everyone at Georges Borchardt, Inc., and to Georges, Anne, and Valerie in particular. Thank you for granting me entry into this world of books. I will be forever grateful.

To all the writers I have had the great privilege of representing, your work has inspired and humbled me.

To Hannah Beresford, Tessa Fontaine, and Annie Hartnett, for your generous encouragement.

## ACKNOWLEDGMENTS

To Clare Beams, Jessamine Chan, Alice Hoffman, Kelly Link, Sophie Mackintosh, Charlotte McConaghy, Rachel Yoder, and Leni Zumas, your books have been my guiding lights.

To my friends, for all your support. To Kaitlin, for daydreaming with me in bars across New York City. To Beth, for listening to me plan and plot for nearly twenty years. To Megan, for allowing me to talk through practically every aspect of this novel (not to mention every aspect of my life).

To Marzenna, Andy, and Anna, for welcoming me into your family. To Annie and Cody, for being such enthusiastic early readers. To my dad, for always believing in the importance of this work. To my mom, for introducing me to my favorite writers, for reading every word I've ever written, for typing up my very first "stories." Without you, this book very simply would not exist.

To my girls, Beatrice and Winnie. You are my dream come true.

And finally, to Adam. I love you. Everything good in my life is because of you.

# ABOUT THE AUTHOR

**Samantha Browning Shea** is an author and the vice president of Georges Borchardt, Inc., literary agency. A graduate of Colgate University, Samantha lives in Connecticut with her husband and their two daughters. *Marrow* is her debut novel.

samanthashea.com

SB_Shea